KATE

Kate Fenton was born in Oldham and educated in Cheshire, Manchester and at Oxford. As a radio producer for the BBC, she has worked for *Woman's Hour* and *Bookshelf* on Radio 4, and also for Radio Wales and the World Service.

She still makes feature and documentary programmes as a freelance and has written two plays for radio.

Dancing to the Pipers is her second novel, and she is currently working on her third. She lives in the North York Moors with her husband, actor Ian Carmichael.

sceptre

Also by Kate Fenton and
available from Hodder and Stoughton paperbacks:

THE COLOURS OF SNOW

Kate Fenton

DANCING TO
THE PIPERS

First published in Great Britain in 1993 by Michael Joseph Ltd

First published in paperback in 1994 by Hodder and Stoughton, a division of Hodder Headline PLC.

A Sceptre paperback

The characters and situations in this book are entirely imaginary and bear no relation to any real person or actual happenings.

British Library C.I.P.

A CIP catalogue record for this book is available from the British Library.

ISBN 0-340-59359-8

Printed and bound in Great Britain for Hodder and Stoughton Paperbacks, a division of Hodder Headline PLC, 338 Euston Road London NW1 3BH by Cox & Wyman Ltd, Reading, Berks.

For my mother,
in love and admiration

And with special thanks to
Jenny Dereham and Richenda Todd

PROLOGUE

I'm rigid with fright because the house lights are dimming. Makes no difference that I'm the merest member of the audience. Not a line to fluff, not a cue to miss. There's a lump of cold dread congealing in my stomach. Hyperactive sense of responsibility — that's my problem. As Henry (ungrateful pig) has so often observed.

All around, a gorgeously perfumed jungle of silk and chiffon rustles and chatters away. Me, I'm silent as an airline passenger who knows that, if she relaxes her armrest-gripping concentration for one second, the plane will plummet out of the sky.

God, I can't even recall the first line of the play ... When did I last read *Twelfth Night*? Probably as a spotty schoolgirl with a titillating paperback tucked under the flabby school text of Shakespeare.

But this production, this whole festival — this glamorously conspicuous consumption of culture — is *not* my responsibility. It's not my fault the house lights have been taken out and nothing — *nothing* — is happening. Not so much as a shiver in the tabs.

Very grand tabs. Bit of a difference from the bald and leaky red drapes that used to hang here. Now we have glimmering acres of blue velvet. Heaven knows what such lavishness cost.

There I go again. As Henry also complains, I have a *loweringly* mercenary mind. Instead of being lost in rapture over the restoration ('A rediscovered Pre-Raphaelite gem' — *Daily*

1

Telegraph; 'Delicious folly' — *Sunday Times*) I find myself computing cost per inch of gilt, per dangler on the chandeliers glittering in every cherubed, curtained box, per yard of luscious carpet — and boggling.

I know what these seats cost. To buy, I mean, not just to sit in. In fact, not to sit in at all, because buying the damn thing does not grant sitting-tenancy rights, only a brass sliver of immortality. Every seat is sponsored, with a plate naming the benefactor. Charities are smart these days. The brass plates sold like brollies in a cloudburst, I'm told. So quickly Nell wished they'd charged more. I thought she was charging quite enough.

Nevertheless, we coughed up for one. Row A, seat 3 is engraved to the memory of Catherine Langham. No, I'm not sitting in it. You have to be joking. We are lurking at the back of the stalls.

A misfired toot from some reedy pipe behind the curtains makes my mouth go dry. Then finally, blessedly, an unseen band begins to play. The music is spare, slow and deeply, deeply Early. All shawms and sackbuttery.

'Sounds like a bloody cat in labour,' mutters the slumped body next to me.

'Authentic,' I murmur, because the word 'authentic' was shot through Richard's plans for this production like Blackpool through the proverbial rock. 'It's —'

But my cultural dissertation is interrupted by a stab in the spine and I concentrate instead on adjusting my zip more comfortably before the curtain finally rises. This frock, however, was not designed for comfort. I'm beginning to doubt whether it was designed for breathing either, but I was (let's face facts) thinner when I bought it. A week-long bout of food poisoning laced with misery had reduced me then to wraith-like insubstantiality. Zipping myself into it for the first time that night, I felt dazzling as a newly hatched butterfly. This evening, I was more the grub, painfully trying to re-encase herself in an iron chrysalis. This garment has more bones than your average chicken. Miracle of modern engineering, Joe had said earlier, admiring the cantilevered cleavage. Typical.

What's more, this outrageous corset with a skirt is scarlet. Scarlet satin no less. With a saucy scattering of sequins and scads of net frou-frouing around the legs. I saw it in a shop window in Oxford, precisely – almost to the day – two years ago. Siren-like, it called to me. How could I resist? If Fate, I remember thinking at the time, had insisted on casting me as The Other Woman (Rejected), I would bloody well dress the part.

I'd never bought anything like it in my life. Not new. Evening gear came from kind friends or Oxfam shops. What's more, this little creation cost a fortune and I was flat broke. So, while the credit card was still twitching, I bought a matching pair of strappy stilettoes too. They're long since lost – I'm not sure they survived that first crazy night – but this gala presented a rare opportunity, in my undressy life, to disinter The Frock. Although I was not without misgivings because, two years ago, I had found myself ludicrously – dear God, *excruciatingly* – over dressed at the dinner for which it was purchased.

I need not have worried tonight. Sequins? My dear, in this darkened auditorium, there are *diamonds* a-twinkle like the tropical sky at night. There is also, bet your life, a cloakroom packed with more furry pelts than Whipsnade Zoo. Well, it's a gala opening, and this isn't a proper theatre. Surprise surprise. Now, it's an amusing hobby for a coven of well-heeled trustees, but it never was more than a toy in the first place and . . .

But all at once, the blue velvet twitches like a horse and bolts skywards. Tighted and tunicked musicians are revealed tootling their pipes in a sylvan glade of awe-inspiring tastefulness. The audience – who know their place – applaud loudly. They're probably so glad to see Shakespeare rescued from a used parking lot, they actually want to applaud. Henry will be

3

chuffed. And so will Richard. I suppress ungracious thoughts and am gratified on their behalf. I clap as loud as the rest. And Orsino, Duke of Illyria, when he strolls on, rotating a hand in a gesture reminiscent of Her Majesty the Queen, is not tricked-out as a Mafia Godfather. No dark glasses, no black leather even. He's dressed as, well, as a Duke. Nice legs. And he is not going to forget his lines.

'"If music be the food of love,"' he intones with thrilling baritone projection (so young but a Shakespearian in the grand old actor-manager tradition), '"play on . . ."'

Relief engulfs me. We have arrived, safely, at the beginning.

> Give me excess of it, that, surfeiting,
> The appetite may sicken, and so die . . .

My own appetite for this play, I confess, is not great in the first place. But, providing the players remember the quotable bits in the right order and don't (as Noël Coward said) bump into the furniture, this audience, afloat in a mellow sea of champagne, will think it's all simply marvellous. And so *frightfully* good for this benighted corner of the county to have Somewhere Like This.

> . . . That strain again! It had a dying fall . . .

I find myself flinching at these words. Even tonight, crossing the courtyard on the way in, I was imagining – for the thousandth time – a body lying shattered on the flagstones. But it can only be my imagination that the actor (the splendidly named Desford Hurley) lingered tragically over each syllable. This guy would wring nuances out of a telephone directory. He is not acting. He is *giving* his Orsino.

I order myself to be sensible.

> . . . So full of shapes is fancy
> That it alone is high fantastical.

You said it, Duke. It's fanciful, fantastical – in fact downright loony – to sit here thinking two people had to die unnatural

4

deaths for this toy theatre to be regilded and recurtained. False logic but ... if either of them had not expired, we wouldn't be here now. Naturally, none of us mention this inconvenient equation, but surely we all, in our own ways, feel guilty.

Well, all except Henry. Guilt, pronounced Henry recently, is the mint sauce of the soul. Sweet-sour, despised by the French and irrevocably associated with low church Sunday luncheons. Henry has forsworn guilt, along with sex, sunbathing and sugar in coffee.

Now a pretty young man has waltzed on to the stage. Hell, mint sauce or murder, I can't work out the rights and wrongs. The only certainty is that this play will last a long time. Shakespeare always does, let alone Shakespeare with a Glynebourne-length dinner interval.

The rest of the audience doesn't mind. For them this is the beginning of the story. For me, it's the conclusion. The beginning was two years ago. I was wandering the streets of Oxford wearing this very dress. And those crippling, soon-to-be-wrecked spike heels. Also an ankle-length mackintosh with a half-bottle of whisky tucked into the pocket. As yet untouched.

It was a summer night, Midsummer night near as dammit, almost half past nine, and it was my thirtieth birthday.

'If music be the food of love,
play on . . .'

or

*A MIDSUMMER NIGHT'S
DAYDREAM*

CHAPTER ONE

For no particular reason, I had arrived at Magdalen Bridge. I was wandering lonely as a cloud — a black thunder-cloud — because I was reluctant to return to St Margaret's College. But the shoes were pinching like hell, so here I was, taking the weight off my aching plates by leaning on the stone parapet of the bridge. And, as the last shreds of daylight faded from the sky, I was gazing down into the Cherwell. Moodily.

If the above has conjured up soft-focus shots of the dreaming spires; of college walls gilded in the melting sun; of punts drifting like lazy swans under the bridge . . . you can forget them. There was a typhoon blowing that night. It was the kind of Oxford summer weather your memory kindly obliterates after you've left the place. You remember the balmy punting evenings. The other six nights of the week were probably as dank and rainily grim as this one.

There were punts below now all right. Roped together for the night, they were heaving and clashing restlessly on the swollen water. Even the ducks had taken refuge on land. Under the arches of the bridge the river oiled angrily. Behind me, cars sliced up into the High like powered water-skiers. As Magdalen clock struck the half-hour, the rain responded by thickening with callous ferocity.

I didn't care. This miserable monsoon seemed a perfectly fitting backdrop. In such a night as this should Becca Haydock celebrate the end of her youth, the end of an affair and, to all appearances, the end of her career.

And was I down-hearted? You bet your life I was.

An amplified drumbeat started to throb somewhere in the distance. The university savages were obviously still revolting the peace-loving natives of the town. For me, as the rain continued to fall with tropical warmth and passion, the drumming only reinforced the Somerset Maugham atmosphere. Oh for a long verandah and a longer pink gin. The river was dark with mud. Easy to imagine a few crocodiles lurking down there. The rain carved glossy brown circles on the surface.

'Looks like the whirls on nut chocolate, dunnit?' said a man's voice behind me. 'Jush – just imagine drowning in chocolate. Bloody wonderful way to go.' The words were slurring together and I recognized, without deigning to look round, that the speaker was drunk. I wished I was drunk myself, but that didn't predispose me to chatting with inebriated strangers. I pretended I hadn't heard. No use. 'Like chocolate, do you?' he enquired.

'No,' I said crisply. Fibber. There was a half-eaten bar in my pocket even now. But I wanted to be left alone to enjoy my wallow in misery. I'm not prone to depression; I'm even less prone to indulging it. So, just this once, I was bloody well going to make the worst of it.

But the man flopped against the parapet beside me, forcing me to look at him. Squat and scruffy, he was clad in a sodden anorak and pale checked trousers which flapped wetly round his stocky legs. 'Swiss chocolate,' he said dreamily. 'Belgian, maybe. None of your home-grown muck. Best things in life are foreign imports.' His teeth flashed white in a grin. 'Like me.'

His accent was certainly foreign, but only to Oxford. His vowels were British, and as solidly uncompromising as a loaf of Hovis. Yorkshire, or maybe Lancashire. An ear for accents was only one of the thespian skills I lacked.

'In France, now,' he went on, 'they take chocolate seriously, know that?' I had no intention of encouraging him, but this was a rhetorical question. 'Over there you can get to be a brain surgeon quicker than a master *chocolatier*. Lotta people die before they make the grade.'

'Really?' I said, and winced because I could hear in my own voice my mother dealing with a door-to-door salesman. For a paid-up member of the Labour Party, Ma can get fearsomely high-horsed when she wants.

'Got their priorities right,' he continued, apparently undaunted. 'Live to eat, they do. Not eat to live. Heard that before? The French —'

'Yes,' I snapped. 'I have heard it before.'

'Not a vegetarian, are you?'

'No.'

'Well that's something, any rate,' he said. 'Want a cigar?'

'I don't smoke.'

'Nor me neither,' he agreed, but he produced from his pocket something resembling a Cumberland sausage. 'What the hell? Best Havana — stink like old socks. Thass what she said.' This seemed to amuse him because he rocked with laughter so violently he couldn't even bite the end off the thing, but it was a curiously sour laugh which ended abruptly as he spat the end into the river. Then there was a protracted frowning pantomime of lighting what was left: no small matter given the driving rain and his condition. He lurched towards me and I stiffened, but he was only trying to use me as a windbreak. So I settled back against the wet parapet while he struggled.

He was shorter than me, but then most people are, even when I'm not bestriding the petty world on stilettoes. I haven't got a hang-up about my size any more. As a gangling teenager, when I first came up to Oxford, I strove frantically to curl myself down to a respectable five foot six. No longer. Towering over the world doesn't bother me. Very handy in supermarkets. But there's no question it bothers some men. Richard, of course, is six foot tall exactly and therefore a whole inch and a half taller than me. It says six feet on his passport and in *Spotlight*, so it must be true — and only my

11

imagination that I can see clean over the top of his head in my bare feet. No prizes for guessing why my feet were unaccustomed to high heels.

What this stranger lacked in height, however, he certainly made up for in breadth. He was built like a tank. His hands curving round the feeble glimmer of a match were the size of dinner plates. On one hairy wrist, in the flickering light, I caught sight of a tattoo. Some kind of bird.

The tip of the Zeppelin finally spluttered and glowed into life. 'There,' he said with apparent satisfaction, coughing violently between inept sucks.

I wondered whether he was a tramp. Oxford had plenty even in my day, and there were probably more in these straitened times. His anorak was disgustingly stained, he was unshaven, and his nose was bent like a boxer's. He had dark, grizzled curls, close-cut, and − I thought − an unusually swarthy complexion. Foreign, like he said.

'What's your problem?' he demanded suddenly.

'I beg your pardon?'

'Saturday night,' he said. 'Here you are. Standing on a bridge in the pouring rain. Looking miserable as sin.'

Chatting with a drunken tramp.

'I'm fine,' I snapped. And I turned away from the parapet, straightened myself, shook some of the rain from my hair, and took half a step in the direction of the city centre. My heel snagged in a crack between the paving stones and I staggered. The tramp shot out a beefy arm towards me.

'"Give me thy hand, O fairest . . ."' he bellowed with the lusty fervour of a bar-stool baritone, grabbing my hand.

'Shut up,' I hissed, holding on to him only because I had to yank the heel free. 'People are staring.'

A lone man was walking his dog on the other side of the bridge. He did not even glance round. You could tell by his hunched shoulders that tramps bursting into grand opera were ten a penny on these rarefied pavements.

'Thass *Don Giovanni*, you know,' said the tramp indignantly.

'I do know,' I snapped (another fib), twisting my foot desperately this way and that.

'"*Your tiny hand is frozen . . .*"' carolled my companion, switching composers effortlessly. Cradled in his enormous paws, my hand actually did look quite tiny. Any minute now he would kiss it.

'Oh no it isn't,' I said, snatching it back, and couldn't resist adding with a smirk, 'and yes I do know that's *Bohème*.'

The song petered out on a strangled rising phrase. 'Too high for me,' he said. And then: 'Sorry. Drunk as a skunk. You're right. Go away and ignore me.'

Of course — perversely — that was what persuaded me to linger. Besides, I was lonely, I like Puccini and what the hell else was there to do? So I found myself leaning on the parapet again.

As darkness closed in, Magdalen tower glowed peachily in the floodlights, and the clusters of globe lamps across the bridge were reflected in white shimmering circles on the wet paving stones. So pretty. Nostalgically, I remembered lingering on this bridge until the early hours, discussing life, the meaning of art and overdraft facilities.

'This,' said the tramp, taking one final puff from his cigar, 'is bloody disgusting.' And he sent it hurtling into the river.

'So why smoke it?'

He touched one stubby finger to the crooked nose with a slightly cross-eyed air of wisdom. 'A Havana a day keeps the girlfriend away . . .'

'No wonder they say smoking's bad for you,' I quipped, quite wittily I thought, but he just gazed at me lugubriously and shook his head.

'Know where she is? Spain. Thass where I was till last night, too. Sitting under a Mediterranean moon. Ice clinking in the drink, pool lapping at my toes. I should still be there now. And where am I?' He looked up at the murky sky. 'After ten hours sweated labour too. What a bloody life. No wonder I'm drunk.'

13

'Well I,' I said, not to be outdone, 'should have spent today on the river, toasting my birthday in champagne.'

'Happy birthday.'

'What's so happy about being thirty?'

'Rubbish.' He belched and attempted, without success, to disguise it with a cough. 'I'm nearly forty.'

'It's different for men.'

'Christ, don't you give me that,' he exclaimed. 'Please.'

'Give you what?'

'Women — age. The biological clock. The race with Mother bloody Nature . . .'

'Who gives a stuff?' I said. 'I'm a day older than yesterday. That's the least of my worries.' I gazed down, but you could hardly see the water or the punts now. Just the glittering reflections of the lights above. 'You know, today we were going to hire a punt,' I sighed. 'Take a picnic. I bought a hamper specially. Proper wicker, with blue china plates and a checked cloth. It would have been so lovely.'

'Not in this weather it wouldn't. You did right to call it off.'

I looked up from the river. 'The weather,' I said, 'was not the reason for the cancellation.'

'No?'

The stranger on the train syndrome. I'd always been reluctant to admit problems even to intimate friends, but here I was trotting the whole sorry saga out. Or rather, spitting it out. Venomously.

'The problem was the Honourable Helena.' Both aitches to be sounded.

'What?'

'The wife.'

'Ah, well,' he said, and continued with the air of a child parroting adult proverbs: 'People who swim in shark-infested waters can't complain if they get bitten.'

'Bit of a swimmer yourself?' I enquired tartly.

'I learned my lesson,' he said. 'Find out, did she? The wife?'

14

'Not as far as I know,' I said tightly. 'In fact, certainly not. Simply, earlier this week, it seems my friend Richard was unaccountably overcome by an attack of husbandliness. A terminal attack . . .'

I'd been planning today for weeks. Everyone knows birthdays, Christmases and suchlike are tough for The Other Woman. She must expect to find herself abandoned on high days and holidays. My view had always been that *other* Other Women didn't plan imaginatively enough. The annual invitation from my old college, which in former years had gone straight in the bin, had instead inspired today's masterly strategy.

You see, I knew Richard's widowed mother-in-law lived in Oxfordshire because, infuriatingly, he was commanded down there by the Hon. Hel. every free weekend.

At first I'd imagined stately weekends in the country pile, forelock-tugging yokels and grouse piled high. It was not Richard, typically, who told me the peerage had been a Labour creation, all of forty-odd years old. But even Richard (who would, an acid-tongued friend once said, include the Hon. on a milk bill) had admitted there was no family seat, just a between-the-wars four-bedroom job. Modest, but nevertheless crumbling. And the longer I knew him, the more vitriolic grew his complaints about the privations of life with the Lady ma-in-law: cold baths, tinned soup, tea-bags used twice over. Even the nouveau aristocracy is not what it was.

So (I had suggested cunningly) if you absolutely must go down there the weekend of my birthday, can't you slip into Oxford for the day? Why not escape the family and the recycled tea-bags and have a heavenly lunch on the river with me? Revisiting the haunts of my youth? And, yes, Richard had thought this was a perfectly terrific idea . . .

'Until Monday night,' I said bitterly to the tramp. 'Out of the blue, he asked me out to dinner. And just as the coffee arrived, told me it was off. I thought he meant my birthday picnic. But no, it turned out he was talking about the whole caboodle. Us. Finito.'

15

'Why?' said the tramp.

A gaggle of children, clad in full evening dress, wandered past us twirling brollies and giggling hysterically. One of them was essaying a tap-dance, while loudly dooby-doing a familiar tune. 'Singing in the Rain.' What else?

'You tell me,' I answered sourly. 'I still don't know.'

I remembered the conversation with Richard through a hideously nauseous haze. I adore you, of course, Richard had said, just as much as ever. But . . .

'But what?' I had snarled.

'Well . . . Helena,' he mumbled, stirring his coffee like a Kenwood Chef. 'Supposing she finds out? What about the boys?'

I pointed out that he hadn't sprouted a wife and two sons overnight, and he'd said the time came when a man must consider not his own selfish desires but his family, blah blah, the future, blah, and with Helena's mother so gravely ill . . .

His ma-in-law? Where did she come in? That was when I lost the thread of the plot.

Believe me, he went on, this hurts me more than . . .

Really. He really genuinely did say that.

But I'd been watching a cluster of black bubbles whirling round his cup and wondering why my stomach seemed to be pursuing them. Round and round. This was not the effect of Richard's protestations of undying devotion but . . .

'Probably the seafood cocktail,' I said now to the tramp.

'Dodgy mussel?' He shook his head. 'Very nasty.'

'Awful,' I agreed fervently. 'My innards were heaving like the English Channel. No way can you play the big love scene dodging to the loo every ten minutes. I had to rush home in a cab — but he's not escaping that easily. I made him promise he'll come round tomorrow afternoon. Now I'm feeling human again I'll find out what the hell's going on. Honestly,' I added, 'you wouldn't believe how lousy I felt. I've not eaten a proper meal all week.'

This appeared to affect him far more profoundly than the

sad tale of the end of my affair. 'Thass terrible,' he said. 'Come on, sweetheart. I'll feed you.'

I stiffened, already regretting my disclosures. 'I'm not hungry, thank you.'

''S'matter of fact,' he said, 'I don't think I could face food either. Which *proves* how bad things are.'

The clock struck the three-quarters with ponderous musicality. The sound reminded me with painful vividness of late-night vigils over essays. It also reminded me that it was time to curtail this bizarre conversation and go back to college. I thought about the walk, and quailed. Instead I tottered, wincing with every step, just as far as the kerb. I would try and pick up a cab. Always the same. The broker I get, the more I spend. In times of affluence, I have been known to be quite Scrooge-like.

'You think you've got problems . . .' the tramp began, strolling across to join me, but I ignored him. I balanced on the kerb, scanning both directions of traffic. A van rumbled past and showered me with muddy water. I muttered curses between clenched teeth.

'What about me then?' he went on. 'Al says I'll be broke by Christmas.'

I snorted, protecting my monopoly in the misery stakes. 'Christmas? You should be so lucky. The cash machine rejected my card today.'

'My partner's left me to get married,' he continued dolefully.

'So what? Mine already is married.'

'Not that kind,' he said, hiccupping. '*Business* partner.'

'Al?'

He looked at me as though I was simple-minded. 'Al's the girlfriend,' he said, and then shook his head. 'I mean, *was*. Once. Long time ago. I'm talking about *Bunny*. Best partner a man ever had and he's gone and got married. Now of all times.' Any minute now, I thought, he would dissolve into richly alcoholic tears. 'Can't do it on my own,' he groaned. 'Can't make the business work, not without Bunny.'

17

'Well I,' I declared, 'haven't had a single offer of work in four months.'

'We sell up everything because of his big ideas. And then he ups and offs.'

'The lease on my flat expires in a fortnight and I can't possibly afford to renew it.'

'And where does he go? New Zealand, for Christ's sake. Why couldn't he fall for a girl from Newbury?'

'I shall be homeless,' I snapped, 'as well as jobless and manless.'

He glared drunkenly at me. 'I've had to come home three days early from holiday. To work. On a scheduled flight too. Cost a fortune.'

'Holiday?' I hooted. 'I haven't had a holiday in years. And what's more' — I delivered the clincher with grim triumph — 'my canary died this morning.'

'Bloody hell,' he said in awed tones — and began to laugh. He had, I must say, a wonderful laugh. The kind of fruity, uninhibited drain-gurgle any sitcom producer will murder to include in his audience.

'No laughing matter,' I muttered. Laughing. I'd lifted the cloth from his cage to find Ringo lying on the bottom, toes pointing heavenwards, eyes closed. What do you do with a dead canary in a fourth-floor London flat? So heartless simply to drop him in the dustbin. But you can't bury him in a flowerpot. Nor cremate him on a gas fire. It had, I confess now, crossed my mind to package him up neatly in a box and brown paper and address him to Richard Seymour. Which is surely how Other Women (Ex) are supposed to behave. Instead I parcelled him up in a brown (biodegradable) paper bag and stuffed him into the verger's compost heap behind St Mark's. Ashes to ashes, dust to dust. An admirably green solution.

'Give us your hand again,' said the tramp. 'We'll jump off the bridge together. Double suicide.'

I didn't take the proffered hand, but I grinned at him. I was warming to him in spite of myself.

'To tell you the honest truth,' he confided with the air of one conceding defeat generously, 'it was a bloody disastrous holiday. When they rang me up in Spain and said half the staff were down with summer flu, I couldn't get on a plane fast enough.'

'As a matter of fact,' I said, not to be outdone, 'I never much liked the canary.'

But the flat was silent as a morgue without his asinine trilling and cage-rattling routines, so I had jumped into the car and come to Oxford after all, even with no Richard and no picnic. A snap decision. A mistake.

Another car splashed past, but I was quicker off the mark this time, and dodged aside. Only when I resumed my vigil did the tramp blink owlishly and ask what the hell I was looking for. A cab, I said.

'In this weather? On a Saturday night?'

'I'm an optimist,' I said, turning and tip-tapping determinedly along the pavement, scanning the road as though sheer intensity of gaze would conjure up an empty taxi.

'That's funny. So am I,' he said, staggering along doggedly behind me. 'Optimist, I mean. Maybe we were meant for one another. Sort our problems out together. Fate.' He sounded — to my alarm — as though he might be about to break into song again. I turned to glare and he closed his mouth abruptly and stared back at me. We were standing under the last of the curly lamps at the end of the bridge. 'Hey up,' he said, blinking with the air of one seeing a vision, 'don't I know you?'

Oh sod it, I thought. Here we go again.

CHAPTER TWO

I'll come clean. Do you remember a series of Mr Frosty Frozen
Food adverts on the telly featuring a hyperactive, permanently
tracksuited mother-of-three? The ponytailed idiot who shinned
up to the treehouse with the beefburgers and zoomed down
the sand dune on a mountain bike with the crispy spring rolls?
The most popular ad was the one where she tripped into the
stream and the youngest lad, with a flashy flying tackle, rescued the plate of Pitza-Bitzas before it joined her in the mud.
Ho-bloody-ho. It took two days of sitting in that mud before
the Creative Geniuses behind the cameras were satisfied.

Well, that was me. Or rather, had once been me. Because
although no one except my bank manager seemed to have
noticed, the series had been terminated. The Creative Genuises
had created a new caring, sharing storyline with an inept,
unironed dad in a bedsit. No doubt targeting the lucrative
divorced parents market. I knew the actor now playing Dad
as a matter of fact. He actually was a divorced parent. Good
luck to him. For hacks like him and me, an advert is a life-
saver. You can slog your guts out, six nights and one matinée
a week for a whole year and not earn as much as you can
with a few thirty-second commercials. It's not hard to put up
with a couple of days in the mud if you can warm up afterwards in a hot bath in the very comfortable flat the ad's
paying for. Yes, adverts are wonderful things, except . . .

If you hit lucky with a running character, like I did, you
find you're recognized all over the place. Now, you might

think this is exactly what every actor craves. Indeed, I sneer myself when I read in my magazine of some twinkling starlet confiding how embarrassed she is to be besieged by autograph-hunters whenever she sticks her exquisitely sculpted nose-job outside the front door. A likely story, I think.

So why am I complaining? I'll tell you why. It's one thing to be a Famous Actor, recognized for your brilliant work, talents, or even for your glorious good looks. (I wouldn't mind a *bit* being recognized for glorious good looks. Fat chance.) It's another to be taken, a mere spring of twenty-six when the series began, for the real-life, almost middle-aged, gormless mother of three lusty lads, called Rosie. I'm not keen on Rebecca as a name, but I can't stand Rosie.

Where d'you get your tracksuits from, Rosie?

More than once complete strangers have asked me that. And, with warnings of the criminal sums advertising agencies are prepared to squander in the pursuit of authentic suburban reality, I tell 'em. When they caution me, with a friendly wink that I'm letting my youngest run a bit wild, I give a cheery grin and agree. Boys will be boys, I say.

Are they mad or am I?

As a matter of fact, it was the ones who *didn't* talk to me who were harder to cope with. The ones who talked about me as though I were frozen inside some invisible television screen and couldn't hear a word they said.

'Looks different, doesn't she?' a woman had observed to her friend that very afternoon, as I pondered the scarlet frock in the shop window.

The friend pursed her lips. 'Preferred her hair the other way myself.'

'So did I,' I had muttered glumly, and she jumped as though the mannequin in the window had addressed her, and scuttled away like an offended rabbit.

'You do look different,' said the tramp now, staring at me consideringly.

21

'Don't tell me, older.'

'Oh no,' he said, and his face split into a distinctly lascivious grin. 'Much sexier.'

Which shows how drunk he must have been. Greta Garbo might just manage to look sexy in an ankle-length yellow mac with rain streaming down her face, but I promise you I couldn't. I looked down my nose at him. I have a long nose.

'Let's go find a drink,' the tramp said unabashed. 'Drown our sorrows together.'

Actually I don't know why I keep calling him a tramp. Tramps don't have cigars in their pocket, ex-girlfriends in Spain and ex-business partners in New Zealand. At least, I shouldn't think so. But he looked so disreputable.

'Well . . .' I said uncertainly.

Dear Lord, how many times since then have I wondered what would have happened if I'd said yes? How many fates swung on my hasty calculation that if I bought a round of drinks I wouldn't have enough left in my purse for a taxi?

I shook my head. 'Better not,' I said, and resumed my limping progress up the High Street. He, equally unsteadily, followed.

'In a hurry to get somewhere?' he enquired.

'Not really,' I admitted. 'More a case of coming *from* somewhere. A Gaudy, if you want the truth.'

He lurched to a halt again and turned to frown at me. 'Gaudy? That a pub?'

I remember noticing his tight curls were full of wobbling rain-drops, glimmering in the street light. 'College reunion,' I explained. 'Annual dinner. Old girls get-together.' The very phrase, now I came to think of it, was profoundly chilling. Old girls. My God.

'Somehow, Miss Haydock,' Dr Dacre had observed over the opening (minuscule) sherries, 'I should not have expected to encounter you tonight.' Sixty if she was a day, and she still had the complexion of a Girl Guide. Did she drink the blood of incoming virgins? 'Not at one of our little Gaudy dinners.'

Dr Dacre was perceptive as ever. I wouldn't have expected to meet me at a Gaudy either. However, I was not about to explain that, when booking, I had viewed the event purely in the light of supper and a cheap bed for the night after spending a day of alcoholic and adulterous passion on the river.

'Oh well, you know how it is . . .' I muttered, which was about the standard of articulacy I had always achieved in tutorials with the woman.

'Good do, was it?' enquired the tramp. 'Bloody fabulous wine cellars in some of these colleges.'

I laughed sourly. 'Not the women's colleges.'

But I too had vaguely anticipated glamorously candlelit long tables, haunches of roast Magdalen venison, witty banter over the vintage port . . .

The strip-lit dining room was a parade square of navy blue. Rank upon rank of neatly buttoned and bowed blouses were tightly tucked into sensible skirts. Even the little black number I'd brought with me would have looked flashy here. As it was, resplendent in my new scarlet frock, I felt like the visiting whore at a Mother's Union convention. Brown soup, brown stew, brown chocolate mousse out of a packet.

By coffee time, with five speeches billed, my single glass of wine was long gone. To wash away the lingering miasma of the mousse, I was glugging water which tasted just as warm and dustily distinctive as the college tap water always had. Meanwhile, the post-prandial chat revolved around helpful husbands and clever (we don't like to use the word *gifted*, but . . .) children.

I studied the (badly typed) programme of festivities. No mention of liqueurs with the coffee. Not even a mint. And five speeches to come. It felt like midnight. I looked at my watch. It was barely nine o'clock.

'And do you have a partner?' enquired a kindly neighbour, having clocked the bare fingers of my left hand.

'I . . .' But then the full misery of my situation rose and

choked me. 'Must get to the loo,' I croaked. 'Before the speeches.' The chair screeched across the parquet. I left the room alone. Did everyone else have cast-iron bladders? By the time I returned to the dining-room doors, the first speech was under way. From inside, I heard a sycophantic tinkle of laughter.

And then I remembered that, once upon a time, there used to be an off-licence not five minutes' walk from the college gates.

'Did a runner eh?' said the tramp.

With the air of one about to flash dirty postcards, I lifted the flap on my pocket to reveal a half-bottle of cheap whisky nestling against the curve of my hip. What else do you buy when you're staying in a college room with no bottle-opener, no ice, no mixers, just a tap and a tooth-glass? But returning with the bottle to that chilly cell, heavy with the shades of undergraduates departed, had been such a sordid prospect, I had instead wandered on. And here I was now. With blistered feet, and dripping hair, ambling up the High in conversation with an unshaven drunk.

'You don't want to drink that paint-stripper, my lovely,' he said thickly. 'Come back to my place. I've single malts, champagne, you name it . . .'

An unshaven amorous drunk.

'Thank you very much,' I said primly. 'But I believe I'll return to college.' And kept right on walking.

Faintly, on a gust of wind, there drifted towards us the thrumming of a highly amplified band. The jungle drums were still beating their own rhythm away to the left.

Memories washed back on the tide of sound. Memories of Saturday nights alone, agonizingly convinced by the irrational hormones of youth, and the parties throbbing on every side, that I was the most unwanted girl in the university.

'Oh *balls!*' I cried in a burst of recognition and nostalgia.

'Beg pardon?' said the tramp.

24

But I was using the word literally. I'd realized belatedly it wasn't simple undergraduate parties making such a din.

'The music. This time of year, end of the summer term: there are probably balls all over the university tonight.'

'You're telling me there bloody are,' he said with an animation which surprised me. 'Why did I come home early from holiday? What d'you think I've been doing all day?'

Another straggle of evening-dressed youngsters giggled past us. Now I realized their destination.

'Straight off the bloody plane and into work I was this morning. No wonder I needed a drink after twelve hundred salmon and asparagus suppers.'

Only now did I recognize the blue-checked trousers flapping damply round his legs as chef's gear. 'Do you work in one of the college kitchens?'

'Are you kidding?' He nodded scornfully in the direction of the throbbing disco beat. 'These joints can't take the strain. We delivered enough strawberries there today to sink Wimbledon.'

'St Benedict's Hall?' I said wistfully. 'We fell in the fountain there one year.'

Abruptly, the pavement ahead of us was blocked by a merry, noisy, umbrella-wielding queue, spotlit in a rainbow of colours under arc-lights bright as a football stadium: the final remnants of the ball queue outside Bendy Hall.

God, I remembered queueing outside those ancient gates. Seemed like only yesterday. You always had to queue to get into balls. Part of the ritual of these annual all-night bashes was a security worthy of a Middle East airline. With tickets costing the wicked amount they did, ball-crashing was a highly popular sport among the young bloods. So the dreaming spires were spiked, the honey-coloured walls razor-wired, and the resultant queue to get through the one, needle's-eye entrance could take anything up to an hour.

We used to pass round the bottles of cheap fizz just like these children were doing. We didn't notice the existence of anyone outside our own glittering circle either. Just like theirs, our queue would part automatically to let grey shadows of the other, grown-up world pass through, without ever actually seeing them. Oh nostalgia . . .

'It's like being a ghost,' I said, stopping in the gloom on the other side of the queue and turning back to survey the arc-lit scene. It was unnervingly like gazing back into my own past.

The boys' evening suits looked just the same as they had in my day. Wrong sizes and wrong eras, the trousers were yanked up under the armpits with braces and the spiv-sized lapels adorned with dewy roses stolen from college gardens just as I remembered.

'I feel like a lost soul,' I said, 'who's wandered back to haunt the place she used to own.'

'Shouldn't go back,' said my companion, with an irritating air of sagacity. 'When something's over, it's over.'

'All these familiar buildings,' I went on. 'Look over there. Where the windows are lit up. I used to know nearly everyone on that floor. I had so many friends in Bendy Hall, and now the whole place — everywhere — is overrun with strangers.'

The girls still piled their hair into messy nests, woven with fresh flowers. Nothing had changed except the faces. Mud and rainwater were seeping up their petticoats like mixed chemicals up a filter paper. They didn't give a stuff. And I was middle-aged enough to be glad my own skirt was short.

'Can't recapture the past, it's gone for ever,' the tramp said, adding with an unexpected flash of poetry: 'like the bloom on a rose.'

'You're so right,' I murmured, but he wasn't talking about me and my melancholic wallowings.

'That's why I should never have gone on holiday. Al and me split up ages back. Should've known the holiday'd only end in tears but . . . You're not listening to me,' he added, sounding rather hurt.

'I'm feeling — dispossessed,' I wailed. 'It's like opening the

26

front door of your flat and finding a total stranger wearing your dressing gown, acting as though they owned the place. Imagine it.'

'Haven't got a dressing gown.'

'Don't be pedantic.'

'Don't even know what it means. I didn't have your education.' He grinned crookedly. 'Sounds bloody rude to me.'

Just look at me, I thought. All dressed up. Fit for a ball. Why, I wondered wistfully, couldn't an old friend somehow materialize out of my past and that queue, brandishing a spare ticket. And, even if they didn't exactly sweep me off my feet (I haven't many friends built on the necessary scale), at least sweep me into the ball. I'll swear that thought really, honestly, did cross my mind and it isn't a retrospective romantic gloss.

Because that's what happened. Almost.

Given a long hot bath, I daresay I could have dreamed up something of the kind because I am a prolific day-dreamer. Never a bathtime passes but that I spin some delicious drama casting myself, according to mood, as a languishingly lovely, wittily worldly, or simply fatally female leading lady. But all storylines, to satisfy, have to be plausible. Have to be rooted somewhere in the nitty-gritty of ordinary life. The events of the next few minutes were so improbable, I would have felt obliged to improve on them.

A bicycle exploded into view, not from the heavily guarded gate but from — or so it appeared — the actual college wall. It shot into the pool of arc-light, scattering the amiable queue and nearly cannoning into us. Then it swerved and juddered into a semi-collapsed heap at the roadside.

'Shit,' said my companion and plodded, arm outstretched, towards the bike, which was hastily righting itself. But suddenly the tramp appeared to change his mind, because he dodged away in the opposite direction. I think he called something about spotting a cab. I couldn't be sure, because I'd lost interest in him. I was staring, dizzy with disbelief, at the bike.

'Oliver?' I breathed, mellifluous as any languishing and

lovely romantic heroine. And then, with a steely projection more reminiscent of Margaret Thatcher as the cyclist began, unhearing, to ride away: 'Oliver!'

The bike wobbled and stopped again. And Oliver Langham straightened one long leg to the pavement, glancing back towards us. Or rather, towards *me*, because the tramp had vanished. Who cared?

'Sorry?' he said dazedly.

That soft, terribly public school voice, that tall angular figure belted into a shapeless mac, that floppy shock of fair hair, even the bicycle clips round the bony ankles: they were all unmistakable. I gathered together every seductive smile I had ever possessed into one magnificent, magnesium-bright beam.

'Hello, Oliver,' I purred.

Let us tread softly now, for we tread upon my juvenile dreams.

I realize Oliver Langham may not strike you as the ultimate object of womanly desire, but I was obsessed with him for the best part of my first term. True, I was in love with a few others at the same time. Well, there were four point seven male undergraduates to every lucky female in those days. Being Up at Oxford was, for me, being up in a continuous high of sexual infatuation, as exhausting as it was exhilarating. Fortunately the terms were short.

But Oliver Langham was different. Maybe his appeal was just that to my newly arrived eyes he was so very — Oxford. Oxford as in Marmalade, Brogues, Accent and Bags. You know, British classics. At any rate, he wasn't mad, unwashed and bad like most men I fell for in those days. Admittedly, no oil painting either — except maybe a Picasso from the most angular period. Oliver always had (at first glance) appeared just such a gangly tangle of limbs, spectacles and hair as you see before you now.

But look more carefully and you see meltingly sensitive

28

blue eyes, teeth of Californian perfection and a delicious cleft in his so-square jaw. What's more, he possesses, I promise you, the most adorably shy smile.

Which, unfortunately, was not glinting at this moment. In fact, he was frozen on the pavement edge, blinking at me through (I'd swear) the identical pair of scholarly horn-rims I remembered so well.

With a quiver of disappointment I realized the thrill of recognition had not been mutual. 'Becca,' I offered helpfully. 'Rebecca Haydock.'

He swallowed a couple of mouthfuls of air.

Of course, he had also enjoyed the inestimable attraction — when I first met him — of being An Older Man. At least twenty-three to my eighteen. A post-graduate replete with a certain air of mystery. Where did he go at night? Why was there no girlfriend?

That sweet air of helplessness, that jawline, those glasses — said my equally smitten chum Jenny — Clark Kent to the life.

'We knew each other years ago,' I offered now.

Not well enough. One invitation to tea, followed by choral evensong. Wow. Just call me Lois Lane. But Oliver Langham didn't have to walk through a swing door to effect the miraculous transformation into his alter ego. He picked up a baton. The tangle of elbows resolved into masterful purpose, and the second alto section of his choir (Jenny and I) melted in unison.

That choir, The Commoners, was one of dozens of hobbies (fencing, the Liberal party, Agatha Christie Appreciation) I had flitted and flirted through in my first term. My interest in Renaissance choral music was limited — but not in Oliver Super-Conductor Langham.

'Don't you remember?' I muttered now, beginning to get desperate. 'I used to sing in The Commoners.' Until Christmas, when quality control and auditions came in — and I went out. And never saw Oliver Langham again. Ah me. I found a new home in the medics' revue. No doubt the Bedpan Blues was more my *métier* than Byrd's five-part Masses. 'I was an alto,' I added finally.

29

The effect of these words was amazing. The talisman which brings the statue to life. 'Alto?' he echoed wonderingly. I actually thought for one moment he had remembered me, and beamed even brighter. 'Do you still sing?' he demanded.

No great perception was needed to see that he urgently desired an answer in the affirmative. Besides, saying 'yes' is a reflexive skill learned in years of auditions. Tap-dance? Wind-surf? Speak fluent Mandarin? You name it, an actress answers yes.

'Sure,' I said. I'd done six weeks on tour with a musical version of Snow White only a few years back, for heaven's sake. A heavy metal version.

'Madrigals?' he said.

The show must go on . . . Besides, if he'd asked whether I fancied swimming the Thames that night I would have flexed my biceps and smiled. As it was . . . Foll lolly loll loll. I shrugged with becoming modesty. 'Somewhat out of practice.' Twelve years or so.

'You can read, though?'

At least I didn't assume he meant newspapers. Besides, sight-reading music is like riding a bicycle. I told myself airily. Once learned, never forgotten. What I chose to overlook was that I had never been much good at it in the first place. I used to stand next to Jenny and tag along. I had an unpleasant suspicion that with madrigals you were stranded one to a part. Still, there's no business like show business . . . Of course I could read.

He twisted the bicycle round to face this way and advanced on me. 'You wouldn't help me out of a hole, would you?'

And as all the clocks in Oxford began striking ten o'clock, the rain stopped completely and a fairly Godmother sang in my head: You *shall* go the ball. You jammy bugger.

Oh, foll lolly loll loll.

CHAPTER THREE

Oxford college balls are strange phenomena. I daresay Cambridge balls are much the same. I know they insist on calling theirs May balls while holding them in June, but I've actually never been to one, so I couldn't say for sure. Maybe they're all modelled on grand London Society balls, but I've never wangled an invitation to one of those either.

The Oxford kind, however, last all night, and offer facilities comparable with your old-style Butlins Camp. With, on the whole, less comfort and very much less efficient bars. I may never have graced the Grosvenor Square Ball, but I speak as one who knows about Butlins camps. I served a whole summer in Minehead as a Redcoat.

Like any holiday camp, a ball offers an eclectic (and free) selection of entertainments: bands and discos, films and side-shows, fortune-tellers and wandering jugglers. There are generally two regimented sittings for dinner with stalls flogging shish kebab, candy-floss and suchlike to plug any gaps. Both institutions can also be relied on for traditional bacon-and-egg breakfasts. The only difference is that holiday campers sensibly expect this when they get up; surviving ball-goers, just before staggering home to bed.

Butlins can generally offer more in the way of fairground rides, although it has been known for dodgems to be installed in medieval quadrangles, and any ball worth its salt ought to be able to field, at the very least, a helter-skelter. This ball — I saw through the well-guarded gateway — had one of those

31

giant bouncing castle constructions just inside the entrance. Taffetaed Lavinias and Sophias were springing, shrieking, into its rubbery billows as soon as they got through the security cordon.

But Oliver did not even approach the main gate. White-Rabbit style he led me behind the queue to a tiny doorway recessed in the college wall and, after riffling through every pocket, produced a key. He unlocked the door, we both stooped, went in, pulled the bike in after us and shut the door on the light and hilarity outside. We were in a kind of stone tunnel with doors on either side. The Alice in Wonderland feeling intensified.

'Where are we?' I said. My voice echoed. I could feel, rather than hear, a disco beat pulsing somewhere nearby.

'Under the Principal's Lodgings.'

He flipped on an electric light and wheeled the loudly ticking bicycle down the flagstones to the far end, where, with the air of long practice, he tangled the handlebars in an elegant wrought iron gate to keep it upright.

'Won't someone be coming through there?' I asked automatically. Can't help it. Even in Wonderland I'm mindful of my social responsibilities.

He glanced up. 'It's only the gate to their garden,' he said. 'Even Constance can't say she's likely to want to go out there on a night like this. Come on. We're late.'

Which is just what the White Rabbit had said too. So, ducking through another medieval doorway, I followed. We emerged past a monolithic slab of lager-swilling security heavy into the main quadrangle, which was seething with damp but determined revellers, all scanning programmes like orienteers with maps.

There's no question that, while holiday camps may have the edge in fairground hardware, balls win hands down when it comes to sheer variety of entertainment. A disco is a disco anywhere, but not many holiday camps have yet thought of offering a performance of *Lysistrata* on the bowling green. In the original Greek. Nor a string quartet playing late Beethoven in the chapel. And nor — come to that — a madrigal group. Wow.

In fact, at a ball, the number of different events crammed into one small space, a tightly printed programme and a short summer night is overwhelming. I could understand why the Lavinias and Sophias were hurtling — map in hand — from one amusement to the next like panicked humming-birds. Stand still for a minute and you're bound to miss something. Since you've paid such an exoribitant sum to come there is an exhausting obligation to extract value for money.

The high cost of tickets is also the reason for the wacky range of entertainments on offer. It isn't so much that ball organizers seek to attract the punters with promises of every imaginable diversion. (Would you be seduced by the prospect of Greek drama in the rain?) No, it's because every scratch orchestra, every scrabbled-together choir or drama group in the University will offer just about anything to secure a gig at a ball — and the free tickets which accompany the booking.

'Unbelievable,' said Oliver distractedly as he shepherded me round the quad. 'They absolutely insisted I pitch for this bloody ball, and then half of them don't turn up.'

'They?'

'The madrigal group,' said Oliver, pausing to let a dancing bear career across his path. 'Common Chord. It's an offshoot of The Commoners.'

'Do you still conduct The Commoners?' I said dizzily. It was like tumbling back through time. To learn the fledgling choir I remembered still existed, that *something* was still unchanged . . .

'Well — yes,' said Oliver. 'I mean, not just — recently. But the baritone left a message on the answering machine. Said he'd got flu.' Oliver scowled. 'He claimed there was an epidemic. First I've heard of it.'

'There is,' I said. 'Or so I gather.'

He led the way up a curling stone staircase of an antiquity you could positively smell. 'Well, everybody I could get hold of claimed to have it,' he said. 'Or they'd already gone down for the vac. Or were revising for a viva. Or singing at another ball. There are three tonight.'

At the top of the staircase was a door with a big sheet of paper sellotaped across it labelled: 'STRING QUARTET, BEAR, COMMON CHORD.'

'We leave our stuff in here,' said Oliver, opening this door and then pushing through another inner door which was felted and festooned with empty drawing pins. 'So, in the end, I felt I simply had to come myself.'

Sydney Carton sounded more cheerful about standing in for Charles Darnay.

'Free ball ticket,' I suggested brightly.

Oliver, holding open the door, eyed me as though I were demented.

The room was poorly lit with one, yellow-shaded bulb and looked pitifully naked. There were grey smears of Blu-tack on the walls, sticky coffee rings on the desk and a pervading air of books and owner lately departed. Now there was only a tangle of coats on the bed and wellingtons tumbled nearby.

'And as if that weren't enough, I got here to find the alto's gone sick too,' said Oliver, bundling off his mac and snapping the bicycle clips off his trouser legs. 'And Elizabeth's first class. One of the best altos in Oxford.'

God, even the dullest man can look alluring in decent evening dress: severe black, plain crisp shirt. I gaped wordlessly – less in admiration of Oliver's tie and tails, however, than in dismay at his description of the absent Elizabeth.

'The best?'

'Well, of the female altos,' he said, considering the matter briefly. This was small consolation.

The room was cold, with the year-round chill peculiar to stone-walled rooms, sunless for five centuries. But I only shivered when I spotted, beside the pile of coats on the narrow pallet bed, a horribly professional-looking stack of dark blue, gold-embossed folders, each thick with music.

'All I wanted was to get this over as quickly as possible and then find Constance,' said Oliver, picking one of these up and riffling furiously through the copies inside. 'But I had to make an attempt, at least, to replace Elizabeth . . .'

"So you were bicycling off an alto hunt, were you?' I enquired with entirely false bonhomie.

'What else could I do? Hopeless quest at this hour on a Saturday night,' said Oliver. 'I mean someone who knows our repertoire, and can read and so forth. There's a woman at St Hilda's I was just praying hadn't gone down yet. Extraordinary I should run into you.' He spoke distractedly, still sorting copies.

'Extraordinary,' I echoed, keeping my mac on and groping in the pockets. 'Um, how many are we?'

'The usual six,' said Oliver, and my heart, which had been vainly hoping for an ensemble more along Huddersfield Choral lines, sank lower still.

When going into battle, first apply warpaint. But I didn't even have a handbag. The spending on my ensemble had had to stop somewhere. In the pocket of my mac I found a comb, and also the whisky bottle, hell, how embarrassing, and stuffed that back. In the other pocket lurked my purse, the melting remains of a chocolate bar and my college room key. Not even a sodding lipstick.

'Do you want to have a look at what we're doing?' said Oliver.

'One minute,' I said desperately. 'Just combing my hair.'

I located a small and dimly lit mirror inside a cupboard door and began combing my sopping locks and biting my lips to give them a bit of colour. Probably a good thing I couldn't see much beyond a dusty blur. I licked a finger and tried to erase the panda smudges under my eyes. Beauty's all in the mind, I thought bravely, pouting at myself. Glitter, my darling . . .

The door exploded open and a tubby, curly-haired cherub with freckles and a crimson cummerbund rolled in. 'We're late!' he roared. '*Oliver!*' You would have thought he had seen a visitor from Mars. 'Christ, I didn't expect –'

'Tom's ill,' interrupted Oliver flatly. 'He left a message on my answering machine.'

'Bloody fool,' said the cherub. I noticed, with surprise, his face had turned quite as crimson as his cummerbund. 'Why didn't he come and find me? Didn't he know? He should have –'

'Probably buried in exams. Anyway, it doesn't matter,' said Oliver, gathering up a pile of the folc rs. 'I'm here now. Someone had to step in. We couldn't let this place down.'

'Well, yes, but . . .' The cherubic cheeks contorted and he seemed unable to frame words. 'Well, if it's OK by you . . .' he said gruffly. 'Better get a move on then. We should be starting the serenade by the fountain in three minutes.'

'Coming,' said Oliver. 'Where are the others?'

'Waiting at the bottom of the staircase. And who's this?' he said, pointing at me.

'An alto,' said Oliver. 'Alastair Frost, um . . .'

'Becca Haydock,' said the alto, smiling nervously.

'Hey! Don't I know you?' said Alastair Frost, which surprised me because undergraduates in my day had better things to do than watch the telly.

'Shouldn't think so,' I said. 'It's about a hundred and fifty years since I was up.' With the bravado of a boxer shedding his towel, I dropped my mac to join the pile on the bed. The strapless scarlet screamed as brazenly in this dim and chilly room as it had in the convent atmosphere of St Margaret's.

'You're wearing terrifically well then, if I may say so,' said Alastair, taking my hand and kissing it. His mouth was wet. A lecher-in-the-making and he looked barely older than my television children. 'Where did Oliver find you?'

'Walking the streets,' I said merrily. 'All dressed up with, as it were, nowhere to go.'

Oliver glanced up. He seemed to find it unremarkable that I had arrived conveniently packaged in full ball attire. 'Have you been drinking, Alastair?'

'I sing better when I'm pissed,' said Alastair, and grinned at me. 'Come right on down,' he said, opening the door for me with a flourish. 'Who do you sing with now?'

'Anyone who happens to share my bath,' I said brightly. 'Oh, is that folder for me?'

I peeped inside. The density of lines and notes was reminiscent of a railway junction at rush hour — and about as meaningful. I snapped it shut again and tucked it confidently under one arm.

I could, I thought, make a run for it. For the second time in an evening. But the madrigal squad was gathered at the foot of the stairs; Oliver, two steps behind me, was between me and my mac; scarlet is not inconspicuous — and I could as easily fly as run in those ankle-wrenching shoes.

'To the fountain then,' said a pale-faced girl with Pre-Raphaelite hair. Both she and the other woman were clad in pointy-sleeved velvet numbers, droopily redolent of lutes, minstrels and such.

'Oliver's standing in for Tom,' announced Alastair loudly, almost as though he was trying to forestall argument. 'And this is Becca.' I smiled glassily. No wonder they looked shocked. I didn't much resemble my idea of a lady madrigalist either. But I fell in with the troupe, retaining as best I could both the folder under the arm and the nonchalant air of confidence. Besides, I could read music. Course I could. Foll lolly loll . . . et cetera.

We assembled in front of the fountain. A straggle of bedraggled audience awaited us. There was no rain now, but the gentle plashing of water which spouted from two growling lion faces made me wish, nervously, I had visited a lavatory. The others shuffled into place round me, and like them I opened my folder. Then I gulped hard, and prayed for inspiration.

Oliver on the other side of the semi-circle, tinged a tuning fork and gazed at us meaningfully, raising one finger.

Whereupon I realized my Fairy Godmother really was on

duty that night. When Oliver had cycled out of the queue, it had seemed likely. What happened next convinced me.

Ball organizers always tend to assume, fondly, that housing a thousand mega-watts of band in a tent will somehow contain the noise as well. At that precise moment, in the marquee immediately behind us on the Founder's Lawn, a rock band struck up its first ear-bombing chorus.

Oliver paused, finger still aloft, and said something.

'What?' roared Alastair. 'Can't hear you.'

'We can't sing here,' cried Oliver, stepping forward.

'Got to,' shouted Alastair. 'It's in the programme.' He turned to me winking. 'Always the same at balls. Like pissing in the Atlantic. Here goes.'

And as we opened our mouths and sang — stray snowflakes lost under a blizzard — I found myself beaming straight into Oliver Langham's searingly serious blue eyes.

I was going to enjoy the ball after all. Foll lolly loll *loll*.

At ten-forty-five precisely, Alastair waved his pocket fob watch with the aplomb of a shop steward. Our spot was over — and never a note heard. The only flaw was his cheerful shout of: 'See you chaps at five by the tower, then.'

'Are we singing again?' I bawled into his ear.

'We're the dawn bloody chorus, darling.'

'Only' — I smiled confidingly — 'my voice is appalling in the early morning.' What an improviser. 'It takes simply hours to warm up to, well, anything passable.' A few actresses I knew — the more intense sort — used to say this, so I didn't see why singers shouldn't have the same problem.

'Oh, mine too,' bellowed Alastair promptly. 'Don't give it a thought. One quick number, that's all, and we're down before we die of exposure. It's bloody cold up that tower and I hope you don't suffer from vertigo because . . . Oh *shit*.'

He wasn't looking at me. He was staring past my shoulder. I turned round. Oliver was stacking the navy-blue folders precariously on the edge of the fountain. My fellow choristers were gathered by the wall of the pulsating marquee. Looking even more busily cherubic than ever, Alastair trotted straight across to them and plunged into conference. A moment later, jerking his head towards me to follow, he led a delegation over to Oliver.

'I say . . .' he began — but not loudly enough. Grimacing, he shepherded Oliver behind a stone wall. I followed determinedly.

'Deafening, isn't it?' said Oliver wearily. 'But don't think I couldn't hear the obscene alternative you were substituting for the refrain in "The Swan", Alastair.'

God, if he could hear that — could he hear me? Or rather, *not* hear me, because I'd mimed the lot with the angelic aplomb of a choirboy on a Christmas card.

'Thing is,' said Alastair, toying with his fob watch, 'we wondered whether we wouldn't be better substituting the 'Maying Carol' at dawn. Just Nige, Fay and me. The rest of you can enjoy yourselves . . .'

I could have kissed him. It never occurred to me that he had not arranged this as an act of mercy to me.

'. . . or of course go home,' he finished hastily.

Oliver shrugged. 'Fine,' he said. 'God knows why I bothered turning out. This mob wouldn't notice if we sang the Highway Code. If you come upstairs we'll sort out the copies.' He strode through an archway back into the quad and began climbing the stone steps to the room again. 'Post them on to me if you want.'

'You're not going?' I said, stopping dead halfway up the staircase. Alastair, glancing rather peculiarly at me — almost as though he were embarrassed — sidled past up to the room.

Oliver turned and looked down at me. 'After I've seen Constance. At least, then I'll . . . well, I don't know. God alone knows . . .' He began climbing the stairs again. 'Alastair's idea seemed sensible to me. I thought you agreed.'

'But you can't bring me in here and then just dump me,' I said indignantly, scrambling up the stairs two at a time after him and following him into the room.

Alastair, who was already riffling through a sheaf of copies, flushed a vivid red and cleared his throat. 'Um, I could show you around,' he offered, with notably less zest than earlier.

'Oliver is going to take me for a drink,' I announced. 'It's the least he can do after hijacking me off the street.'

'Fine,' said Alastair, laughing uncertainly. 'Well, why not? I've got the copies here. Um, see you around later. Maybe. If not, well, um . . .' Rather to my surprise, he shook Oliver's hand – but not mine. 'All the best, mate.' He waved at me, warily I thought, and, thrusting a roll of music into one pocket, he shuffled out. He seemed anxious to get away.

'Well?' I said expectantly. Like a child who has been promised a treat and is not going to be fobbed off with excuses.

'Look, I don't think I'm really up to it. This sort of thing,' said Oliver.

'What sort of thing?'

'Balls. Dancing – drinking. Well . . . anything really.' He was leaning on the desk, head bowed.

'Oh,' I said. And deliberately let the disappointed silence quiver in the air. It's just possible I may have permitted my chin to quiver as well.

Oliver loosened his bow tie and dashed the stray lock of hair back from his forehead. It was a scene, I thought, from a 1930s movie. His tall tie-and-tails elegance belonged to the era of Noël Coward and Jack Buchanan. So did his accent, come to that. He straightened and gave me a weary half-smile. Gosh yes, perfect, I nearly exclaimed aloud. He ought to be about to tell me, through bravely clenched teeth, that he couldn't leave his wife after all. That he was most terribly, terribly, sorry, Amanda, but . . .

'I don't want to be a bore,' he said. 'But just the thought of going out there . . .' He shrugged. 'Life has been –' he began, and I'd swear I remember these words perfectly: 'Life has been – rather ghastly recently.' Which proved, in retrospect, to be stiff-lipped understatement worthy of any British vintage screenplay.

I did not perceive that at the time, however.

'Join the club,' I said. 'Mine's been foul.'

Such a well-brought-up boy. He immediately said politely, 'I'm sorry to hear that. What's the matter? Or perhaps you'd prefer . . .'

But I was bored with my troubles. Besides, I'm a terminal optimist. Something was bound to turn up. And if it didn't of its own accord, well I'd just have to give Fate a helpful shove. Speaking of which . . .

'Today is my birthday,' I said cunningly. 'And because you yanked me in here it's too late, now, to celebrate as I planned.'

With a lonely tooth-mug of whisky and a half-bar of chocolate?

'Oh God,' said Oliver. 'I'm sorry.'

'And,' I went on, wide-eyed with guile, 'I'm not sure I can get back into college.'

'Surely — it's not even eleven yet, is it?'

'St Margaret's used to shut the gates at eleven. Of course, in the good old days they had a night porter and gate hours. Now I've noticed a push-button job to the side of the lodge door. And,' I concluded with triumphant truthfulness, 'I don't know the code.'

He winced. 'What can I say?'

'I suppose,' I sighed, confident as an angler who knows, even if the fish doesn't, that the bait has been irrevocably swallowed, 'there might still be the low wall into the kitchen yard. Always was in my day. They used to leave a dustbin on the other side to make climbing over easier. Goodness knows if I can manage it dressed like this. Still . . .'

'Well,' said Oliver, straightening his tie again with a reluctance which I blithely ignored, 'I daresay the least I can do is buy you a drink first. Um, did you happen to notice where the bar was?'

CHAPTER FOUR

Imagine a rickety, formica-topped table. Innocently laid out on it — before festivities began, I deduced — had been a small chopping board, a blunt knife, the odd piece of fruit and a limp handful of mint. Scraps and juice now testified to this. Beneath the table would have stood a cardboard box with a few bottles of lemonade, a couple of Pimm's and a tray of glasses. Now, put behind the table one cowering, underpaid skivvy with no small change. In front of him looms a slavering horde, fifty or more strong, all roaring for immediate refreshment.

I suppose it took us about ten minutes to get to the front. Oliver put me in mind of a saint being jostled by the mob to his martyrdom. I clutched his arm and edged us purposefully forward.

One or two people glanced at me — or so I fancied — curiously. But I was used to attracting funny looks.

'Does this make you feel as old as it does me?' I said and, catching the eye of one of the reinforcement skivvies now labouring behind the table, boldly demanded two pint glasses.

'Two *pints*?' said Oliver.

'You're right,' I said, impressed. 'Better make it four. It could be dawn before we reach the top of this queue again.'

It was tricky juggling two large glasses apiece through the throng, so at my suggestion we downed one immediately.

'Actually,' said Oliver, halfway down, 'I don't really drink.'

'Don't worry,' I said in disgust. 'They've barely coloured the lemonade.'

'Quite — thirst-quenching.' He drained the glass and added defiantly, 'Maybe I needed a drink.'

I smiled approvingly. 'That's the spirit.'

That night, in that mood, had there been a fireplace handy I might have felt inclined to hurl the empty glasses into it, with a lusty Slavonic oath. Instead, I tucked them out of harm's way on a windowsill and, remaining glasses in hand, we wandered off to find some peace, amiably colliding as we ducked under a Gothic stone archway. Eventually we settled, side by side, on a bench in front of a rose-bed to watch the ball roll by.

The air was warm, if a little damp, and the noise of the rollicking rock band in the marquee had temporarily given way to a string orchestra somewhere else. Rather out of tune. The first dinner sitting piled in past us and, as the crowds thinned, so did the clouds overhead. A pale, fat moon peered shyly over the college roof and I heard a peacock yowling from on high. Velvety roses bled sweet perfumes into the darkness behind us. The trees were glittering with fairy lights, and Oliver Langham's profile, as he gazed at his feet, was of Roman-coin nobility. If an emperor can be imagined in specs.

'It's like a time warp,' I observed after a few minutes. The thought was more poetic than the words.

'Sorry?' said Oliver, startled out of his reverie.

'Finding myself back here in Bendy Hall. And you still here, looking just the same.'

Actually, he had improved with age. Men tend to. Irritatingly. At twenty-four Oliver had looked, even to my fond eyes, a fogyish thirty. At — what? — thirty-six, he had, I decided dispassionately, advanced to a really rather distinguished-looking thirty-one. The tail suit helped. But he was certainly unchanged in manner. So shy. So diffident. So not-quite-in-this-world. A sophisticated soprano had declared Oliver Langham must be gay. Just because he hadn't invited her to choral evensong . . .

'So what have you been up to for all these years?' I enquired heartily. 'Wife and six kids at home?'

43

Oliver jerked round to stare at me. 'God no . . .' he began —
but, in jerking round, he sloshed Pimm's over the expensive
frills of my skirt, and I leapt to my feet, flapping. Then there
was the usual volley of apologies and reassurances: feeble
quips about the drink nearly matching the colour of my dress.

'No,' muttered Oliver, when I eventually resettled on the
bench beside him. 'No wife. No — children.'

He spoke noticeably bleakly. As for me, I thought the
evening's prospects were brightening by the minute. I can't
claim the flame of love had burned unflickeringly in some
corner of my heart for the last dozen years. Be reasonable.
Whose tastes, at thirty, are the same as at eighteen? But the
night was young, I was thinking, and Oliver had such a
delicious dimple in his chin . . .

'You and me both,' I said chirpily. 'Unencumbered, I mean.'

He didn't seem to hear, let alone respond in kind. Mind, I
can't say I was entirely surprised to find Oliver Langham still
wifeless. When we grew out of the Clark Kent joke, Jenny and I
had diagnosed Oliver more realistically as your dyed-in-the-
wool Oxford bachelor. Ex-public school, scholarly, and thus
terminally shy of the female of the species. Look at C.S. Lewis,
said Jenny. And as for Lewis Carroll . . . Oliver was better
looking. And not — we agreed determinedly — gay. In fact she
predicted — odd how clearly I remembered this — he was
destined to fall romantically and hopelessly in love in his dotage
with some blushing child virgin. The fact we were both ourselves
virgins did not inhibit us from using the term pejoratively.

At this moment, the shy bachelor was glugging the remainder of his Pimm's as fast as a camel in an oasis. Suddenly I
knew what he was after: escape. Any minute now, he would
plonk down the empty glass and declare home time.

'Must find Constance,' he uttered rather thickly between
mouthfuls, confirming my suspicions.

'So what do you do, Oliver?' I said smartly.

He lowered the glass and seemed to find it hard to bring
the question and me into focus. 'Um, teach.'

'Here?' I said, before he could raise the dregs back to his lips. 'At the university?'

'Convent school. Down the Woodstock Road.'

'Oh,' I said, and a certain disappointment may have leaked into my voice. I'd imagined a more splendid destiny for Oliver Langham than a convent classroom. God, if only you could have seen him on the podium. Music flowing through his veins had much the same effect as a shot of adrenalin on lesser mortals. He conducted like a soul possessed. I fancied he might be inspiring choirs and viol ensembles across the world.

'I still conduct The Commoners,' he added a touch defensively. 'And there's my research. I'm preparing a performing edition of some early Florentine motets ...' Suddenly he shrugged. 'Fearfully boring, I know. Boring as hell.'

The curious thing was, he didn't say this with the shy laugh I would have expected. Oliver had always been charmingly self-deprecating. He spat the words out with truly painful self-loathing.

'No ambition,' he said. 'One of life's rut-dwellers.'

Hamlet, I thought. That was it. Hamlet in a modern-dress production. Exactly the right air of confused misery was clouding the noble profile. At that moment (at most moments) I would have preferred an ardent, free-booting Romeo. Still ...

'Is something worrying you?' I said.

He jumped like a startled gazelle. 'No, I mean ... So tell me what you're doing these days.'

I didn't believe him. Here was one unhappy man lost in his own troubles and only manufacturing an interest in me. But that he showed no disposition to pour out his woes on this sympathetic (if naked) shoulder was in his favour. Like I said, I lack the confiding impulse myself and I'd served a year and a half as an all-purpose confessional: priest, mother, agent, accountant, and even marriage guidance counsellor, to Richard.

Richard believed, ardently, in the necessity for externalizing (his word) emotion. What, after all, is acting? (His words.) If we cannot understand our own innermost workings, how can we begin to portray those of the rest of humanity? And so forth. In other words, Richard was a A Serious Actor to my comedian. He was also a good actor, while I, frankly . . .

'What did you say you did?' enquired Oliver.

'Act,' I said. I could have replied type, chauffeur, waitress or walk dogs. And that was only careers since Christmas. Par for the course. Ninety-whatever per cent of the profession are out of acting work at any one time. 'But not for much longer,' I added.

'Oh really,' he murmured, stifling a yawn. 'Why?'

'There comes a time when you have to grow up and face facts,' I said bleakly. Thirtieth birthdays inspire pronouncements like that.

'Ah,' said Oliver, and stared at the drink remaining in his glass like a mountaineer viewing the last hundred feet of the Matterhorn. 'I say, are you sure this stuff isn't alcoholic?'

'Hardly at all,' I said, although my own head was swimming pleasantly, and I was waxing philosophical about large questions (The Future: Whither?) which is always a bad sign. 'Thing is,' I said, 'I'm not much good at it. Never have been.'

'What?'

'Acting.'

'Oh surely,' said Oliver, sounding oddly strained, 'all performing careers go through bad patches?'

'No,' I said. And, no, this wasn't thespian modesty. I wasn't waiting to be pressed into confessing that well, maybe I wasn't quite so bad. Critical acclaim for me had been the *Oldham Star* pronouncing my performance to be perfectly adequate under the circumstances.

Oliver drained his glass. 'Well, it really is getting rather late and —'

'I only stumbled into acting by accident,' I interrupted ruthlessly, although telling one's life story is not the most alluring of ploys. 'Up on the Edinburgh Fringe after I left here. Terrible revue but we were sharing a cellar with a professional company and a pipe burst.' I knew I was gabbling, but if I drew breath he'd bolt. 'I fixed the pipe and they offered me a job. Assistant Stage Manager. I mean, an Equity card, just like that. So, on the road it was for two glorious years . . .' Glorious? Who wrote this script? Two years of damp beds, greasy bacon, chronically sick transit vans and half-empty, echoing halls. Still, people look back to the Blitz fondly, don't they? 'Until,' I added, 'the company went bust.'

That unexpectedly pinioned his attention. 'Oh Christ. That's the heartbreaking thing about these small touring outfits, isn't it?' It could only be a frog in the throat, but he almost sounded on the brink of tears. 'I know. My —'

'No, no — best thing that ever happened to me,' I protested. 'Because then —'

But just as I was about to regale him with my single spell of glory on BBC television (as a green furry kangaroo in *Storybox*) I was interrupted by a voice with all the charm — and certainly the penetrating qualities — of a chainsaw. The kind of voice adapted to ruling anywhere, from outposts of the Empire to vicarage jumble sales.

'Oliver! Great Scot, it really was yours . . .'

He was looking past me, and I swivelled round to see a short, trimly stout woman in a ruffled white blouse and black skirt which was either too long, or not long enough. The silver sandals thus inelegantly revealed were sturdily strapped like surgical appliances. Her white hair was twisted back into a bun. A double string of pearls had knotted round her spectacle chain; also in the tangle was a lumpily crocheted black shawl.

'Constance,' exclaimed Oliver, springing up with ill-judged haste. He wobbled noticeably before managing to peck the air beside her cheek. 'I want to see you.'

'I went down to let the dogs out,' she said, clasping his arms at elbow height and peering up at him. 'And I saw the bicycle.'

47

'Hell, I'm sorry,' said Oliver. 'You've asked me a hundred times not to block the gate, but I thought on a night like this —'

'No, no. It was just the shock. I hadn't seen it there since ... well, anyway. But darling, I'm so sorry, I've put guests in your room.'

'Doesn't matter,' said Oliver. 'I never intended staying tonight. In fact, the sooner I'm through with all this, the better.'

Terrific.

'I'd simply no idea you were planning to come,' she went on. 'When I saw the bike I — well, I was dumbfounded. But here you are.'

'Can we go somewhere to talk?' hissed Oliver. But she was not listening. She had released his elbows and was gazing enquiringly at me.

'Oh, sorry, yes,' muttered Oliver. 'This is Rebecca Haydock. My aunt, Lady Berisford. My uncle's principal of the college, you know.'

Well, no, I didn't know. But at least that explained the private entrance through the college wall. I promptly stood up to shake hands and it says everything about Lady Berisford that although her inquisitive nose was no higher than my cleavage, she nevertheless contrived to look down on me.

'Rebecca Haydock,' she repeated, tasting the name dubiously as she shook my hand.

An Aunt, I thought, in the grand Wodehousian tradition. I tried to remember if Constance was the gorgon or the good sport with a French cook.

'Oliver needed a spare alto,' I said gaily, 'and he chanced to bump into me.'

'You're a *singer*?' she said, leaving no doubt that in her careers A–Z, singing was classified somewhere between shop-lifting and smack-dealing.

'Becca's an actress, actually,' said Oliver, which seemed downright foolhardy if singers were so low on his aunt's preferences.

'An old friend of Oliver's,' I chipped in hastily.

'An actress?' said Lady Berisford, giving it the full five-syllable treatment. 'Good God, so you are.' She let out a guffaw of laughter. 'I've seen you on the telly. With those Pitza things. Your uncle's potty about them, you know,' she added to Oliver. 'And an old friend too.' If she had invested actress and singer with sinister meaning, she made a positive novel out of this innocent description of me. 'Come up from London, I dare say?' And she gave what I could only describe as a knowing smile. 'No problems with the trains today?'

'Actually,' I said bemusedly, 'I drove.'

But she was already patting my arm, rather as one would pat a promising filly. 'Well, well, well. I'm delighted to meet you at last.'

It was like the notorious actor's nightmare. The one where you find yourself floundering on a stage and everyone knows what the play is except you.

'But I don't think,' she added with friendly confidentiality, 'that you want to be wandering around here, do you? Why not come up to the Lodgings? I've gathered in the senior contingent and we're all having supper. Get out of this crush, eh?'

'I really don't think . . .' began Oliver.

'Nonsense,' boomed Lady Berisford, rising higher in my estimation by the minute. 'Now you *are* here you must come and have something to eat. You look like a skeleton, child. Only a few old friends,' she added to me, as though by way of reassurance.

Her dining room was dark panelled and hung with heavily framed portraits of earlier principals; a sour-faced crew. A long and highly polished table was festooned with salvers of salmon and asparagus and, behind them, sparkled crystal bowls of strawberries. Enough strawberries to sink Wimbledon . . . I wondered, momentarily, where the drunken chef had melted away to. I don't like loose ends. The least I could have done was bid him a polite goodnight.

'You must help yourselves,' said Lady Berisford while shovelling alarming quantities of food on to our plates. She poured wine with equally reckless generosity, and shepherded us into her drawing room.

There was a sea of grey, chattering heads. But, having been reduced by the young ball-goers outside to feeling myself on the verge of crumbling senility, I was undaunted. In fact, my heart skipped with the recognition that here at least I was the merest child. So I flirted with youthful outrageousness with a retired philosophy don as I juggled plate, fork and glass, and went on to discuss The Drama (which *proves* the Pimm's can't have been as weak as I thought) with a visiting reader in English from Harvard, and generally rather enjoyed myself. Oliver was ensconced on a sofa between two bosomy matrons. Out of the corner of my eye, I saw him glance imploringly at his aunt, but her only response was to flit past and refill his glass.

Eventually, she bustled across to me and filled mine too. I had soon abandoned the plate. I've never really mastered the knack of eating on the hoof. Besides, my still-delicate digestion was reeling from the Gaudy supper.

'So, my dear,' she said. 'Tell me all about yourself.'

This was a command, not an invitation, and she continued to bark questions while topping up my glass with piston-like regularity. It was rather like filling in a verbal job application: name, age, status, education . . .

'St Margaret's woman?' she said approvingly. 'Well, that says something.' I wasn't sure what, but I smiled obediently. 'To be frank, you're not at all what I expected,' she went on. 'Very much better in fact.'

What? I thought, but then assumed she was talking to me as the girl off the advert. At that moment a red-nosed toad bulging out of his brocade waistcoat rolled up to ask where the gin was hidden. Far be it from me to cast stones when it comes to counting glasses under the bridge, but he looked to me as though he'd already consumed quite enough.

'And who,' he bellowed, nearly falling into my *décolletage*, 'is this pretty chicken?'

Lady Berisford — or rather, as she insisted, Constance — grimaced at me apologetically. 'Becca is a friend of Oliver's. A very *old* friend,' she said with puzzling emphasis. My uneasy sense of not being entirely *au fait* with the plot intensified.

'Well, I don't know if I would put it like that,' I began, incurably truthful. More a young acquaintance, I was going to quip, but the toad spoke first.

'Oliver?' he spluttered, goggling. 'Is young Langham here? With *this*?'

Lady Berisford and I both glared at him. Her look would have deflected a ballistic missile.

'This gorgeous creature, I mean,' he went on, apparently by way of apology, spraying consonants and gin-scented spit liberally as he looked from me to Constance and back. 'But . . .' He opened his mouth and closed it a few times, evidently lost for words. He grasped my arm and pulled me towards him. 'Have I got it wrong?' he said in a pantomime whisper audible on other side of the quad, never mind the room. 'Wasn't Melinda telling me —'

'The gin is on top of the fridge, Hector,' interrupted Constance. 'And Oliver is about to take his old friend out for a dance. Oliver!' Oliver looked up in unmistakable alarm. 'Becca's getting bored with us old fogies,' said his aunt breezily. Several old fogies heard this and smiled with visibly strained tolerance. 'I've promised her you'll be a sweetie and take her round the place. The band in the big marquee later on is supposed to be rather good. Can't think of the name, Death's Door or something, but the students assure me they're the latest hot ticket. Off you go.'

'Rotten dancer, I'm afraid,' mumbled Oliver into my ear, ten minutes later.

We weren't exactly dancing. By then, I could barely walk, let alone dance. Because of the shoes, not the alcohol. Besides, Death's Door (or whoever they were — I never found out)

51

had not yet materialized. Instead, a Highland pipe ensemble, fully gift-wrapped in hideously lurid tartan, was wailing a lament for the dead of Culloden. So we, like everyone else, were mooching, zombie-slow, round a dance floor which, being both dimly lit and lumpy, was potentially lethal.

'You're the best partner I've had in years,' I said, which at least made him laugh. Disbelievingly. 'True,' I continued. 'I hardly ever get anyone to dance with who's actually taller than me.'

'Well, that's something, I suppose,' he said and stumbled in one of the holes, his body cannoning into mine. Rather pleasantly, as a matter of fact. 'I'm afraid I'm . . . slightly drunk.'

'Not really,' I said soothingly.

'Not really,' echoed Oliver in my ear. Drunkenly.

'Hold on to me,' I murmured, 'and you'll be fine.'

Oliver actually had, I found myself thinking, a surprisingly good body. Not so much thin, as delectably lean and tautly muscled. And, still companionably entwined, we wandered on through half a play, a discotheque, a firework display . . . I forget what else.

'You're being terribly kind,' mumbled Oliver at some point.

'Not at all,' I cooed.

I also recall rescuing an orphaned half-bottle of fizz from an empty table.

'Makes you feel better, doesn't it?' said Oliver indistinctly between swigs. 'This stuff.'

'Famous for it,' I said.

Ball fatigue, in my experience, had always tended to set in around four in the morning. The hour when night is darkest, deadest and coldest and dawn quite unimaginable. This was the watershed hour which sifted the wimps from the bloods, the creepers home to bed from the heigh-ho bacon and Bucks Fizz at dawn mob. In years past I had always, naturally, prided myself on being one of the latter. Age will tell. The spirit was willing but the flesh was shivering.

'Is there anywhere we can get warm?' I croaked. Somewhere

in the distance, the disco was still pounding like a tired migraine. My teeth were chattering.

Oliver blinked like a cross-eyed owl. 'Warm?'

'What about your aunt's?'

It was I who led the way back to the Lodgings and pushed open the front door. The hall was deserted, lit only by one green-shaded lamp. A clock was ticking ponderously stage left.

'In here?' I said, opening a door at random.

'Uncle's study,' said Oliver, stumbling in after me.

I switched on a desk lamp. The walls were thick with books. There was a glorious fireplace, a massive monument carved in stone, but inlaid with the ugliest of green institutional tiles — mostly cracked — and containing, instead of the requisite roaring logs, a cold and tinny wire cage of electric bars. But at that moment I was not interested in aesthetics.

'A fire,' I said, with the wonderment of one discovering the Holy Grail, and switched it on.

'Oh wow,' breathed Oliver bending forward to warm blue fingers over the mean orange bar, swaying. Poor boy. No head for liquor. I collapsed on to the hearthrug, kicking off my shoes.

'Move the fire this way a bit,' I said, stretching out weary legs, 'so I can thaw my toes.'

He bent to shift it, staggered, and collapsed heavily on top of me, luckily without having picked up the fire.

'Idiot,' I said, giggling. He was floundering among frothing petticoats when, with the precise inevitability of farce, the door opened on Lady Berisford. The silver sandals had given way to pom-pommed men's slippers, which were at my eye level.

'Ah,' she said, pale blue eyes surveying the tangle of limbs on the floor and swiftly drawing the wrong conclusions. 'I think the pair of you should be cutting along home, don't you?'

'Actually . . .' I began blearily. How the hell, I was thinking,

53

was I going to get back into St Margaret's at this hour? Earlier on, talk of locked gates had been the merest ploy. But here I was, at four in the morning, genuinely without the means to get back into college. 'I'm not sure . . .'

'Come on, come on,' she said, chivvying Oliver to his feet. 'Home, James.' And she whispered briskly to me, 'My dear, at my age nothing shocks me.'

There was a dreamlike sensation of years sliding away, of becoming once again a misbehaving teenager, caught at the end of a party in illicit mid-cuddle when the parental lights were switched on. I almost shook my head, expecting to wake up. But Lady Berisford was unmistakably flesh and blood. 'I couldn't give two hoots, myself,' she was saying, 'as long as it makes him happy. But – really – not in the college. His uncle is the principal, and you know what men are like. Besides, we've a house full of guests.'

'Mush talk,' said Oliver to his aunt with a drunk's fixity of purpose. 'Important.'

'Not tonight, Josephine,' she said, firmly but not unkindly. 'You two run along and find your coats. I'll ring for a cab.'

And within minutes we were tucked into the back of a taxi with a bacon sandwich apiece, heading for Harecombe Gatehouse. God alone knew where that was. Or at least God and, I hoped, the taxi driver, because Oliver was snoring with his head comfortably cushioned on my shoulder and I hadn't a clue.

CHAPTER FIVE

It's always disorientating, waking up in a strange room, in a strange bed — with a strange head on the other pillow.

The first thing I noticed was the sunshine. I supposed that was what had woken me. A high-noonish sun had rolled above a skylight and was blasting down on my face like a blow-torch. I was in an attic bedroom. Cottagy, with sprigged wallpaper and white woodwork. A mess. On a chair in the corner, like a blowsily collapsed poppy, lay my frock.

Wriggling into a sitting position I looked down and saw I was wearing a man's shirt. Oliver's evening shirt, yawning indecently open. I bundled it closed.

My first coherent thought, having remembered why and where I was, formed itself into gratitude that the hangover wasn't as bad as might have been expected. The second thought was that it probably hadn't started yet. I knew, with absolute certainty, there was no chance of returning to sleep. And that's generally a bad sign.

The fair head at the other side of the bed shifted and flopped back into the pillow, muttering. As gently as I could, I dropped my legs over the side of the bed. Wrapping the shirt round me, I padded out of the room and downstairs.

The sitting room looked even worse in the daylight that it had last night: books, papers and clothes spattered everywhere. And not, I thought, kicking a sock out of my path with a bare toe, *clean* clothes either.

Poking through the mess was a harpsichord painted

nauseous green. A recorder-like tube lay on top, and a tin, round which buzzed two bluebottles. Rice pudding, half eaten, with a teaspoon still in the can. I shuddered. The only uncluttered surface was the sofa.

I remembered helping Oliver to shift the debris off that. Or rather, doing it myself while he watched helplessly. Even if he hadn't been pie-eyed with alcohol. I doubt he would have been of much assistance. This place showed the measure of Oliver Langham's practical abilities. Jenny would have nodded wisely: truly a bachelor pad in the grand old tradition. But I couldn't help boggling a bit. Oliver wasn't that much older than me. He ought to be one of the new-man, self-sufficient-in-shirts and wizard-with-a-wok brigade. Maybe every evolutionary stage has its throwbacks.

Harecombe Gatehouse was not large. There was only the one bedroom upstairs, and this sitting room occupied the whole ground floor of what I judged to be the original building. A kitchen and bathroom were tacked on in a lean-to at the back. I walked through now. The condition of the kitchen would have turned stronger stomachs than mine, but I managed to scrub clean a mug and make some weak tea. One milk bottle in the odiferous fridge was, at least, white and unopened. I smelled it with the glaring caution of a *vigneron* sampling the new vintage, before pouring a little into my tea. Then I took tea — and refuge — in the garden.

Did I say garden? A patch of scrub behind the kitchen, enclosed by a ragged privet hedge which had nearly overgrown a rickety gate. But the stormy night had given way to a most glorious day. The sky was that intense blue which always makes me long to dive up and swim among the frail shreds of cloud, and a sympathetic breeze was ruffling the leaves of two lines of beech trees which stretched away to the rear, flanking a chalky drive.

It occurred to my bleary brain that Harecombe Gatehouse was literally a gate house. Square and satisfyingly symmetrical as a child's drawing, it was blessed with the intriguing, curlychimneyed charm of those lodges that perch coyly on country roads, hinting at the existence of some stately pile. The front door, where the taxi had delivered us, opened directly on to the road, but this side wall supported a farm gate giving into the chalky drive. The drive wound up and away across billowing curves of quintessentially English parkland. Sheep-cropped grass was studded with trees, each as perfectly formed as a botanical drawing. And beyond that rose a wooded hillside, atop which peeped — a touch of fairy tale perfection — what appeared to be the turrets of a castle, tinged rosy-pink in the sunshine. Too good to be true.

Somewhere in the hedge a bird was singing Vaughan Williams arrangements. I sat down on the dry grass, stretching my legs to soak up the sun, and sipped my tea. The peace, the warmth and the sweet meadow scents were intoxicating. A fat bee lazily circled my head. There were crickets chirping nearby. I closed my eyes and listened. Not a car, not a plane. Then, dimly, from far away, I heard church bells ringing. Of course, it was Sunday morning, or nearly — I opened one eye to squint at my watch — afternoon. Getting on for twelve. How wonderful not to be in London. I hate Sundays in London. All the nice shops closed; streets full of tourists; tubes behaving eccentrically; Richard invariably *en famille* and out of reach all day; and only Monday to look forward to.

And then, even as I drained my mug of tea, I remembered Richard was not going to be *en famille* all day. He was coming to see me. At, oh lummy, two o'clock.

No chance.

I scrambled to my feet and hurried through the back door, blinking in the dark kitchen and trying to ignore the ripe stink from the bin. In the sitting room I located first a telephone answering machine, then, by following a cable from the windowsill, the instrument itself, which was buried under a table.

With the frisson of danger which always accompanied this action, I dialled Richard's home number; imagined the phone trilling on a frilly peach and turquoise table. Oh, I'd never actually been inside the Prescott residence but I had – I'm ashamed to admit – peered through the window. Well, I was on my way to other friends in Fulham, wasn't I? Sorry, Chelsea. Richard always gave his address as Chelsea. His was your typical tiny over-chintzed terrace, the kind where even the gas bill is pinned up with a swag and a bow.

Now I held my breath as I imagined the Hon. Hel. – tiny, pretty and frilly. I had no doubt, as her nest – scurrying to pick up the receiver. I waited poised, to slam mine down.

'Prescott,' snapped Richard's voice. He was the only person I'd ever known who answered the phone with his surname.

'Hi,' I said. 'It's me.'

The voice changed to a strangled croak. 'Rebecca? Darling, why are you ringing me at home?'

'Is she there?'

'No, she's with her mother.'

'Phew. So why are you whispering?'

'I'm not.' A two-octave shift of pitch: 'Anyway, what about you? I can hardly hear you.'

'I'm trying not to wake the house up.'

'House? Rebecca, where are you?'

'Well, to be honest, I'm not exactly sure. Somewhere in the midst of terribly English countryside. Quite heavenly, actually.'

'You mean you're not in London?'

'Yes. Or do I mean no? Sorry, my brain feels like it's been pickled.'

'Darling, you *insisted* I came round this afternoon.'

'Yes, Richard, I know. I'm – um – sorry.'

'For heaven's sake, I've only stayed in town because of that. I should be at Nebworth with Helena – and her poor mother.'

'Poor mother?' I said. 'What's up with her?'

'Darling, I *told* you,' said Richard. 'Over dinner.'

'I was not at my best that night,' I said huffily. 'And thanks a lot for asking if I'm recovered. What's wrong with Helena's ma anyway?'

'It's her heart.'

'They've finally found she hasn't got one?' I suggested, rather wittily I thought, considering the scrambled condition of my brain, but it didn't raise a laugh. Richard's own care with his cash, it had to be admitted, was a byword in the profession, but this had never inhibited him before from lambasting the miserly mother-in-law.

'Margaret's been desperately ill,' he said with a syrupy concern worthy of Dr Kildare. 'I'm afraid, well, they've warned us to fear the worst. Helena is with her twenty-four hours a day. It's all been terribly distressing.'

'Richard? You can't *stand* your mother-in-law. She wrecked your marriage, remember? She —'

'Becca,' he interrupted smartly, with only the faintest shimmer of embarrassment audible. 'This is a matter of life and death. Not a time for picking over old quarrels. Try and understand . . .'

Oh piss off, I thought.

Sometimes I wondered what I ever saw in Richard Prescott. He had bounded into my life, clad in white flannels, through the drawing-room windows of a farce entitled *Two in a Four-Poster*. Apt title, considering where we ended up by the third week of the tour. Such 'anyone for tennis?' larkery was, of course, beneath Richard's towering talents, but he looked dishy in the flannels. Also without them, when the plot demanded they were dropped. But it wasn't just his elegantly sculpted kneecaps which riveted the audience. Richard oozed Presence, that indefinable, supremely enviable quality in an actor which effortlessly draws all eyes. And even if, off-stage, his clean-cut handsomeness was beginning to look a little preserved in the careful way peculiar to actors of a certain age — shoes and eyes a mite too shiny, accessories almost too immaculately matched — he was more than desirable enough still for you to wonder what *he* ever saw in *me*. Or perhaps more to the point, used to see in me.

'I wanted to meet,' he was saying reproachfully. 'I wanted

to part – friends.' He had a marvellous voice, too, resonant as a cello; and, even via the reductive medium of the telephone line, he could inflect pathos into every thrilling syllable.

'I'm very sorry,' I muttered. He was right, after all. I'd made him promise to come round. 'Last night got a bit out of hand.'

'What? Darling, can you speak up? Where are you?'

'I told you, I don't know.'

'I can't hear you.'

'And I'm trying not to wake anyone up. This is a very small cottage.'

The mellifluous cadences sharpened up markedly. 'Is there a man with you?'

'Oh shut up, Richard.'

'Rebecca – *are you with another man?*'

'Not in the way you ... Well, blimey,' I exclaimed, forgetting to whisper. 'Why shouldn't I have twenty men here with me? I'm a free woman, aren't I? You gave me my marching orders!'

There was a pause so pregnant and so long I was on the point of shaking the receiver when he said, 'Christ, darling, you amaze me. You really do.'

'What are you talking about?'

'Do you think I haven't been through hell all this week?'

I began to feel dizzy. Surely, I was thinking, those are *my* lines. 'I rather understood,' I said tightly, 'that I was the injured party.'

'My *God.*'

Another long, crackling silence.

Any minute now we would be into subtexts. Richard was hot on subtexts. Of the kind where the heroine says, 'Hasn't the weather turned nasty?' and means (of course), 'I'm planning to murder my lover on Wednesday.' I am, I accept, depressingly literal. I actually say what I mean.

'Are you telling me,' I enquired doggedly, 'you *didn't* want to give me the boot last Monday?'

'Of course I didn't want to ...'

I waited for my heart to skip with elation. Didn't miss a beat. Just as well.

'. . . but, as I tried to explain over dinner, witnessing near-death at close quarters . . .'

'Mine or hers?'

'. . . forces one to, well, take stock of one's own life. A man has to —'

'Do what a man's gotta do?' I snarled.

'*Please*, you're making this very hard. I realized it was time I began to think of my family, face up to my responsibilities. That's what I've been trying to explain, only you won't listen. Becca, we can't discuss this over the telephone.'

I twisted the telephone cable sulkily round my fingers. 'What more is there to say anyway?'

'Christ, relationships can't just be chopped up like bits of firewood. A relationship's a — a living organism. Surely it's better cauterized gently,' he went on, getting into his metaphorical stride, 'to stem the flow of —'

'Lifeblood?' I snapped. I can fight with metaphors too. 'And just how long have you been gently cauterizing Helena? Since years before you met me. And after eighteen months of subjecting me to post-mortems on your marriage,' I finished triumphantly, 'you suddenly tell me the corpse wasn't dead after all.'

'Darling,' hissed Richard in his Noël Coward voice, 'much as I adore you, there are times when you prance across the minefield of human emotion with all the subtletly of a clog-dancer.'

'And I suppose you,' I whipped back, 'are Rudolph bloody Nureyev.'

Yet another silence — Richard was a master of the significant pause — and then he said with great weariness, 'I should have guessed. You're doing this to punish me.'

'Doing what?'

'Hurtling into another man's bed. Then ringing to tell me. To gloat. To —'

'I'm not in bed. I'm in the middle of the floor, if you must know.'

'My *God*. An orgy.'

'Don't be ridiculous.'

'In a place you can't even name. Do you know *his* name, by any chance? Christ, do you ever think about risk? You ought to come home for your own sake, if not mine. And if you set off now –'

'Can't be done,' I said briskly. 'The car's still in Oxford, there's less than a fiver in my purse and if you think I'm hitch-hiking across the countryside in an evening dress and high heels . . .'

There was only a strangled groan.

'It's not as bad as it sounds,' I added reluctantly. Nevertheless, I thought, blanching. I really would have to return to college to collect car and belongings. In the middle of a Sunday afternoon. In full evening dress. 'None of your business if I stay a week,' I finished with a spurt of bad temper.

'If you insist,' said Richard coldly. 'I just hope, during this impromptu vacation, you haven't forgotten Ariel.'

Oh hell. Ariel, winged spirit. Ariel, known to plebeian me as Ringo. Well, he had that kind of fringe. But Ringo had been a present from Richard in our first week together – and an absolutely typical Richard Prescott present. Heavy on romantic symbolism, low on cost. Richard had actually (I later learned) cadged the bird free off the landlord of his digs in Birmingham, who bred them. He decanted it into a wonky Chinese lantern of a cage and – with the prettiest speech about lovebirds – presented Ariel to me.

So, to avoid prosecution from the RSPCA, I'd had to spend a fortune on a mobile aviary with all mod cons, and then cart it round for the rest of the tour. To give him his due, Ringo didn't eat much. But soon there were the vet's bills, because Ringo (delicate as all pedigree specimens) was prone to every disease known to bird. There are few sadder sounds than a canary with a cough.

'Ah, Ariel . . .' But euphemisms have never been my strong point. 'He's dead,' I said.

'Dead?' ejaculated Richard. *Dead! and . . . never called me mother?*

'He looked very peaceful,' I offered, and then remembered the man on the bridge, laughing his head off.

'Rebecca? You're not *laughing?*'

'Course not.'

'My God. How too utterly bloody symbolic . . .'

'*Symbolic?*'

Well it would be, wouldn't it? Even a canary has a subtext.

'. . . of *us*. Our relationship.'

Which also, after eighteen months, and just as abruptly and inexplicably, had turned up its toes and died. Yup, I could actually grasp a subtext here, though I doubted it was quite what Richard had in mind.

'Don't take it to heart,' I said. 'Hadn't you better get a move on, if you want to get to the . . .' About to say 'death-bed', I amended it tactfully to sickbed, and we said an almost-civilized goodbye.

I tried, but failed, to replace the receiver without tinging the bell. However, there was still no sound from upstairs, so I reboiled the kettle, washed my face, brushed my teeth with one finger and a smear of toothpaste, and then ventured back to the bedroom carrying two mugs of tea and a sugar bowl on a tray.

'Oliver?'

He was sprawled diagonally across the bed, as if dead. Tentatively, I touched one shoulder. No effect. I shook a little harder. He rolled round with alarming speed, opened his eyes and wailed, 'Cathy?'

CHAPTER SIX

'Um, no,' I said amiably, 'Becca, actually.'

He blinked a couple of times, tried – with evident difficulty – to focus on me, and then muttered less than flatteringly, 'Oh God. Sorry. Oh – thanks.'

This for the mug of tea which I was offering him.

'Sugar?'

'Please. Two.'

I had guessed he was a sugar man. Funny how you can tell. I ladled in a couple of spoonfuls and stirred vigorously. He really did wince as the spoon struck the cup. Hangovers are, of course, proportionately worse the less you are accustomed to drinking. I guessed, therefore, that his might be of cataclysmic dimensions.

'Who's Cathy?' I enquired, lowering myself on to a chair beside the bed and sipping my own tea.

'My wife,' he said.

His *what*? This archetypal rice-pudding-out-of-a-tin bachelor had a wife?

I gritted my teeth. 'What a dashing life I lead,' I murmured. 'Straight from one married man to another.' And reflected that this only confirmed the direst forecasts about spinster life after thirty. T'other side of the big three-oh, the wise sisters moaned, you could guarantee any halfway attractive man was going to be gay or married. I'd never believed them.

'But you told me you didn't have a wife,' I protested. 'I distinctly remember –'

'No, no, you don't understand,' whispered Oliver painfully, and only a mouthful of tea prevented me offering some sour jest about married men *never* being understood when he added: 'She's dead.'

Of course I didn't know what to say. That kind of line is a silencer coming from someone in the age group where widower-hood is, if not exactly to be expected, at least a natural hazard. But from Oliver Langham?

'Dead?' I repeated numbly, and grimaced because it sounded like Richard asking about that damned canary.

'I was dreaming about her just then,' said Oliver, lying back on the pillow and closing his eyes as if trying to recapture the image. 'I dream about her all the time. But, you see, in the dreams she's not dead.' A film of sweat glimmered on his forehead. 'At least, even in the dream, I know she is dead really — I remember *everything* — but she's getting up and walking towards me, and she can't talk.' He was gabbling. 'I know I ought to be happy to see she's alive, except I know she can't be, and I'm terrified, and . . .' He sounded terrified, too. Almost hysterical. 'She looks awful, grey-coloured, and she stares at me as though —'

'Typical,' I interrupted briskly.

Oliver opened his eyes. 'What?'

'It's one of the standard dreams people have after they've lost someone they love.'

I am, you understand, a passionate armchair shrink. Never miss an article in the papers and magazines.

'Common as dreaming about flying, or your teeth dropping out. I know, long after my grandfather died, I was still dreaming about him. Suddenly, Grandpa would be there at a family tea party, only not quite taking part. And he didn't look — right, somehow. And we'd all be embarrassed because we knew he was actually dead but in a terribly British way no one liked to mention the fact to him.'

Oliver felt obliged to smile. Such a wretched little smile. 'It's not — quite like that.'

'Same kind of thing, though. It's all to do with your subconscious not being able to accept the fact of death. The dreams go in the end. At least, mine did.'

'I thought I was going mad,' said Oliver.

'Lord, no.'

He gazed at me silently. Battalions of thoughts were galloping behind the sad blue eyes.

'Is it long since — Cathy died?' I asked gently.

'Just now — waking up — it seems like a lifetime ago,' said Oliver dazedly. 'Almost as though it all happened to someone else. Extraordinary.'

Being more conversant with the perception-warping effects of hangovers, I did not find this so very extraordinary. Poor boy. 'She must have been terribly young.'

'Twenty-two . . .'

I choked on a second mouthful of tea. Dear God. Not quite in his dotage but he really had fallen for a child bride.

'She would have been twenty-three now,' continued Oliver desolately. As if it made a difference — but this was no time to raise questions of cradle-snatching.

'I — I'm so sorry,' I muttered, wishing I had Richard's gift for infusing trivial words with rich emotion. 'I don't know what to say.'

'No one does,' said Oliver.

Now I understood why the house was such a mess. It looked as though it had been deprived of the housewifely touch for years, but evidently not long enough for Oliver to learn how to fend for himself again.

'How did she . . .' So difficult to know whether one should show concerned interest, or draw a tactful veil. I baulked at the word 'die', and compromised on: 'What happened to her?'

I expected him to say cancer. Maybe one is conditioned, these days, to think every premature death must be caused by cancer. Oliver set his chin defiantly. 'She fell,' he said.

'*Fell*? You mean — Was she a mountaineer or something . . .?'

He looked at me as though I were half-witted. 'She fell from a roof. It had been raining, you see. The tiles were slippery. The police never thought of that.'

A bluebottle zizzed past my ear. I flapped it away numbly. All I could think about was this gingerbread cottage. But one would be hard put to break an ankle tumbling off this roof.

'They were so sure she jumped,' continued Oliver, still staring at me rather unnervingly. 'The police. They had all their theories worked out. They were quite convinced. Nothing I said . . . They just didn't take any notice.'

'Do you mean,' I murmured, soft-voiced as an interviewer in one of those intimately probing television documentaries, 'Cathy took her own life?'

'Mad, isn't it? I thought they were all mad. And they wouldn't have said that if they knew her. I mean she might talk — threaten — but Cathy would never actually do a thing like that. *Never.*'

The amateur psychiatrist naturally disregarded this outburst — a refusal to face the truth is a typical defence mechanism of the bereaved — but I was helpless with pity. 'How — Christ, how agonizing for you . . .'

'When I realized she was dead, I just wanted to kill myself,' he declared.

I seized his hand. 'You mustn't talk like that,' I said fiercely. 'You mustn't even think of doing anything — silly.'

'I don't. Not any more.'

'I should hope not.'

'I — haven't the nerve. I mean, at the time, I — I tried taking sleeping pills. A whole bottle. But they only made me feel lousy. I couldn't even make a decent job of that.' His eyes widened. 'That's what Cathy said to me, you know. That I was too much of a coward. Whereas she . . .'

'Hush,' I said. 'Hush, darling.'

The endearment was automatic, like soothing a distressed child. But Oliver glanced up warily, and I felt his hand twitch under mine. I hastily released it on the pretext of picking up my mug.

Then we both sipped our tea in uncomfortable silence. I was perched on the chair beside the bed, shirt-tails primly tucked round to hide my thighs.

'I . . .'

'I . . .'

We had both started to speak at the same time.

'No — you first,' insisted Oliver.

'I'm afraid I used your telephone for a long-distance call,' I said conscientiously. 'Rather a long one.' This may seem irrelevant to you, but actors have a bad name for borrowing other people's telephones. Also money, beds, food and anything else they can scrounge. Fledgling canaries for instance.

'Help yourself,' he said listlessly.

Without his glasses, Oliver was revealed to have unexpectedly long lush eyelashes — the kind a woman would kill for — and he looked heartbreakingly young.

'Nice tea,' he added humbly. Poor lost boy.

The sun had moved round again. It shone across the crumpled sheets which were, I noted belatedly, none too clean. There was a faint whiff of hamster's cage shimmering in the warm air. Some people apparently find a ripe and rumpled bed like this suggestively sexy. I am not one of them. I like fresh white linen, orderly bedrooms and bodies which smell of soap and toothpaste. It says a lot for his eyelashes — or the lingering rose-tint of nostalgia — that Oliver, unwashed, uncombed and bleary-eyed, slumped under greying sheets, could still strike me as being more than passing attractive.

'You were about to say something too,' I prompted.

'Oh,' said Oliver, turning away. 'I — um . . .' He was staring out of the window now, apparently studying a distant tree. 'I don't even know how to . . .'

Dim of me really. I just continued to gaze at him enquiringly.

'I mean,' said Oliver, glancing back towards me positively

shiftily, 'I've never had to ask this – I'm not used to drinking . . .
but, um, did we . . .?'

Understanding dawned.

'Hell, no,' I said. 'No, of course we didn't.'

Oliver was blushing furiously.

'God, I'm sorry,' he whispered. 'How could I even . . .?'

'You were going to sleep on the sofa downstairs, don't you
remember? Although I offered to kip down there. But you
insisted. Anyway, we shifted all the books –'

'That's right,' he said, his face clearing miraculously. 'Yes, I
remember that.'

'But that sofa's so small, you nearly had to bend double to
lie down, and I'm not much shorter than you. And besides, I
couldn't find any blankets.'

'Blankets? I, er . . . have we got any?'

'Don't think so. None in either of the wardrobes anyway. In
fact, there hardly seemed to be anything in the wardrobes at all.'

'No,' agreed Oliver desolately. 'Now all Cathy's things are
gone.'

I cursed myself afresh for tactlessness.

'Anyway,' I said bracingly, 'by then we were both simply
dropping with exhaustion. So when we'd, um, got you un-
dressed . . .'

His eyes widened with alarm and he tried to glance, surreptitiously, under the quilt.

'You're quite decent,' I said, amused. Quite, quite decent.
Oliver, typically, wore the kind of baggy white cotton under-
pants I seemed to remember my father favouring.

'You had to undress me?' he moaned.

'Not really.'

Not much.

'Just helped you – well – balance. That's all. I'm afraid we
lost a few buttons off your shirt, though.'

When he fell out of my clutches, with me holding the shirt,
the buttons had pinged off like bullets.

69

'So I thought you wouldn't mind if I borrowed it to sleep in. And we both collapsed in here at something past five.' I smiled. 'All perfectly innocent.'

Oliver flushed. 'I'm so terribly sorry. How could I even imagine . . .?'

'Don't apologize. Kind of thing anyone might think.'

I'd thought of it myself, as a matter of fact, last night. *En passant*. But Oliver had been snoring even before I pulled the quilt over us.

'I'm so embarrassed. I've never been in such a state . . . You were terribly kind to look after me like that.'

'Pleasure,' I said, sipping my tea with the airy composure of a vicar's wife. 'So nice to see you again, after all these years.'

Oliver glanced at me uncertainly. 'The thing is,' he began, 'I — Well, under the circumstances I hardly know how to say this . . .'

'What?'

'When, exactly, did we know one another?'

'You don't remember me?'

'I've a shocking memory,' said Oliver.

I gave an exaggerated sigh. 'And I was *agonizingly* in love with you.'

'Don't be silly,' he said, bridling like a schoolboy. At least he sounded a bit more cheerful.

I grinned. 'The day you invited me to choral evensong, I spent half my grant on a new coat.' I sighed. 'And I didn't eat any of the walnut cake you'd bought for tea because I thought nuts made one's breath smell. That,' I added, indulgent of the innocent child in her blue corduroy coat, 'was in case you kissed me. Which of course you didn't.'

'You're making this up.'

'Not a word of a lie.' I was quite transported on my cloud of nostalgia. 'I kept hoping, of course. We stood for ages outside the college gates, I remember, talking, and then —'

'Did your hair used to be longer?' he demanded suddenly.

'I used to be able to sit on it.'

70

'And – darker?'

''Fraid so.' Now it had more highlights than the Blackpool illuminations.

He shook his head. 'How stupid of me,' he said slowly. 'You haven't really changed . . .'

I beamed.

'I was scared stiff of you,' he said.

Thanks a bunch. 'Now it's you who's making things up,' I said in minatory tones.

He began to shake his head, then winced and stopped. 'You were so – frightfully busy.'

'Rubbish.'

'No – when I asked you out to tea, I remember you taking out your diary.'

'Bluff.'

'Truly – and it was simply a mass of engagements.'

'Madly exciting things like reminders to hand essays in, and wash hair. I'm an obsessive organizer. Always was. Ma said I was the most unnatural child she'd ever encountered.'

'I'm a mess,' he said with what was almost a laugh. 'Aunt Constance used to say I couldn't organize myself out of a paper bag. No wonder I hardly dared speak to you. Christ – Constance,' he added, the smile snuffed out abruptly. 'I meant to see her last night . . .'

'You did,' I began. 'Don't you remember?' But he only shook his head slightly and drained his mug of tea. 'I needed that. I feel as though I could drink a bathful. Is there any more?'

I held out my hand for his mug and, as I did so, the buttonless shirt gaped open a few more inches than was decent. I clasped it to my bosom at once, but Oliver was already colouring like a traffic light.

'No, no, I'll get it myself,' he said hastily, swinging long bare legs over the side of the bed and standing up – and then immediately subsiding again. 'Maybe in a minute,' he concluded, in a strangled whisper. And this sudden collapse was not caused by alcohol. At least, not directly.

May I propose a motion for debate? *This house believes excessive consumption of alcohol powerfully stimulates the masculine libido on awakening.*

Or, to put it more economically: hangovers make men randy. I throw the proposition open because I don't know if it's physiological fact, or mere coincidence. In lists of aphrodisiacs from ginseng to Rachmaninov, I've never seen a mention of the phenomenon. But several female friends concur. Bad-temperedly, because they, like me, find a hangover inclines them towards making love about as powerfully as it does towards waving football rattles. Men, however, are strange creatures. And, when Oliver had so unwisely clambered to his feet, evidence to support my hypothesis had been unmistakable. And how.

'Gosh,' he muttered, puce with mortification. Poor baby.

What's more, my own hangover was definitely in remission. On the point of enquiring when he would be fit to give me a lift back into Oxford to collect my car and worldly goods, I paused to reconsider plans.

'I'm most terribly sorry,' whispered Oliver. 'I . . .'

After all Richard bloody Prescott had already assumed I'd been orgying all night. And read me a lecture. Oh he of little faith. Wouldn't it just serve him right if . . .

I took Oliver's mug and put it down on the bedside table. He glanced sideways at it and twitched.

Why the hell, I was thinking, should I be hanged as a boring little lamb, when the grass in the sheep's field was suddenly looking so green? Besides, the poor lad obviously needed cheering up. It was almost my public duty. A far, far better thing. Et cetera.

I flicked my hair back and stared him straight in the eye. 'Don't apologize,' I purred with Mrs Robinsonish languor. Never mind that I was younger than Oliver. He made me feel at least old enough to be his mother. 'A woman should be . . . flattered.'

'You — she should?' he croaked, as if I'd confessed to a penchant for eating glass.

I smiled what I trusted was an understanding, woman-of-the-world smile. 'You've been on your own a long time.'

'Well . . .'

I let the shirt slip open a little, and resisted a temptation to pout. I haven't the face for sultry pouts.

'Shall I . . .' I began, so huskily it made me cough, and I had to up the voice to normal pitch before continuing. 'Shall I go and get some more tea, then?' I did not, you can be sure, stir. But I'd swear Oliver would still have squeaked yes please, had I not been staring him into submission like a cobra mesmerizing a rabbit.

There was a long, meaningful silence.

The snake's tongue flickered round her parted lips in a manner reminiscent — she hoped — of Brigitte Bardot.

'You know, I'm sorry . . .' began Oliver at length, and the poor bloody cobra nearly hissed. So much for mesmeric powers.

'I told you, there's nothing to apologize for,' I growled, preparing to rise.

'No — you don't understand,' stammered Oliver, the sad blue eyes slipping away from my gaze. 'I, well, I suppose, finding you here — and me — you know, in bed, I meant, just for a moment, I was sorry — in a way — that . . .' He was scarlet-faced, and suddenly I felt a reckless surge of hope.

'Yes?' I whispered and carelessly let the shirt fall open to the waist. Oh, shameless hussy. Asking for everything she got, this one.

'I mean, I'd never imagined . . .'

I hardly dared breathe. I felt I was willing every word out of him. 'But you were sorry, perhaps,' I whispered, 'that we . . .?'

'Well,' said Oliver hoarsely, 'that we, um, you know . . . *didn't*.'

And so naturally we, um, you know . . . *did*.

ENTR'ACTE

'Is that it then?' whispers a stout man immediately in front of me into his wife's twinkling earring. 'Time for dinner?'

He is halfway to his feet before she hisses him into subsiding. His hopes were evidently raised by the stage being plunged into mysterious darkness. Suddenly, however, the instrumental ensemble strikes up another catchy little Renaissance number. And I mean suddenly. It began with the kind of startled bang which suggests they were late on cue. No doubt they were supposed to be papering over the cracks in Henry's carefully orchestrated scene and lighting change. I imagine Henry jigging up and down in the wings and smile. And the band's still determinedly tootling as the lights brighten on a new configuration of actors, poised for action and looking sheepish because they can't start until the musicians shut up.

The fat man sighs and his head drops lower between his shoulders.

I sympathize. But that's not 'it', no.

Nor was that it when I so brazenly seduced Oliver.

That, really, should have been the end of the story. It seems to me there were at least two possible outcomes. One, we could have tumbled not just into bed but wildly in love, and gone on from there. You know, lived happily ever after.

OK, so that's not very plausible. Anyone could see, even by then, that Oliver Langham and I had about as much in common as Tinkerbell and Tolstoy.

Alternatively — and this, no question, was what I had in mind at the time — we would revel in our all-too-brief and glorious encounter. A single Midsummer-night idyll. It would cheer us both up no end. Mend Oliver's bereaved heart. Salve my wounded pride. And we would kiss — and return to our very different lives. Cue sweepy strings. The End.

Wrong. I got it wrong all the way along the line. For a start, I should never have behaved as I did with Oliver. I'm not being prissy simply because I'm a respectable married woman these days, in training for solidly middle-class middle age. I'm just trying to look back honestly. What was it Richard accused me of? Clog-dancing across the emotional minefield? Beast — but he was right then.

There's a laugh in the audience round me, and for a moment the play distracts my train of thought. Rich, isn't it? A member of an audience complaining because the play is distracting her. You can see why I eventually gave up the theatrical profession. But you need a mellow and relaxed mind to enjoy this kind of entertainment. Coming back here has screwed me so up-tight, I find it hard to tolerate gentle comedies of misunderstanding. There has been far too much of it in real life. I feel irritably tempted to march up to the stage, give them all a good shake, tell them who's who and what's what, and then we can all get our supper.

Instead, another act has to be endured, and I face it stoically. *Che sarà sarà* and what have you. And, by the same token, what has been, has been. If you see what I mean. Water under the bridge, spilled milk and no profit in weeping for the endless might-have-beens, as the Richards of this world do. I can disapprove, but I can't whole-heartedly condemn myself for that long past Midsummer madness. And I couldn't possibly say I regretted it.

On the contrary, I staunchly remind myself that, for a few hours at any rate, Oliver and I were happy. It's important to remember that. Well, maybe he was just grateful to be anaesthetized for a spell. Sunshine, nostalgia and unbridled lust are a potent brew. What the hell. I enjoyed it, didn't I?

'Give me excess of it, that, surfeiting,
The appetite may sicken, and so die . . .'

or

THE TRAGEDY OF ERRORS

CHAPTER SEVEN

I've never really understood this post-coital *tristesse* business anyway. I never feel in the least *triste*. Just then, I felt pretty damn terrific. Oliver, I noticed even at the time, wasn't quite a matching picture of contentment — more your condemned man who's been allowed his last cigarette — but I was lying back with a satisfied yawn, when I saw the woman.

For a nasty moment I thought we had been disporting ourselves under the gaze of the deceased wife, but the photograph was black and white, the satin evening dress cut along distinctly New Look lines and the tightly coiffed blond goddess wearing it bore an unmistakable resemblance to Oliver.

'My mother,' he confirmed, after raising himself on one elbow to peer myopically at the picture. 'Taken years ago, of course. She died soon after I came up to Oxford.'

'She was very beautiful,' I said, and he nodded.

If it was odd that Oliver's bedside table should feature a picture of the late mother rather than the late wife, I don't think I considered the matter then. I was absorbed in tracing the likeness between mother and son.

'The image of you.'

'Hardly,' said Oliver, with a rather bitter laugh. 'She used to ask how she'd produced such an ungainly child.'

The woman was standing, I observed, in the curve of a grand piano, one gloved hand across the lid.

'She was a singer,' he explained. 'Soprano.'

'So the music came from her as well. Did she perch you on a piano stool in your nappy?'

'God no. My mother didn't really take much interest in me.' He shrugged, adding as though this explained everything: 'She never wanted children.'

'She told you that?' I said indignantly. 'Your own mother?'

'I'm afraid I put an end to her career. She had a terrible time giving birth to me. She hardly sang at all after I was born.'

'What about your father?'

'I scarcely remember him. I was only nine when he died.'

Poor, poor boy, I thought, my heart swelling to overflowing. Unloved and orphaned as well as wifeless. No wonder he looked so glum. The least I could offer was a little practical comfort.

'Hey,' protested Oliver. 'What — what are you doing?'

'Isn't it nice?'

'Well, yes,' he said. And then: 'Oh God . . . *yes*.'

Poor lamb.

'Christ, it's like — coming back to life,' he gasped minutes later. 'Almost feeling — there's something worth living for — I mean, wanting to live for — after all.'

This clog-dancer across the nation's emotions didn't turn a hair.

'I should bloody well think there are things worth living for,' I said, seizing him by the shoulders and pretending to shake him. 'No more of that rubbish.' As far as I was concerned, carnal pleasure mingled deliciously with a high-minded consciousness of Doing Good.

'But you don't realize . . .' began Oliver, with a weighty sigh which reminded me momentarily of Richard. I released his shoulders and he flopped back on to the pillows. 'The guilt —'

'Guilt? Because you're in bed with me?' At least I refrained from saying that the wife could hardly object now she was dead. I do have some tact.

80

'You see, I loved her so much,' he declared with, I couldn't help thinking, unnecessary fervour under the circumstances. 'Oh God, what am I going to do?'

I raised myself on one elbow, and looked him in the eye. 'Everyone suffers from agonizing guilt when the partner they love commits suicide.'

Oliver flinched. 'It was *not* suicide —'

I was not to be deflected mid-sermon. 'Dies in ambiguous circumstances, then. It's human nature. You loved her —'

'I *did*,' he cried, as though I needed convincing. 'And —'

'And so inevitably you put yourself on the rack, wondering what you could have done — *should* have done — to prevent her death. Anyone would. But — no, listen, Oliver — however Cathy died, whatever you feel you might have done to stop her, it can't make any difference now, can it? However much you blame yourself, it won't bring Cathy back.'

Oliver gazed at me without speaking.

'There comes a day for everyone,' I declared, 'when they have to close the door on a tragedy. Put it behind them.'

'You don't understand,' muttered Oliver, not for the first time but with markedly less conviction than before. 'You can't possibly. How could I even —'

'What about a holiday?'

Just send all your problems to Aunty Becca, address at foot of page.

'Holiday?' echoed Oliver, as though the word were alien. I could almost see the idea evolving in his eyes. It was like watching a chicken chip itself out of an egg: the same painful slowness. Oliver frowned, and his mouth formed itself round several words before framing: 'Italy . . .'

I pounced. 'Italy?'

'Years ago,' he said, wonderingly, 'before I even met Cathy, I'd planned to go to Florence — take a sabbatical — to follow up some research. I suppose I —'

'Brilliant.' I settled back on to the pillows. 'Get away from it all, I would.' I was thinking that if all good-deeds-for-the-day were this enjoyable, I might have stuck with the Brownies.

And I was still rosily pleased with myself and the world a few hours later when I wandered out on to the kitchen step to admire the sunset. The elegantly spindly sound of Oliver playing his harpsichord drifted out on the warm evening air as I sipped a post-prandial whisky. Oliver's kitchen cupboards had proved to be innocent of the demon drink, except for half a bottle of Campari which I loathe. Luckily I'd remembered the cheap Scotch in my mac pocket. The kitchen had been equally free of food, and since sex and hangovers give one a hell of an appetite, it was as well I'd thought to pick up some bacon and eggs when I returned to Oxford to collect my clothes and car.

There had been a minor hiccup over getting back into town. Oliver, it turned out, not only had no car, he had never even learned to drive.

'How the hell do you get into work?' I had demanded.

There was a bus from Harecombe village, he said unconcernedly. And during the summer, he generally cycled in. No wonder, I thought, he had such admirable muscle tone if he regularly pedalled the ten miles into Oxford.

'And Constance keeps a room for me in the Lodgings,' he added. 'Great help if I'm rehearsing late. I've got a key and I can stop over whenever I need. Hell — I left the bike in college last night, didn't I?'

He had actually seemed to think I would have borrowed his bicycle for my own return journey to Oxford. Ho ho. But he kindly offered to pay my cab fare back to St Margaret's which was just as well because the contents of my purse wouldn't have covered it.

Now, the cluster of towers etched against the skyline darkened from pink to black. Positively Disneyesque. When Oliver eventually abandoned Scarlatti in favour of me and wandered out, I asked him what they were.

'That? That's the castle,' he said, glancing up at the silhouette. 'Harecombe Castle.'

'Real castle?'

I had to repeat the question before he seemed to hear.

'Victorian folly,' he said. 'Monstrosity.'

He lowered himself on to the step beside me, which was a relief because I was developing a crick in the neck. 'Built by an ancestor of Constance's — well, of mine too — but she doesn't own it now. It should have been knocked down years ago.'

'It looks rather pretty,' I protested. 'When did it pass out of your family?'

Oliver shrugged. 'The place was requisitioned during the war. It was such a wreck afterwards the family had no choice but to sell. They let the castle go with the patch of ground it stands on, but they held on to the estate.'

'Still?' I said, impressed. 'Is it large?'

'Constance owns all the land this side of the castle. Tenanted out to a couple of farmers, of course.'

'Of course,' I echoed with the airiness of one entirely familiar with estate management. 'And this cottage?'

'The Gatehouse belongs to Constance too,' he said. He began to scuff a circle in the gravel path with his toe. 'I was quite happy in Oxford with her and Uncle Michael. But when this house fell vacant, Constance seemed to think I should have a place of my own.'

I offered him my glass of whisky but he pushed it away, shuddering like a man whose hangover has frightened him off alcohol for life.

'What about the castle?' I said. 'What happens there now?'

'God only knows,' snapped Oliver with surprising bitterness. 'It's been put to any number of uses since the family sold up. The latest talk is of it being turned into an hotel. Until last year it was a kind of finishing school — glorified secretarial college. I don't know what you'd call it exactly.'

'If it was like some of the joints in Oxford,' I said, 'more a glorified marriage agency for dim-witted girls from the home counties. Mummy and Daddy paying the earth for darling

Emma to learn flower arranging by day and meet nice eligible undergraduates from Christ Church at night. God, there was one party I was invited to where –'

'Actually,' said Oliver quietly, 'Cathy went to Harecombe Castle.'

From then on, we were downhill all the way. Oh, it wasn't just my clanger about secretarial colleges. Looking back, I realize my innocent curiosity about the castle had really been the drop of rennet which began, inexorably, to sour the cream of the Midsummer idyll.

I stammered something about Harecombe being, no doubt, nothing like those colleges, then ditched the salvage attempt and enquired instead, with brightly false interest, 'Was that how the two of you met? When Cathy was at college in the castle?'

Oliver shook his head, then unexpectedly took my glass and swallowed half the contents in one gulp. 'She'd just left. Cathy lived in Harecombe village. Soon after I moved here, they asked me to conduct a carol concert in the local church.' His smile was at once sweet with reminiscence – and quite heart-wrenchingly sad. 'But I shouldn't talk to you about Cathy.'

'Why not?' I said nobly, one of the let-it-all-hang-out generation. 'If it helps, talk about her all you want.'

And so he bloody well did. I began to think inhibitions were grossly undervalued commodities.

Cathy, I learned as I washed up the supper pots, was not from your estate-owning background. More your estate-dwelling – as in Harecombe council estate. Dad had debunked with another woman when she was still toddling, and Mum had typed her fingers to the bone to rear the child alone, actually taking, years later, a poorly paid job at the said Harecombe Ladies' College (which incidentally sounded *exactly* like the joints I was talking about in Oxford) to secure reduced fees for her daughter. But, after two years of deportment, napkin-folding and desultory commercial studies, Cathy had — quite understandably — found the local amateur operatic society more alluring than her new job in a solicitor's office. Greasepaint roars louder than Tipp-Ex.

The Am. Dram. Soc. had fielded half the choir at the above-mentioned village carol concert. Oliver had picked up his baton and one voice soared above the chorus.

'Heavenly, bell-clear soprano,' said Oliver.

He accepted a tea-towel with an air of faint puzzlement. His mother had been a soprano too, I reflected. Men are always supposed to be trying to marry their mothers, aren't they?

'How old was Cathy when you met?'

'Nineteen. Absurdly young, I know,' he added with swift defensiveness. 'But at the time it never occurred to me — for God's sake, when we met, I wasn't even thinking of Cathy as . . . as . . .'

'A woman?'

Oliver did not cringe at the corny dialogue.

'I was comfortable. I'd almost begun to assume I wouldn't marry — not me. Seems crazy now. Incredible, because marrying her changed everything. It was like switching the lights on. As though I'd been living in the dark for years. And now, I couldn't possibly imagine a life without —'

He broke off as he realized, quite transparently, that he was indeed facing a life without Cathy. For an unsetting moment I thought he might blub but I reckoned without British grit.

'What I mean to say is,' he resumed, with a fleeting, ghastly smile, 'she took me by surprise. At first I just saw a talented soprano. I asked her to sing in one or two things I conducted in Oxford.'

Pygmalion, I was thinking as I passed him a wet plate, because it emerged that Oliver, Professor Higgins-style, had taken this promising young singer's musical education in hand. To be honest, his shyly confided, sugary love story was irritating me more than a little. I was beginning to feel like the original tart-with-the-twenty-two-carat-heart who wise-cracks her way through cowboy movies. The one who shares a smouldering moment with the hero, but is destined to be shot and to expire, repentantly and conveniently, in his arms, thus releasing Our Hero for the gingham-frilled virgin-next-door, who has real blonde hair ... instead of a mop of peroxide streaks.

At least, it looked real in the wedding photograph. Cathy was as golden-haired as she was golden-voiced. Following Oliver up to bed, I had surreptitiously poked around in the chaotic sitting room and found the picture face down on a sideboard. It was one of those ghastly would-be arty jobs with grease-smeared margins. The happy couple were framed between the branches of an old cedar tree. Oliver looked as wood-faced as you'd expect. She, however, was your picture-book bride. Not merely pretty in her frothing clouds of tulle, but radiantly happy. I squinted into the glowing little face and wondered what the hell had driven her, barely a couple of years on, to kill herself.

Ten minutes after capsizing into bed, I thought I knew. Oliver, who was already propped up against the pillows de-scribing the singing teacher he found in London for his so-talented bride, was reminding me tiresomely of a born-again Christian who feels impelled to tell the world about Love. Except the God Squad are at least happy as well as claptrappy. Think of it as therapy, I told myself crabbily, clambering in beside him and pulling the quilt up to my ear. Talking about the late sainted consort — not just beautiful but talented too — was probably doing Oliver untold good.

Anyway, I ascribed the rhapsodies about Cathy's talents to husbandly fondness, until I learned with a flicker of reluctant respect that she had actually begun to sing professionally: solo engagements and a short spell with a touring company. Even more interesting — at last a tang of vinegar in this saccharine saga — Oliver clearly hadn't been too happy with her fast-blossoming career.

'Cathy had the perfect Mozart voice,' he said, 'but she hankered after the big romantic repertoire: Verdi, Puccini...' From the way he said this, you'd think Puccini was a Mafia hoodlum. 'I thought she was taking on too much, too early. She was putting her voice under terrible strain.'

Oh yeah? Her voice or her marriage? I smiled cynically into the pillow. The Professor Higginses of this world never like it when the Elizas begin to carve their own destinies.

'These opera-on-a-shoestring outfits seemed to be springing up all over the place,' he went on. 'God, *Bohème*, with an out-of-tune piano in a church hall. Can you imagine?'

'As one who's played *Private Lives* in a Working Men's Club, yes,' I said, 'without too much difficulty.' I did not bother to stifle my yawn.

'That was with Wessex Opera.'

'I've heard of them,' I said, momentarily surprised out of my torpor. 'They were supposed to be good. Wasn't there a fuss because their grant was under threat?'

'They folded completely,' said Oliver. 'Cathy was devastated. Her first big leading role. They'd signed her up to sing *Tosca*.'

'Tosca?' I squawked, sitting up abruptly.

Tosca – who concludes the opera by flinging herself off the battlements?

'Yes – why?'

'It didn't occur to anyone that Cathy might have been inspired to do what she did –'

'Cathy did not –' began Oliver furiously, then crumbled. 'Shit, Becca, I'm sorry. You don't want to hear all this.'

We were both apologizing, me for my tactlessness and he was penitent like a child repeating a lesson. He must learn to accept it. I was right. Cathy was dead and –

'Shall we just forget it?' I suggested. 'And get some sleep?' But Oliver had other ideas.

And it occurred to me, in a sudden and unwelcome insight, that Oliver wanted me with exactly the same unloving passion an addict needs a fix. Heroin and sex are both effective pain-killers. Only now, really, did I notice how tight shut he kept his eyes. He wasn't making love to me at all, I thought outragedly. He was thinking of his bloody wife.

He dropped immediately into a coma afterwards. I lay back and reflected that dead wives could prove even more of an intrusion into one's love life than the extant variety.

The moral was clear: Other women's husbands should be left alone. What I should do was find myself a nice, unencumbered model.

Back to London, I thought grimly, first thing in the morning.

CHAPTER EIGHT

Which is what I said to Oliver over the toast and tea next morning. That I must get back to London, I mean, not that I was looking for an eligibly fancy-free bachelor.

Oliver had woken before me and proceeded downstairs to work out some ideas on the harpsichord. There can be few sounds more murderously grating on the waking ear than seventeenth-century counterpoint improvised on a harpsichord. Like needles being dragged across corrugated iron. If that was his usual practice at eight in the morning, I began to think Cathy Langham had earned canonization.

Happily, the smell of burned toast had eventually lured him into the kitchen. 'I'm afraid I've got to go into town,' he said.

'Into school? I guess you're up to your eyes in the end-of-year scramble.'

'Actually I've only got to tidy up odds and ends. They've let me off the Speech Day and end-of-term concert round.'

'Lucky old you,' I said, too absorbed in hunting through my handbag for my diary to register that, of all members of staff, the music master might be the least dispensable employee on these occasions.

'But I thought I might ask about taking time off,' he said, 'To go to Italy.'

'Terrific,' I said, wandering over to the open doorway. 'Want a lift into Oxford? I'll drop you on my way back to London.'

'London?' he said. 'Must you go straight away?'

I wasn't looking at him, I was admiring the morning. Another heavenly day. I chucked a crust towards a blackbird, who jumped on it with bright-eyed enthusiasm, and then opened the diary to see what exciting treats were in store in the new week.

Rarely had the pages looked quite so spectacularly unsullied. Day after white day. Only one forthcoming event rated capital letter billing, a fortnight tomorrow: 'FLAT LEASE EXPIRES'. Wow. What a life.

I only realized Oliver had approached when, awkwardly, he threaded his arms round my waist. 'Do you really have to go?'

I suppose he did sound rather forlorn. I suppose a small voice of conscience did whisper to me that I might have strayed into dangerous waters; that one really shouldn't play fast and loose with sad — and undeniably vulnerable — souls like Oliver. I ignored the voice.

Besides, I was absorbed in deciphering the single scribbled entry under today's date. Uncle Gordon? Oh hell. Ma had made me promise if I was around I'd go home and support her through lunch with this guardian of the nation's morals on his annual visit to Sin City. Great-uncle Gordon's views on The Youth of Today made Mary Whitehouse sound like Fanny Hill. And he was teetotal.

'Well . . .' I said. After all, it was a peach of a day. Heaven-sent for pootling around in the countryside. So much for moral lectures to self. I released myself from Oliver's embrace to attend to the toaster. 'I guess I could stay another night. If you like. More toast?'

'Great,' said Oliver, taking two more slices. Poor old thing, I thought. Not been feeding himself properly.

'I suppose Cathy did the cooking?'

'Cathy?' said Oliver, his mouth inelegantly full. He paused to swallow. 'God no. She hated cooking. Hated everything to do with housework, come to that.'

In the middle of wiping down the sink, I found I was gritting my teeth. 'Really?'

90

It was bad enough feeling sleazy, the ageing tart to her blushing bride, but now I felt boringly domesticated as well: a plodding Martha to her airy Mary. I began to regret my snap decision to stay.

'So how on earth,' I enquired sweetly, 'did the two of you manage?'

'We muddled along,' said Oliver with the now all-too-familiar tragic smile. 'Pamela used to come round and clean sometimes. Mucking us out, Cathy called it.'

'Finish your toast,' I said. 'I'll run you into town and I'd better buy something for dinner. In my mundane experience,' I added waspishly, 'man cannot live for ever on bed alone.'

I quite enjoy cooking, but I've always been stronger on self-confidence than actual technique.

After dropping Oliver off outside St Benedict's Hall to pick up his bicycle, I found a supermarket which took credit cards and allowed myself to be tempted by a duck. Inspired by a cookery book I'd borrowed from the kitchen shelf in the Gatehouse — which had cracked open, incidentally, with the air of a volume still virgin from the printers — I returned to Harecombe, laden with bags of exotic and expensive ingredients specified for *Canard à l'Arlésienne*.

On reaching home, I read the recipe more carefully. The book calmly instructed that the duck should be boned. Simple as that. With a few spindly diagrams of a kind I thought I'd left behind after Biology O Level.

The only apron I could find in the kitchen was a soppy frilled pinny, featuring a mop-headed girl clutching a bunch of flowers. Yuck. Moreover, no sooner had I finished scrubbing the kitchen to a standard suitable for such a tricky surgical procedure, and boldly split the beast down the backbone, than there was a knock at the front door.

I walked through the sitting room, wiping the blood off my hands and the sweat from my forehead with a paper towel, and opened the door.

The front door of the Gatehouse gave directly onto the lane, so the small, thin woman was standing in the middle of the road. She was surveying the windows for signs of life. As a matter of fact, she reminded me rather cruelly of one of those small grey animals that get splattered across the highways daily. A little vole or a shrew. Her hair was exactly that mousy pepper-and-salty colour. She had pale, timid eyes and a pointed nose. She wasn't old — her skin was clear as a nun's — but her dress was depressingly middle-aged. A sludge-coloured shirtwaister buttoned to the neck, in the kind of synthetic fibre that makes you sweat just looking at it, in weather like that. Tights too.

'Can I help you?' I said, with less than open-hearted friendliness. She was carrying a flashy navy suitcase — crocodile effect, if you can imagine a blue crocodile — and I assumed she was selling something. Or worse, was a member of an obscure religious sect with a bag full of Bibles. She had, I diagnosed, the slightly loopy look of a fanatic.

'Pardon?' she whispered. Not a Bible-basher, then: no ingratiating smile, no sales patter. She took a couple of uncertain steps towards me and put down the case. 'You're the woman — off the television.' What was really odd was the absent-minded way she said this, as though voicing an irrelevance.

'Got it in one,' I agreed.

But she was staring as if I had six legs.

I admit I wasn't looking my glamorous best. Jeans, hair hitched up in a rubber band. Actually, it was the apron which seemed to pinion her gaze. It occurred to me that she was the kind of woman who wouldn't dream of answering the front door wearing an apron. Probably, like my gran, she would have whipped it off and tucked it under a cushion.

'Is . . . Mr Langham at home?' she said eventually.

''Fraid not,' I said. 'Can I help? Take a message?'

'I . . .' There was sweat on her forehead and her thin lips worked silently. For one ghastly minute I thought she was succumbing to heatstroke.

'You'd better come in,' I said. 'Would you like a cup of tea?'

The reviving effect of this offer was miraculous – but not in the usual way.

She drew herself up smartly, snatched up the case and said, 'Please tell him Pamela called.'

'Pamela?' I said, the mental computer clicking into operation. 'Oh yes. Don't you sometimes' – liberal sensitivities baulked at 'clean'. Surely cleaning, like dustbin-collecting, had been superceded by grander job descriptions – '*do* for Oliver?'

She gasped. Stared at me as though I'd accused her of running a child porn-ring.

Whoops, I thought. Not *that* Pamela.

'Mrs *Metcalfe*,' she snapped, as though that explained everything. She fastened both thin paws round the handle of the case, as if afraid I might wrest it from her. 'Tell him I must see him. Urgently.'

'Certainly, Mrs Metcalfe,' I said apologetically, with my best smile. She was not to be won over. With one final stare, in which incredulity and disgust seemed equally mixed, she hurried off to a small white car parked in front of my own study in rust and polyfilla. I remember thinking at the time it was an unlikely car for a woman like her. Small and sporty with go-faster stripes down the sides and a cute name monogrammed on the back. Trendy or Candy or something.

I shrugged and returned to the kitchen. About a quarter of an hour and one bloodied thigh bone later, I heard another car in the lane. The engine stopped. A door slammed. Then there was silence. I flung down the knife and marched into the sitting room.

It wasn't her again. That much was evident, because I could see a red car bonnet through the window now. I walked over and peered out. Well, well. A long lean beast like something out of a Bond movie. Open-topped with – I blinked – tiger-skin seats. Of a non-endangered acrylic species, naturally. No owner visible and, oddly, the boot lid was gaping. I shrugged and went back to the kitchen.

There was no one at the back door either. I was just picking up the knife again when, out of the window, I could swear I saw a face peer through one of the gaps in the privet hedge, then dodge out of sight. I stared. After a minute, the face appeared in the next gap along. Male, with a healthy suntan and square, very black sunglasses, which winked at me enigmatically.

I walked to the back door.

I couldn't see the owner of the face at first, but I quite distinctly heard a baritone voice mutter, from behind the hedge, in apparent astonishment, 'Well, bloody Nora.'

Then he appeared at the garden gate, which he kicked open.

He was short, but very broad. Built, as my apron-hiding gran who was also one of nature's Bowdlerizers used memorably to say, like a brick potting-shed. Mighty shoulders brushed the hedge both sides as he walked through the gateway. This moving mountain of muscle was encased in breathlessly tight white jeans and a jungle-patterned shirt, which gaped open nearly to the waist, exposing a hugely hairy expanse of chest. And there was nestling among the black matting — yes, honestly — a gold medallion. His forearms, sturdy as young tree-trunks, were equally hairy. The shirt-sleeves were pushed back but it was hard to imagine a cuff ever fastening round those colossal wrists. The impression was of primitive man bursting out of the flimsy trappings of civilization.

'Hello?' I said, goggling.

Once inside the gate, the hulk paused and smiled. Or rather leered. He had very white teeth, lots of them, and he exuded sheer animal sexuality with the subtlety of an air-raid siren.

'Surprise, surprise,' he drawled. 'How ya doing?' The accent hovered unhappily between Beverly Hills and Bradford. Any minute now, I thought, he would whip out a microphone, wiggle his pelvis and croon a hit number from the Latin lovers' songbook.

I gave him the Red Queen stare. 'I beg your pardon?'

Grinning, he lifted the sunglasses, and only then did I recognize the close-cropped curls, the crooked nose, the chocolatey voice. Even the tattoo on the hairy forearm.

'Blimey,' I said. 'It's the man on the bridge.' He was clean-shaven now, but the jaw was still profoundly blue. No longer a tramp, more a bouncer strayed from a Costa Lager nite club.

'Got it in one, sunshine. Anyone at home?'

'Only me,' I said faintly.

'Well, that suits me,' he said, strolling across the scrubby grass and kissing me on the cheek. In fact, on both cheeks. Quite unperturbed, it seemed, by having to reach up to do so. I stood like a dummy, reeling in a cloud of expensive cologne.

'Where's —' Suddenly he broke off and eyed me shyly. Or as shyly as such a hirsute slab of machismo can look. 'Where's Oliver then? In school?'

'Yes,' I began. 'He's — you mean — do you *know* Oliver then?'

He shrugged.

'Sure.' He threw his car keys in the air and caught them in a one-handed slam. 'I thought it was you two I saw disappearing into that little door in the wall,' he said. 'But I could hardly credit it. One minute you were there in the street, talking to me, and the next?'

'It was you vanished first,' I protested.

'And here you are now. At Harecombe Gatehouse, no less,' he said, ignoring this and gazing at me eyebrows raised, as though awaiting the answer to question. 'What a turn up for the bloody book, eh?'

CHAPTER NINE

'What's so very amazing about that?' I said, flushing under the intent scrutiny. 'Small world, as they say.'

'Is Oliver a — friend of yours, then?' The innuendo dripping from the word 'friend' made it clear he wasn't speaking in 'just good friends' terms. What's more, he sounded frankly incredulous.

I bridled. 'I've known Oliver Langham for years. We met at university, as a matter of fact.'

'Did you now?' he said. 'And you just — happened to meet him again t'other night?'

'That's right.'

'You're actually staying here?'

'I have been. Yes.'

'For long?'

'What is this? Some kind of interrogation? I'm going back to London,' I said, 'tomorrow morning.'

'Bloody good thing I came round today, then,' he drawled, eyeing me up, apron and all, with the unashamed lechery of a Benidorm beach bum. 'Bloody terrific.'

'What is?' I said, hitching the neck of my shirt closed.

'Finding you here today.' The deep voice slid round every syllable like double cream. 'I've been kicking myself, you know, letting you disappear like that. I never even asked your name.'

'So you didn't.'

'I've been thinking about you ever since.'

'Oh yeah?'

He moved a little closer. 'Just this morning, I was wondering how the hell I could get in touch with you.'

'Well, here I am now,' I said, hopping smartly backwards into the kitchen doorway. 'What can I do for you?'

Stupid question.

'I can think of any number of things, but maybe not here in the garden.'

'Pack it in,' I said — but I was laughing.

'I really did want to see you again,' he protested. 'Hey, you've got amazing eyes — did you know that? Now what's so bloody funny?'

'Well, honestly. What a corny line.'

'They're an unusual colour,' he said rather huffily. 'I hadn't noticed in the dark, that's all. Very green.'

'Pea-soup colour.'

'Not the way I make pea soup, baby. And what's wrong with telling someone they've got beautiful eyes?'

'Must be the way you tell 'em.'

He straightened abruptly and gazed up at the sky with an air of martyred resignation. 'OK, give me the works,' he said. 'Smash what's left of my ego — which, I'm here to tell you, isn't much. Tell me I sound like an ageing gigolo, the originality of whose vocabulary in sexual encounters — now, let me get this right — would not stretch the boundaries of a Max Bygraves lyric.'

'Wow,' I said. 'Who told you that?'

'Al.'

'What on earth had you said to her?'

'Nothing. She came out with it in Spain after she found me chatting up the barmaid.'

I laughed. 'Well what did you expect?'

'What did *she* expect, more like? But, we won't go into that now,' he said, propping himself against the door jamb and leaning towards me confidentially. 'We weren't talking about Al. We were talking about you, sweetheart. You and me.'

'Oh no we weren't. How do you come to know Oliver anyhow?'

That distracted him. He straightened and turned away. Kicked a pebble across the path. 'Well, I've been friendly with his aunt for years.'

I considered the combination of Constance Berisford and him . . . seeing me boggling, he protested: 'She's one of our best customers. And we're nearly neighbours now, aren't we?'

'You and Lady Berisford?'

'Well, in a manner of speaking, I guess. She owns the estate, doesn't she? But it was Oliver I was talking about.' Suddenly, he twisted round, waving a stubby finger at the horizon. 'See those towers, ma'am?' he roared. 'You're only looking at the finest eating house in the West Country. You're only looking at a small, but ultra – and I mean ultra – luxurious country hotel. You're only looking at the venue all the society weddings, conferences and dances will be falling over themselves to book. You're looking at –'

'Shut up,' I said, grinning. 'I get the picture.'

'You're also looking at,' he added, dropping the sales spiel, 'the biggest bullshitter in the county.'

That bit I could believe.

'And you're going to be working there?' I enquired. 'Or just selling it to the world?'

'Excuse me, baby,' he said grandiloquently. 'I own the joint, Well, nearly. I was just going up there to – oh, give us a break. What's the joke now?'

'I suppose you own that Batmobile out in the road too?'

'Bet your life.'

'You told me you were bankrupt.'

'On the brink of, I bloody am, as well. Did you hear me say I owned the castle? Told you I was a bullshitter. I should think I own a couple of chimneys. The bank owns the rest.'

'Even so . . .' I said, marvelling. 'You know, I thought you were a tramp.'

'But you loved me anyway. Just for myself. Kiss me, honey, and I'll turn into a prince.'

'You have to be a frog for that.'

He promptly croaked and hopped towards me, at some risk, I couldn't help thinking, to the tight white trousers.

'Lunatic,' I said, flapping a tea-towel at him. 'You've left your boot open, did you know?'

'Oh yeah.' He straightened, shrugging. 'I — thought I'd better see if anyone was home first. I don't suppose you know where —' He broke off to stare at the tea-towel.

'Sweetheart, you haven't murdered anyone have you?'

'What? Oh, is it bloody?'

'Don't let me interrupt if you're dismembering Oliver's corpse.'

'Not Oliver's corpse,' I said bitterly. 'A bird's.'

'Strangled another canary, have we?'

'What a memory,' I said admiringly. 'But I didn't strangle poor Ringo.'

'Is that the bird or the boyfriend?'

'Same difference. They're both down the chute. So to speak.' I sighed. 'God, it seems a lifetime ago I was on that bridge, moaning about my troubles.'

'Not to me, it doesn't. I'm only just facing the world again. I spent yesterday in a darkened room with tea-bags on the eyes.'

'Bad hangover eh?'

'Jet lag.'

'From Torremolinos?'

'Torremolinos?' he said scornfully. 'Do you know Spain?'

I shook my head.

'Then there's no point giving you directions. We were staying in a little corner of paradise. What should have been paradise anyway. Father Xavier was right,' he said, adopting an Irish accent now. '"Walk carefully when you t'ink you've found paradise, son, dere's snakes in de bluddy grass." And speaking of snakes, I daresay Al's still sunning herself there.

Or . . .' He glanced at his watch. 'Or she was until an hour ago. So what's your problem?'

'Problem?'

'With the bird.'

'I think the beast's deformed,' I said. 'None of the bones are where they're supposed to be. Maybe because it's a duck, and the diagrams are of a chicken. They say you bone them the same way.'

'You do, by and large. Want a hand?'

'Can you bone ducks?' I said dubiously.

'Can I bone ducks? Are you kidding? Blindfold and whistling *Traviata*. But only if you offer me a drink.'

'Tea?' I said, leading the way into the kitchen.

'It's lunchtime,' he protested. 'Well, OK. Hang about a minute . . .'

And to my surprise, he sprinted out of the garden again. I heard him mutter a curse as, I deduced, he scrambled over the farm gate, then I heard a car boot slam. When he reappeared in the kitchen doorway, he was holding a bottle of champagne, no less, in his huge fist. A bottle just running with condensation. A bottle just ready, in other words, for drinking.

'Convenient,' I observed.

He grinned a touch self-consciously. 'Never travel without it. Got a couple of glasses?'

While I ransacked one cupboard after another, he – I could tell – was surveying the room curiously. I resisted an urge to apologize for the mess. Eventually I found some glasses. He proceeded to lever out the cork with such smug nonchalance I hoped it might explode in his eye, but it sidled out with only a steamy sigh.

'Here's to you, gorgeous,' he said, raising his glass. 'I never expected to be drinking this with you, but I couldn't be happier.'

I raised my own glass. With surprise – and a passing twinge of conscience on Oliver's account – I found I agreed. With this gorilla. With this grinning, over-sexed, underdressed hunk of animal. Even though hairy chests make me sneeze, and as for gold medallions . . .

'Down to business,' he said, beckoning. I gulped. 'Come here, baby.' I edged towards him, but he only wiped my forehead with a damp cloth, tutting. 'More blood than a Hammer Horror.'

Then he turned me round and removed my apron, taking his time untying the strings while breathing unnecessarily close to my neck. I found I didn't mind in the least.

He donned the apron himself. The frills made him look like a bull in a lingerie shop, but he didn't seem to worry, just washed his hands with the meticulous, between-the-fingers soaping of a surgeon. Then he sneered at the knife I handed to him, and retreated to the back step where he whisked it back and forth with a noise that made the hairs on the back of my neck twinge.

'Of course, you're a chef, aren't you? Or should I say *were*,' I added kindly, 'before you became a tycoon.'

He glanced satirically across at me, and informed me that the day he stopped cooking was the day the business would stop too. He ran an outside catering company. Specializing in — he grinned at me crookedly — *balls*, and banquets; weddings and the like. But I mustn't be deterred. No job was too small for Flying Duck. Even boning out this one. For free.

'That really what the business is called? "Flying Duck"?' And, as I asked, I noticed the bird tattoo on his wrist actually depicted just that.

'Yup, that's where Bunny got it from,' he said. 'I thought it was a bloody silly name, but he was the ideas man, and he was right. People remember it.'

'Is my duck beyond rescue?'

He gave me a look of ineffable superiority, took another swig of fizz, and began whistling '*Sempre Libera*' as he applied the knife to the mangled carcase, only breaking off — as he cast a white wingbone aside — to ask what I was planning to do with the bird. I picked up the book and read him the recipe.

He pursed his lips, as though tasting the ingredients. 'Bland, I'd try a bit of cayenne.'

'No chance. I haven't bought any, and this kitchen doesn't run to anything more exotic than salt and tea-bags.'

'Not surprised,' he said. And then glanced sideways at me. 'Cathy, bless her, never struck me as the domesticated type.'

He said the name awkwardly, as though testing it on me. This didn't surprise me. People often speak awkwardly about the dead, and here we were, in her kitchen.

'So Oliver tells me,' I said, just to illustrate Oliver and I weren't embarrassed to talk about the late wife. 'How well did you know Cathy Langham?'

He seemed momentarily at a loss for words, and applied himself to easing out the main skeleton.

'Well, Al knew Cathy years before I met her,' he said. 'They were brought up next door to one another in the village here. It was Al introduced me to her.'

'And Al's ... your girlfriend,' I said, twirling the glass between my fingers. 'The holiday companion with the deadly arsenal of put-downs.'

'*Woman* friend,' he muttered grimly. 'Very keen on Politically Correct terms is our Alison. Ex-girlfriend, anyway.'

'The holiday was that bad, eh?' What I was after, I admit, was proof of the real McCoy: your actual, unencumbered bachelor.

'Oh, Al and I split up ages ago,' he said. 'Last year.'

'And went to Spain together last week? For old times' sake?'

'I wouldn't quite put it that way,' he said. 'The holiday was all her idea.' He began whistling again, quietly, through his teeth.

'But you were telling me about Cathy,' I prompted.

'Got something to put these bones in? You'll want them for the stock. Yeah, well, I met Cathy last autumn, when she sang at a dinner we were doing. Big job. Hundred and eighty covers. Fabulous voice,' he added.

'So I've gathered,' I murmured acidly, and he looked at me speculatively for a moment before returning to his labours.

'She sang all my favourite arias. I'm a great opera fan, mad about —' He broke off so abruptly I thought he'd cut himself, but no, another bone pinged into the bowl and he continued: 'Well, I like the tunes, that's all. Don't know the first thing about it, for Christ's sake. But it was that night, after the dinner was over, Cathy tipped us off about the castle. The college had packed up and she'd heard it was coming on the market.' He paused, pulling a wry face. 'That night, in the roaring mood I was in, I'd have discussed buying Balmoral. The next day I'd already forgotten. But Rupert was on to it like a flash.'

'Rupert?' I enquired, sipping my champagne.

'My partner, Rupert Hare-Smith.'

'Oh, *Bunny* . . .' I said, and he gave another of his crooked grins. The broken nose was undeniably endearing.

'Sharp as a box of knives, Bunny. Next thing, we were selling the restaurant — we used to have a bistro down St Giles's. Sold the wine bar, too. And here I am now, with only the outside catering left, and a bloody castle. Well, a castle all bar a bit of red tape. With luck they'll have sorted that while I've been in Spain.'

'And no Bunny.'

He looked at me in surprise. 'Did I tell you all about that too? I really must have been pissed.'

'He's gone off and married an Australian,' I said promptly.

'New Zealander. Same difference. Bunny met her at a Valentine dance we did the buffet for — your actual whirlwind romance. Bloody hell. Still, I can't entirely blame him,' he added fair-mindedly. 'She's a cracker and her dad owns a vineyard.'

It wasn't clear which attribute was most to be envied. I laughed and he joined in.

'Well, there's your duck. Finished.' He patted the flesh back into shape. 'I've poured half my life story out to you and you still haven't told me your name.'

'Becca Haydock,' I said, warming to him even further as I admired his immaculate handiwork. 'Thanks a lot.' He was washing his hands again, and stripping off the pinny. Not a speck of blood on the white trousers either. For a tycoon, he was handy with a knife.

'Joe Duff. My pleasure.'

Joe, I thought, suited him. Short, square and solid.

'Are you cooking this tonight?' he said.

'Course I am.'

'Pity,' he said. 'I was hoping to persuade you into my car, so I could whisk you away and seduce you with my own brilliant cooking. Way to a woman's heart — or so I keep hoping.'

'*Canard à l'Arlésienne* will be quite brilliant enough, thank you,' I said, firmly suppressing a twinge of regret.

He grinned, 'I'd be happy to seduce you without the food.'

'What?' I squawked. 'Honestly, you're beyond belief.'

'So are you,' he said, taking the champagne bottle out of my nerveless hand and filling both our glasses. 'I mean it, I really like you.'

He sounded as though he meant it, too. But there's your would-be Don Juan for you. A hundred and ten per cent sincerity has to be their stock in trade.

He strolled out into the searing sunshine again, glass in hand, cockily sure I would follow. Which, OK, I did.

Fastidiously brushing crumbs of earth out of the way, he lowered himself on to the grass. 'I think it's Fate, don't you? Our bumping into one another again like this.' He had dark, liquid eyes. Very soulful. 'We shouldn't kick against destiny, baby.'

'Destiny?' I said breathlessly, sitting down at a wary distance from him. 'I don't believe in destiny. "I am the master of my fate: I am the captain of my soul".' I paused. 'Or is it master of my soul and captain of my fate?'

'Any room for a stowaway on board?' enquired Joe Duff.

'You're impossible.'

With an agility remarkable for his bulk, he rolled across the grass, and ended up lying beside me.

'It's the Latin in me,' he murmured. 'I just accept that certain things were meant to be.'

I had no doubt what things he had in mind.

'After all, here am I,' he said, touching his icy glass to my bare forearm, and grinning when I yelped. 'And here are you. Fate.'

'I'm not sure Oliver would see it quite that way,' I felt obliged to say.

Joe put down his glass, looking suddenly more amazed than amorous. '*Oliver*?' he said. 'I mean — I didn't like to ask, are you and Oliver . . .?'

I found I was blushing. 'Well . . . *no*,' I burst out. 'Course not.'

I won't say a cock crowed, but a blackbird certainly piped up in the hedge.

'I've just been here for the weekend,' I said. 'Back to London tomorrow. Like I said.'

'Good,' said Joe Duff. 'At least, good, if I can persuade you to give me your phone number. I come up to London quite often.'

'Do you?' I said, torn between gratification and guilt.

He smiled and nodded, draining his glass. Then he rolled away, and clambered to his feet. I felt let down. I was ready for him to sweet-talk my address out of me. Instead, he started brushing grass off his trousers.

'I suppose I can't ask . . .' he said tentatively, and I looked up, prepared to dish out the phone number on demand. 'I mean, tell me if the question's out of order, what with you being here and that . . .' Sitting on one man's lawn, making assignations with another, well, yes, I could see his point. But I was prepared to overlook the irregularities. He thrust out a hand, and yanked me to my feet. 'But,' he said, 'where's Cathy?'

*

If he hadn't been holding my hand I swear I'd have fallen back on to the grass. I stared at him aghast. 'Don't you know?'

'I'm sorry. Obviously a tactless bloody question. I mean, I guessed they'd had some sort of row . . .'

'Look,' I said, scrabbling my wits together, 'was Cathy a close friend?'

'Was?' said Joe. 'What do you mean, *was*? Shit, earlier on I noticed you asked how well *did* I know –'

'Oh God. I'm sorry. There's no easy way to say this. Cathy Langham's dead.'

At least he didn't blench, or stagger. He just stared in blatant disbelief. 'Cathy? Dead? For Pete's sake – when?'

I shrugged helplessly. 'I don't know exactly. Not terribly long ago. I think – well, some time in the last year . . .'

His face cleared. 'Don't be daft. She was alive and kicking t'other day. Take my word for it.'

The blackbird began singing his little head off again.

'This is mad,' I said. 'At least, one of us is mad. *When* are you talking about?'

'Fortnight ago?' said Joe. 'Yeah, fortnight ago to the day. I was packing when she rang. Night before I went on holiday and . . . Becca? Becca, what's the matter?'

At moments of crisis your whole past life is supposed to whiz past you. All I can say is, the last thirty-six hours whizzed through my dazed – and stupid, God how could I have been so stupid? – brain in ten seconds flat.

106

CHAPTER TEN

'When did she die?' I demanded an hour later when Oliver, flushed and glistening from his long cycle ride, strolled into the kitchen.

'What?' he said. 'Shit — what's that?' He had tripped over my weekend bag, which was packed ready by the door.

I took a deep breath and — I hoped — a grip on myself. 'A friend of yours came round,' I said. 'Joe Duff. And he said —'

'Friend of mine?' snapped Oliver. 'That oily yob?'

'He told me,' I said, 'that he saw Cathy, or spoke to her anyway —'

'He *what?*'

'A *fortnight* ago, Oliver. For Christ's sake, tell me when Cathy died.'

Oliver turned away, kicking my bag up against the wall again. 'They don't seem to be able to tell exactly. The police were saying today that —'

'The *police?*'

'They wanted to see me again,' He scowled. 'Needn't have bothered. They couldn't tell me anything I didn't know already and —'

'Oliver. When did it happen?'

He snorted. 'If you listen to those so-called experts any time between eleven p.m. and —'

'Not the time,' I nearly screamed. 'I mean, when? For pity's sake, she is dead, isn't she?'

*

'Are you all right?' Joe Duff had said worriedly. So much for breaking the news gently to this friend of Cathy Langham. I was the shell-shocked and shaking one. 'Look,' he said. 'I think you'd better come inside and sit down.'

Sheep-like, I followed him and capsized on to a kitchen chair. My brain was under bombardment from remembered snatches of conversation, agonizingly vivid fragments of scenes. I could feel the flush of mortification prickling up from my bra to my ears. The more I remembered, the hotter grew my shame.

'Tea,' said Joe Duff, opening one cupboard door after another. 'I guess we could both do with some.'

The ball, I thought. That fucking ball. No wonder everyone was so astonished to see Oliver there. No wonder – oh, no wonder – he had been reluctant to dance. What was it he'd said? *Life has been . . . rather ghastly?*

'Sugar?' said Joe Duff, and I shook my head.

Oh, Oliver, I was thinking desperately, why didn't you tell me? Instead of letting me drag you round like a puppet on my arm? No wonder they stared – knowing Mrs Oliver Langham was barely cold in her grave. But was she in her grave? Dear Lord, had they even held the funeral?

'When was it you saw her?' I demanded, so sharply Joe Duff splashed milk over his hand.

'Drink this,' he said, handing me a dripping mug. 'Like I said, Cathy phoned me Monday evening. Two weeks back. I was finishing the packing because the flight was crack of dawn next day and I had to pick Al up from her mother's on the way . . .'

I had already stopped listening. No more than a fortnight ago, I was thinking. Cathy Langham was sitting here in this kitchen.

'You see, Cathy'd borrowed a bit of money off me and she rang to ask if I wanted it back straight away, because some job she'd been counting on had fallen through. Course I told her not to worry . . .'

Automatically, as I sat down, I'd picked up the apron lying on the chair and folded it across my knees. *Her* apron. I jumped to my feet and stuffed it into the washing machine. Then thought about – of all things – the sheets on Oliver's bed. On *their* bed. The not-very-clean sheets. Sheets she might even have slept in. I hugged myself in horror.

'But she knew that anyway,' Joe Duff was continuing. 'I'd always said she could pay me back whenever. And if you ask me, why she'd really rung was because she'd heard I'd got the castle.'

Now I was staring at my mug of tea. With the real 'is this a dagger which I see before me?' glare. The mug featured a teddy bear holding a balloon. *Her* mug, no question. I was sleeping in her bed, with her husband, even drinking from her cup. I slammed it down on the table.

'Something wrong with the tea?' said Joe.

I shook my head. I couldn't begin to explain. But I couldn't drink the tea either.

'Matter of fact, I was glad she phoned because there was this legal quibble,' he went on, as though pouring out every detail would convince me the woman wasn't dead. 'You see, if I'm going ahead, we'll need access through the side gate here – there's a bridge over the moat at the front of the castle, too narrow for builders' lorries. But Constance Berisford has to agree to us using the back drive. I knew she'd ask the Langhams if they minded. Cathy said – Christ, I remember her saying this on the phone – she would fix it. And then . . . Look, Becca, are you sure?'

How the hell, I was thinking, had she contrived to vanish so utterly from the rest of the house? OK, an apron. A teddy bear mug. But what about the rest of her? All I'd seen was Oliver's mess. And the yawningly empty wardrobes . . .

I realized Joe was staring at me.

'What?' I said.

'This might sound daft. But are you sure there hasn't been some misunderstanding? I mean – about what's happened to

Cathy? I know she and Oliver had a row. And I've not heard anything . . .'

'What?' bellowed Oliver. I hastily apologized.

'Didn't mean it,' I muttered. I didn't, I had known all along Cathy Langham was dead. No one — let alone Oliver — could have acted the bereaved husband so convincingly. As I had told Joe Duff. The only thing I didn't know was *when*.

'Two weeks ago,' said Oliver. 'Monday night. She . . . Becca, don't look at me like that. What on earth's the matter? You *knew*.'

'Of course I didn't know,' I snapped — before remembering I was dealing with a recently widowed man who merited, at the very least, gentleness.

Besides, by this time, I suppose I should actually have been relieved to hear Cathy Langham had been dead for a whole fortnight. In the interminable wait for Oliver to come home, I'd begun to wonder whether she hadn't passed away mere hours before I rolled, like a lusty tidal wave, into her grieving husband's life. I didn't blame Oliver for what had happened. He'd been swept along, helpless as a leaf on the Severn Bore.

'I thought it'd happened ages ago,' I said. 'Last year some time. You said, oh I don't know, that she was twenty-two, that she'd be twenty-three now . . .'

'Her birthday was — would have been — a couple of days after she died.'

'Oh God,' I breathed. 'A fortnight.'

'Does it make a difference?'

'Well of course it does.'

'Why?'

Why? Exactly. I'd been asking myself that for the past hour. Contemplating the moral dilemma. Why should it be so profoundly shocking to learn the man you've been sleeping with (the man you seduced. The man you damn nearly *raped* . . .) was widowed only days ago? I'd known his wife was dead, hadn't I? But I'd automatically relegated the event to

110

some date respectably in the past. Was there a watershed? Some mysterious dividing line after which it became accept-able to consort with a widower? Wherever this mythical line fell, there was no question Oliver was well the wrong side of it.

'I can't explain,' I said. 'It just feels — awful, that's all.'

So much for worldly, unshockable me. Feelings aren't logi-cal. I felt I'd violated some profound taboo. And if I'd managed to offend myself, how must it appear to less emancipated sectors of the world?

'What must *you* have thought of me?' I added stiltedly. 'I can only say — I would never have behaved as — as I did. Not if I'd known.'

'I thought you were being kind to me,' said Oliver with shaming simplicity.

Kind? Kind as a slavering she-wolf offering shelter to an orphaned lamb.

'And what the hell . . .' I moderated my tone with difficulty. 'What were you doing, anyway, going to a *ball*?'

'God knows I didn't want to. I'd shut myself up here, switched the answering machine on. I told you, Becca, all I wanted was to die . . .'

The tins of food, I thought. The empty fridge. The sordid, dismal mess.

'But I found this bloody message on the machine saying Tom couldn't sing. I suppose it made me realize I couldn't just sit here for ever, and it was Aunt Constance's college we'd be letting down. So I made my mind up to come in and' — he grimaced — 'face the music. Then I met you.'

'Yes,' I whispered, wondering at a Fate which steered me towards St Benedict's College with such malign precision. Five seconds earlier or later, and Oliver and I would never have coincided.

'You made me . . . see sense. The way you talked to me, I realized —'

I actually groaned aloud, remembering the brazen Brownie,

111

briskly telling a man whose wife died days ago to pull his socks up. Put it behind him. Take a holiday.

'But you were right,' he protested passionately. 'Nothing I do can bring Cathy back. Christ, I'd do *anything*, give my soul, I loved her so much.'

'I behaved unspeakably. I can only repeat how sorry I am.'

'Sorry? You don't know — you'll never know — what you've done for me. For the first time last night, I didn't dream about it all. I didn't have the nightmares. Because of you.'

'Fuck,' I breathed. 'I mean, good. If I've done anything — that helps, of course I'm glad. But . . . look, I'm sorry, Oliver, but if you can bear it, I think you'd better tell me just what really did happen to Cathy. Now.'

'I've seen no one since I got back from holiday,' Joe Duff had said wonderingly. 'Not who knows Cathy, I mean. Or do I mean *knew* her? It just doesn't seem possible.'

'You can say that again.'

'For God's sake, what's supposed to have happened to the girl?'

'Don't ask me,' I wailed. 'I think I've been blind and deaf.' Freshly remembered details, like poisoned darts, were flashing home by the quiverful: the photograph by the bed. Of Oliver's mother. Well, of course. Why would he need a picture of Cathy if her face had been on the next pillow until now?

'Car accident? Al's always said she was a lunatic behind the wheel and —'

'No, no,' I said, burying my head in my hands and wishing he'd shut up and go away.

And what about Constance Berisford? That was what I was thinking now. At least I could understand why she got so worked up, walking into her study and finding us, as she thought, *in flagrante*. But it was Lady Berisford who then packed us off in a taxi. Virtually flinging us into bed together. What kind of behaviour was that for an outraged aunt? I even remembered her saying that nothing shocked her. Well, it bloody well shocked me now.

Joe was still waiting for an answer.

'I'm sorry,' I said reluctantly. 'No — no accident. Cathy, um, apparently she took her own life.'

'No,' said Joe Duff. 'No. Not Cathy. She'd never kill herself. Not in a million years.'

'That's what Oliver said too. But it seems she did. Threw herself off a building. I don't know where but —'

'Bollocks,' interrupted Joe Duff, sounding all at once hugely relieved. 'I know she didn't. Al was there, for Christ's sake. She told me Cathy was only playing games . . .'

'I don't usually come home at all on Mondays,' said Oliver. 'The Commoners rehearse in the evening, and then I stay overnight with Constance. But Cathy had been away that weekend.'

He was sitting opposite me at the kitchen table, exactly where Joe had sat. Hot, mid-afternoon sunshine flooded through the open door; the same sun which had blasted down on our naked bodies yesterday afternoon. Today, in spite of the heat, I was shivering.

'She always went up to London for her singing lessons, but she didn't usually make a weekend of it,' Oliver took a deep breath and seemed to be forcing himself to concentrate, to order the facts. 'But she was working hard, learning Tosca. So that Monday afternoon I biked home from school specially to see her. She got back just after I did. I was sorting through the post when she walked in, looking so happy. And without even thinking I gave her the letter.'

He got to his feet and walked over to the window.

'It was from bloody Wessex Opera. Saying they were packing up. At first, she didn't speak. Just held the letter out to me, as though she couldn't believe it. You see, Cathy couldn't bear to — fail. Not when she'd set her heart on something. She was convinced this was her big chance. She said — she actually told me — she'd been prepared to do *anything* to get it.' He shut his eyes for a moment before continuing. 'God, I was so crass. I tried to suggest she look on the positive side. I'd always said Tosca was too heavy for her voice.'

I grimaced.

'I know, I know,' Oliver cried. 'Poor darling. That was the last thing she needed. She turned on me then. Said I was a snob. That I despised the kind of music she wanted to sing and — oh, what does it matter now? Even then, I knew she didn't mean the half of it. The point is, she slammed out of the house and got into the car.' He sighed, and walked back to the table. 'The side gate here was open and when she turned into the castle drive, I was relieved. It's a shortcut, you see, up past the castle, into the village. I thought she was going to see her mother. But she wound the window down and screamed she was going to kill herself. I tried to grab the handle on the door but she roared off up the drive and I followed. Lord, this must sound too bloody ludicrous for words. I followed on the bike. But, honestly, I didn't take her seriously. I mean, I hated her being so upset but I knew she wouldn't dream of killing herself and —' He broke off and glanced uneasily out of the window. I could see the castle on the horizon, turrets glowing rosily.

'There's one huge tower, like a lighthouse, on this side. They call it the Lady Tower. And by the time I arrived, she was up there, leaning between the battlements, yelling at me that she was going to jump. I knew it was only a game, but I froze. I mean, supposing she slipped . . .' He took a shuddering breath. 'And then I heard another voice, from inside, shouting to her not to be so — so stupid. A friend,' he added. 'She used to be a neighbour —'

'Alison,' I interrupted flatly. 'Yes, I know.'

'Al told me all about it on the way to the airport next morning,' said Joe Duff. 'She'd walked up to the castle that

114

afternoon, to see what I was buying, and there was Cathy letting herself in, obviously in a hell of a temper.'

'Letting herself in? Cathy had a *key*?'

'There's a kind of theatre tacked on the back of the castle,' he said impatiently. 'The locals have the run of it. They hide a stage-door key under a brick. Lord knows why they don't just leave the place unlocked. Every bugger for miles around knows where to find the key. Anyway, Cathy ignored Al, and charged into the castle shrieking like a banshee that she was going to throw herself off the Lady Tower. You see' — Joe looked at me almost pleadingly — 'Alison told me all this as a joke. She didn't take it seriously. Not for a minute.'

'For Christ's sake, the girl was running up a tower threatening suicide.'

Joe shrugged. 'Tantrum. Lovers' tiff. That's what Al said it was. She swore Cathy only started laying on the melodrama when she saw Oliver arrive. He panted up to the roof too and Cathy burst into tears. Al said it was farcical. She asked Cathy to reconsider jumping, if you please, because a suicide wouldn't be good for trade if I was turning the place into a hotel. You see what I mean? It was all a joke. And Cathy walked down the tower with the other two.'

'Are you sure?' I said dazedly.

'Alison was very good,' said Oliver. 'By the time we got her down to the bottom of the tower, Cathy was actually laughing. But she didn't want me to come home with her. She insisted she'd be perfectly all right and told me to go to my choir rehearsal and leave her in peace. But I couldn't abandon her, not in that state. I watched her drive down the hill and then I cycled into the village to get her mother . . .'

'I know Cathy went home to the Gatehouse,' declared Joe Duff. 'I know she was OK. She telephoned me, didn't she? I told you.'

'But — how did she sound to you?'

'Fine,' he said irritably. 'Absolutely fine. She wanted to know all about the castle, what I was planning, and –' Suddenly he broke off, and stared not so much at me as straight through me into some world of his own. 'She couldn't,' he whispered dazedly. 'Could she?'

'Her bloody mother was out,' said Oliver. 'So I cycled home again on my own. Cathy actually seemed cross I'd come back, but she was behaving normally. Cathy was like that. Up and down like mercury. She really did seem fine.'

'That's what Joe Duff said. She rang him up. Did you know?'

'I gathered she'd talked to him,' he said stiffly. 'I remember she said there was some access agreement he wanted.'

Behind the kitchen door stood a pair of green wellington boots. It was perfectly obvious – now I thought about it – that these didn't belong to Oliver. They were child-sized. Cathy Langham's traces were everywhere. I had just failed to see.

'Even so, I wanted to stay with her,' said Oliver. 'Besides, by then it was too late to cycle into Oxford for the rehearsal. But Cathy insisted I mustn't miss it, mustn't worry. And – and to go back to the Lodgings afterwards as usual. In fact, she said she'd run me into town because it was her fault I was so late. She drove like a mad thing and managed to get me there by half eight.'

'Half past eight?' I said. 'But she . . .' If there were discreet euphemisms for suicide I couldn't think of one then. 'She didn't – well, didn't the police tell you nothing happened until after eleven? Where did she go after she dropped you?'

'Christ knows,' Oliver burst out. 'I've been asking myself that ever since.'

'I don't suppose,' said Joe Duff – it was as though he could barely bring himself to voice the thought – 'she could have gone back to the castle later?'

116

I'd never seen a man with a rich Mediterranean tan manage to look so ashen.

'You mean to try again?' I said. 'Seriously this time? When there was no one there to stop her?'

Oliver only nodded convulsively when, an hour later, I asked him the same question.

The madrigalists had known, I suddenly thought. They who had so kindly and firmly insisted on taking over the dawn chorus, which was to be sung from the tower in St Benedict's College. And I'd blithely assumed it was me they were trying to spare.

'She went back to the castle,' I said. 'Late that night and . . .'

'She fell,' roared Oliver, then he plunged his face into his hands. His shoulders began to heave with the agonized coughing sobs of a man who doesn't know how to cry.

Joe Duff looked terrible. As though someone had clouted him mid-forehead with a mallet.

Lost in my concerns, I had to remind myself how shocked he must be. How awful it must be to learn that a friend you were chatting to on the phone only the other day had taken her own life.

'I can't believe Cathy was the type,' he kept repeating. 'However angry or upset she was. Surely she wouldn't *kill* herself?'

I had to wait for the sobs to subside before I could ask. This time yesterday, Oliver and I had been entwined together in bed. Now, I was reluctant even to put a comforting hand on his shoulder. My very presence in the house was indecent.

'The police are quite sure, are they,' I began carefully, 'that it *was* suicide?'

Oliver nodded without looking up.

'How can they tell?'

'They'd learned all about that stupid scene in the afternoon, for a start,' said Oliver. 'Alison Laverick had told her mother, and it was all over the village. But what I couldn't believe, was that Cathy actually left a letter.'

'A suicide note?'

He flinched. 'That's what they insist on calling it. A letter, anyway. To me. I mean, I didn't find it. The police did. Someone found her — the body . . .'

His voice was cracking apart again.

'I'll make some tea,' I said helplessly. What else?

I chose for myself the ugliest, plainest beaker from the back of the cupboard. A beaker Cathy Langham would never have chosen to drink from herself.

Oliver quelled the sobs soon enough, the Britishly stiff lip much in evidence, and, red-eyed, accepted the mug. His hand shook.

'They found her the next morning. An old chap was up there looking for his dog. He knew Cathy; told the police who she was. They said the letter was in her pocket. Saying . . .' He clenched his teeth. 'Oh, that her life was getting nowhere. That *we* were getting nowhere. That our marriage had obviously been a mistake' — his voice trembled, but he continued — 'for both of us. That I knew how desperately she wanted to sing with Wessex, and that she was sorry. She did actually say that. She was sorry.'

The mug rattled against his teeth. 'They've still got the letter, but they showed it to me. Even offered me a photocopy.' He made a noise of contempt. 'Becca, I couldn't believe it. But the words were there, in her handwriting. On — her paper.'

'Oh, Oliver,' I murmured.

'The funeral was ghastly,' he said abruptly — and all I could feel was relief that at least they had held the damn thing. 'Horrible. The vicar didn't know her and he kept spouting meaningless platitudes about art and free spirits . . . and the bloody curtain was closing on the coffin. Christ Almighty . . .'

118

I took his hand and squeezed it. What an inadequate gesture. 'I'm so sorry,' I whispered. 'For — everything.'

Oliver's head jerked up. 'Nothing for you to be sorry for. If it weren't for you I — well, I can't imagine where I'd be now.'

This only piled the guilt on thicker. Surely any halfway intelligent being would have sensed the freshness of tragedy in the air? 'For heaven's sake, where is she?' I burst out.

Oliver, not surprisingly, looked baffled.

'In this house,' I said. 'I mean, there are bits and pieces of Cathy's, but where are all her things? Her clothes?'

'Oh, that's her mother,' said Oliver. 'Constance was worrying about me, the state I was in. I wouldn't let her touch anything. Just told her to leave me alone. So the day before the funeral she asked Cathy's mother to see if she could sort me out a bit, I suppose. Anyway, she turned up and I — I just couldn't bear to speak to her, let alone argue. I left her to it. Stupid misunderstanding, that's all. Pamela packed up all Cathy's stuff.'

I shut my eyes. No, please, I was thinking. Not this. '*Pamela* packed it up?'

Oliver drained his tea. 'People think it's upsetting seeing clothes, things like that. Rot. But I got back and found she'd stuffed everything in black plastic bags. I was beyond objecting. She meant to help. She said she'd sort it all out, give it to charity. I just wanted her out of the house. I told her to take Cathy's car as well — no use to me — and then she could drive it all down —'

'Pamela Metcalfe?' Surely, surely, I'd behaved badly enough without *that*? But I knew the truth already. I now knew Cathy had once driven a flashy little white car. Probably used to own a navy mock-croc case too.

'Pamela Metcalfe, yes,' said Oliver, adding with an incongruous flicker of indignation, as though it had never occurred to him before: 'She didn't even tidy the place up.'

I wanted to crawl under the table and hide. Race back to London and pretend none of this had happened. I hadn't experienced such paralysing shame since adolescence. No wonder the poor woman had stared at me. A fortnight after Cathy's death, I had opened her daughter's front door, quite evidently at home, with, just for good measure, her daughter's distinctive apron tied round me. And mistaken her for the cleaner. She would have been well within her rights, I thought, to shoot me.

'You must go and see her,' I said to Oliver, after recounting every shameful word of our exchange. 'Tell her ... oh God, tell her you had a distant cousin staying. Anything. Anything that she'll believe. A married cousin. Who's now gone back to her husband. In London.'

I stood up.

'You're not going?' said Oliver.

'Are you going?' I had said to Joe Duff. Not in any anxiety to keep him there – I badly wanted solitude to sort out my thoughts and pack my bag – but because, frankly, he hardly looked in a condition to drive.

'I think,' he said, 'I'd better go and meet Al's plane. Tell her what's happened.'

'I can't possibly stay. Surely you can see that?' I said to Oliver. I'd ripped a page out of my diary and was scribbling wildly. 'My address, number. Ring me. Come and see me – if you want.'

If you *must* was what I was thinking, and that's probably what it sounded like, too, because Oliver shook his head, with a forlorn smile.

'Thanks all the same,' he said as I scrambled into my car. 'Thanks for everything.'

I'd never felt such a bum in all my life.

CHAPTER ELEVEN

It was a stuffy, stifling Sunday evening and the flat looked like a rag-and-bone yard. I'd never have believed I could have accumulated so much junk in three short years of living there. I'd been ferrying furniture, one piece at a time in my sardine can of a car, across London on and off for a fortnight, and still there were parapets of books and pans yet to be scaled. And by Tuesday noon I had to be out. No way could I afford the luxury of a removal firm. As things stood, I couldn't even afford another flat.

So I was going – where else? – home to mother. At thirty.

Strictly temporary, I had said. I won't be here long.

I was trying to reassure myself more than my mother. Ma was typically unperturbed, in fact delighted to be welcoming me back into the bosom of the family home. As she said, another body about the place wouldn't make much difference.

Ma doesn't run a home, more a refuge centre for half the student population of London. Like nature, she abhors a vacuum. As soon as my two older brothers and I flew the nest, she promptly filled the gaps with substitute chicks. Why cook a casserole for two, she reasons, when fourteen is just as easy? My dad has a shed at the bottom of the garden and a good nature.

Don't get me wrong, I love my mother. As mothers go, she's League Division One. But over the past fortnight, ever since I'd fled shamefacedly back from my escapade in Oxford-shire and begun the weary process of traipsing my chattels across town, I'd realized it wasn't going to be easy living with her again.

'Don't say I didn't warn you about married men,' she had observed this very afternoon, moulding and thumping a lump of clay with vigorous competence. Ma is a potter. She teaches ceramics part time. 'Shared lust' — *clump! slap!* — 'isn't half as dependable as a joint mortgage.' And a good deal more of the same.

I think she wishes the world were as satisfyingly malleable as a piece of clay. The mini-sermon referred to Richard. I was too embarrassed to tell anyone about poor Oliver Langham. One day, I thought, it might make the kind of grisly morsel you'd produce for a girlfriend at the end of the second bottle of wine. But not yet. I'd heard nothing from him. A week after leaving — a week ago today — my conscience had finally driven me telephone him. The phone had rung three times, and then clicked into a breathy silence.

'Oliver?' I'd said nervously. 'Just rang to see how you were getting on and —'

Then I broke off because a female voice — a golden voice — was cooing: 'Sorry we're not here to take your call. This is Cathy Langham. If you'd like —'

I'd slammed the phone down and felt obliged to pour myself a stiff drink. You don't have to believe in spirits to hear voices from the other world. Why couldn't Oliver, silly bastard, have changed the message? On reflection, I realized the mechanics of answering machines were probably beyond him.

I hadn't tried again. Even if I'd felt up to it, my phone had been cut off four days ago. Moving both out of the flat and into the red, I had put off paying the bill too long. Now, sitting amidst the wasteland of boxes, I was sorry. Not that I was moved to ring Oliver (although I felt I should — but it could wait until I'd moved, couldn't it? Got myself straight? Found a job? Say next year . . .?) but because I *hate* a dead telephone. Enough to make you feel you're the last creature

122

alive on God's earth. Even the batteries in my bloody tranny were running flat. I picked up another stack of books and began slotting them into a too-small box.

When the doorbell rang, I assumed it was the caretaker yet again, complaining about my car parked illegally across the entrance. I picked up the entryphone.

'Yes?' I barked.

'Ah, Becca?' said an oddly familiar corncrake of a voice. 'I'm so glad you're at home. This is Constance. Constance Berisford. May I come up?'

'I'm on the way to Washington,' she announced as, numbly, I opened my flat door to find her unknotting her headscarf. 'But we're staying tonight with friends in St John's Wood. I thought you wouldn't mind if I called *en route*, as it were . . .'

How Pimlico could conceivably lie on a route from Oxford to Washington via St John's Wood was beyond me, but naturally I ushered her into the sitting room.

'Charming,' she said, picking a skilful path across the rubble to gaze out of the window. 'So important to see a little green in this benighted city, don't you think?'

I muttered something ungracious about this being nearly the last day I could enjoy my green and pleasant view, and she cocked an eyebrow with an expression of quite unnerving attentiveness.

'You're moving?' she said, and I explained as I tried to clear a space for her to sit down.

'I shall be perfectly comfortable here,' she announced, planting herself on a pile of blankets and cushions with the aplomb of Queen Victoria visiting the Bedouins. 'Work keeping you busy, I dare say?'

I soon disillusioned her on that head too, and plunged without further ado into a tangled apology for behaving as I had at the ball. With her nephew. That I hadn't realized —

She silenced my incoherent flood with a wave of the hand. 'No need to apologize to me,' she said. 'We're old friends, aren't we?'

We were?

The new-old friend was smiling brightly up at me, rather like an expectant squirrel perched on a toadstool, pondering the best way to make a ripe nut fall into her lap.

'Would you like something to drink?' I faltered, wondering where I'd packed the mugs. 'Coffee?'

'Do you know,' she said, 'I feel positively awash with coffee. I should tell you I spent two hours this afternoon with Oliver. One ought to be grateful one's beloved nephew is immune to the demon drink, but there's something so depressing about abstainers, don't you find? Now, if you happened to have a little gin . . .'

While I located the box which held the rattling skeletons of my drinks cupboard, hoping the gin wasn't as empty as most of the other bottles, I asked, awkwardly, how Oliver was.

'That,' she declared magisterially, 'is what I've come to talk to you about. Just a tidge of tonic. Such a nasty taste, I always think. Yes, that's splendid.'

'I did try and ring him,' I began.

'And I tried to ring you,' she agreed, 'having inveigled the number out of Oliver, but there seems to be a fault on your line. Wretched things, telephones. Ah, thank you. Here's mud in our eyes.'

I couldn't help warming to Lady Berisford, even if she was sporting prominently on her lapel the enamelled brooch of one of the Hon. Hel's pet charities: The Cancer Foundation, meetings second Thursday of the month and a helpful variety of *ad hoc* events. Richard's wife was a very reliable do-gooder. I'd sometimes thought I ought to make a donation to the Foundation: I owed them a large proportion of my love life. But Richard seemed a lifetime ago now. Oliver's sad shadow had almost blotted out the memory.

'I'm worried about Oliver,' Lady Berisford announced, as though she'd read my thoughts. 'My dear, don't look so alarmed. I have *always* worried about Oliver. Ever since the day, at the age of nine, he turned up on my doorstep one summer morning, in his prep school blazer, asking politely if he could possibly stay with us. Until September. His mama had waltzed off to the Caribbean with her new lover. Not three months widowed, if you please.'

She paused to take a swig of gin, sublimely unaware that I might find this observation pertinent to my own recent behaviour.

'Do sit down,' she added kindly. 'I have shocking arthritis in my neck. Has Oliver told you about his mother?'

'That she was a singer,' I said, perching on a box of books. 'I got the impression she perhaps wasn't the most loving of —'

'Don't you think the explanations of all of us lie in our parents? I do. Of course,' she said, 'the modern trend is to *blame* everything on one's parents, which is not the same thing at all. However, I do feel allowances must be made for Oliver. You must make allowances for me too,' she added. 'Oliver is very dear to me. Very dear.' Then, as though this admission required apology, went on briskly: 'I never bred, myself. Married too late. Not surprisingly, I see Oliver as my adopted son. I have done since long before Vivienne died, and with good reason. As far as she was concerned, the pregnancy was simply a mistake.'

She paused to rummage in her large handbag, murmuring, 'She was forty-one, you know. Nothing nowadays, when girls feel obliged to secure their seat on the board before investing in nappies, but it was damn nearly a medical miracle then. And the fuss she made . . . My dear, would you mind?'

She drew from her handbag a packet of slim cigars. I stole the saucer from under a wilting ivy and handed it to her.

'The agony, the suffering . . . all of which she blamed on my brother Peter. I'm not surprised he drank. It's my view he harassed the poor fellow into an early grave . . .' She screwed up her face and applied a match to the tip of the cigar. 'I hope it's peaceful up there. He earned it, living with that noise for twenty years. She had one of those shrill wobbly voices which make your teeth ache. Every time I hear that damned laughing song, I think of Vivienne.'

'But the baby finished her career, didn't it?' I said. 'That's what I remember Oliver telling me. Having him.'

'Rot. She had hot and cold running nannies from the day Oliver was born. Her career had been declining for years. But naturally it had to be the fault of the child. Really, they were quite alike in many ways.'

'Oliver and his mother? Yes, I've seen —'

'His mother and Cathy,' she said impatiently. 'Singers, the pair of 'em, but more than that, there was something in Cathy's manner, her *attitudes* ... However, I dare say the Freudians would tell me that sons will always try to marry their mothers. It makes one almost glad one never had children. I truly believe the only real kindness Vivienne ever did her son was to die before she'd got through all Peter's money. But that, I assure you, was unintentional. You could never imagine Vivienne killing herself. Never.'

'People say the same of Cathy . . .'

Oliver and Joe Duff did anyway.

'Well, yes . . .' Lady Berisford blew a reflective column of smoke up towards the ceiling. 'I suppose I was surprised when I heard what Cathy had done. *Shocked*, I should say.' She did not sound unduly perturbed, however.

'Lady Berisford . . .'

'Constance, please.'

'You . . . Didn't you much like Cathy?'

'I have no wish to malign the dead gratuitously. Besides, I'm biased, as Michael would tell you. He says no girl would have been good enough for my pet lamb, and I dare say he's right. I'm sure she had her charms,' she added unconvincingly, 'but, no, Catherine simply didn't — *fit*. If you know what I mean.'

I could guess. Looking at Constance Berisford upright on the pile of rugs, square-shouldered, bright-eyed and as solidly daunting as the figurehead of a ship — a very British ship — I felt a twinge of sympathy for anyone who did not *fit*.

'I admit,' she went on, 'I've asked myself a number of times over the past two years – since they married, you know – whether I did right in casting Oliver out into the world.'

'Casting him out?' I echoed and she gave a braying laugh.

'Into the Gatehouse, I mean. He was quite content living with us and, naturally, I was delighted to house him. But he was getting into his thirties and I feared . . .' She broke off and smiled oddly conspiratorially. 'You, of course, will think this ridiculous, but I was afraid Oliver was turning into what we used to call a confirmed bachelor. Vanishing breed, but you can still find 'em in Oxford. Fifty-year-old schoolboys, wolfing down the college Spotted Dick, locked into their books and their enclosed masculine little worlds. I felt it was up to me to give Oliver a shove. I freely confess I was hoping he might find a nice young woman. So off he went to Harecombe – and met Catherine Metcalfe. Ah me. Naturally, I've always kept his room in the Lodgings to make life easier for him with rehearsals and so forth. Well, easier in every way. As you know.' Another, faintly conspiratorial smile over the rim of the glass.

'So Oliver told me . . .'

'Although I use it for guests when we've a houseful. As, I'm sorry to say, we had on the night of the ball. But you understood my dilemma that night, I know.'

Madmen look at one with just such an expectation of understanding when they confide the problems of being King. Not that I could doubt Constance Berisford's sanity, but there was, without question, a mystifying gap between her perception of the world and mine. She swept on, however.

'I just thank God the poor boy was staying with us when that wretched girl took it into her head to – well, to tread in Violet's footsteps. As it were.'

Now I really was losing track and said so.

'Hoary old legend,' said Constance impatiently. 'In fact, hardly a legend because the germ's true enough, but it's passed into local folklore as these things will. The wife of my disreputable forebear, Sir Montague Rivenhoe, builder of Harecombe

Castle, chucked herself off the self-same tower after a marital tiff. Oh, if you insist, just a couple more fingers. Thank you.'

She waited, graciously, until I'd refilled my own glass before resuming. 'Without question, that was in Cathy's mind. She was exactly the type of girl to be influenced by such romantic twaddle. A perfectly disgusting way to go killing oneself.'

I found myself wondering if there were U and non-U methods of suicide. Would a shotgun in the shrubbery have been more acceptable?

'So horribly distressing for those left behind,' Constance went on. 'I could hardly bear to put it into words — to tell Oliver.'

'You were the one who had to break the news?'

'Who else? He was with us. Fortunately, the local police sergeant knows me because I sit on the bench, and he had the sense to telephone me when they were trying to locate Oliver. After they found, well, the body, they went down to the Gatehouse. Empty, of course. Then to the village but Catherine's mother was away. And finally me. I'm grateful, although it was —' she stared into her glass — 'the most appalling task I've ever had to undertake in my life.'

The silence yawned long. I could hear my alarm clock ticking somewhere amid a jungle of pot plants.

'I remember it was a heavenly morning,' she said quietly. 'One of those days when the world looks washed clean. We'd driven home late from a party in London the previous night through an absolute torrent. After Sergeant Jones rang, I went into the garden to collect my thoughts. It was nearly nine, and for one cowardly moment I confess I hoped Oliver might have gone out already without breakfast — he often forgets to eat. But no, the bike was in the passage, and I remember clutching it — absurd really — and praying. I don't often pray. I always assume God has a fairish idea of what's afoot. But just then I prayed.'

'I would have,' I said fervently. 'How on earth did you . . . find the words?'

'Oliver was still asleep. He was working terribly hard, poor boy, with the end-of-term concerts and exams and so forth. I shook him. I couldn't bring myself to tell him outright. I said there'd been an accident. Cathy was ... hurt. He was half asleep, but he bounced up then, wide-eyed. God knows, I never cared for the girl, but at that moment, I would have given my own life to bring her back ...

'I'm sorry,' she said abruptly. 'You don't want these maudlin outpourings. There is a point to them, as a matter of fact. Oliver was stunned. I don't choose the word lightly. He looked like my dog Polly once did when she'd run head first into a plate-glass door. He couldn't focus — his eyes, or his brain. He was gripping my hand and repeating: "Killed herself?" as though the words didn't mean anything to him. No tears — but, my dear, the look in his eyes. Even the policeman when he arrived to take the statement was nearly blubbing.

'The thing is, I was terrified Oliver would do something — foolish. You know? I would never have expected Cathy to take her own life, but Oliver? He was always such a sensitive little boy.'

I shifted uncomfortably on my box of books. 'He did try. Didn't you know? He told me he took some pills.'

She recoiled, as though I'd hit her.

'I'm sorry —' I began.

Already she was resuming command of herself, however, and, after a minute, said with painfully careful composure, 'No. No, I didn't know that. When?'

'I'm not sure. Only enough to make him groggy anyway. And he said he hadn't the nerve to try again.'

'Well, thank God for small mercies.' She swirled the gin round in her glass before swallowing a mouthful. 'Naturally, I didn't want to let him out of my sight. But he insisted on returning to the Gatehouse, shutting himself away. He kept switching that bloody machine on to his telephone ... Oh, I drove out there daily, on one pretext or another, but he didn't want to let me in. He'd just be sitting at his desk like —

like a dead man. Heart-breaking. Staring into space while the mess piled up.'

'I can imagine,' I whispered.

'There was the funeral, and then that damned ball to cope with, and a house full of guests — and to my utter disbelief I saw his bike tethered to my gate again.' Suddenly her face brightened. 'I go in search, and what do I find? Oliver with an attractive blonde clinging to his arm.' To my astonishment, she was beaming at me. 'Frankly I couldn't believe my luck. Oliver's mystery woman made flesh at last.'

'Mystery woman?' I croaked, but she was sweeping on.

'Bugger what the old fogies might be whispering in my drawing room. For the first time Oliver was showing signs of returning to the land of the living. I could have embraced you myself and —'

'Constance,' I interrupted firmly. 'Look, I'm sorry, but this is completely mad. *Mystery woman?*'

'Ridiculous turn of phrase,' she agreed promptly. 'It's just, well, not knowing your name, that's how I've tended to think of you over the past few months and —'

'Constance,' I repeated, stemming the tide of exuberance with difficulty. 'There's some horrible misunderstanding here. The last time I saw Oliver — before the ball, I mean — was my first term at Oxford.'

Constance, you could tell, was not the sort readily to welcome challenges to her perceived view of events. 'But, my dear, we've talked on the phone. Don't you remember? You were coming to meet Oliver — the trains . . .' Her voice tailed away.

'No,' I said. I could feel the blush scalding my neck. 'You and I haven't talked. And I haven't seen Oliver. I just bumped into him that night, outside the college gates, for the first time in twelve years.'

'Dear — *Lord*. A — a chance encounter?'

I nodded, trying to look as coolly nonchalant as a boiled lobster can.

'And I,' she said wonderingly, 'packed you off home together . . .' Suddenly, unbelievably, she gave a hacking guffaw
of laughter. 'I even ordered the taxi,' she hooted. 'My dear,
how simply priceless . . .'

She was laughing so much she had to put her glass down
and grope for a handkerchief. After a few stunned seconds, I
could only join in.

'What must you have thought of me?' she said at length,
wiping her eyes. 'No wonder my poor husband thanks God
he didn't pursue an early inclination for the diplomatic service.
Still' – she picked up her glass and raised it in my direction –
'all's well that ends well. As they say.'

I wasn't sure I'd have put it quite like that. But instead of
opening that can of worms I asked about her so-called mystery
woman.

'Well, yes, that's a puzzle,' she conceded. 'Over the past
few months, a woman has telephoned the Lodgings two or
three times. Asking for Oliver. She and I even – as you might
have gathered – had a brief but most enlightening discussion
about the London train timetable and I took it into my head,
well, that Oliver had . . .'

It was her turn to blush now. The merest scarlet smudge,
mind you, atop the cheekbones.

'I'm talking, of course, about before Catherine died. To be
frank, I rather thought my nephew had found himself a –
what's the current expression? – a *bit on the side.*'

CHAPTER TWELVE

'Oliver?' I gasped. 'I − honestly, I'd swear . . .'

'No, that's what Michael always said,' she agreed with an unmistakable touch of regret. 'But there was something in the voice, the way she said his name − one has a certain womanly intuition about these things, don't you find? But, as my lawyer husband frequently reminds me, intuition is not evidence.'

'Not Oliver,' I said positively. 'I shouldn't think he ever so much as looked at another woman. While, um, Cathy was alive, I mean.'

'Ah,' she said, looking at me keenly. 'I dare say you're right. That puts me in a tricky spot, doesn't it?'

'Does it?' I said warily.

She picked up her cigar and studied it. 'You see, I'm anxious about Oliver. There's something wrong. Yes, yes,' she said, cutting off my expostulations, 'I know the poor boy is devastated by Cathy's death. But since the ball, I've noticed it particularly: there's something beyond that . . .'

Like a scarlet-frocked trollop clog-dancing into the wreckage of his emotional life and straight out again? I gulped half my gin.

'Suddenly I don't understand him at all,' she went on earnestly. 'Quite out of the blue, he's declared he's going to Italy.'

'Italy?' I echoed, wincing. My fault again. 'Mightn't that be a good idea?' I faltered. 'Getting away?'

She snorted. 'He's no idea where he's going, staying, let alone what he's planning to do. But nothing I say will dissuade him. And now,' she added, in a dizzying change of tack, 'Michael and I have to fly to Washington. Fund-raising, of course. Our American Friends. Being principal of an Oxford college these days has little to do with learning and everything to do with lucre. I shall be back for the inquest, naturally, even if the jet lag kills me.'

'Inquest?' Somehow, 'inquest', like 'atomic bomb' or 'tarantula', while being a familiar enough noun, sounds quite alien when it crosses one's own path. 'Hasn't the inquest happened already? Before the funeral, surely?'

'Oh, they open an inquest immediately,' she said. 'For so-called identification purposes. As if we didn't know who she was. But then they adjourn the damned thing – all red tape you know – to put their evidence together. We have to troop back for the second and final instalment this Thursday.'

'Poor Oliver,' I said. 'Having to go through it all again.'

'Exactly. He's dreading it. And now, of all times, I'm forced to desert him. I simply have to support Michael on this trip. So I've been racking my brains for someone who can keep an eye on Oliver. I thought about Pamela Metcalfe, but the poor woman's naturally distraught herself, and some time ago when I asked if she'd look in on him, well, wires got crossed and it was rather disastrous.'

'She tidied Cathy out of existence,' I said uneasily. I had a inkling of what was coming.

'And you,' she said, smiling serenely, 'particularly given our little misunderstanding, seemed the obvious candidate. In fact I couldn't understand Oliver's reluctance to phone you himself when I suggested it. Now,' she added reflectively, 'I see I may have been a little tactless. As it was, I'm afraid I was reduced to telling him you'd promised some help with one of my charitable projects when we met at the ball. And that I'd lost your address. Not *wholly* untrue. After all, surely this is the most charitable of projects?'

'What is?' I growled. As if I didn't know.

'Well, I wondered,' said Constance Berisford, 'if you might

be kind enough to look after my poor darling. Just for a couple of days, say.'

'Why me?' I gasped. 'Surely there must be someone else, someone closer to him?'

'You're the only living creature who's managed to penetrate, well, this awful *shell* of despair round him.'

'More like the only idiot crass enough to charge in where anyone else would be too sensitive to tread.'

'Nonsense.'

'Constance, I'm a working woman.'

'I rather gathered,' she purred, taking ruthless advantage of earlier information gleaned, 'work was a little thin on the ground?'

'I still have to earn a living.'

'Of course.' She started rummaging in the handbag again. 'I though, perhaps, you would accept a small contribution for –'

'God, no,' I exclaimed, horrified as a cheque book and pen appeared. 'I wouldn't dream of it.'

'You'd allow me to cover your petrol, surely,' she said. Christ, she was worse than a time-share salesman.

'What would people think?' I said, trying a fresh tack. 'Me staying with Oliver when Cathy's barely a month dead?'

'I don't believe idle gossip should deter one,' Lady Berisford pronounced with magisterial disdain, 'from doing what is clearly right, do you?'

'Oh come off it. Look what you said yourself about Oliver's widowed mother going off with a lover.'

'*Touché*,' she said cheerfully. 'So tell people you're his cousin. That's what you instructed Oliver to say to Mrs Metcalfe, didn't you? Very sensible. Most unfortunate she should have called round unexpectedly.'

'Unfortunate? I can't bear to think about it.'

'Quite, quite. Well, we'll say you're one of my nieces. I have dozens, you know. Michael's sisters were all frightfully prolific. What could be more natural than my asking you to look in on the boy?'

I marched to the window and stared down at the square, mutinously. But Constance Berisford's lot had not ruled the Empire for generations without learning how to counter rebellion in the ranks.

'A last little drink, I think,' she said, and I heard a chink as she filled the glasses. 'What does gossip matter anyway? It's not as if you knew anyone in the neighbourhood.'

'Yes I do,' I said indignantly. 'I know Joe Duff.' And then broke off, thinking, yes, there was always Joe smoothy Duff. Oliver's new neighbour . . . The hesitation was a mistake.

'People are so mealy-mouthed these days,' Constance declared, sidling up beside me and slipping a glass into my hand. The tonic seemed to have eluded her. I took one sip and nearly choked.

'It's common knowledge in Harecombe that my ancestor — the castle-builder, you know — had a floozy in his bed while his wife was still laid out in her coffin.'

I turned round, startled out of my sulk. 'After the poor woman jumped off the tower?'

'Lord no,' said Constance. 'Or rather, yes, that's the wife in question. Violet. An actress, wouldn't you know? The stage has always held a disastrously fatal fascination for the men of my family . . . Good Lord.' She gave a hoot of scandalized laughter. 'Forgive me, Becca, I was forgetting. You don't somehow *strike* one as an actress.'

'No,' I said, resignedly. Actresses, as is well known, are witty and glamorous, with long fingernails and longer anecdotes.

'Old Sir Montague had plucked Violet out of some chorus line. Just like a novel, really. He was fifty-odd and besotted. He actually built a theatre for her, as if his castle wasn't monstrous enough already. But, of course, contrary to the novels, no rake was ever reformed by love. He soon got up to his old tricks and Violet threw herself off the tower. But she didn't die. All she managed was a fractured leg and a few bruises. It was always speculated that the crinoline acted as a kind of parachute.'

135

She took a last appreciative puff from her cigar and threw the butt, with the accuracy of a darts player, through the open window.

'The cream of the jest, though, is that old Monty, who was superstitious as hell, saw his wife's deliverance as a sign from the Almighty and gave up his philandering ways forthwith. Which no doubt explains why poor Violet produced a sprog a year from then until her untimely — but perfectly natural — death. Which brings me back to what I was saying. Monty regarded her demise as a release from his promise and pounced on the nearest tart. He tumbled into his own grave soon afterwards. And serves him right, too.'

She laughed heartily, and I joined her. Fatal. Never laugh with someone if you're about to turn them down.

'So you'll pop down and see Oliver?' she said.

'Well . . .'

She smiled up at me; brisk, square-shouldered as an officer inspecting the troops. 'From the first, I thought you were the kind of girl one could count on,' she said.

That's my trouble. Everyone always does recognize in me the reliable, good-hearted, responsible type. A deliverer of fish fingers to the nation. Why can't I be mad, bad and dangerous? Towering over Lady Berisford, I nevertheless felt like a raw cadet, about to have a medal pinned on me.

'When is the inquest?'

'Holiday in the country?' said Moyra, Agent to the Stars, when I telephoned from Oliver's on Wednesday morning with wan optimism and my Oxfordshire number. 'Lucky old you, darling. I simple adore that part of the world.'

'It's not a holiday,' I growled. 'I'm . . .' Then I glanced over my shoulder into the kitchen where Oliver was washing up the breakfast pots. Well, stirring the water with a mop, 'I'm staying with a friend,' I muttered, 'just until tomorrow.'

Baby-sitting was the expression which had sprung to mind. Constance had airily dismissed my last-ditch attempt to persuade her a grown man would be unlikely to welcome an aunt-despatched guardian angel foisting herself upon him. 'Nonsense,' she had said. 'Tell him you —' she glanced around — 'you're exhausted after the move, and want a breath of country air. He'll never suspect I had anything to do with it.'

'Constance has been on to you,' Oliver had declared, as soon as I rang, hoping against hope the machine might answer again. It hadn't.

'Not really,' I said feebly. 'Oliver, are you OK?'

'She's worrying about nothing.'

'Are you eating?'

God, I sounded just like my mother.

'Look, I don't want you to feel obliged.'

But I did feel obliged, in more ways than one. And when a thin, unshaven, unironed, heavy-eyed Oliver opened the door of the Gatehouse on Tuesday evening I was glad I *had* yielded to Constance Barisford's blandishments. I had also yielded, I'm ashamed to admit, to a cheque forcefully stuffed into my hand which would enable my little car to drive to Australia and back. Oh, I felt obliged all right.

Anyway, once here, I'd bustled around. Warmed up the stew I'd borrowed from Ma's capacious freezer with some garbled tale of an ailing friend, and force-fed the boy half a bottle of Bulgarian red. That put a bit of colour in his cheeks at least.

I hadn't hesitated, once that was inside him, to tackle head on the question of the so-called mystery woman. Possibly a subtler approach would have been wiser.

'What?' Oliver had roared.

'Constance mentioned something . . .' I faltered, feeling as though I'd questioned the virginity of Mary in the presence of the Pope.

'I don't know what the hell she's talking about,' snapped Oliver. 'Hundreds of people ring me at the Lodgings. Singers, colleagues, students. She must be mad.'

I assured him soothingly that I dared say I'd got the wrong end of the stick, that I hadn't meant to imply . . . then gave up and offered him some of Ma's apple crumble instead. He was touchingly appreciative of that, and confided, awkwardly, that he was glad I'd come.

Which brings us to the other major hiccup of the evening. Bedtime. I mean, what do you do? I was feeling sorry for Oliver; fond of him even, in the most maternal, feeding-up-the-poor-lad way. But that's not the same thing, is it? And whoever heard of a romantic idyll supervised — and paid for — by an aunt? I just couldn't do it.

I dithered around downstairs for as long as I could. When, finally, I walked into the bedroom, Oliver was already in bed and he pulled back the covers with a shy smile.

I'd thought about explaining how knackered I was after a long day shifting the final boxes, but rejected it as being cheaper than pleading a headache. Then I'd thought of being honest. Frank, direct, woman-of-the-worldish. Discussing the ebb and flow of sexual desire. The natural inhibitions one might have about rolling into a dead woman's bed.

I thought about it — and muttered: 'Afraid it's the wrong time of the month. You know . . .'

And poor Oliver had blushed just as vividly as I'd known he would and accepted without protest the consolatory cup of cocoa I'd made for him.

Well, I reasoned, curling up chastely beside him, the excuse wasn't *wholly* untrue, as Constance Berisford would say. And tomorrow, I'd tidy this dump up and bake him a nice chocolate cake. It was the least I could do to earn my petrol money.

These admirable plans — once I'd rung Moyra the next morning and rescued Oliver from the dregs of the washing-up bowl — were set back by a slight difference of opinion between the grieving widower and myself. Well, more than slight.

I was briskly organizing Oliver with a shopping list. Since he was cycling into the village to execute it, I took the opportunity to remind him, tactfully, that I was figuring as his cousin. As he'd told Cathy's mother.

'Oh, I haven't spoken to that woman,' he snapped. 'Not since she took all Cathy's things away.'

'Not spoken to her?' I exclaimed. 'Not at all? But that day she came here – a whole fortnight ago, Oliver – she told me she wanted to talk to you. Urgently. And shit, you mean you never explained to her about my being here at all?'

'I met her neighbour in the village,' he said impatiently. 'I told her I'd had a cousin here. Mrs Laverick's the biggest gossip in the county. You can bet Pamela knew all about it within five minutes.'

'But, Oliver,' I said, 'the woman was in a terrible state. For heaven's sake, this is Cathy's mother we're talking about.'

'I know that,' he shouted. 'She keeps coming round here, wailing about her daughter –'

'I thought you said you hadn't seen her?'

He set his jaw obstinately. 'I pretended I was out.'

'*Oliver*! I don't believe I'm hearing this.'

'It was you who told me I should try and put it behind me. Pamela just wants to dig over the whole thing again and –'

'Bloody hell, Oliver. When I was spouting all that claptrap, you know I'd no idea how recent –'

'Anyway, Pamela never liked me,' he said. 'Said I was too old. She didn't think Cathy should have married me.'

'Half the men in the world say their mothers-in-law hate them,' I retorted. 'Where do all the bad jokes start? Oliver, you must go and see that poor woman.'

Slowly the obstinacy faded into his usual look of haunted misery. 'Oh shit,' he said. 'I suppose you're right. Better get it over with then. I'll go round after I've done the shopping.'

I didn't actually pat him on the head – 'I may be some time,' he warned darkly – but I sped the reluctant Captain Oates on his way with promises of a nice tidy house when he got back.

I won't say I enjoy housework, but there's something very satisfying to my soul in putting things in order. Imposing symmetry and pattern on chaos. Proto-fascist nature, a kind friend once diagnosed. Nevertheless, after a couple of hours with the vacuum and dusters, my back was aching and the miasma of lavender scented polish was making me feel distinctly sick. I decided the bedroom would have to wait until Oliver returned to lend a hand. Then I heard a car stop nearby. I thought nothing of it until a deep voice muttered something about this bloody gate giving him a hernia one day.

Joe Duff.

I straightened and suddenly, like Mole, felt the time had come to cast down the brushes and venture into the outside world. I stripped the rubber band from my hair and tripped into the back garden. To my disappointment the car — a long purr of red — was past the garden gate and disappearing up the hill. But it could only be going to one place, couldn't it?

With a scribbed note to Oliver and a flick of mascara I set off for the castle.

CHAPTER THIRTEEN

Harecombe Castle did not merely bask pinkly in reflected sun. I realized, as I strode up the drive towards the wooded ridge on which it stood, that the place actually was pink. This so-called castle was built of brick. The architect, though, had not allowed such a plebeian medium to dilute his grandly medieval notions. Anything Edward I could do, he could do better. Between trees, as I climbed, I glimpsed battlements and arrow-slits galore.

At length, the drive, with a cunning twist, delivered me behind what had clearly once been the castle stables, a building of Christmas-card prettiness, with carriage arch below and the dinkiest clock tower overhead, complete with — or so I thought at first sight — a weather vane. On closer inspection this proved, less romantically, to be a television aerial, suggesting the stables had been converted for human habitation. I squinted through a window and found I was looking into a shabby kitchen, I dodged back, in case there was an occupant, and strolled under the archway into a flagstoned courtyard.

To my relief, the Batmobile was there, parked beside a weed-infested dish which had once been a pool. A green, fat-stomached boy clutched over his shoulder a fish whose open mouth gaped dry. The car was equally devoid of life. I wondered where to look for the owner.

The courtyard was roughly square, with one side open to a dry hayfield of a lawn. The stable block lay at the rear, the castle at the front and occupying the third side was a windowless monolith, tacked on to the back of the castle, which could only be Sir Monty's theatre. The unmistakable box of a fly tower squatted incongruously amidst the crenellated grandeur.

The castle itself was smaller than I'd expected, however, and a real mongrel. Château-style French windows were shuttered beside quaintly Dickensian bays. Art nouveauish portholes were dotted between the arrow slits. Pink brick, like raspberry ice-cream, was sliced with vanilla stone sills and lintels. Gargoyles growled, the guttering blossomed in Tudor roses and every chimney pot flaunted a different frilling.

The cocktail had a certain charm, but I was reminded of those Gothic asylums our Victorian ancestors planted, at a safe distance from their comfortable lives, on the outskirts of towns. A zigzagging of fire-escapes enchanced the impression. More workhouse than Camelot. I thought with an unexpected shiver, but I was already thinking of more recent history. There was no mistaking the tower.

As soon as I'd entered the courtyard I had known. The others were mere puny ornaments. This jutted out like a lighthouse, dominating castle and courtyard alike. It wouldn't take a feminist to spot here a giant phallic symbol. I wondered briefly if christening it the Lady Tower was a Maypole-type jest, or could the Lady in question be Sir Monty's sad suicidal wife?

Narrow windows were slotted up its mighty stem, which was not rendered any more beautiful by a twisting black fire-escape. It was so bloody high, topped with — I squinted up into the sun — what looked curiously like a coronet. Elaborate battlements formed the peaks. A tiled roof rising within was the puff of velvet, and pale stone circled the outside like a strip of ermine. Did Cathy step between those battlements, I thought, out on to that narrow sill? Did she stand there long before . . .?

Just the thought made my stomach lurch. I glanced down at the flagstones, as though expecting them to be spattered with blood. Suddenly a strapped and studded door in the base of the tower crashed open.

142

'Christ, men are so fucking *thick*!' a female voice was shouting. 'Just forget it, can't you?'

'Easy enough for you to say that' — Joe Duff's chocolatey voice was unmistakable — 'but I don't like it.'

Hers then moderated to a more persuasive tone. 'Just tell me what good it would do. Do you want to dig up the whole sordid mess again? OK, OK, so you say it's not the same. Who the fuck cares? You got rid of it, didn't you? Well, *didn't you*?'

The reply was inaudible, but must have been in the affirmative, because the woman said, less stridently, 'Fine. Then no one need ever know anything about it.'

Life would be so much more interesting if one had no inhibitions about eavesdropping, I thought, reluctantly warbling: 'Um, hello?'

The woman didn't so much walk out of the doorway as explode through it, like a brawling cat chucked from on high. She had a shock of hair in a purple-brown which can only come from a henna pot, yards of leg shrinkwrapped in leopard-spotted leggings, and a scowl which would have stopped a fleet. A tight black *bustier* revealed a lot of suntanned skin but not much in the way of *buste*. No prizes for detecting a certain womanly sourness in this description so don't be misled. I had a suspicion who this might be, and if so, then, even without her fortnight-in-Spain's bronzing, Al was an enviably lean and handsome creature.

Joe followed close behind, bulging out of a white singlet like a navvy. I smiled sunnily and he gaped back as though hard put to place the face. Great. At least, just as I was on the point of prodding his memory, he managed, disjointedly: 'Becca? Hell, I — didn't expect to see you. Sorry . . .' He glanced uneasily at leopard-legs growling by his side.

'I'm interrupting something,' I said. A girl can take a hint. 'I was walking past and —'

'No, not at all —' Joe began.

'We were only having a row,' she snapped simultaneously.

'I was just saying that anyone buying this ugly great folly must be off their head.'

Oh yeah? Joe looked flummoxed too, but he rose to the bait. 'Well, this is a bloody fine time to tell me. When the deal's finally signed, sealed and delivered.'

'I told you when Bunny quit you were mad if you went ahead,' she declared. 'But oh no, the macho entrepreneur has to prove he can go it alone, minus half the necessary capital.'

Ignored, I traced the pattern of the flagstones with one idle toe waiting for a ceasefire.

'The bank's given me a good deal, Al. Bunny set it up.'

Al it was indeed. The girlfriend, or ex-girlfriend, according to Joe Duff.

'But Bunny's not here to see it through, is he?' Unexpectedly she turned on me. 'I've tried to explain to Joe. It's a question of personality type. The three Cs.'

Joe gazed up at the sky. 'Spot last month's masterly article.'

I half smiled, until I caught sight of Alison's face.

'Cerebral, creative, or craft-orientated,' she said. 'Some people's talents lie in their brains.' She whipped round to address Joe again. 'Bunny, for instance.'

'I'd call our Rupert pretty bloody crafty.'

'Whereas with artists, writers, musicians,' she said, ignoring him, 'their work at best flows straight from the soul.'

'Thank you, Madam Dostoevsky.'

Advantage Duff. I glanced up, suddenly wondering how long it would take to reach the ground if you stepped off that stone sill glinting halfway to heaven. Shit, *halfway to heaven* . . .

'And then there are Nature's craftmen,' she declared, 'who should recognize their *métier* is working with their hands.'

'In my book, cooking takes brain, heart and soul as well as hands,' Joe retorted. 'It's a bloody art form, which you'd realized if you weren't an anorexic rabbit.'

I stifled a laugh, prepared to concede the game to him, but she zipped straight back.

'You're missing the point. What you can't do, Joe Duff, is cook the fucking books.'

Oh well played, madam. By now the voices were echoing round the courtyard. A rook flapped out from the tower, squawking in alarm.

'Cooking the books? We've always run a totally straight –'

'You need someone with Bunny's talent for organization. Face facts, Joe. You couldn't run a vicarage tea party.'

Up to that point I felt this quarrel had been fought before. The insults were hurled like second-hand snowballs: frozen to a vicious solidity, maybe, but lacking the explosive *élan* of the freshly gathered sort. Now, however, Joe stiffened.

'I'm only amazed you were prepared to consort with such – such *peasant* stock. I can't believe my uneducated brain fitted the Laverick blueprint.'

This innocuous-looking shot must have packed spin because she snorted audibly and with that they were down at the net slogging it out for dear life.

'Your brain would be a damn sight better if it wasn't ruled by your balls,' she hissed, and I caught my breath.

'That,' growled Joe, 'didn't seem to be the trouble on holiday. Quite the opposite, in fact.'

And – mystifyingly – this clinched game, set and match. I thought Alison might actually hit Joe, but with a visible effort of will, she folded her arms and turned away. Two suntanned shoulder blades heaved above the black bodice in eloquent silence. Blimey, she really was upset. All at once, I felt uncomfortable, that I shouldn't be witnessing all this, and began to sidle away.

'No, hang on,' said Joe distractedly, and walked across to Al, putting a hairy arm round her shoulders. She twitched. 'Sorry, love,' he murmured. 'Below the belt.' Then, in spite of himself, he grinned. 'So to speak. Sorry, sorry. Look, come and meet Becca.'

She shook off his arm, and turned to face me as Joe performed perfunctory introductions. Unnecessary as far as I was concerned but, more surprisingly, when Joe muttered something about my having been at Oliver's, Alison Laverick exclaimed, 'Oh, are you Oliver's cousin then?'

'Cousin?' echoed Joe, in understandable puzzlement.

I managed a nod and was spared awkward explanations by her reminding Joe, impatiently, that her mother had said a cousin of Oliver's had been round to see him. The gossipy neighbour, I deduced. Al was brought up next door to Cathy . . .

'I'm glad there's someone keeping an eye on Oliver,' she said, shaking my hand, 'with the inquest tomorrow. How is he?'

'Fine,' I stammered. 'Well — as fine as can be expected.'

'Poor sod,' she said. 'Give him my love. And, look, I'm sorry about just now. I've a filthy temper, not improved by the vagaries of British Rail.' She looked at Joe. 'Have you much to do here?'

His mouth twisted wryly. 'Only the odd lifetime's work.'

'I'll see you later, then,' she said. 'I'd better walk down and tell Mother I've arrived safely. Although what she thinks can happen between Paddington and Oxford stations God only knows. You don't mind dropping my bags down when you've finished here, do you?'

As Joe nodded I inferred, interestedly, that Alison Laverick was visiting from London, and that Joe had met her train. But, if that was where she wanted her luggage, she was staying here in Harecombe with her mother — and not with Joe Duff. Well, well . . .

'Nice to meet you, Becca,' she said. 'If you want a laugh' — she smiled satirically — 'ask *Bluebeard* here to show you round his castle.'

And with that she was gone, Joe watching her in grim-faced silence. I cleared my throat, like a walk-on constable in a bad cop opera. Ahem, ahem . . .

'Sorry,' said Joe, collecting his thoughts with a palpable effort. 'Did you, um, want to see round the joint?'

If this was Bluebeard at his castle door, then I was an unsolicited double-glazing salesman. 'What's up?' I said.

He almost managed a smile. Shrugged. 'An Englishman's castle is his ulcer.'

'Oh come on. Last time I saw you, you were absolutely full of how fantastic it was going to be. What's gone wrong . . .?'

Stupid question. The great black shadow of the tower was right under our feet.

'Bound to take the gilt off the gingerbread, isn't it?' agreed Joe affably.

'Look, I owe you an apology,' I said. 'That day you came round to Oliver's, I'm really sorry for the crass way I broke the news about – the tragedy. It must seem absurd – I still can hardly believe it myself – that I could actually be staying in the Gatehouse and not know what had happened to Cathy but –'

'Forget it,' he said. 'Come and look round the castle if you want. I wouldn't mind,' he added, under his breath but with perfectly audible ferocity, 'if I never had to hear that poor bloody girl's name again.'

CHAPTER FOURTEEN

We walked into darkness at the foot of the tower. Dimly, to the right, a spiral staircase coiled up and away. Joe caught the direction of my gaze. 'Yup,' he said flatly. 'That's the staircase to bloody Paradise. Up four floors and through the fire door.'

I was planting my ghoulish foot on the first step, but Joe almost hustled me past and threw open a hefty oak door, which squealed like Dracula's coffin. 'Ladies 'n' gennelmun, kindly mind the 'oles in the floor. 'Ere we 'ave the Great 'All. Note the genu-ine Victorian dirt on every surface, the lingering haroma of Jeyes fluid . . .'

'Wow,' I said.

In the shuttered gloom of the hall you expected to stumble into armour-clad knights, dozing under centuries of cobwebs. Instead the shadowy lumps proved to be a couple of scarred tables and an easel. There was, nevertheless, a gallery fit for minstrels. I danced up a curving staircase, sighing 'Romeo, Romeo, wherefore . . .' etcetera, and leaned over the balustrade. But Romeo had wandered away and was kicking some panelling.

'Hope that's not bloody worm holes,' he said.

Flattened, I descended and trudged out of the hall after him. The other rooms were no less theatrical. Everywhere, there were cornices and dados elaborate as the icing on a wedding cake, and fireplaces like Russian Orthodox altars.

'Al calls it the Victorian version of Disneyland,' said Joe as we walked into what he'd informed me would one day be the main dining room. 'A monument to smug bourgeois kitsch.'

'She packs quite a turn of phrase, doesn't she?'

'She's paid to,' said Joe, running a finger along some carved panelling. 'She's a journalist.'

'I think it's got fantastic potential.'

'That's what Bunny reckoned,' he said, studying his black fingertip gloomily. 'But that guy could sell a skating rink in the Sahara. Al's right, you know. It's not going to be easy without him.'

'Well, I'm dead envious,' I retorted. 'I'd love to have a toy castle to play with.'

He grinned tiredly. 'Wanna job?'

All I wanted was a few laughs. Gloom and doom I could get down at the Gatehouse with Oliver. And just what had happened to the soupy-eyed Latin lover, whispering about destiny? All he could talk about now, as he led me along the flagged passageways, was his debts.

'There's a theatre here somewhere, isn't there?' I enquired with determined brightness.

Joe halted and strode back down the passage. At the end, he groped in his pocket. I was faintly amazed such a fat bunch of keys could have been squeezed into the pocket of such painfully tight jeans.

'Police told me I should lock the pass door into the theatre,' he explained.

'The police?'

He grimaced. 'She came through here. So Plod suggested to me, as a responsible property owner, blah blah. As though access to the bloody tower is an invitation to jump. No one else has this century and the village has been using the theatre for donkey's years.'

After trying several keys, he opened the door.

Strangely, the first thing that hit me was the smell. The smell of a theatre is unmistakable, don't you find? A rich cocktail of damp and dirt which has festered for decades in the dark. There are echoes of scent, hairspray, mothballs from granny's fur coat and, underlying that blend, a powerfully sweet tinge (or so I've always thought) of choc-ices. I sniffed the air appreciatively as I followed Joe into the darkness.

Then he switched on a few lights and I gasped. I'd been expecting a glorified village hall. Silly, really, considering the wacky theatricality of the rest of the castle.

As I walked down the centre aisle a hundred golden cherubs winked at me. Curtained boxes, ornate as sedan chairs, lined the side walls. The circle overhead was garlanded, gilded and graped, and supported by four trumpet-blowing goddesses with breasts like missile nose-cones. In the dim light, I didn't notice the damp and peeling ceiling, the balding velvet, the chipped paint. I was just thinking old Sir Monty had done his wife proud. If anyone had been besotted enough to build a place like this for me, I'd have been happy to overlook the odd chambermaid.

'It's fantastic,' I breathed.

'Not bad is it? Shame really. Bunny was full of plans for a conference centre but —'

'Conference centre? That's criminal. This is a *theatre.*'

'Don't you start,' said Joe, following me down to the front of the auditorium. There were spindly battalions of music stands in the orchestra pit, an open piano and a couple of Coke cans. Joe sat down on the front row, the seat creaking loudly under his weight. 'The Harecombe Am. Dram. bunch have already had a preservation order slapped on the interior. I told 'em they needn't have bothered. With Bunny gone, I can't afford to touch this place. A restaurant and hotel's more than enough. They can put their shows on until the cows come home — or the roof falls in.'

'But you could do so much here,' I exclaimed, scrambling across a rickety ramp to stride centre stage *à la* Sarah Bernhardt. Oh for a follow spot. 'Plays. Recitals. Imagine restoration comedy in a place like this . . .' I'd always fancied myself in restoration comedy. You know: sex, jokes and pretty frocks. 'God, it would be *marvellous.*'

The acoustics were thrilling too: the house was resonant

150

as the inside of a piano. 'Chamber opera,' I declared. 'Mozart, maybe —'

'Pack it in,' said Joe's voice from down below. 'You're daft as Cathy.'

That pricked the thespian bubble. 'Cathy?'

He looked forlorn in the middle of the front row, toying with his keys.

'Forget it. Nothing.'

'No, please. You were saying?'

'Cathy seemed to think this place was heaven-sent to be an opera house. Little Glyndebourne of the West Country. As though it were the easiest thing in the world. Must have been out of her tiny mind,' he said. 'Well — she was, wasn't she?'

'Was she?'

'To do what she did? Are you kidding?'

I was quite ready to continue the discussion, but he rose, kicked the creaking seat upwards and stomped back up the aisle.

'It's opening time,' he called from the doorway. 'Fancy a drink?'

I hopped off the stage and reached him just as he was flicking off the panel of houselights.

'Where?'

'There's a new wine bar in the village. May as well suss out the competition. I'll ring Al. See if she wants to join us.'

That wasn't quite what I had in mind and, as I followed him out of the theatre, I said maybe I ought to be getting back to Oliver, after all.

'And you're his cousin,' said Joe. He was striding ahead so he couldn't see the contorted purple of my face as I stammered something about distant and second and removed. He wasn't paying attention anyway, just concluded, before picking up an antiquated telephone receiver: 'It figures.'

And somehow, bizarre as it seemed at the time, he sounded disappointed.

*

Harecombe village surprised me. I suppose I expected your typical calendar-cute West Country village, but we rounded the corner of the castle to be confronted by a sea of suburbia lapping right up to the castle gates, with ever newer orange roofs glaring far into the distance.

'Mushroomed in the last twenty years,' said Joe as we strolled down the castle drive. 'One Executive Estate after another. The dread spread of dormitoryland, Al calls it.' He gave a fleeting grin. 'I call it captive customers.'

This front approach to the castle was much grander than the winding lane at the rear. A battlemented portico frowned down a lamp-lined drive to a moat. The moat, sadly, was a swampy ditch now, but still surmounted by the prettiest of arched stone bridges.

'Sweet,' I exclaimed.

'Bloody useless,' said Joe. 'Try getting a scaffolding lorry over here.'

'Oh, yes,' I said, remembering. 'You needed access by the Gatehouse, didn't you?'

He looked blank for a moment, then snorted, 'Storm in a lawyers' teacup. Turns out there was always a right of access down the back. I needn't have bloody worried, need I?'

The castle gates, one of which still bore a peeling sign for Harecombe College. 'Tradesmen please to rear door', were slumped open, looking as though they had been dozing in exactly that position for decades. We walked between them into a square which, in spite of the pay and display carpark, still preserved vestiges – some half-timbering, a giant oak tree, a charmingly tumbledown pub – of the old village which had once nestled outside Sir Monty's gates.

As we threaded a path between the cars towards what had patently once been the local co-op, now painted the equally unmistakable bottle-green peculiar to wine bars, a voice hailed us. I turned, and saw Alison was not alone.

'Look who I found,' she called. 'Next door.'

Oliver, wheeling his bike with two bulging carrier bags

dangling from the handlebars, aimed at me the self-righteous smile of one who has done his duty. Then he saw Joe, and stopped smiling.

'Just been viewing the castle,' I said, before the tactlessness of the words crunched home. 'Amazing to find that theatre,' I added hastily, 'here, in the middle of nowhere . . .'

If the face is the window of the soul and most people's panes are, as it were, frosted or at least discreetly leaded, Oliver's was plate-bloody-glass. I knew at once I'd said something wrong.

'Gilt and cherubs and red plush,' he retorted. 'It reminds me of a fairground organ.'

'Horrendous,' agreed Alison. 'How could anyone appreciate a play with all that screaming for attention?'

Well, that placed Alison Laverick, didn't it? The world, if you ask me, divides into those people who like their stages bleak as a sauna with the odd splash of significant stainless steel, called something enticing like The Pit, and, on the other hand, those vulgar souls (me for instance) who still hanker after the gilded palace school. When I was a child, my toy theatres were always called the Alhambra. My tastes haven't advanced.

'I've been to see Pamela,' said Oliver, pushing his spectacles back up his nose.

'And I rescued him on the way out,' added Alison.

'Rescued is the right word,' he said with a grateful flicker of a smile in her direction. 'Honestly, Becca, it was frightful.'

'Pamela can't come to terms with it at all,' said Alison. 'My mother's been telling me the whole gory story.'

'Do you think she's actually going round the twist?' demanded Oliver. 'I mean, she —'

'Menopausal,' interrupted Alison. 'I left an article about hormone therapy for her months ago, but —'

'For Christ's sake, Al,' said Joe. 'The poor woman's just lost her only daughter. Isn't that enough?'

'It's well known the menopause can make women behave irrationally, Joe. That's all I'm saying.'

'And I suppose grief can't?'

Seconds out for Round Two, I was thinking, and, What a jolly little drink this is going to be, when I realized Oliver was addressing me. 'She's obsessed,' he was saying incredulously. 'Totally and utterly obsessed with some fucking suitcase.' The obscenity, coming from him, was shocking.

'I need a drink,' said Joe, breaking off from his squabble. 'Coming?'

'Joe!' snapped Alison.

'She's pestered the police with it,' said Oliver. 'I told her they'd already asked me. How the hell am I supposed to know what Cathy did with a suitcase?'

'Mrs Metcalfe had a case with her when she came round to the Gatehouse that day,' I said uncomfortably. 'A flashy crocodile job. Blue.'

'Matching pair,' responded Oliver. 'She showed it to me, too. Apparently she gave them to Cathy for her eighteenth. I dunno. Cathy seemed to have dozens of bags and cases. Heaven knows what she did with this one. But that's not all. Her mother's now saying clothes are missing too. She's been sorting them out for Oxfam. My God, that woman must have kept an inventory of everything in Cathy's wardrobe. This was gone, that was. What did she imagine I'd done? Flogged the stuff?'

Joe turned and walked away. Alison smiled tightly. 'Maybe we all need a drink. Oliver?'

'What in God's name does it matter anyway?' he went on. 'Cathy could have left half her frocks at the dry cleaners for all I know. She was always losing things. What? Drink? Oh, no thanks. No, really . . .'

Alison shrugged and followed Joe into a murky doorway under a gilded bunch of grapes the size of tennis balls.

'Oh come on,' I said. 'I wouldn't mind a drink.'

Oliver shuddered – anyone would think I was suggesting a quick slug of strychnine. 'But you go ahead,' he said ungraciously, remounting his bicycle.

Neither playing piggy-in-the-middle to the warring ex-lovers nor Florence Nightingale to Oliver's wounded soul was exactly an alluring prospect. But it was a long, hot walk home and Oliver was on his bike. So I waved him off and walked into the wine bar.

CHAPTER FIFTEEN

It took me a few minutes to locate them in the cool liquid gloom of The Drunken Fox. They had retreated downstairs to the cellar bar. I clattered down a spiral staircase and followed the buzz of quarrelling voices, which broke off as soon as I stuck my head round the brick-lined alcove.

Joe scrambled to his feet. 'I'll get a bottle. White OK?'

'Water for me,' said Alison. 'Still — and no lemon.'

'Sour enough already?' said Joe, and smartly dodged round the corner.

'When God invented Adam,' she said, chucking a desultory cocktail stick after him, 'she was certainly having an off day. Bloody men. Who needs 'em?'

I laughed warily.

Alison wasn't laughing. She continued to glower at the wall while I picked up a beer mat and studied *The Amazing History of Hops, Part V*. 'Just ignore Joe and me,' she muttered when I'd got to the competition on the flip side. 'We've — well, we've always fought like cat and dog.' She yawned, flexing her long thin body. 'Pity we couldn't persuade Oliver in. He's pretty wretched, isn't he? God knows what he did to deserve this.'

'Terrible tragedy.' I responded piously.

'Her death?' said Alison, 'Or Oliver marrying her in the first place?'

Blimey.

'I — um — I thought Cathy was a friend of yours?'

Alison eyed me speculatively, pursing her lips. Hers was, I noted with envy, the kind of full, luscious mouth models buy with silicone implants.

'Well, we were brought up next door to one another,' she conceded. 'But she was years younger — barely out of nappies when I went to university. Besides . . .' She picked up her sunglasses and toyed with them for a moment before asking: 'How well did you know Cathy?'

'Never, um, actually met her,' I said, wishing, not for the first time, I hadn't coined the brilliant idea of posing as Oliver's cousin. Alison, however, didn't question the relationship.

'But Oliver's talked to you about her, obviously?'

'Oh yes,' I said. 'And so has Lady — Aunt Constance.'

Alison cocked an eyebrow. 'And do you think you would have liked her? If you'd known her?'

'Well . . .'

She leaned forward, her face all at once delightfully conspiratorial. 'Believe me, you wouldn't,' she said, and I was preparing to settle down to a little cosy character demolition when Joe rounded the corner of the cave with two bottles in one fist and three goblets, like knuckledusters, protruding from the other. Alison's smile snapped off like a light.

'I ordered some sandwiches too,' he said. 'Smoked salmon OK?'

'Yuck,' said Al, 'I'll eat the garnish.'

I just couldn't work out the chemistry between her and Joe. It was easy to see what physically had attracted each to the other and the undercurrent between them still sparked at high voltage, but it wasn't sexual somehow, not any more. Or was that wishful thinking?

'Know how I met Al?' Joe said, nudging her along the bench so that he could sit down. 'She came to write a piece on our restaurant. Personally I think editors should be sacked if they employ food critics who are vegetarian, teetotal, and eat less than the average sparrow.'

'I'm none of those things,' retorted Alison.

'You're vegetarian.'

'Unlike some people,' she said, eyeing his bulk, 'I try and exercise a little self-discipline in life. Actually,' she added earnestly to me, 'I have a huge appetite.'

Women built like neglected whippets always say that.

'Anyway, you can't complain,' she said to Joe, 'I gave you a very good write-up.'

Joe grinned. 'Only because I came out and chatted you up.'

'My oh my. Listen to the overweening vanity of the male of the species.'

'Do you always write a food column?' I interpolated before they could lock horns again.

'God no,' said Alison. 'Features. For women's magazines mainly. That piece was just a one-off — and look what happened.'

'I wasted a bottle of my best white Burgundy on you, you ungrateful trollop,' he said amiably, 'when you wouldn't have known the difference between Montrachet and this crap.' He poured the wine into two glasses and handed me one. 'So what am I missing? Make my day. Tell me you've been talking about me.'

'Cathy Langham. The true story,' said Alison.

Joe stopped grinning. 'Oh Christ, do we have to?'

Why, I found myself wondering throughout that lunch, did Alison dislike Cathy with such venom? Dim of me. Very dim.

Once she was launched on the subject, there was no stopping her. But on the face of it, everything she said made sense, fitting entirely with Constance Berisford's version — and filling in the home background too. Cathy's mother, deserted by her husband, had lavished labour, love and loot on her little girl who, said Alison, was as grateful as spoilt children usually are. While Mrs Metcalfe toiled for a pittance in the college office, Harecombe Castle, for a reduced fee, taught her daughter a minimum of typing and a load of snobbery.

'Makes you wonder why we want to have kids at all,' Al added – and I thought Joe gave her a very odd look – but she just swept on. 'Honestly, I find Pam's kind of devotion almost frightening. It's unstoppable as a primeval force. Whatever Cathy did to her, she just went on oozing love.'

'Smoked salmon – that's us, sweetheart,' said Joe, taking the plate from a prettily bottomed waitress who giggled coyly. 'Got any horseradish?'

'But it doesn't fit, surely?' I said doggedly. 'Someone as self-centred, as secure as you – and Constance too – describe Cathy Langham, committing suicide . . .'

'Cheap smoked salmon,' pronounced Joe in tones of satisfaction, having lifted the lid of one of the sandwiches. 'Scrag-end bits, and not many of them either. And,' he concluded triumphantly, 'it's sliced bread. Bloody hell.'

'Well, she'd lost the job she really wanted. Cathy,' Alison added, glancing at Joe, 'would do *anything* to advance her career.'

'Pack it in, will you?' said Joe. 'The girl's dead.'

'That doesn't mean we have to canonize her.'

'But to end it all for a single lost job,' I said, taking a sandwich. 'Hell, I've had more parts melt away than I've had hot dinners. I've never felt inclined to kill myself over them. Murder the odd director, possibly . . .'

'Cathy didn't intend to kill herself,' declared Alison, nibbling a lettuce leaf. 'If you ask me it was a cry for attention.'

Having just bitten a piece out of the sandwich, I nearly choked. 'Jumping off a bloody great tower? A cry for attention? You're joking.'

'Do you know,' said Joe, 'I don't even think this is butter. Oh thanks, darling.' This for a plate containing three plastic sachets of horseradish.

'I rescued Cathy from her first so-called attempt in the afternoon,' said Alison. 'Believe me, Becca, I've never seen anyone less inclined to suicide in my life. She was playing the scene to the hilt. She never intended to jump.'

'The fact remains,' I said, 'that when she went back,

she did.' I took a sachet of horseradish and offered one to Joe.

'Wouldn't touch that commercial muck,' he said. 'I didn't want horseradish anyway. I just wanted to see what sort they'd offer me.'

'She probably fancied herself as a latter-day Lady Violet,' said Al, adding acidly, 'in more ways than one. Wouldn't you agree, Joe?' But Joe was steadfastly ignoring her and had leaned round to pluck a menu from an adjoining table. 'You probably don't know the local legend,' she said to me. 'Montague Rivenhoe built the theatre —'

'Chicken paprika,' Joe began muttering. 'Venison in sodding port.'

'Oh yes, I do,' I responded. 'His wife found he was screwing a chambermaid and she jumped —'

'And survived,' interpolated Alison smartly. 'Thus ensuring his undying devotion. Just like Cathy intended to.'

'Bollocks,' growled Joe — and I agreed.

'Barmy,' I said. 'Cathy already had Oliver's undying devotion.'

'Oh, what the hell,' said Alison. 'She might have tripped. She might have been drunk. But no one,' she concluded intensely, 'will ever make me believe Cathy Langham intended to kill herself that night.'

Strangely, she was addressing this to Joe who was staring back with equal intensity. Just as I began wondering afresh what on earth was going on between them, Joe ostentatiously resumed his study of the menu again.

'Anyway,' said Al, shrugging, 'we'll just have to see what they come up with at the inquest tomorrow. I should think Oliver will be glad when it's all over. I can't say I'm much looking forward to it myself.'

'Are you going to be there?' I said in surprise.

Joe lifted his nose from the menu. 'Just as I thought. All boil-in-the-bag stuff. I don't think I need lose sleep over the competition. What, go to the inquest? Not bloody likely.'

'I am,' said Alison calmly. 'That's why I've had to come down from town. They're calling me as a witness.'

It was soon after that Joe threatened to leave if we didn't change the subject. We were carrion crows feasting on the remains of the dead, he said, which I thought was rather poetic. But it was Al who stalked off, saying that if he wanted her, she was at her mother's.

Which left Joe and me. And which, I admit, suited me just fine. We forgot Cathy Langham and swapped life stories instead, in a lingering tête-à-tête in our brick-lined cave. He had been, he told me, touching the crooked nose ruefully, a thug when young. A terror in the neighbourhood, a trial to his poor sainted mother. Yes, he confirmed in answer to my question, mother was dead. Father?

'No,' said Joe.

'What do you mean, no?'

'She was an unmarried mother,' he said. 'They hadn't invented single parents in Burnley in the fifties. I was a souvenir of a holiday in Morecambe. He, apparently, was a waiter in the Empire Hotel, but she never told me that. I only found out from an aunt at her funeral.' He grimaced. 'Mum was a stubborn old bird. The only thing she would ever tell me was that he was Italian. She said I'd got his eyes.'

'I can believe that,' I said.

No, this wasn't murmured huskily across the dimly lit table. It was plain observation of fact. We weren't playing mating games. I don't say the possibility didn't wing across my thoughts as his knee brushed mine, but Alison had barely departed and, besides, I liked Joe Duff better when he dropped the Latin-lover act.

I learned he had gone into the army at eighteen and joined the Catering Corps, which was where he had eventually encountered Major Rupert Hare-Smith, and through him, he said frankly, all the good things in life. Bunny was a great bloke, a great partner. Joe raised his glass. Absent friends. Never looked

161

back, since meeting Bunny. Leaving the army together, they had bought and sold their way through a bewildering variety of businesses of which only Flying Duck now remained . . .

'And a castle,' I said.

Joe looked glum again.

But we both agreed we were basically optimists, and both quite uncharacteristically dismal about our immediate futures. We agreed about a lot. And, when we drained the bottle, he suggested — almost shyly — that we exchange telephone numbers. I put the shyness down to guilt, because of Al. Whatever, this hardly seemed the wolf who had lounged into Oliver's garden a fortnight ago, chewing the stem of his sunglasses.

He gave me a lift back to the Gatehouse. I waved him off down the lane before tapping on the front door, which snapped open even as my hand was poised for the third tap.

'You've been quite a time,' said Oliver.

I recollected, with a belated twinge of guilt, that I was here to keep a surrogate auntly eye on him. 'You know how it is,' I said vaguely, walking into the sitting room, 'when you get talking . . .' The sitting room was aglow with polish. Full of wine and good company I was pretty well aglow myself.

'Talking about what?' demanded Oliver.

Only then did it occur to me that Oliver was looking distinctly miffed. Thunder-faced even. In fact — if it wasn't so ludicrous — I'd have said he looked like your classic jealous lover. Jealous? Of me? 'Joe was asking about you,' I protested. Truthfully, Joe had enquired after Oliver's welfare in tiresome detail. Bad as Constance. 'He seemed most concerned.'

'Did he indeed?'

'Alison Laverick was there too,' I said hastily. Well, almost true. 'She — she's a writer, I gather.'

Oliver nodded, the cloud-base lifting fractionally. 'She actually interviewed me a while ago for an article. About teaching. I told her I was terribly boring, but she seemed to think it was worth while.' He picked up a pencil from the desk and

162

began toying with it. 'I never saw the finished piece. Did she happen to mention it?'

'Um, no,' I said, floundering. 'She told me she used to live next door to Cathy and —'

Oliver stopped toying with the pencil. 'You were talking about Cathy?' The way he said this made it sound as though we had been guilty of grossest indelicacy.

'Only — in passing.' Come to think of it, when I remembered what Alison had been saying, maybe the conversation had been pretty gross. But that was hardly my fault.

'With Joe Duff?'

'All of us,' I said uncomfortably.

The pencil between Oliver's fingers snapped. He threw it aside.

'And did Joe Duff happen to mention,' he burst out furiously, 'that he had an affair with Cathy?'

CHAPTER SIXTEEN

It was so obvious, wasn't it?

No wonder Oliver was green-gilled with jealousy. Bugger all to do with yours truly.

'Joe and Cathy had an affair?' I echoed, sinking on to the sofa. I was remembering that sunny afternoon Joe had rolled up at the Gatehouse. I could see him now, creeping behind the hedge like a burglar, peering through the gaps, *looking to see who was at home*. The bastard was looking for Cathy, wasn't he? Avoiding Oliver – and finding me.

'He didn't mention it?' said Oliver grittily. 'Funny, I thought he'd be just the type to brag about the – the notches on his bedpost.'

And with Cathy mysteriously absent, the lecherous pig had wasted no time in transferring his slimy attentions. Destiny, my foot.

'How could he?' I hissed.

'The man has the morals of an alley cat,' said Oliver, misunderstanding my indignation. 'He's a – a shameless womanizer.'

Shameless womanizer? *Never darken my doors again, sir, or I shall ask you to name your friends* ... But I was in no mood to laugh. Just then, shameless womanizer fitted the bill. Cad, bounder ... and, besides, uglier suspicions were occurring to me. Tentatively, I said, 'Didn't Cathy telephone Joe the day she died?'

'Apparently.' Oliver walked over to the desk. 'Something about the castle,' he added over his shoulder.

'There wasn't — do you suppose — any connection between Joe and . .'

'Cathy dying? God no, I can't blame *that* on him.' Oliver glared out of the window. 'It — the affair — happened, oh, nearly a year ago. One bloody night, that's all it was. *All* . .' He gave a sour barking laugh.

It wasn't a year ago Joe Duff had crept round here. More like two weeks, with — now I came to think of it — a bottle of champagne. Conveniently chilled. The effrontery of this brazen Jack-the-lad took my breath away. I could see him now, raising his glass to mine, drawling that he hadn't expected to drink this with *me*.

'Are you sure?' I prompted.

Oliver spun round. 'I know every last sordid detail. Last autumn, I was away with the choir and Cathy was booked by him to sing at some function.'

'A banquet?' I enquired chattily. Oh, the blinkers were off now. A banquet he'd said. Where she had sung all the great Latin lover's favourite arias.

'He got her tight afterwards, so tight she hardly knew what she was doing. Took her back to his flat and . . . oh, you can imagine. When I found out I wanted to kill him. Really, honestly. I — I've never felt rage like it.'

'How did you find out, Oliver? Did Cathy tell you?'

'Yes — well, no. Not exactly.' He shuddered. 'Becca, it was excruciating. Like some cheap farce. Alison apparently found' — his mouth puckered in distaste — 'She found one of Cathy's earrings. In his bed. And recognized it. She came tearing round here with the damn thing, shouting at Cathy. Didn't realize I was upstairs until it was too late. Shit, I don't blame Alison. I know how she felt: we were in the same boat. The only person I blame — Cathy poured out the whole miserable story then — is that *bastard* Duff.'

And so say all of us.

'I gathered Alison and Joe Duff had split up last year. Was it over this?'

Oliver nodded. 'Poor girl. At first I felt I couldn't forgive Cathy either, but she was so distraught. And anyone can make a mistake once, can't they? It never happened again.'

Oh Oliver, I thought, you poor fool, and he sensed something because he added fiercely, 'Cathy loathed Joe Duff. She told me so. The very day she died, as a matter of fact.'

Oh yeah? And that surreptitious visit to the Gatehouse wasn't all. Didn't Joe tell me he'd lent Cathy money? Not last year, recently. On the point of asking Oliver if he knew, I saw the anguish in his face and shut my mouth again. Not my can of worms. Cathy's secrets could slumber on in the grave as far as I was concerned. God knows, I'd clambered into the woman's bed with her husband, cooked in her kitchen, drunk from her cup. All I needed was to discover I'd toyed with the idea of inheriting her lover as well.

I felt sick. And not metaphorically. My stomach was churning as it hadn't since the bout of food poisoning. I put it down to cheap wine until, having bolted to the bathroom and been luxuriantly sick, I groped in my soapbag for my toothbrush and a box of tampons fell out. Bought, with my customary efficiency, nearly a week ago. And still unopened.

I started adding up days.

Field Marshal Montgomery, when asked by a foolhardy admirer how he kept the garden of his retirement years in such immaculate condition, is said to have barked, 'Weeds do not grow on *my* lawn.' With similar pugnacity, I told myself that alien life did not sprout in *my* womb. My body functioned as reliably as Greenwich Mean Time. Admittedly, this period might be a little late. I hadn't warded Oliver's advances off with a total fib. The time of the month had truly been nigh. I'd put the uncharacteristic delay down to the stresses and strains of moving house. You know, trans-London jet lag.

Now I had to concede a more scientific diagnosis was required.

With the inquest the next morning, Oliver retired early

166

with a biography of Palestrina by way of soothing bedtime story. Evidently it worked. I was able to assure Constance, when she telephoned from some airport – two thousand miles not diminishing the bray by one decibel – that he was already sound asleep.

'Good show,' she roared. 'You'll deliver him to me at the Coroner's Court then? Know how to find it?'

All the time we were talking I was staring at the carrier bag in front of me as though it contained a live grenade. As soon as I put the receiver down, I made myself a cup of tea, closed the curtains conspiratorially against the balmy summer evening, and fished out of the bag the shinily wrapped pregnancy testing kit I'd slipped out to buy that afternoon.

I stripped off the cellophane and arranged the contents of the box gingerly in the middle of Oliver's desk. A toy chemistry kit, I'd always loathed chemistry. According to the instruction leaflet, I couldn't conduct the test until the morning. I sipped my tea and swotted up the procedure.

A gentle rap on the window immediately in front of me made me catapult tea over the leaflet. I bundled everything into the carrier bag and stuffed it under the desk before hastening, flushed and guilty, to the front door.

To my surprise, Alison Laverick stood there, a glamorous ghost in a white leather jacket which drooped, expensively big, over the leopard-spotted legs. She looked surprised to see me, too. 'I saw the light at the desk,' she said. 'I assumed it was Oliver.'

'He's in bed,' I whispered, jerking my head upwards. 'Asleep.'

'I'm taking Judy for a walk,' she said, and I saw a scaggy sheepdoggish beast sniffing in the hedge opposite. 'I thought I'd call to see if he was all right, with the inquest tomorrow. I didn't realize you were staying here. Knowing this rabbit hutch, I assumed you'd be with your aunt.'

'She's in the States,' I said grimly. 'Unfortunately. That is, well, the, um, the sofa's bloody uncomfortable . . '

We eyed one another for a moment in awkward silence.

'By the way, I meant to ask you earlier,' she said unexpectedly. 'You did the Frosty Food commercials, didn't you?'

When I admitted that I used to, yes, she said an acquaintance of hers was a copywriter at the agency producing the ads and named him. I did know him slightly, as a matter of fact. But ... 'I didn't get on — *fantastically* well with him,' I ventured.

Whereupon her face split into a deliciously malicious grin. 'Total and utter prick,' she purred, expressing so exactly my own sentiments I invited her in for a cup of tea.

'The dog will be fine outside,' she said, following me into the sitting room. 'To be honest, I don't like dogs, but the animal hasn't had an outing for weeks and my mother twisted my arm. It's Pam Metcalfe's. I'm sorry, am I interrupting something?'

I assured her, with unnecessary emphasis, that she had interrupted nothing. 'I'm glad of company,' I said. True — I was grateful for any distraction on what promised to be one of the longest nights of my life. Until, that is, as I poured Alison's tea, I saw out of the corner of my eye the chemist's bag slowly — like a cat yawning — uncrumpling itself under the desk. Directly opposite her. Any moment now, I thought, it will burst open and expose me.

'Oliver tells me,' I babbled, hopping across the room to a chair far from the desk, 'that you interviewed him for an article. He — he was wondering what had happened to it.' It was the first fatuous remark to come into my head. Anything to glue her attention to me. So I was surprised by the shifty look which crossed her face.

'Oh that,' she said. She eyed her fingernails for a minute before saying, 'For Pete's sake, don't tell Oliver this, will you?'

At that moment the carrier bag expired sideways with a soft sigh, leaving the contents concealed. I sighed too, and collected my wits enough to assure Alison her secrets were equally safe.

'It's always the same,' she mused. 'You talk to someone for one piece and something completely different crops up. I was writing about convent schoolgirls actually. I rang Oliver because he teaches at the Sacred Heart. But . . . Oh shit, why am I telling you this?'

I settled back in my chair. 'What on earth did you write? Don't tell me Oliver was having a raving affair with the head girl?'

She smiled wryly. 'Sod all about convent schoolgirls. I wrote that piece all right, but Oliver couldn't contribute a sausage. To him, pupils are sopranos and altos, O levels and A levels, or whatever they call exams now.'

'I can believe that.'

'But, naturally, we got to talking about . . . other matters. And I was also researching another feature. I disguised him in the final piece,' she added hastily. 'I called him Jeremy. I don't suppose he'd ever recognize himself if it weren't for my byline at the top.'

Now I was intrigued. 'What was this article about then?'

Alison glanced up the ceiling and took a sip of tea before saying softly, 'Unlikely as it must seem . . . adultery.'

Well, I might have guessed. Didn't all conversational roads round here lead straight back to Catherine Langham? She was smiling mistily down from the mantelpiece, her frame gleaming with the polish I'd applied myself this morning. Al caught the direction of my gaze.

'You must admit Oliver's a rarity these days,' she protested. 'I thought they stopped manufacturing his sort along with the Morris Oxford. He's amazing, don't you think? So wonderfully, *Britishly* straight and decent. So utterly faithful. Mating, like a swan, for life. I just couldn't resist quoting him – your archetypal wronged husband – but it felt immoral. I knew he'd be appalled to end up in print. He only talked to me so freely because, oh . . . I may as well tell you. After Cathy had sung at a dinner, she and Joe –'

'Don't bother,' I said. 'Oliver told me himself.'

She recoiled as though I'd hit her. 'Did he? The poor guy was shattered. I've never felt so fucking guilty in my life.'

'*You* felt guilty?' I exclaimed. 'Why on earth –'

'Oliver need never have known a thing if it wasn't for me and my foul temper, storming round here,' she said. 'Why couldn't I keep my big mouth shut? After all, what's one drunken night of lust? Oliver wouldn't see it that way, of course, but most of us aren't exactly without sin when it comes to throwing –'

'One drunken night of lust?' I interpolated, having the sense this time, to keep my face firmly in neutral.

'Well, I imagine Joe was both drunk and lusty,' she said. 'If the two are not mutually incompatible. Personally, I always suspected Cathy was as capable of passion as a Barbie doll. But –'

'No,' I said cautiously. 'I meant, only the one night?'

'Hell yes. Once I blew the gaff that was it. Oliver suicidal, Cathy gushing contrition. As well she might. Honestly, that girl would have slept with the devil in hell if she thought there were job prospects. Pity she didn't realize Joe books singers about as often as Covent Garden hires centre forwards. Or at least, not until after she'd hijacked him into bed.'

'Oh, hang on,' I protested. 'Cathy? *Hijacked* Joe Duff? Oliver says . . '

Alison mimed a world-weary yawn. 'I know what Oliver believes. He's repeated to me all the twaddle she gave him. His innocent wife. The vile seducer forcing brandy down her throat. Honestly, if you'd known Cathy you'd laugh your head off. But it was hardly up to me to disillusion Oliver.'

'It, um, takes two to tango,' I said tritely, draining my mug.

'Sure,' agreed Al. 'And she found a willing partner there. I could have throttled Joe – I gave him the boot, one night or not. But we were going nowhere fast. If that hadn't bust us up, something else would.'

Once I'd have welcomed this disclosure for my own sake.

170

Now I was glad for Alison's. She didn't know how well out of it she was.

'But it was different for Oliver,' she went on. 'Truly, even at the time I felt sorrier for him than I did for myself. He — adored Cathy. And she led him a rotten dance. She couldn't give a fuck about him. Never had.'

The bride twinkled enigmatically down at us.

'Then why,' I demanded, 'did she marry him? And why stay?'

Alison blinked at me. 'For the money, of course.'

'Money?' I echoed incredulously, glancing round the shabby sitting room.

'For a cousin,' she said, 'you don't seem too clued-up on family affairs.'

> I'd as lief crawl through yonder thorny thicket,
> As say pooh to a callow throstle . . .

. . . is what a friend of mine swore she always came out with if she dried in a Shakespearian speech. Inflect it with the appropriate emotion, she told me, and no one will suspect a thing.

In real life, when stuck for words, I tend to offer a drink.

'Well . . . OK,' said Al. 'What the hell?'

I liked her more by the minute. As Constance said, there is something so depressing about abstainers. The smell of white wine, however, as I pulled the cork, provoked a reminiscent wobble of nausea. I told myself desperately I was imagining things.

'A teacher's pittance,' said Alison, accepting her glass, 'wouldn't have kept Cathy in tights. I remember Oliver tying himself up in knots when he admitted — I forget how it came up — he had an income left by his parents. So very English. I tell you, I wouldn't be embarrassed by a private income.'

'Me neither,' I agreed, sipping my wine and wondering why it tasted like metal shavings.

'And I doubt he ever thinks about what he might inherit.

171

But you can bet your life Cathy did. She told my mother quite openly she expected Lady Berisford to leave the lot to him: Harecombe Estate; the whole caboodle. What do you reckon?'

'Well,' said this distant cousin, striving, queasily, to look wise. 'Constance hasn't any children of her own.'

'So I gather,' said Alison, twirling her glass between her fingers. 'Poor woman. At least — would she have liked children?'

'Oh yes, I think so,' I said, on safer ground now. 'She told me she'd married too late.'

'Tell me the old, old story . . .' murmured Alison. 'God, isn't life unfair?' I wasn't clear what she meant, and said so. She seemed disappointed by my lack of perception. 'It's easy for the male of the species, isn't it?' she said. 'They're not ruled by the biological bloody clock. Recently, half my friends have been rushing down the aisle like demented lemmings, marrying the most cretinous men, just to get themselves pregnant. Have you got a regular partner?'

I shook my head.

'Hasn't it got to you yet?' she went on. 'The child-bearing years ticking away?'

Now I gulped and had consciously to restrain myself from looking at the white carrier bag. 'I've, um, I've never thought about it.'

'Give it time. You're younger than me. I'm thirty-six next birthday and it bloody well has to me.' She began teasing a thread out of the arm of the sofa. 'But Joe and I didn't quite see eye-to-eye on the question. As on most other fucking things.'

She wasn't being flippant any more. She was in dead earnest. I was astonished. Was this wise-cracking, worldly, *what's one drunken night of lust?* Ms Laverick confessing that what she really longed for was a house, a husband and a baby? Whereas Joe *Don Juan* Duff . . . Oh, poor Alison.

'Joe doesn't believe in marriage?'

172

She snorted. 'Of course Joe believes in marriage. Like any good Catholic boy.'

'But not for himself. I mean, not to you?'

'Hell, I wouldn't marry Joe Duff if you paid me.' She was grinning; a bit sourly, maybe, but she sounded as though she meant what she said. Now I really was confused. 'He's a good lover, or rather . . .' Then her face puckered momentarily as if with pain. Or was it anger? 'He was once anyway. But not,' she added disgustedly, 'husband material. Not in a million years. Joe and I have absolutely nothing in common. The holiday in Spain proved that, if nothing else.' She drained her glass. 'I should never have suggested that trip. Never.'

'Have another drink,' I said, but she shook her head.

'I'll get maudlin and you can do without that. Besides, I've a lousy head for booze and I've got to be intelligent in the morning.'

'Oh, the inquest,' I said as she got to her feet, and picked up her jacket. I stood up too, and we agreed, with more warmth than usual in such promises, that we must meet in town.

'I might not get a chance to talk to Oliver tomorrow,' she added, embracing me, 'so give him my love, won't you? I'd offer to give him lunch afterwards but I suspect it's not the kind of thing you do after inquests. Tell him — tell him I'll give him a ring next week, maybe. Is he staying here or going back to his aunt's, do you know?'

About to say I wasn't sure, I was struck by a suspicion. More in the nature of a blinding light, actually. 'Al,' I said, 'have you telephoned Oliver before — at St Benedict's, I mean?'

Halfway into her jacket, she paused. 'Once or twice. I didn't want to ring here for obvious reasons after last autumn's soap opera. But I had to fix the convent school interview. I took him out to dinner, and we've met a couple of times since.' She zipped up her jacket, grinning wryly. 'I wouldn't say we were crying on each other's shoulders, more a case of Oliver crying on mine, but —'

173

'You're not going to believe this,' I declared. 'At least — look, just tell me you discussed train timetables with Constance.'

She raised her eyebrows but, after a moment, nodded. 'I've never actually met Lady Berisford. She sounds quite a character.'

'A character and a half,' I crowed. 'Know what she thought you were? Wait for it. Only Oliver's bit on the side. Her very words, I promise you.'

To my disappointment, my new friend didn't seem to find the joke quite as rich as I did. 'Me having an affair with Oliver?' she gasped. 'Christ, the combined lures of Marilyn Monroe and the Mata Hari couldn't have tempted . . . Your aunt actually thought . . .'

'Oh, sod the aunt lark,' I said. Alison Laverick had confided in me and I wanted to cut the tangled web. Besides, if ever a girl yearned for a sisterly and sympathetic ear at this moment, I did. 'You won't believe the mess you got me into either. For heaven's sake, don't breathe a word in the neighbourhood . . .' And, pouring us both another glass of stainless-steel-flavoured wine, I plunged into the true story of my chance meeting with Oliver, Constance banishing us back here . . .

'Sweet innocent sex and sunshine,' I hooted, 'as far as I was concerned, until Joe creeps into the garden, bottle of champagne in his fist, and asks me where Cathy is. I swear, I nearly died . . .'

Alison was not laughing. And too late I noticed her face was not exactly aglow with sisterly sympathy, either. In fact, she looked murderous. And that was when it occurred to me that even the most determinedly ex of ex-girlfriends might not be enchanted to learn her erstwhile lover, freshly returned from their holiday, had rushed immediately round to visit Cathy Langham. Oh well done, Becca. Straight in with the size eights again.

'Don't worry, I can let myself out,' she said tightly. 'Tell Oliver I called, won't you? Judy? Here girl . . .'

CHAPTER SEVENTEEN

If I slept at all that night, I wasn't aware of it. Beside me, Oliver lay like the dead. I envied him as I shifted in and out of that wakeful doze where commonsense is comatose but imagination races on, turbo-charged. Faces and voices, facts and fancies were swimming in and out of focus, all contradicting one another crazily.

Joe and Cathy. She despised him, hisses Oliver. A likely story. They were lovers — but I remembered Joe muttering he'd be happy never to hear that poor bloody girl's name again.

Joe and Alison, then. Oh knickers, Alison. My big mouth. But could she really, still, be hankering after Joe? Mostly she gave the impression of, well, not hating him. Hate's much too close to love. She had seemed indifferent. Until I put my foot in it.

It was one of those clear, moon-bright summer nights. I must have got up hourly to trudge down to the bathroom with ever-dwindling hope. Once, on the way back, I parted the curtains to squint up at the dark pinnacle of the tower etched on the horizon. A mistake. Next thing I was dreaming I was walking up there. In my nightshirt. Oliver running behind me, begging me not to do it . . .

I woke up, shivering with sweat. This time, I went downstairs, made tea, and sipped it, wondering afresh what had made Cathy climb the hill — the tower. No one really knew, did they?

Her mother apparently wouldn't believe it, but what loving mother could ever accept her only child's suicide? Oliver was the same. The truth was presumably too painful for those who loved her to endure. Constance, though, who had no love for Cathy, admitted it surprised her. Joe put it down to madness; Alison to thwarted ambition, but even Alison had seemed anxious to claim Cathy never intended actually to kill herself. A cry for attention? Rubbish.

Richard's voice drifted across my incoherent thoughts. Richard and his bloody onion thesis. 'An actor should treat the character he's playing as an onion. The words on the page are merely the brown paper skin. It's up to the actor to get underneath that. Peel away the layers and reach the very essence of the person.'

I used to wonder if Richard had ever encountered a real live onion. Keep peeling away and all you find is more of the same. You end up with a pile of scraps – and floods of tears.

Consider the outside of Catherine Langham, though. Oliver's pretty, smiling child bride. A bride, according to Constance, who didn't quite *fit*. Peel that away and you find Joe Duff's mistress. Alison sees inside that a calculating, ambitious bitch. Well, as they say, she would, wouldn't she?

I left half my tea, and climbed the stairs again.

However selfish, however ambitious Cathy might have been, no one denies she was well loved. She was no latter-day Lady Rivenhoe. Cathy was adored by her mother. By Oliver. By – Joe Duff? But, like an onion, the tears are there at the centre. Got to be. Dreadful, tearful despair. Which drove her to jump.

If she jumped.

The thought made me jerk upright, and Oliver muttered a sleepy protest. No one had so much as breathed any other possibility. Constance dismissed the inquest as a formality, Oliver dreaded only the ordeal, but might the police be hatching some other explanation? A little push . . . Hell no. The girl had a suicide note in her pocket.

I settled back. Closed my eyes. Maybe the morning would produce some answers. Inevitably, my last dozy thoughts shifted back to questions closer to home. The morning would certainly produce an answer to that. One way or t'other.

'These home test kits are pretty reliable,' said the doctor, lifting off her glasses to look me in the eye, in exactly the way a soap-opera medic would. 'Although this is still very early days. But from what you say, it's possible.' She smiled sympathetically. 'I find women often know instinctively.'

I had dropped Oliver off at the Coroner's Court, ready to hare back to London, but he'd pleaded with me to meet him afterwards: give him moral support, maybe even persuade Constance it was a good idea for him to go to Italy.

'You're a grown man,' I said. 'Tell her yourself.'

But he looked so drawn and haggard that I relented. Besides, I was curious about the outcome of the inquest.

So instead I'd driven straight to the surgery I had known in student days. A shabby semi-detached house had been replaced by a rubber-planted, air-conditioned Health Centre. Dr Brown had been put out to grass, but the new incumbents had kindly granted me an emergency appointment. Yes, it was a bloody emergency. No way could I wait even another day until I returned to London for my own doctor to establish the awful truth. Besides, I wasn't sure I wanted Dr McKinnon to know. He was a fatherly old buffer and Catholic to boot, so unlikely to be immediately forthcoming with the necessary remedies. He'd be upset. If I was . . .

'How?' I said now indignantly. 'I take the pill. The same pill I've taken for years and years and I've never even had a scare. Every night I wind my watch and swallow my pill. I'm conditioned like Pavlov's dogs. I only have to hear ticking and I start salivating.'

'Did you forget to take one?'

I had already worked this out, of course. Not hard. Counted backwards to the night of the ball. When I didn't go to bed or take my watch off, and the pills were locked away in my college room until the following afternoon. 'But everyone forgets to take the odd one occasionally, or takes it a bit late,' I protested. 'For heaven's sake, women I know have come off it for years trying to get pregnant.'

She was quite human actually. She did not point out now — as I could imagine other doctors doing — that the packet instructed you to take one tablet, at the same hour every day, and if not . . .

'It's unusually unlucky,' she said. 'Can you think of any other reason why your cycle might have been disrupted? Stomach upsets for example?'

Stomach upsets.

That was the moment this outrageous suspicion began to look horribly plausible. I couldn't even claim ignorance as a defence. I read every pill scare story in the newspapers. I could recite the list of risks to effective contraception like a creed.

'A bout of food poisoning,' I mumbled.

'Can stop you digesting the pill,' she said. 'Still, we don't know yet that you are, do we?'

Oh yes we did.

And I doubted that even the Field Marshal, once the damned dandelion had had the temerity to take root, could simply will it out of existence. Stronger measures were called for.

'Thanks,' I said. 'You've been very helpful.'

'Rebecca?' croaked Richard, like one recognizing a voice from the other world. 'Why are you ringing?'

Nice to hear from you too, buddy.

I was ringing because I'd time to kill before Oliver emerged and I ached to talk to someone. A familiar voice. Also, because it happened to be the second Thursday of the month.

'Isn't it one of Helena's Good Works days?'

'No — I mean, possibly, but —'

'Is she there?'

178

'She's with her mother still, but ... Rebecca, why are you ringing from what sounds like the middle of a street?'

'It is the middle of a bloody street. It's the first telephone box I've found that works.'

'Becca?' he said, sounding a bit more like himself. 'Why, darling, is something the matter? You're crying.'

'No I'm not.'

Yes I was. It was being called darling. I wanted someone to rock me in strong grown-up arms and tell me everything was going to be all right. And I blew my nose ferociously a few times, while Richard whispered soothingly — there, there — that I was a poor possum and other such nonsense, before asking again what the trouble was.

'I'm pregnant.'

The burble of endearments ceased.

I am pregnant, I repeated silently to myself. It was the first time I'd actually framed the words. Extraordinary: they were quite meaningless. Like saying, I can fly. But I watched two mop-headed girls cycle past, wobbling and giggling and felt very, very old.

'It can't be mine,' said Richard at length. 'I had the snip after Thomas.'

'Of course it's not yours. I haven't seen you for — *What?* Are you telling me, Richard Prescott, you've been letting me stuff myself full of unnecessary hormones for eighteen months when all along you'd had a vasectomy?'

'One can't be too careful, darling. Accidents will happen. As you've found.'

So much for the comfort. I sniffed loudly.

'This is rather a shock, Rebecca.'

'You're telling me.'

'Do you know who the father is?'

'Of course I bloody know. What kind of a life do you think I've been living?'

'You're upset.'

'Bet your life I'm upset.'

179

'Well, God, so am I. Barely have we agreed our ways should part . . .'

'*Agreed?*' But I spoke without heat. The split with Richard was old history, as likely to inflame me now as the Wars of the Roses.

'And you leap into bed with some stranger.'

'I have known Oliver Langham since I was eighteen.'

'Is that what he's called? At least I have a name now, when I imagine you in another man's arms.'

'Oh for God's sake, I've always known Helena's name.'

'Helena is my wife,' he said, unanswerably. 'After you phoned me from that man's house, I went through *hell*. And I won't say I *warned* you at the time, but −'

'Then don't. Sermons I can do without. I've been very unlucky. Even the doctor admitted that.'

'Well, I'm sorry, darling,' said Richard briskly, 'but what with the school fees and −'

'*What?*'

'I assumed you wanted to borrow some money.'

'I *never* borrow money,' I said magnificently. Except from the bank, naturally. 'I . . . I just wanted a shoulder to cry on, I suppose. But it's all right. I've stopped crying now.'

That's my big brave girl, as my mother used to say. Becky never cries for long. With the result that sensitive souls like Richard Prescott believe one doesn't actually have feelings at all.

'I know you, darling. You'll have it sorted out in a trice,' said Richard.

See what I mean?

'The National Health,' he went on suavely, 'is terribly good about these things nowadays.'

A purple-faced woman with tight shoes and a shopping trolley had braked outside the telephone booth and fixed me with a piggy eye. I stared back equally malevolently. 'What things?'

'You know what I mean, darling.'

'An abortion?' I snarled, and the piggy-eyed woman jumped, and turned away. 'Why not say what you mean?'

First time I'd put that into words either. Abortion. Ugly word. A safeguard you know is there, but, like fire-escapes and life insurance, will of course only ever be required by other people. The sort of people who get themselves into messes.

'What other option is there?'

None whatsoever. It had been a toss-up between ringing Richard and one of those advisory services. But the phone box lacked a directory. That didn't stop me saying pugnaciously, 'I could have it.'

'And support it how? There isn't a huge call for pregnant actresses. And I don't know if you've ever looked into the costs of child care but —'

'Is money all you ever think about, Richard?' I shouted, all the angrier because he was right. 'Would you be talking like this if it was yours? If it was a little scrap of you inside me now?'

'Look, you're upset. And so am I — I'm terribly, terribly distressed for you, love. You must let me know when you've got it all sorted out. You will, won't you?'

'OK,' I sniffed, mollified. 'I'll give you a ring.'

'Probably safest, actually, if you were to write to me care of Penny.'

'What?'

'You know Penny, darling. At the agency. Quentin's new —'

'Richard?'

'Darling?'

'Fuck off.'

Nothing like a row to buoy one up. Sympathy could have reduced me to a puddle of maudlin tears. As it was I marched down St Aldate's like a storm-trooper.

The Coroner's Court was tucked down a cul-de-sac in a

181

squat building as distinguished as the average municipal lavatory. The door was shut, and the place looked as dead as it had when I'd deposited Oliver. The little lane, however, was no longer empty. Joe Duff was slouched in his smug, vulgar red motor on a double yellow line, one tattooed forearm resting on the door, while Pavarotti blasted 'E lucevan le stelle' weepily into the shimmering summer air from powerful speakers. Joe's head was back and I presumed his eyes were closed because he didn't seem to see me stomping along the pavement towards him.

'Pretty crass choice of tape,' I said loudly, stopping by the car.

'Compact disc,' he murmured, opening his eyes, and then he recognized me and gave a big, sickly, welcoming smile. 'Hey, Becca.'

'Tosca chucked herself off a tower too.'

'Christ,' he said, and snapped the music off, then eyed me more attentively. 'What's up?'

'Nothing.'

'Yes there is. You look like you've been run over by a bus.' He leaned across and pushed open the passenger door. 'Sit down.'

Suddenly my knees felt less than reliable. I got in.

'Sweetheart,' he said, shoving a heavy, hairy arm round my shoulders. 'What's the matter?'

Sympathy. Coming from almost anyone else it could have been fatal. But not Joe Duff. I wriggled away and he retrieved his arm without visible embarrassment.

'Just worrying about my future,' I said glibly. And wished it weren't true. 'Where I'm going to live, what I'm going to do. Same old things.' As we were talking about yesterday, in a dim wine bar, your knee touching mine. You lecher.

'Funny you should say that,' responded Joe smartly. 'You know, I've been thinking a lot, since then. What we were talking about − in fact, I was hoping I might see you here. Although I guess' − he glanced towards the door of the courtroom − 'this is hardly the ideal time and place.'

For what? Unless . . .? But, no. Not even Joe Duff could resume the Fate and destiny routine outside an inquest over his dead girlfriend with her husband and his own ex-partner in there to boot . . .

'You know I'm on my own now,' he began.

. . . could he?

'And from what you've told me, you're pretty much at a loose end too.'

I don't believe this, I was thinking. I just don't believe this.

'Look,' he said. 'You'll probably turn me down flat.'

Dead right. I couldn't wait. 'Go on.'

He took a deep breath and stopped playing with the steering wheel. The brown eyes were awash with entreaty. 'It wouldn't suit you to come and work for me for a while, would it?'

'What's so bloody funny?' demanded Joe. 'Look, this may not be the best job offer you've ever had, but even so —'

'No, sorry,' I spluttered. 'Stupid joke.'

I almost wished I could share it with him. Hysteria mounts fatally when there's only you laughing. I hadn't had to exercise such mighty will power since Canon Chasuble left his flies undone. I was blinking away tears as Joe explained — rather huffily — that he'd decided he really needed someone to keep an eye on the work at the castle. Look after the office side of things.

'Why me, for heaven's sake?' I said shakily. 'I'm an actress.'

'You've done lots of other jobs, though, haven't you? You told me. And —'

'No. I mean, thanks very much and all that, but —'

'Things in the pipeline, eh?'

It was his choice of words. Biological diagrams of female tubes swam before me. *Only one little embryo*, I wanted to say, and I nearly started laughing again, but if I had I would have burst into tears. Hysteria cuts two ways.

'No,' I said unsteadily. 'Nothing, exactly, in the pipeline.'

Practically nothing. Certainly not a baby. A speck of spawn. Gone in a trice. I hoped the National Health was as accommodating as Richard said. I could do without explaining this requirement to my friendly bank manager.

'I never thought you'd want the job for ever,' said Joe, misunderstanding my hesitation. 'I was only suggesting it as a stopgap, to tide you over. Because, well, to be honest, Al said she saw you last night, and told me how things stood between you and Oliver. I'd wondered, obviously, that day I came round to the Gatehouse, but . . .'

This, at least, killed any lingering urge to laugh. I shut my eyes. 'Shit,' I said.

'No, don't get me wrong,' said Joe urgently. 'I can see how difficult it must have been. But, truly, I think it's fantastic. You're the best thing that could have happened to the poor bugger. And if you wanted to stay on at the Gatehouse with him . . .'

I opened my eyes. 'I'm not staying another day in the bloody Gatehouse. My car's in the multi-storey with my bag in the boot and I'm going straight home.'

'I suppose it is awkward,' said Joe swiftly. 'With Cathy's mother and that. But look, if you wanted, there's the Stables — up at the castle, I mean. Tatty, but quite habitable. Bunny was going to move in there while —'

'Joe,' I interrupted. 'I am leaving Harecombe for good and all.'

He stared at me. 'But what about Oliver?'

'Oliver?'

'Well — look, why do you think I suggested this job?'

'Out of concern for *Oliver*? Is this some kind of joke?' At least he had the grace to blush. 'Fine time to worry about Oliver now,' I snarled. 'You have an affair with his wife, and now —'

'Affair?' he roared and then glanced guiltily round the empty street before lowering his voice. 'Becca, would you call one night an affair?'

184

'Oh, don't you give me that. Please. I've had it from Oliver. And Alison —'

'One night,' interrupted Joe. 'I'm not denying what happened. Last year. She'd sung . . .'

'At a banquet,' I said frigidly. 'About the only thing I can't do is recite the menu.'

'It was a big function. Important to us,' said Joe. 'And it went like a song. Afterwards, well, it must be the same after a show. You're high as kites. Relief, triumph. We were knocking back the left-over booze and, OK . . . Becca, I'm not proud of what happened.'

Do you know, for a few moments, suppressing all evidence to the contrary, I almost found myself believing him? Of course I could imagine the euphoria. Maybe Joe hadn't, as Oliver claimed, exactly forced the alcohol down her throat, white-slaver style. Maybe they were all drinking together, acting the goat. Like you do . . . The soupy brown eyes would have convinced more cynical hearts than mine.

'If you really want the truth,' he growled, as though this final admission was being dragged out of him, 'I wouldn't have planned for it all to end there. Cathy was — gorgeous. But Al found the bloody earring and all hell broke loose.'

He was a masterly liar, I thought. This last admission would have convinced many a wavering jury. But I'd had time to assemble my case. 'So why,' said the prosecuting counsel, grim-faced, 'if you and Cathy are such distant history, did you creep into Oliver's back garden a fortnight or so ago? Don't tell me you were bringing the champagne for me.'

At least he didn't attempt to lie his way out of this. In fact he looked wary as a cornered rat. 'So I was coming to see Cathy. A bottle of fizz — between friends. That's all.'

'And — purely as a friend — she'd telephoned you.'

'What is this? An inquisition?'

'The day she died,' I continued remorselessly.

'So?' snarled Joe. 'I've yet to learn you can commit adultery down a telephone line.'

185

'And you saw her.'

'What?' shouted Joe, swivelling round to stare at me.

'Well, you must have done recently. You lent her some money, didn't you?'

'Oh shit, that, what did I go telling you that for? Yes, I lent her some cash. A week — two? — before she died. Honestly, she turned up out of the blue on my doorstep and asked if she could borrow a few quid. Only three hundred, for Christ's sake.'

'Three hundred pounds?' I squealed, so shrilly a pigeon pecking at the hot tarmac exploded away in a flurry of winged indignation. '*Only* three hundred?' Only more than I owned in the world at that moment.

'Shut up,' hissed Joe. 'No need to tell the whole world. And no need to mention it to Oliver either.'

'Don't worry,' I said disgustedly, 'I wouldn't dream of it.'

'Look, Becca. You can think what the fuck you want. But I'm telling you I went to bed with Cathy once.'

I sat in prim silence, listening to the heedless buzz of city traffic behind us.

'And believe me,' he added fervently, 'if I could undo a single night of my life, it would be that one. But like Father Xavier used to tell us, there's no un-committing a sin. And no such thing as a sin without consequences.' He grimaced and continued in a bad Emerald Oyle accent: 'It's like dropping a pebble in de Liffey, sonny. Dere's no getting it back, and no way to stop de bluddy ripples spreading.'

I laid a hand across my perfectly flat stomach. The merest ripple, I thought. So small no one will ever notice it before a helpful doctor melts it away.

'Don't talk rubbish,' I said.

'You're obviously not a Catholic,' retorted Joe, more aptly than he knew. Suddenly he swivelled round. 'Hell, they're out.'

The little brown door had opened and Alison was standing on the step, sharp-suited in acid green. Joe tapped the car horn and she stalked down the pavement towards us, like a glossy praying mantis descending on a couple of fat grubs. A short, grey-haired matron followed more slowly.

'So what happened?' said Joe. 'Hey, what's up?'

Alison Laverick strode round to Joe's side of the car, ignoring me. 'Well, I was wrong about there being no great revelations in there,' she snapped. The woman was fizzing, I suddenly realized, with hot, venomous anger. 'God knows why I bothered coming to this fucking charade. They'd got it all worked out. One simple motive topped the list. Cathy had got herself inconveniently pregnant.'

CHAPTER EIGHTEEN

I hadn't fainted since First Form, when passing out in Assembly attracted a cup of tea plus Marie biscuit in the school secretary's office and was thus an accomplishment to be envied. Even then I'd never managed it more than once, but I recognized now, twenty years on, the symptoms. That sensation of tumbling backwards down a drainpipe, the world a bright circle at the top, getting smaller and quieter by the minute.

I remembered as an eleven-year-old thinking triumphantly: So *this* is how you do it, and sinking to my knees. Now, I swallowed and blinked and willed myself back up the drainpipe. I was sitting in the car, so at least I couldn't fall over. In fact, as I groggily focused on Joe and Alison again, it seemed they hadn't even noticed anything amiss. Joe was talking to the plump grey-haired woman, who had joined Alison beside the car. He called her Mrs Laverick. Alison's mother, I thought, and was stupidly pleased with my brain for working this one out. Alison was leaning on the bonnet, drumming her fingers.

'I'd better get back to Pamela,' Mrs Laverick was saying. 'She's in a sad way. The judge was kind enough but . . .'

'Coroner, mother.'

Cathy Langham was pregnant. Just like me. I'd slept with her husband, flirted with her lover . . . Whatever I did, I was thinking wildly, whatever happened to me, it seemed Cathy, like Kilroy, had got there first.

'But you could tell the judge was getting impatient,' Mrs

Laverick continued imperturbably, 'when Pamela was going on about all Cathy's bits and bobs she reckons she can't find and –'

'He swept that right out of court,' said Alison sharply. 'Oliver told them he hadn't noticed anything missing and everyone could see Pamela was hysterical. She just kept repeating her daughter wouldn't do such a thing, as though the record had stuck.'

'Alison!' said her mother, tutting. 'Poor Pamela was shocked to the core, as well she might be. Hearing about the baby like that. That could have been her grandchild. No wonder she's in a state. And as for poor Oliver . . .'

Oh God. Oliver. What kind of a state might he be in? Learning he'd nearly been a father?

'I must go and find him,' I said, fumbling for the door handle. My brain seemed to be rolling loose round my skull. Fortunately, no one was looking my way.

'Suicide then,' Joe was saying. 'Straightforward –'

'No,' said Alison and, one foot on the pavement, I froze.

If she jumped . . .

'They always try and avoid saying suicide. Something about taking her life while the balance of her mind was disturbed.'

This time I did lever myself out of the car, and felt better for standing upright. 'Where's Oliver?' I said.

Alison looked at me with no trace of our one-time camaraderie. 'Your *cousin*,' she said with cold emphasis, 'is in the keeping of an elderly female Rottweiler I assume is your *aunt*.'

Give us a break, I was thinking. If I could apologize, I would. But hardly here and now.

'That's no way to speak about Lady Berisford,' said her mother, smiling and nodding at me.

'She was lecturing Oliver as though he were a mentally retarded child,' retorted Alison. 'And dismissing the rest of the world – me included, when I dared approach – as though we were deaf servants. There they are now.'

Sure enough, Oliver and Constance Berisford were on the

189

step of the courthouse. Oliver looked washed out. I raised a hand in greeting. Neither acknowledged it. Terrific. I turned back to the car briefly. ''Bye,' I said and set off up the cul-de-sac.

'Becca,' called Joe, raising himself at the wheel to look over the windscreen. 'Think about the job. You've got my card, haven't you?' The look Alison was giving me would have disabled a tank. So I pretended not to have heard, and walked on with a wave of farewell. 'Ask Oliver what he thinks,' Joe bellowed.

I reached Oliver just as a tall, dark-suited man emerged and claimed Constance's attention with gravely outstretched hand. Oliver dangled behind her like an abandoned puppet. I grabbed his sleeve.

'Alison says . . .' I began in a furious undertone, then collected myself enough to continue more compassionately: 'Oliver, did you know Cathy was having a baby?'

'Yes – *no*,' stuttered Oliver. Two policemen walked past us with sympathetically lowered eyes. 'She wasn't having a bloody baby.'

'Oliver,' bellowed Constance. 'Mr Marshall has come out to talk to you. Giles . . .'

She just looked through me. Well, I guess the last thing a man needs at the inquest on his wife is a one-time *bit on the side*. Let alone a pregnant bit on the side. So I hung back and tried to blend into the scenery.

I gathered the tall dark suit was the Coroner himself. I couldn't catch all the words, but enough to realize he and Constance were on the same dining circuit. Trust her.

On the other side of the road, Alison climbed into Joe's car. It purred off and her mother bustled back towards us. At the same moment, a party of camera-laden Japanese tourists rounded the corner, evidently having stumbled off the historic Oxford trail. They milled up the dull little cul-de-sac like puzzled sheep.

'Good idea,' the man was saying, nodding, as Constance rabbited determinedly on.

I leaned against the wall and willed her to shut up and let me grab Oliver, until I realized she was talking about Oliver's plans for the future. Something about research.

'. . . Renaissance choral music,' she was saying. 'I'm encouraging him to go to Italy for a spell.'

Encouraging him? What had inspired this *volte face*? Had I misheard? I wished I could hush the chattering of the bewildered tourists who had now reached me and were flapping their maps.

'How sensible,' the man said, nodding.

'I have friends in Tuscany,' said Constance. She would. 'With whom he could perhaps stay for the summer. But a longer-term arrangement in Florence itself would be preferable. As Oliver and I have just been discussing.'

Oliver looked as capable of discussion as a tailor's dummy, standing there while ideas were pinned and fitted on him.

'Splendid,' said the suit. 'When do you plan to go, Oliver?'

Behind them, a thin figure materialized in the doorway. Dressed in grey and red-eyed with tears, Pamela Metcalfe looked more like a sad little mouse than ever. There was a policewoman holding her arm, and Mrs Laverick now marched up to support the other one. Oh Lord, so-called cousin or not, I was probably the last person Mrs Metcalfe wanted to see now. Not easy, when you're five foot ten and fair to melt into a party of Japanese camera clickers, but I did my best.

She didn't look towards me, though. She paused on the step, glancing from Oliver to Constance, like a starving gerbil hoping for a friendly nut to be chucked her way.

No nuts were forthcoming. Oliver studied his feet and Constance dismissed her with a smile of regally glacial sympathy before resuming her conversation.

Then Pamela obviously recognized the man in the suit, and her face darkened. I feared she might actually charge over and accost the Coroner. However, Mrs Laverick whispered in her ear and, with the help of the policewoman, steered her off down the road. Words like 'travesty' and 'miscarriage' drifted

191

back to me. I must say, even in the midst of my own anxieties. I felt sorry for Pam Metcalfe. Sorry that circumstances prevented me hurrying after them and at least showing her some kindness. Can't have been fun, not *fitting* with Constance's notions of family.

At length, the suit walked back into the courthouse, and I stalked over to rejoin Oliver. 'A decent chap,' Constance was saying. 'No nonsense. You were lucky to get him today.'

It occurred to me as I drew closer that Constance Berisford, despite the bracing tone, looked haggard. Years older. Jet lag, I supposed. It seemed to take her a moment or two to focus on me. And there was no trace of the grateful smile I was expecting.

'Ah, Becca,' she said. 'Still here?'

'I asked her to come back,' said Oliver. 'Thanks, Becca.'

'Good. Then perhaps she'll be kind enough to run you home. That won't inconvenience you too much, will it?'

Not so much a deaf servant. More a minor helper at the Conservative garden party. I could hardly expect fulsome tributes for my baby-sitting services with Oliver standing beside us, but even so . . .

'Although I know you'll be anxious to return to London as soon as you can,' she added.

Perhaps she was just too tired for niceties, but this, honestly, sounded less a social pleasantry than my marching orders. It seemed my usefulness was at an end. Troop dismissed. Bloody hell.

Whereupon the CO – having established where my car was parked – observed that St Benedict's Hall lay on our route home. She didn't wait for the lift to be offered, just hitched her handbag to the approved queenly angle in the crook of the elbow, and led the way out into St Aldate's.

'What happened?' I said to Oliver as we followed in her wake, frustratedly aware that she could hear everything.

'It was a madhouse,' he spat. 'They'd crawled all over Cathy's life – and they thought they knew everything. Saying the stupidest bloody things . . .'

We paused to cross the road.

'And *Alison*,' he went on furiously, 'was the craziest of the lot. I couldn't believe it. She's always been so kind. She was standing there, telling them about that afternoon when she found Cathy up the tower as though she really had stopped Cathy from jumping. Going on about how suicidal Cathy was because of the job falling through. But Alison knew she wasn't. Surely . . .'

'Al didn't believe Cathy ever meant to kill herself,' I agreed bemusedly. 'She said so to me. She —'

'Miss Laverick gave her evidence like a sensible woman,' pronounced Constance, without turning her head. She strode across the road, and a bus trundled between her and us.

'Oliver — the baby?' I whispered, but Oliver was already talking.

'Pamela never stopped looking at me. Her eyes are just like Cathy's. Isn't it funny? She's such a withered old stick, I'd never noticed before. But today it was as though Cathy was there, staring at me. Oh God . . .'

'Hush,' I murmured, putting an arm round him and shepherding his lanky frame across the road. Comforting this six-foot adult as though he were a wretched, confused child. A child with Oliver's eyes. A little boy, I found myself thinking, with Oliver's eyes . . .

Hell, no. I mustn't even think like that. This wasn't a child inside me at all. It was a couple of cells. A few alien dots with no right of tenure.

'Come on, you two,' roared Constance, and we hurried forward. She paused on the pavement to address us. Pep talk to the troops. 'We'll have no more post-mortems.' Even then, I couldn't help thinking was a typically ill-chosen turn of phrase. 'It's finished. I've told Oliver he must put it behind him. What's done is done. However sad and regrettable. All we can do is try to forget it. And get on with our lives as best we can.'

Almost exactly my own long-ago advice to Oliver. So

innocently, so clumsily offered. But now I found myself applying the brusque little homily to myself. *However sad and regrettable — forget it — get on with life* . . . Translated as: one quick trip to the clinic and Bob's your uncle. Oh God.

Oliver and I subsided into matching flattened silences all the way back to the carpark. The journey was enlivened by Constance machine-gunning instructions at Oliver: passports, possessions, addresses, blah, blah, blah. You had to hand it to Constance. She never lost the ability to surprise. In fact, you would think, I reflected rebelliously as we finally pulled up at the side door of the Lodgings, that Oliver's going to Italy was a scheme entirely of her creation. She did not invite us in. She did thank me. For — stiff nod — *everything*. If I'd had a chauffeur's cap, I dare say I might have raised it.

I watched her unlock the door in the wall. Watched it shut with a bang after her.

'My God,' said Oliver, slumping back into the passenger seat. 'Let's go home.'

But I turned the engine off and he glanced round in surprise. 'Oliver,' I said gently. The drive had given me time to muster a few shreds of tact. To remind myself that if this had come as a shock to me, it must have been a bloody sight more distressing for Oliver. 'Cathy was pregnant?'

'Yes,' said Oliver flatly. 'That is — no . . . Shit, where does this thing go?'

I took the seat belt from Oliver's limp fingers and clicked it into place. 'Oliver? You're not making sense.'

But he was. I was already guessing exactly what he meant.

'She — had it *terminated*.' His voice was the barest thread, almost lost in the rumble of traffic. 'That's what they called it. Euphemisms. As if — a different name makes it better.'

Three youths in academic gowns staggered past the car, ties askew, wine bottles waving. I recognized post-exam euphoria, the certainty that life could never be so ghastly again, and envied their innocence.

'Cathy had had an abortion,' I said. I didn't ask why. Silly question. Because she didn't want to have a baby, that's why. Just like me. Even in the abortion clinic, Cathy was there first.

One of the youths crashed against the wing-mirror. I jumped violently, but Oliver didn't even notice. The boy grinned an apology and reeled off towards the college gates.

'When?' I said.

'Sunday. The day before — she died. Private joint in London. She'd told me she was going up to see her singing teacher.'

Oliver studied the back of his hand, flexing his fingers. His knuckles were white. 'You know what she'd always said, Becca? When — when I'd talked about our having children? Cathy always said she wasn't going to be like my mother. And wreck — her career for a child. Isn't that,' he suddenly burst out, 'just too bloody ironical? She did it for the sake of her career, for that lousy Wessex Opera Company. And she gets back from the hospital to find a letter telling her it's fallen through. Killing — a baby for the sake of a non-existent job.'

'It's — not *killing*,' I said faintly.

'No? What would you call it? Shit, when she told me what she'd done, I almost didn't know whether to laugh or cry.'

I'd been watching a piece of paper flap across the road in the draught from a passing car, repeating to myself that killing didn't enter into it. That Oliver was only talking like this because he was upset . . . Now I swivelled round to stare at him.

'When she — when *Cathy* told you?' I said dazedly. 'I thought it had only just come out now? Mrs Laverick was saying how shocked Cathy's mother was . . .'

Oliver shifted in his seat and began muttering that, well, yes, possibly he should have told Pam. As the police had suggested to him. But the woman had been in such a state and who was to know they'd make such a song and dance about it in there today —

'Oliver,' I said, cutting ruthlessly across these garbled self-justifications. 'Are you saying you knew all along Cathy had been pregnant?'

195

'I *didn't* know she was pregnant,' he snapped. 'That's the whole bloody point. She didn't tell me until it was too late.'

'But you knew before she died,' I retorted, my voice rising. 'You knew Cathy had had an abortion. The police knew. And you never even *mentioned* it to me?'

'Why the hell should I?' he exclaimed. 'It's ghastly. I didn't want anyone to know. Becca, why are you looking at me like that. Why should it matter to you?'

Why indeed? I took a grip on the steering wheel and, I hoped myself. 'At the very least,' I said carefully, 'I would have thought the baby — the abortion — might go some way to explaining what Cathy did.'

'That's what they claimed,' he snorted. 'Idiots. For them, it explained everything. Depressed after the operation; because of the job.' Suddenly he groaned. 'Oh Becca, why didn't she tell me first? Before she'd got rid of our child?'

I shut my eyes and told myself Cathy and I had nothing in common. Nothing. That our plights were entirely different. 'Maybe because,' I whispered, 'Cathy was afraid that if she told you there was a baby on the way, you might have tried to persuade her to have it.'

'Of course I would,' Oliver exclaimed. 'But not if she really didn't want it. Honestly, Becca. I'd have understood. Well, I'd have tried to understand. Maybe even . . .'

Maybe even what? Helped her to organize the operation? Was that what he couldn't quite bring himself to say? But I didn't need help. I would manage on my own, thank you very much.

'What's the point?' said Oliver desolately. 'She just went off and did it. I don't even know where she got the money from. It wasn't from me.'

I caught my breath. 'Money?'

'That all came out, too. I didn't know about that before today. I'd never considered it. That she might have had to pay, I mean. But they had the bloody bill in court. It was in her handbag. Do you know what it costs? To kill a baby?'

196

I'd been wondering for the past two hours, but I could hardly tell Oliver that.

'There's no mention of killing of course,' he said contemptuously. 'It's all anaesthetist's fees, and pills and meals . . .'

Now I realized I'd already learned the answer.

'. . . and Cathy never had that sort of cash. She was always running out of money. She always had to come to me. But,' he added fiercely, 'I didn't tell them that in court. I didn't even look surprised.'

'Three hundred pounds,' I enunciated slowly.

Only three hundred quid . . . Shit . . . what did I go telling you that for . . .?

I wanted to scream. To tell Oliver exactly where Cathy had obtained her three hundred quid. But . . . *No need to mention it to Oliver . . .* As Joe bloody Duff had said.

'That's right,' said Oliver, beyond wondering how I knew. 'Three hundred pounds for a tiny, six-week life.'

The size of a pebble? A pebble in the Liffey . . .

Suddenly Oliver let out a howl. The agony of weeks exploding, shockingly, in one animal wail. 'Three hundred quid — to get rid of it.'

But it was his words which made me recoil. The actual words triggered the memory, *Get rid of it.* God Almighty, *Alison* knew too, I thought. She must have done. I could hear her now, quarrelling with Joe in the castle, unaware of me, screaming at him: *You got rid of it, didn't you? Well, didn't you?*

He had. Joe had indeed got rid of it. And said to me — Jesus, what kind of a heartless monster was he? — that he'd be happy if he never heard Cathy's name again.

Oliver was convulsed with harsh sobs. 'Cathy didn't kill herself . . . whatever those madmen think. But she bloody well killed our baby.'

Our baby? Oh Oliver . . .

I unfastened my seat belt and stuck an arm, awkwardly, round his heaving shoulders. Would it comfort him to know it wasn't his child? Would it hell. Besides, who could say?

Six-week-old foetuses aren't issued with labels of provenance. But Joe Duff was happy enough to cough up the cash. To get rid of it. *No need to mention it to Oliver.* The lying, cheating, selfish bastard.

'Sorry, sorry,' Oliver gasped. 'Be all right – in a minute.'

Cry all you want, you poor bugger. I was thinking. And I wondered how Alison had found out this time. She must have kept her mouth shut in the hope of sparing Oliver exactly this agony. No wonder she was angry when the facts came out in court today. At least no one had suggested Joe was responsible.

Oliver straightened himself. Shrugged off my arm. 'Didn't mean all that,' he mumbled. 'I mean – Oh God, I suppose I've got to say – now – Cathy – did kill herself.' He gave a long shuddering sigh, as though throwing off some huge weight. 'Nothing will bring her back. Or the child. It's finished. But at least it wasn't my fault, that innocent little thing ending up in an abortionist's dustbin.'

'Shut up,' I breathed. 'Please. Don't . . .'

But Oliver didn't hear me. 'What did it ever do,' he concluded bitterly, 'to deserve that fate?'

The St Benedict's clock began tolling the hour. Two o'clock. The same clock which had measured the essays and tutorials of my undergraduate life. The same clock which struck ten as I had inveigled myself, so triumphantly, into the ball here. Into Oliver's tragedy. Oliver's bed . . .

He was settling back in his seat. 'It's all over,' he said. 'I still can't quite believe it. Finished.'

Maybe it was over for him. But I finally, bleakly, recognized it wasn't over for me. In fact it was only just beginning. I fastened my seat belt again and switched on the ignition.

I might be in the same plight as Cathy Langham. Pregnant by a man I wasn't married to, career at risk, but that's where the parallel stopped. The paths – Cathy's and mine – parted here.

I adjusted the mirror. At least I could look myself in the eye again.

Cathy Langham had killed her inconvenient — but innocent — baby.

I flicked the indicator lever grimly. The road ahead was horribly clear.

No way, I now realized, could I do the same.

INTERVAL

The setting sun is hovering flirtatiously beside the Lady Tower as we troop out of the dark theatre — at long last — for the dinner interval. Even the weather reminds me of that glorious summer of two years ago. So warm, so cloudless, so un-English, dammit.

Nevertheless, you can spot the old Glyndebourne hands. They are shaking out damp-proof rugs, scissoring open chairs and braying for matches for their dinky wind-proof lamps. As if one needed lamps on this golden evening. They are also the ones regretting, loudly, the lack of a lake for chilling the Sancerre.

My dear, don't you find these cold bags simply *freeze* wine to *death*?

I feel I should apologize for having filled the moat with daffodil bulbs instead of water.

But I notice, as I quit our party to cut across the courtyard, that some enterprising wine chillers have made do with the fountain dish. Several bottle-necks protrude from the clear water. Retrieving them is the problem. The green boy's fish spouts a healthy jet of water now, and warm gusts of breeze spray it with haphazard generosity across the guffawing dinner jackets.

My work, I would like to inform them. I personally cleaned up that little statue. I personally located the stopcock, just behind the tower door. If I didn't personally dredge decades of mud and dead leaves from the bowl, then it was at least I who caused it to be done. But, of course, I don't say anything of the kind. Just give them and the spray a wide berth and hurry across to the stable block.

The Stables — from the outside — look much the same. Prettily clock-towered as ever was. The interior, however, is far from the dingy dump I once knew. Now it's sprigged and spruced fit for *Country Homes and Interiors*. Of course that was always the intention; the final stage of Joe Duff's great plan. When the castle had been transformed into his wonderful restaurant and hotel, the Stables would be converted into an equally luxurious dwelling for the owner. Well so it has been, in the end. And how. But not for Joe Duff.

I open the door and walk in. Inside, barely a wall remains where it was. But young Linda has made herself quite at home. Everything's fine, she assures me abstractedly. She is watching a video on the matt-black miracle of micro-chippery which sits, funnily enough — in this transformed palace — exactly where our old Bakelite monster of a telly used to. The screen is heaving with passion.

'Better than cruddy Shakespeare,' she tells me.

I'm inclined to agree. I promise I will drop in some supper for her on my way back to the second half. She glances up from the screen only long enough to tell me she likes my dress (in a voice which suggests women of my age should know better) and reminds me that she doesn't like fancy muck. I promise to do my best.

As I walk from the courtyard over the close-mown lawn to rejoin the party, which is comfortably encamped by the ha-ha, I wonder if there will be anything to tempt Linda's conservative palate in the mountain of cardboard boxes beside Joe. We may be less grandly damasked and porcelained than our Glyndebourne neighbours but, with Joe catering, I'll bet we're going to eat a lot better.

He is already playing Mine Host. His favourite role. To which end, he has shed his dinner jacket and rolled up the dress shirt-sleeves. Typical. The bow tie will follow any minute. His face positively shines with hungry anticipation — no one enjoys his cooking more than Joe Duff himself — as he unwraps and arranges and scatters pepper over one delight after another.

Constance Berisford is Mole on this picnic, and exclaims noisily as each dish is unveiled. Look! Breast of duck, is it? And quail — stuffed with what? Boned and filled with muscat raisins? Michael, isn't that simply miraculous? Sir Michael amiably agrees but is too thin to play the gourmet convincingly.

A flight of starlings wheels noisily in the clear sky above. Below, clean-looking sheep nibble the park beyond the ha-ha in a businesslike fashion.

'Isn't this just too heavenly?' demands Constance. She is ensconced on a folded cardigan, silver-sandalled feet planted inelegantly apart, with a large glass of wine in her hand. Then she glances with obvious wistfulness towards the castle. 'Such a shame Oliver can't be here to enjoy it with us.'

Sipping my own wine, I forbear to remind her that Oliver would be unlikely to appreciate this fancy muck any more than my Linda. I just smile and nod. After our long estrangement, I am surprised to realize how fond I feel of Constance Berisford. At this distance in time, I can acknowledge that, loving Oliver as she did, Constance must have suffered more than any of us. Yet she has bounced back undaunted, if not unscathed. I admire that. She is advising Alison now, to sample the lobster tartlets.

Al, to my surprise, accepts one. 'Fish is a great protein source,' explains Ms Vegetarian to me.

Pregancy has mellowed Alison. Filled out her cheeks to a becoming rosy pink. Even her hair curls these days. I doubt if she's four months gone but she's already swapped the sharp suits for billowing smocks. She is kneeling on a corner of the rug like a milkmaid. I wonder how pregnant she actually looks under the frills. Funny, I did my damnedest to hide my condition and managed to do so for the best part of seven months. Alison has been advertising hers since conception.

Now she is looking up and beams, radiant as a baby-food advert, at someone behind me.

'But soft,' hisses Henry into my ear. 'Here walks our Petty Princeling.'

I turn, Richard is hurrying distractedly across the lawn towards us. He is quite as handsome as ever. The frosting of silver at his perfectly groomed temples is a master-stroke. He is eye-catchingly clad in dinner jacket of dull blue velvet.

'Noël Coward, would you say?' murmurs Henry. 'Or Dandini? I warned him. Not blue, I said. Everyone will think it's an offcut of the bloody curtains — but would he listen?'

Richard kisses Alison, then Constance — then me. 'All well, darlings?'

This is a cue for us all to express our appreciation of the evening so far. Joe dishes compliments as lavishly as he does food. The smooth toad. Shakespeare, he had whispered to me earlier, reminded him of Wagner without the music.

Henry picks up plate and fork with the finesse of a surgeon, 'I'll say one thing for you, pet,' he observes almost absent-mindedly as he munches. 'Your taste in men has been wonder-fully Catholic.'

'Shut up,' I growl, and add: 'Your mayonnaise is dripping.'

It isn't, but the risk to his pleated shirt is enough to distract Henry's attention. His taste is immaculate in every detail: cream dinner jacket, a single rosebud, silk socks. Beside him, tongue lolling in the heat, sits Miranda, his labrador. With his receding grey hair and gold-rimmed half-moon specs, Henry looks your classic English country gent. Maybe he should have been an actor after all.

'No, no,' murmurs Richard to Joe. 'I simply couldn't swallow a morsel. Not yet. *Impossible.*'

This last pronounced *à la française.*

'That boy,' pronounces Henry, dabbing his thin lips with a very large, very white handkerchief as he watches Richard retreat across the lawn, bowing left and right, 'is fast becoming more camp than me.'

'*Impossible*,' I murmur, then regret it because Henry's smile glints maliciously in my direction.

'Do you know, I think I must propose a toast?' he says, but his glass is empty and he has to look round for the bottle. Thereby he loses the initiative. Joe, one of life's career celebrators, has caught the word 'toast' and has already raised his own glass high.

'The Queen, the actors, the weather, the test match, ourselves — and Absent Friends!'

Never short of causes for rejoicing, Joe Duff. And he roars this compendium with such gusto that several diners on surrounding rugs raise their glasses along with us.

'Absent friends?' murmurs Henry, still smiling in a distinctly unsettling way. 'Who on earth can he be talking about?'

'Bunny,' I reply promptly. 'Old friend. Married and went to live in New Zealand. Joe always drinks to him.'

'And to whom are the rest of us raising our glasses?' sighs Henry. 'Those absent from this picnic — or from this world? The quick or the dead? But I mustn't pre-empt my speech.'

'Speech?' I echo, uneasily. 'What, at the end of the play?'

Joe, I note, has now rolled across to one of the parties who joined in our toast. He is bearing, shoulder high, a plate of delicacies, obviously feeling their own provisions are inadequate. Joe adores feeding people. Left to his own devices this restaurateur would be bankrupt within weeks. Lucky for him he had Bunny. I only wish I could claim I had contributed more to his present prosperity.

It is a minute or two before Henry replies. He is watching Joe's philanthropy with a benevolent eye.

'Henry?' I growl.

He starts, as though interrupted from a pleasant reverie. 'But, darling, of course I must say a few words if called upon,' he murmurs plaintively.

Joe returns to our party with an empty plate, a happy grin and a lipsticked kiss on one swarthy cheek. Henry smiles gracious approval while adding, *sotto voce*, 'It's almost in the nature of giving thanks for a miracle.'

'Please, Henry. Can't we simply be thankful in silence? Can't we enjoy the present and consign the past to where it belongs?'

'But it lives on in us,' he declares. 'We wouldn't be here otherwise, would we?'

Satisfied that he has seriously impaired any pleasure I might take in the second half of the play, Henry now ignores me and beams round the assembled company.

'Isn't that right, loves?' he says, popping a lobster tartlet into Miranda's waiting mouth. 'Whoever would have guessed we'd all end up here like this, tonight? Is it Fate?'

'Ah, Fate,' nods Joe, raising his glass again and smiling first at Alison, then at me, in quite the old, soulful way.

Rubbish, I want to retort. But I don't. I'm not quite as robustly unsuperstitious as I used to be.

'Fate,' continues Henry thoughtfully, 'with a not inconsiderable helping hand from me.'

I agree with that at any rate. Henry Blayne himself has played a more active role than any formless force of destiny. We've all danced to Henry's piping. And who brought him in?

Me, of course.

I raise my glass to Joe.

'Fate,' I whisper.

'That strain again . . .'

or

LOVE'S LABOUR'S LOSING

CHAPTER NINETEEN

The Stables
Harecombe Castle
15 November

Dear Oliver . . .

Fifteen minutes of solid concentration and all I had achieved
was two words. Dear Oliver . . . Why did I find even the
shortest note to him so impossible to write? Crisp demands to
suppliers, charming confirmations to clients, neatly totted-up
invoices: all these I could bash out so swiftly the ancient
Remington knitted its innards in panic. But Oliver?

Dear Oliver,
  *Hope you are well and not eating too much spaghetti — and
  by the way I'm five months pregnant with your child . . .*

Joke.

My condition was strictly between me and the medics —
and the longer it could stay that way, the better.

Oh, I had thought about telling Oliver. For at least five
minutes . . . No, really. From that first bleak moment, sitting
in the car outside St Benedict's Hall, when I recognized I was
going to have a baby instead of a sensible, tidy abortion, I
had begun wondering whether to tell Oliver. By the time we
got back to the Gatehouse, however, all of half an hour later,
I had assembled a string of compelling arguments against.

For a start (I argued) I didn't strictly *know* I was pregnant.

It would be downright cruel to the man, battered and vulnerable as he was, to panic him with unconfirmed fears. Anyway, even if I were, I couldn't see what bringing him in on the act would achieve. Marriage? Sure, I could imagine someone as old-fashioned as Oliver feeling duty bound to stiffen the upper lip and do the decent thing.

The very idea made me swerve momentarily into the path of a juggernaut, which honked a protest. Oliver glanced round in alarm. I smiled back reassuringly. Unlike Oliver, I was not old-fashioned. Not even for a second did I contemplate hustling him down the aisle. That way lay certain misery and madness.

It might solve trivial quibbles like how I was going to feed, house and support the infant — and myself, come to that — but money, paradoxically, struck me as yet another good reason for *not* telling Oliver. When I refused the offer of his hand, he would undoubtedly feel impelled to press money on me. No way was I going to accept that either. Getting pregnant had been my fault, fair and square. It may take two to tango, but there was no question who had choreographed that dance. Why should Oliver pick up the tab?

This wasn't a baby, you see, it was a problem to solve. And it was my problem. I'd manage. Such a big brave girl. Ma would be proud of me. Oh Lord - *Mother*. She'd have to know eventually, I thought, zooming round a tractor within inches of death. But not yet. First I must get myself sorted out.

I turned off the main road into the lane resolving that I would work like crazy for the next nine months. Earn myself a comfortable egg, so to speak, to line the nest.

Just how I was going to earn this nest egg was less clear. One of the most trying features of the actor's life for me had always been the passivity required. You can make scads of admirable resolutions about working your socks off. Keeping them is another matter. It's not in your hands. An actor can only wait by the telephone for the offers to roll in — which they never bloody well do when you need 'em.

210

But I was not going to let that deter me. Maybe it was time to find what my boring grown-up brothers would insist on calling A Proper Job. So, unemployment was up, so what? I was prepared to do anything, within reason. As Joe Duff had said earlier today, I'd done plenty of jobs in my time. As *Joe Duff* had said . . .

The germ of an idea began to sprout.

Dear Oliver,

Well I daresay you're enjoying warmer weather in Florence than we are in Harecombe. A wind worthy of a Wuthering Heights soundtrack is whistling under my office door. I hope you're . . .

Hope you're what? Well? Enjoying yourself?

A fresh sheet of paper had gone into the Remington. But it brought no fresh inspiration. Even the most conventional wishes for Oliver's health and wellbeing paralysed my typing fingers. Dammit, I knew he wasn't particularly well or happy.

Oliver was an irregular correspondent, but his near-illegible scrawls had made clear that the people with whom he was lodging (an Italian university professor and his English wife) were alcoholic, chain-smoking lunatics. (They sounded just my type.) What's more, the food was greasy, the roads lethal for a cyclist and the choir at the girls' academy where he was teaching tone-deaf.

Oh yes, Constance had managed to wangle some part-time post at an exclusively small educational establishment for her nephew, providing him with a little extra pocket money and plenty of free time to pursue his research. At the time I had found myself wishing, sourly, that I was blessed with a helpful aunt to sort out my life for me. As it was, I'd had to make my own arrangements.

These had taken the form, once I'd waved goodbye to Oliver at the Gatehouse, of driving a few hundred yards up the lane and then stopping to fish from my handbag Joe Duff's business card. I studied it thoughtfully before restarting

211

the engine. I didn't drive home, however. First, I took a small diversion via Harecombe Castle, where I peered, with the hammiest air of casual indifference, into the windows of the stable block, and then I continued back into Oxford.

A piece of cardboard stuck in the window of Unit 14B of a small industrial estate announced the nesting place of Flying Duck. I took a deep breath, knocked on the door and, when a young man in chef's hat opened it, announced I'd come to see Joe Duff.

'About the job,' I explained when Joe himself appeared behind the young chef.

'What?' exclaimed Joe.

He looked so blankly incredulous I began to wonder if I'd imagined the whole thing. He motioned me into the kitchen, however, and told the chef, distractedly, that he might as well pack up for the afternoon. That he would lock up now, but tomorrow morning . . .

While they talked fishmongers, I inspected with interest the premises of Flying Duck. There was decidedly temporary look to the place: cheap shelving, more wooden boxes than cupboards. Later I was to learn that Joe had only intended renting the unit for a matter of weeks. Everything was tidy however. The giant steel cookers and sinks were all scrubbed down. It felt like a railway station in the lull between rush hours; the place almost echoed with frantic traffic recently departed. A smell of disinfectant mingled, not unpleasantly, with a rich beefy broth aroma from a lone cauldron glugging on one stove. A glowing violet bulb fried a large fly noisily as the young chef departed with a cheery salute and a slammed door. A butcher's block was piled high with papers and ring files. Joe bundled them into a pile and motioned me to a stool.

'Now then,' he said. 'What's all this?'

'You offered me a job,' I said brightly. 'You said to ring you. Since I was here, I thought I'd call in person.'

'But I gathered . . .' he began. 'Well, from what Al overheard this morning . . . isn't Oliver going to Italy?'

'Flying Monday, all being well. What's that got to do with it?'

There was a chilling pause. Joe wandered away and turned down the gas under the cauldron before saying awkwardly, 'You know, it's not much of a job. Not for someone like you. Answering letters, phone calls, keeping an eye on the builders.'

'Sounds perfect,' I said — and God did I mean it.

To me it spelled not just a regular income but somewhere to live, too. I didn't mention that I'd already been up to the stable block virtually measuring for curtains — well, he'd suggested I could live there, hadn't he? Tatty maybe, but it was a home offering fresh country air and an escape from curious London friends. This job was the answer to a maiden's prayer if, like me, the maiden chanced to be pregnant, homeless and unemployed.

'Surely not,' said Joe. 'You'd be bored out of your skull.'

He'd changed his mind. My so-brilliant plan was just — if I hadn't felt so wickedly disappointed I might have laughed — a castle in the air, no sooner glimpsed than it was melting away.

'I'm never bored,' I said, trying not to sound too pathetic. I wasn't going to plead. Not with Joe Duff.

'I never really expected you to take it on. I shouldn't have asked you.'

I swallowed a lump of tears. 'You've offered it to someone else. Well, never mind . . .'

'Don't be daft,' said Joe with a touch of impatience. 'Since this lunchtime?'

My spirits rocketed up again. Pregnancy, I later came to realize, can have that effect: hormones transforming the sleepiest suburban commuter line of a personality into the whitest-knuckled of emotional roller coasters. 'So what about it?'

'Well . . .' said Joe.

Months later, I would still blush hotly when I recalled the rest of that conversation.

I had not scrupled to calculate what I thought was a fair salary with accommodation thrown in. But Joe, recovering from the surprise, offered more. Which I accepted without a qualm. I even saw a poetic justice in the arrangement. If this pig could dish out hundreds of pounds to abort inconvenient bastards then I, I reasoned, was a positively worthy cause.

And, yes, Joe supposed I could live in the Stables. In fact, it would suit him — now he came to think about it — to have someone on site, as Bunny had once planned to be. Joe Duff sounded keener by the minute, only checking himself to warn me that, ultimately, when Harecombe Castle Hotel was ready for business, the plan was for the builders to move into the Stables and transform the block into a decent home for himself. But that would be next year some time . . .

I suppressed a triumphant laugh, and told him crisply that I could accept the job only for a strictly limited period. Until March.

'Well, if you want,' said Joe. 'See how it goes, eh? If your feeling change by March . . .'

The only change in feelings I was likely to experience was the onset of premature labour pains. The baby was due (according to my own, naturally precise, calculations) on the eighteenth of that month.

'Come the spring,' I said airily, 'I'm planning, well, a certain reorganization of my life. But until then I find myself with a gap to fill.'

'Oh *right*,' said Joe, and he sounded, all at once, alarmingly enlightened. His face split into what I can only describe as a knowing leer. 'Seems a bloody long time. Is that what her ladyship considers a decent interval, then?'

'I beg your pardon?'

'Al told me she heard Oliver's aunt virtually ordering him out of the country.'

'Well, hardly,' I said. 'I mean, Constance is a bit high-handed but . . .'

'I'd have credited Constance Berisford with more sense. It's like something out of a Victorian novel. Meeting you was the best thing that could possibly have happened to her precious nephew. She should be bloody grateful to you. As for banishing the poor bugger abroad just because she's afraid of what people might say . . .'

Was that what he thought? Blimey.

'Keeping up *appearances*.' Joe spat the word out disgustedly. 'My mum wore a Woolworth's wedding ring for thirty years for the sake of bloody *appearances*.'

I suppressed a pithy retort about Constance Berisford's cock-eyed views on appearances. If Constance had only acted in a manner befitting an aunt I would never have got into this mess.

'I'm surprised Oliver didn't tell her to get stuffed,' said Joe. 'Al told me she was laying down the law like nobody's business. Where he was going, what he was going to do —'

'I think getting away is exactly what Oliver needs,' I said stoutly. 'And so does he.'

Not that you would have guessed this, I admit, from Oliver's face when we had parted.

'Oliver, you do *want* to go to Italy, don't you?' I had to ask. Any change in his plans would throw a fatal spanner into mine, so I was relieved when he snapped back that of course he did. But I rather got the impression he was regarding the trip like a visit to the dentist. Necessary and ultimately beneficial but hardly to be relished. Typical man, I thought. His aunt unexpectedly approves the idea, so he begins to toy with second thoughts. No wonder I had blithely promised to write to him. I would've promised to pay his airfare just so long as it got him out of the way.

'At least you'll have him back soon,' said Joe, clearly thinking he was bolstering my flagging morale. 'March will be here before you know it.'

I choked back a derisive laugh. Why disillusion him? If Joe Duff was dumb enough to think I would take a job at Harecombe Castle just to wait patiently for Oliver's return — a latter-day chatelaine, stitching tapesteries, as it were, while her knight went off to the Crusades — then that was fine by me. Saved me the trouble of inventing another story. The real reason, I thought grimly, would emerge in its own good time . . .

'. . . and until then,' concluded Joe, 'Oliver's loss is my gain. I just hope you won't be lonely, stuck out at Harecombe on your own. Still, I'll be coming over all the time.'

I'll bet he would, the lecherous bastard. 'Don't worry,' I said sharply. 'I won't be lonely.'

After all, I wouldn't be entirely on my own. When I finally climbed back in my car and waved goodbye to Joe, I had looked down at my stomach and whispered experimentally, 'We won't be lonely, will we, kid?' It felt even dafter than talking to the canary.

Harecombe Castle
27 November

Dear Oliver,
   Well, here we are, nearly December . . .

A week and a half later, and I still hadn't managed the letter. I'd finished a pile of invoices, and was grittily determined to cross item 6, *Write Oliver*, off my pending list.

   . . . and the pace of progress on the castle means I can understand for the first time why your average cathedral took three hundred years to complete . . .

Ha bloody ha. I'd made this joke in a batch of letters I'd written recently to friends in London, but it was unlikely to amuse Oliver. He'd never seemed keen on jokes, and he was, understandably I guess, even less keen on my working at Harecombe Castle.

I'd told him about my new job in my very first letter, mendaciously over-stressing the temporary nature of the arrangement. His reply had winged back by return, but even

216

so, from Italy, it took a couple of weeks. I read that Oliver was surprised by my news. He wrote, with typically Oliverish reserve, that it seemed a very odd sort of employment to appeal to me. And, between the lines, in glaringly outraged capitals, I read: *Very odd sort of EMPLOYER to appeal to me* ... But, being Oliver, he never even mentioned Joe Duff's name. And thereafter, he also studiedly avoided mentioning Harecombe either, or anything to do with it.

In subsequent letters to him, however, I'd determinedly recounted stories of work on the castle. What else could I write about? You can't fill three sheets with polite enquiries.

Even so, my heart wasn't in it. I have to confess that in those far-off days when I was young, unpregnant and went to smart little dinner parties in Islington, my heart had always sunk when the conversation turned (as it always does at such dinner parties) to the infamies of the building trade. Skipfuls of anecdotes, each longer and grislier than the last.

Believe me, though, the worst Camden Terrace conversion story was a nursery rhyme compared with the epic I could relate after four and a half months at the castle with George.

George was our Master Builder. Capital M, Capital B. A dapper squirrel of a man, he was jauntily moustached with a fresh handkerchief tucked every morning into the breast pocket of his immaculate overalls. Immaculate, I thought acidly, because he rarely did any work. George was, after all, having a busy year. He was also a Master Mason of the rolled-up trouser leg variety (currently Worshipful Master of the local lodge) and a Meistersinger: he was a pillar of the local Operatic Society. He had 'em rolling in the aisles in *Hello Dolly!* I know because the performance took place in the castle theatre and my attendance was mandatory. Joe (who, naturally, had also received the unrefusable offer in the form of complimentary ticket and programme) hummed along with all the choruses and found the real life George equally entertaining.

For me, George's extra-curricular activities were beyond a

joke. I could hear him singing somewhere down the corridor even now — and glared. I ripped the sheet of paper out of the typewriter, and was about to insert yet another when the phone rang and a chocolately voice drawled, 'Hiya, gorgeous. Doing anything tonight?'

'Only the accounts,' I said hopefully.

'We're a bit short-handed, that's all.'

I prayed silently that I could still get into my black waitressing skirt and said he could count on me.

'What's the latest from our Master Craftsman then?' Joe did not mean the latest anecdote.

'I spoke to him this morning. He *promises* mid-December now. But honestly . . .'

We were talking about the castle kitchens. The plan, naïve as it now seemed, had always been that the cellar here would be fitted out immediately, enabling Joe to shift the outside catering operation from that expensively rented box on the outskirts of Oxford into the castle. Here we were at the end of November and the basement was still a dusty concrete desert, sprouting only forlorn stumps of pipes and twisted wires.

'Couldn't possibly move in December anyway,' said Joe. 'Not with the Christmas stampede. Things'll be quieter in the New Year. Not to worry.'

'Another month — at least — paying the rent on that place.'

'Won't bankrupt us, will it?'

'It won't help,' I said grimly. 'Oh God, I'm sorry, Joe.'

'Not your fault, sweetheart.'

But it was — it was.

'About the marquee job next week . . .' he said cheerfully — Joe was unfailingly cheerful — and we went on to sort out staffing and table hire.

CHAPTER TWENTY

It had been apparent from the day I moved in that someone was needed to do more than field letters and phone calls and brew tea for the builders. I found I was taking on two quite separate jobs, anyway – even without occasionally donning a black skirt and understudying for holidaying waitresses. On the one hand, there was the castle to look after. George and his merry men were supposed to be working upwards from Joe's dream kitchens in the basement, via baronial dining rooms on the ground floor to, ultimately, four-postered bedrooms and marbled bathrooms up above.

The logic was elegantly simple. As soon as the kitchens were fitted out, Joe would move Flying Duck here. When the ground floor was finished – February, according to the original plan – the Harecombe Castle Restaurant could open its doors. And in the summer the bedrooms would be ready to cosset a discerning stampede of (preferably) wealthy American tourists on the Oxford-Stratford trail.

Hardened veterans of the building war will already be sniggering. Of course, the work progressed neither on time, nor according to this neat logic.

Once in, builders, plumber and associated tradesmen swarmed all over the building like ants. Heaven knows how Joe had ever expected to manage alone, because while all this was going on, he always knew he would have to continue running the outside catering operation from the hired kitchen miles away. Oh, Flying Duck also employed two sous-chefs and a motley band of skivvies. Not to mention the dicky-bowed front-of-house mob. But it was Joe ran the show. For important functions (and Flying Duck produced everything from Thomas the Tank Engine birthday cakes, via ritzy cocktail canapés to a whole roast pig for a Young Farmers' orgy) he had to be there, presiding over his steaming kitchens like the chief devil in hell.

Which brings me to the second half of my own job. The outside catering. Joe turned out the food and stage-managed the events with panache. But there's more to catering than catering, and clearly someone was needed to do everything else.

In my first week at Harecombe, Joe had arrived daily with bulging plastic carriers of paperwork.

'Chinese to me,' he said.

Mostly, it was to me too. But I flexed my calculator, assumed a look of intelligence and ploughed in. Brazen self-interest might have inspired me to take the job, but − even without the generous salary Joe was paying − common decency would have compelled me to carry it through as best I could.

Within days, I established my office in the castle, in a kind of Gothic broom cupboard overlooking the courtyard, and installed a scarred old warhorse of a desk. I press-ganged two of the builders into erecting shelves, bought a couple of cabinets cheap in a junk shop and applied myself to creating a filing system. Within a fortnight I recognized − rather to my surprise − I was enjoying myself. In fact, I was having the time of my life. Imposing order on the debris of paper which had gathered after Rupert Hare-Smith's departure, despatching winged invoices and orders to all corners of the country, I felt like God creating Eden out of chaos.

Maybe I should have remembered Father Xavier's warnings about Paradise, as once quoted by Joe Duff. But, at first, I saw no snakes in the bluddy grass at all. I sat at my tidy desk typing like fury and congratulated myself on my cleverness, in between mouthfuls of a herb tea which stank of compost heaps but was supposed to curb the nausea.

It didn't. My pregnancy was not like the soft-focus magazine photographs, all bloom and expectant glow. My hair was lank, my skin a bubbling porridge of spots and I was sick in irregular bursts which could, perversely, encompass afternoons and evenings as well as mornings. I was also dog-tired twenty-four hours a day, but that didn't stop me working. Work in fact, was the only thing that made me feel human.

And it was only natural, once I'd shuffled the papers into some kind of order, that I branched beyond clerkly filing and correspondence. When I suggested hesitantly — that the estimated costing for a wedding reception seemed on the cheap side, and that we were, after all, aiming to turn in a profit, Joe beamed and said I was a stingy bugger — just like Bunny. This was, I recognized, the highest compliment he could bestow. A day later we had our first pitched battle over the necessity (or otherwise) for real caviare to garnish a soup — and never looked back.

Yes, I got on just fine with the job. No more waiting for a telephone to ring: I was in control. Master of my fate, captain of my soul, and holder of the casting vote on bathroom fittings. George and Joe favoured streamlined chromium. The architect (a dimimutive, dandruffed worrier) had suggested leggy, old-fashioned four-pronged taps, gold-coloured. I agreed. And that's what was ordered. To my immense satisfaction.

I also — as you will have gathered from the above — got on just fine with Joe Duff, too.

Well, maybe at first I had indulged in a little dark brooding over his role in the Cathy Langham tragedy. But I simply haven't a nature which can keep a cauldron of grievances stewing long. You read about characters in books smouldering over wrongs for thirty years and hundreds of pages. I barely managed thirty minutes. After all, I could hardly take the moral high ground on extra-marital affairs.

Besides, it would have been easier to despise Joe Duff, shameless womaniser, more wholeheartedly if he had actually behaved like one. He did not. Towards me, I mean. He flirted rumbustiously with waitresses, customers and the rest of the world, but his manner towards me, from the day I arrived, was exemplary. He treated me with the careful deference appropriate to, say, a favourite maiden aunt. Or — I sometimes thought — a pregnant woman. If I didn't know Joe couldn't possibly know, I might have wondered . . .

'Hello, beautiful,' he would say when he strolled into my office, dropping an avuncular kiss on my acned forehead, and then settle down to discuss the wiring.

Not that I judged him to be a reformed character, I just looked at myself in the speckled miror on my mothball-perfumed dressing table over in the Stables and knew why anyone might be prompted to talk less of twin destinies and more of twin thirteen-amp sockets. Hello, beautiful . . .

'Actually, you're looking a bit peaky,' Joe observed one morning. 'Are you eating properly?'

At the time, I was still throwing up with disgusting regularity, but I could hardly tell him that.

'Come out to dinner tonight,' he suggested. Not for the first time — this was summer and trade was slack. But, as always, I refused. I wasn't afraid I would end up disentangling myself from hairy ape-armed advances. I refused only because I would not accept expensive meals without returning them, and I was saving every penny of my pay against the non-earning days ahead. So I'd resigned myself to baked beans in front of the ancient telly again when, that evening, he turned up at my front door with no warning, a grin and a box of provisions which he insisted on cooking for me in my own kitchen. 'Working dinner,' he said, ignoring my protests. 'We've got a lot to talk about.'

It was the first of many such evenings — sometimes at the Stables, sometimes in his flat — but that first dinner was the longest and the merriest. We talked late into the night. Talked — argued — laughed. Mostly about the business, because it really was a working dinner. But we worked through three courses and Lord knows how much wine. Joe had to ring for a taxi finally, to get home to Oxford — but then he'd drunk all the wine. I, you may be sure, swigged only mineral water. I was running my pregancy according to the book, or rather personal library of ante-natal textbooks. I explained my abrupt conversion to teetotalism as a health kick, which Joe fortunately didn't question — although he didn't approve either.

'Just like Al,' he grumbled. 'Next thing, you'll be demanding nut cutlets. I hope you realize that if the health lobby wins the day, people like me will be out of a job.'

The odd thing is, I remember feeling quite as recklessly euphoric as if I'd been drinking glass for glass with him. I recall raucously insisting we must have a palatial loo. I told him I always judged restaurants by the loo. Joe roared back that no restaurant of his would be judged by the bloody lavatory.

And — that night — I realized he was right. Funny, but the most piercingly vivid memory of the evening is a taste. Joe wouldn't think that funny at all. He would regard it as right and proper. But only that night did I learn, where food was concerned, Joe Duff was an artist.

I don't mean he composed colourful masterpieces on the plate: there were no spider's-web-patterned sauces or sculpted carrots, nor even nosegays of obscure herbs. But I had simply never eaten lamb which tasted so distinctly and succulently of lamb. What's more (although I could not pass on this ultimate accolade) I reached the last spoonful of pudding without a single flutter of nausea.

'It's going to be out of this world,' I said wonderingly, 'our restaurant.' For the first time — quite naturally — it was 'our' restaurant.

'Well of course it is,' said Joe, raising his glass. He had an authentic artist's ego about his cooking, too. 'Don't say you ever doubted it. Here's to us. A great partnership. Long may it last.'

That damped my elation. 'To us,' I repeated carefully, raising my mineral water. I could hardly drink to the long continuance of our partnership. 'To . . . March,' I said. As it

223

chanced, our projected opening date for the restaurant was then the first of March.

But Joe was not deceived – or at least, not entirely – and his face fell. 'Oh yeah, March,' he said. 'When you leave for better things . . . Speaking of which, I'd better get a move on home.'

I had long since realized, as I settled so comfortably into the job, that Joe was hoping my leaving date would prove as flexible as all the other dates in the Harecombe Castle plans. The truth would emerge soon enough. I wasn't looking forward to telling him he had employed a pregnant woman. And had come, I knew, to trust and depend on her. How could I condemn Joe Duff for his guilty secret when my own was growing in size (literally) by the day?

Besides what had Joe actually done? At least he'd paid for the abortion which had to be one step better than leaving Cathy to cope alone. He wasn't to know – no one could – that it would lead to such tragic consequences. Although as my own mood, in those early months of pregnancy, ricocheted between elation and despair, I felt I could understand what might trigger a less stable personality towards suicide. Particularly with the baby – the cause of all the exploding hormones – gone. I would find myself closing my hands protectively over my own gently swelling belly.

Joe had also told me a load of lies. This, strangely, rankled more. Joe always seemed so utterly, transparently honest, it was unsettling to know he could tell whopping fibs with exactly the same open-faced conviction.

But no one, I thought, could help liking him. Least of all – let's be honest – me. Life in his company, even four foot-slogging hours of waitressing, bounced along in a perpetual bubble of laughter. Conversely, things could seem pretty flat when we were apart. We might argue about his taste in bath-taps (his taste in anything other than food, come to that) but we agreed about the important issues in life – or at least we comfortably assumed we did, while we joked about everything else. The only topic, in fact, which never gave us a laugh was the Langhams: Oliver and Cathy.

Well, Joe conspicuously avoided mentioning her name at all. I only wished he would exercise the same restraint over Oliver. But no, he enquired after Oliver's health and progress with punctilious regularity. My replies grew shorter and tetchier by the week. I didn't reciprocate by asking him awkward questions about Cathy. In fact, like him, I never mentioned her either.

It once occurred to me that Cathy Langham was the skeleton in the castle cupboard. Neither of us wanted to reopen that particular door.

Someone with a more pessimistic nature than mine would, I dare say, have already been thinking it was all too good to be true. Looking, in other words, for the snakes in the bluddy grass. Not me. It was only as the summer had melted gracefully into autumn that I had begun to feel a little less complacent.

Mastering the day-to-day running of affairs had been, I prided myself, a piece of cake. Coming to terms with the underlying structure, the direction we were headed — our 'Business Plan' as I learned to call it — was a different matter.

Business Plan was just one of many bits of jargon I had acquired from the articles which began to appear in newspapers and journals around this time, analysing the problems of small businesses. No doubt such articles had always been written and I had simply taken no interest in them before, but as the boom in the economy dwindled to more of a slow, faint thud, the flow of journalism on this subject undoubtedly increased. I devoured case history after case history of struggling and collapsed small enterprises. It took a long time for my armour-plated smugness to be pierced by the odd dart of recognition. One dart was quickly followed by an Agincourt torrent. I began sending off for Government advice pamphlets and borrowing books from the library, and I studied them all with feverishly mounting anxiety.

Because Bunny had quit the partnership, taking half the money with him, Joe had borrowed heavily to finance the castle. Now, costs were escalating (costs, in every article, *always* escalated — there didn't even seem to be a word for them moving t'other way), deadlines were melting into the future and — God — I began to see us in every sad little case history I read. No doubt anyone literate in balance sheets would have spotted hazards sooner. In fact, gallingly, someone with plain commonsense and no more business training than me had indeed foreseen the danger: Alison Laverick.

I remembered now her prophecy that Joe would be bankrupt by Christmas. I remembered, too, her swingeing 'three Cs' assessment of Joe's abilities. She had been both right — and wrong. Joe was nobody's fool, but he was a craftsman first and foremost. He really loved his work. What greater pleasure in life could there be, he was wont to say, than feeding people well? The haste with which he delivered the administrative reins into my hands showed just how magnificently uninterested he was in matters inedible. As for economy . . . I soon learned suggesting he substitute sirloin for fillet was akin to offering Kreisler a banjo.

So, in early October, I had called him up to the castle for a proper meeting. He arrived mid-morning. There'd been a sharp frost earlier, but now the day was mellow, glowing and autumnally fruitful. Just like me. My body was characteristically punctual. At the end of the third month of pregnancy, exactly as the textbooks said, the sickness and spots had melted away.

So, less happily, had the last shreds of fog clouding my perception of the accumulated accounts of our enterprises.

'You're looking well,' said Joe, strolling into the office and dropping the usual kiss on my forehead.

'Joe, I'm worried,' I said, sitting primly behind my desk as he, still damp from a shower and exuding lemony gusts of cologne, lounged on one corner, swinging an expensively loafered foot.

226

Despite the nip in the air, he was bulging out of the skimpiest of white T-shirts. Later I was to realize Joe Duff didn't possess a winter wardrobe at all. Not only did he not feel the cold, I sometimes fancied he radiated inner warmth like a child in one of those old-fashioned porridge adverts.

'I've had draft proposals and estimates from three design firms,' I began. 'For decorating the interior.'

'Pleased with them?'

'Completely knocked out,' I said and, as his face lit up with innocent delight, continued sternly, 'by the cost. The amounts they're quoting are stratospheric.'

'We can't afford them?'

'We couldn't afford to carpet this office at the rates they deal in.'

Joe shrugged. 'Better get them to revise their ideas a bit, then.'

I tried a fresh tack. 'You do realize we can't possibly hope to open the restaurant until after Easter. Probably' — best to face facts — 'not until May at the earliest.' Next century if present experience was anything to go by. 'As for the hotel —'

'Can't we?' interrupted Joe, with the air of a child whose promised bag of sweets has been whipped away. 'Whyever not?'

So I explained. Like I said, there's nothing more tedious than builder stories, so I won't begin to catalogue the disasters (minor hitches according to George) which were besetting our plans.

'We'll manage, won't we?' said Joe.

And then I launched into my calculation of escalating costs. The shortfall of income generated by Flying Duck to offset them. Note the flashy terminology; shortfall, offset . . . I even got on to fixed costs, because I had been doing the hard sums. Fixed costs, I had deduced, was the staggering amount of money we required just to *be* here at all, before a single customer crossed the threshold. And I went on to tell Joe what we would have to charge in the restaurant, just to cover those inescapable fixed costs. Let alone buy food or pay staff.

Only then did he begin to show real interest.

'Per head? For dinner? Not bloody likely. I want to feed a dining room full of hungry punters, not two tables of anorexic billionaires.'

As far as I could see, what would be required was two dining rooms full of greedy and dipsomaniac billionaires. Every night. But I couldn't bring myself to say that. I wish I could claim it was inherent optimism that silenced me. 'We're getting into debt,' I said.

Deeper into debt, was what I meant.

'The bank's happy enough to lend the money,' said Joe.

'But we'll have to pay it back.'

'Course we will,' said Joe. 'Anyway, property's the best investment you can make, isn't it? Matter of fact, a bloke from the Country Leisure Group was snuffling round only t'other day, to see if I was interested in selling the place.'

'Was he?' I said faintly.

'Offering a lot more than I paid, too.'

'What did you say?'

Joe grinned crookedly. 'Told him to bugger off, of course.'

'Was, um, that wise?'

I wished he wouldn't look at me so trustingly.

'What are you saying, sweetheart? You don't want me to sell up, do you?'

CHAPTER TWENTY-ONE

I can offer all sorts of excuses. I was an actress, not a business-woman. And in those days everyone, not just Joe and I, blithely believed the unwieldy juggernaut of the property market could only lumber forwards. Sometimes faster, sometimes slower, but always in the same direction. We weren't the only ones to be astounded by the discovery of a reverse gear. Nor were we the only ones who were going to be ambushed, on the retreat, by traffic-cop bank managers slapping down fines in the form of ferocious interest rates.

In fact, why not blame the bank manager? Ours was, I could argue in my own defence, just another sob-story which had begun in that seductive golden age when kindly banks scattered money like confetti over romantically inclined small businesses.

I could go on. With purpler metaphors and more self-justification. But the excuses don't wash because, even by then, I had learned enough to recognize we were in trouble. Over-confident, over-extended, over-schedule, over-exposed — every bit of jargon fitting our position seemed to begin with *over*. Except overdraft. Which is what all the other labels meant, but bank-speak for our debt was something like: Business Expansion Credit Facilities. An overdraft by any other name, huge and still swelling.

'Shall I ring this guy?' said Joe. 'Let him make me an offer I can't refuse and book the world cruise?'

Joe may have sounded flippant but I had no doubt, if I'd said sell, he would at least have considered the offer seriously.

I nearly did. So nearly. In my memory I see myself sitting behind the desk. The sums in front of me are neatly ruled in red and blue ink, but the conclusions are inescapably black. What they tell me is, yes, Joe should take the money and run.

But I'm glancing through the prettily paned window of my office, towards the Stables. My refuge until the baby arrives. I'm thinking of the comfortable· income drip-feeding my hungry bank account, now firmly in credit, which is my precious insurance against non-earning days ahead. I'm even thinking, wistfully, how much I like this job, how much I enjoy working with Joe Duff, and if he sells up . . .

'We'll manage,' I said. 'I'll think of something to cut costs.'

'That's my girl,' said Joe with a brimmingly confident smile. 'You nearly had me worried then.'

What I thought of — within twenty-four nail-shredding hours — was Henry Blayne.

Henry was one of my oldest friends, in both senses of the word 'old'. His actual age was one of the best-kept secrets of the theatrical profession. He had discovered, he once told me, fifty to be a profoundly comfortable figure and thus had decided to linger there awhile. Several years on, he was still elegantly lingering. I had encountered Henry with that first touring company I joined after leaving university. He was a designer and, in his day, successful. He certainly earned a lot of money. And just as quickly spent it on an exotic menagerie of dogs, monkeys, parrots — and impecunious young men. All chosen with exquisite taste and maintained in expensive luxury. Not so much a theatrical designer, someone had once said of Henry, more a travelling circus.

In recent years, work and money had thinned out. So, inevitably, had the entourage. Rumour had it that the monkey had strangled the parrot, but it may have been one of the young men did the deed. I wouldn't have blamed him. The parrot was a cantankerous old bugger.

Anyway, Henry's opulent penthouse in Soho was swapped

for a flat in Victoria and, latterly, a very much smaller flat in Earls Court. No room there for animals, and the young men, too, seemed to melt mysteriously away. This, Henry claimed (he was admirably free of self-pity) was a blessing. He had at last learned what a time-wasting business love was. And so *messy*. However, like a reformed smoker with weaklings who have not yet kicked the weed, Henry was noticeably more waspish these days about the sexual peccadilloes of his friends.

His taste, though, remained exquisite and his advice was sought when any of his friends decorated. He dispensed it with the same reckless largesse which had dissipated his fortune. The drawback to consulting Henry was that, where he advised, he also tended – with the airy fastidiousness of your true nomad – to move in.

I knew he had had to abandon the Earls Court pad, and I eventually ran him to earth at the house of mutual friends, a house which had been fabulously transformed under his direction. Three months after the decorators had packed up their brushes, Henry was still occupying the guest bedroom.

'One should be thankful for small mercies,' muttered his hostess, Rosalind. 'At least he doesn't travel the zoo with him these days.'

So it wasn't clear who was most delighted with my invitation to come and cast his professional eye over Harecombe Castle, Rosalind and her husband, or Henry himself. As for me, when his tall, soberly mackintoshed figure emerged from the train at Oxford, I threw myself into his arms.

'Darling girl,' said Henry, patting his scarf carefully back into position, 'to what do I owe the honour?'

And I told him. I didn't stop talking all the way back from the station to Harecombe. Well, I didn't confide quite everything. I didn't tell him about the impending Happy (ha ha) Event. However, he had already learned (trust Henry, also known as Reuters Blayne) that Richard and I had parted, from mutual friends. Unlike several of those friends, though, Henry expressed no dismay at my quitting the theatre for this eccentric new occupation. But then Henry, with typical frankness, had long since advised me my talents would be better employed in another profession. Like the army.

'If we're losing the nuclear deterrent,' he had said earnestly, 'this country needs you.'

I sometimes wondered why I liked Henry as much as I did.

'My God,' he cried, as we drove through the gloom into the castle courtyard, 'Child Henry to the dark tower came ... And you've been living here alone? But then, you always were such a distressingly phlegmatic creature.'

'That's right,' I agreed. Only this morning, I'd heard George regaling his crew over one of their interminable tea-breaks with spine-chilling tales of the shadowy Lady Violet climbing the spiral stairs. Interrupting his *salon*, I had pointed out with Debrettish pedantry that, correctly, she was not The Lady Violet, she was Lady Rivenhoe. A much less satisfactory name for a ghost.

But on gloomy evenings like this, as I led Henry in through the tower door, I found myself glancing up the staircase and thinking about plain, untitled Mrs Langham. Cathy, q.v. *Wuthering Heights*, is an unpleasantly evocative name for a ghost.

'Well, I'd have been spooked to death,' Henry declared, surveying the chaos of scaffolding and dustsheets in the hall through narrowed eyes. 'It's all very *Scottish Play*, isn't it?'

Henry would no more have named *Macbeth* than worn tartan trousers. I, on the other hand, was not superstitious. I blamed any occasional jumpiness firmly on the hormones.

'I sense a lingering miasma of tragedy,' Henry was murmuring dreamily — and this was before I'd filled him in on recent castle history. 'Already I am thinking deep crimson. We need to enhance that feeling of blood being spilled on stone.' He shivered deliciously.

'Solid brick throughout,' I said. 'I've got a stew in the oven. Shall we go across and eat?'

Henry was less enchanted with the Stables. Understandably. The stable block – grateful though I was to be living there – was not the most comfortable or welcoming of dwellings. You could see that it ought to have been charming and indeed that one day, no doubt, it would be. But the building had been converted to house humans instead of horses long before conversion had become the high art form it is these days, with everyone transforming every barn, stable and bus stop they can lay their Black and Deckers on. There was none of today's slavish retention of original features; no daring split-levels, no sculpting of space. The aim of that long-ago builder had apparently been to coerce the interior into as close a replica as possible of a conventional semi, c. 1953, with a clutter of cardboard dividing walls, shiny brown fire-places and lumpily-tiled lowered ceilings. My own bits and pieces were shuffled in among the inherited furniture, looking uneasy as package tourists on a native bus.

The place was surprisingly big, however. Henry could take his pick from three spare bedrooms and stay as long as he wanted. He curled a lip at all of them, but it says everything for his talents that, even before he came down to eat my stew, his artful disposal of his own silk bedspread and an arrangement of photographs on the wall could almost make one overlook the glaring paper and seedy furnishings.

What's more, it took only a few minutes of conversation the next morning to convince Joe that the answer to our problems lay in Henry Blayne. I had been horribly nervous of introducing them. Not just because I was putting forward a friend for a job – although it was little enough we were offering to pay him – but because I was painfully anxious they should like one another as much as I liked both of them. My apprehension was unfounded.

'A hairy hunk of perfection,' murmured Henry in my ear. 'Love the tigerskin seats.'

'The guy's clearly a genius,' said Joe, as he climbed into his car and roared off back to Oxford.

233

I consigned to my out-tray the sketches and estimates from the interior designers. Henry had sneered at their lumpish lack of imagination. But cost, I said sternly to him, must be our guiding principle. He could give his soaring vision free rein as long as the results were cheap. This was a mistake. Henry replied stiffly that the day his name was associated with anything *cheap*, he would put Judy Garland on the record player and cut his wrists. The need for *economy*, however, he understood intimately. Only too intimately in recent years.

Even George was bowled over by Henry, recognizing in him a true Man of the Stage. My untheatricality had, I knew, proved a disappointment to George. Whichever famous actor or production he named, with the eagerness of a sparrow waiting for titbits, I could almost guarantee not to be acquainted with him, her or it. Henry, on the other hand, scattered Larries and Johnnies lavishly across George's path and spoonfed him juicy backstage anecdotes.

I could only marvel and be thankful. George's hours of attendance at work shot up. However, his fast-blossoming hero-worship led — indirectly — to an early tiff between Joe and Henry. George was anxious to show this consummate artist of the theatre the sets, still gathering dust on the stage, from the last production of the Harecombe Players. Henry — inevitably — walked into the theatre and fell in love. Not with the *Hello Dolly!* sets, but with the toy theatre itself.

'Ravishing,' he breathed to Joe later, shutting his eyes in an agony of creative ferment. 'Quite simply, it's everything I have ever dreamed of. What we could do with that little gem hidden in our midst . . .' (For Henry, note, it had become 'we', 'us' and 'our castle' within five minutes.) 'So many ideas are racing round my head, I can't even begin to articulate them.'

'Don't try,' retorted Joe. 'Just forget them now and for good. Contrary to popular opinion, I'm trying to open a hotel and restaurant here, not a bloody Palace of Varieties. We can

234

hardly afford to renovate the boiler, let alone waste money on that barn.'

I was surprised at the rudeness with which Joe spoke, but also dismayed at what he said. This was the first time he had really shown any sign of recognizing the precariousness of our finances. He was realizing, I thought, that I had advised him wrong. That he should have sold up. My knot of guilt twisted tighter.

Even worse, as Henry and Joe glared at one another, I began to fear I would have to retrieve Courtenay Design Consultants from the out-tray, but already Joe was apologizing and Henry — equally graciously — accepted the apology.

'I always was a pushover for a strong-minded man,' Henry said to me that evening. But I couldn't help noticing that the pad on which he was sketching was emblazoned with missile-breasted goddesses suspiciously similar to those supporting the circle in the theatre.

'No way, Henry,' I said.

'Oh, not now, maybe,' said Henry, smiling at me seraphically. 'But one day. At long last, I realize I have found my destiny.'

Harecombe Castle
29 November

Dear Oliver,
    Well, Christmas is coming . . .

. . . the goose might be getting fat, but luckily I wasn't. Or at least, nothing baggy sweaters couldn't hide. Being tall helped. Oh Lord, would I ever get this damn letter to Oliver written? The wastebasket of my office had been choked with rejected attempts for a fortnight. I was just wondering how I could save this one from the same fate when the telephone on my desk rang.

Twenty minutes later, I resumed my letter, on a briskly fresh tack:

*You'll never guess who phoned just now — quite out of the blue —
none other than your Aunt Constance . . .*

'May I speak to Joe Duff?' she had begun, after I had cooed
my glueyly charming 'Good morning, Harecombe Castle' in
best hotel-receptionist style. All the world's a stage, and every
job just another part.

'My name's Berisford,' she bellowed, after I explained —
trying to ignore the drill which had begun squealing outside
my door — that Joe was not here. It was strangely dislocating
to find myself talking to Constance after all this time. I almost
felt that, in writing to Oliver, I had conjured her up like a
genie out of the telephone. 'Joe's an old friend,' she was
continuing, 'and I wondered if he could help me out of a
hole?'

Leaving no pause for me to identify myself as another old
friend — and one, moreover, she had coerced into helping her
out of another hole not so long ago — she demanded to know
when we were opening for business. So I told her, with a
sparkling confidence which required real acting talent, spring.

*In spring time, the only pretty ring time, When birds do sing,
hey ding a ding, ding . . .* the castle would be finished and pig-
a-ligs would land on Mars.

'It all sounds a shocking botch-up,' she went on, and for
one unpleasant moment I thought she was referring to the
work in progress here. But it turned out she was trying to
organize a charity function. 'Personally, I loathe balls,' she
said. 'They always mean trouble.'

I suppressed a snort of sardonic laughter. How true,
Constance, I thought, how true. If only you knew who you
were talking to, and the trouble the St Benedict's Hall ball
has meant to me . . .

'Um, Lady Berisford . . .' I tried again, but she was ploughing
on.

'In past years we've always held the Foundation bash in
February, and here we are at the end of November with

nothing planned. You must think us unbelievably incompetent. I can only say that the moving spirit of the ball sub-committee for the past umpteen ... Dear me, did I say spirit? Unfortunately apt turn of phrase because she's been dying, you know – or rather not dying, which is much more inconvenient. But now she's demanding to know –'

'She's recovered?' I chipped in, following the monologue with difficulty between intermittent wails from the drill.

'Happily, yes,' said Lady Berisford, sounding not at all happy. 'And – well – in short, circumstances are such that my fellow committee members and I have felt obliged to *imply* plans for the ball are well in hand. As of course they should have been. Everywhere that could possibly accommodate us in February seems to have been booked up months ago.'

The drill raised its pitch to a shriek of anguish and I winced as I told Lady Berisford there was no question of our being open by February.

'But *spring*?' she said eagerly.

'Late spring,' I said, resisting the temptation to cower. Any minute now I felt sure a spinning bit would nose out of the wall beside me. 'By the way, we ...'

'I met Colin Howard when I drove out to Harecombe yesterday. He farms the south end of the estate, you know, and he was talking about the goings-on at the castle which naturally set me thinking this might be our salvation. I wondered whether a contingent of ladies from my committee could possibly come up and have a look round? Of course, I myself am pretty well acquainted with the place because it actually used to belong to –'

'To your family,' I managed to interrupt at last. The drill had stopped. And I identified myself.

'Good Lord,' she said. 'Becca.'

The change in her tone was too marked, surely, to be imagined. A minute ago she had been merrily confiding in me as a stranger. Telling her my name was like opening a fridge door. A damp chill settled over the conversation.

'Do you keep in touch with Oliver?' she said stiffly.

'As a matter of fact I'm writing a letter to him at this very minute,' I responded virtuously.

'Good Lord,' she said again. 'And you're actually working for Joe Duff, at Harecombe? What an extraordinary change of vocation.'

I assured her I had always been capable of turning my hand to a variety of jobs and that this one was only temporary.

'You know Oliver will be staying in Italy for a full year?'

'Well of course I do . . .' I began.

And it was only then I started to wonder, incredulously, whether Constance Berisford too might be deducing I had taken the job at Harecombe just to wait for the return of the Prodigal Nephew.

'Oliver is unlikely ever to come back to this neck of the woods. As a matter of fact . . .' There was a pause before she rattled on: 'The reason I came out to Harecombe yesterday was to take a look in at the Gatehouse. I'm planning to lend it to a young mathematician from Trinity. I'm — sorry.'

Sorry? And she sounded, yes, embarrassed. Anyone would think Alison and Joe had been right, and that Constance in best Victorian auntly tradition really had banished Oliver abroad to detach him from his actress floozy. (*The stage has always held a disastrously fatal fascination for the men of my family . . .*) But this was barmy. It was Constance who had once bludgeoned me into coming back to Harecombe . . .

'Lady Berisford,' I said, judging the Constance days were gone, 'I — I wouldn't want to you to, well, get the wrong idea. About my working here. As far as Oliver is concerned, whatever there was between us finished long ago. There's nothing now . . .'

'. . . beyond simple friendship' was how this stilted speech was meant to conclude, but I found I was cupping a hand over the curve in my stomach. This was not a lump of simple friendship. 'At least, not in the way you might be thinking.'

'Great heavens, I wasn't thinking anything of the sort,' she

238

declared with a notable lack of conviction. 'You're a sensible girl. And, well, under the circumstances I'm sure it's for the best.'

But I noticed the strangled vowels relax and, after she had made arrangements for a viewing party to visit the castle, she bid me a positively cordial goodbye. And that really annoyed me. I thought Constance Berisford ought to have been touched — grateful even — to think I might be waiting patiently here for her precious nephew. Didn't I *fit* either? In fact, I was so irritated by the conversation I totally abandoned my letter to Oliver. Instead, I rang Joe and told him he had to give a conducted tour to the ladies of a charitable committee the day after tomorrow.

'Why me?' protested Joe. 'I'm up to my eyes in Christmas bloody puddings.'

'If we're going to get the business, they'll need persuading to delay the date until May. And what's more, I should think they'll take some convincing this disaster zone will be habitable before the end of the decade. In other words,' I added, 'the job needs someone with a king-size talent for sweet-talking women.'

'Oh well, if you put it that way . . .' said Joe.

A few days later a blue linen-grained envelope arrived, addressed to him in a loopy and distinctively feminine hand.

Joseph Duff Esquire himself appeared minutes after the postman, looking mildly harassed and dressed already in his chef's trousers and jacket. I liked the austere white chef's tunic. Reminiscent of a surgeon or a priest, and an improvement on his dodgy taste in shirts.

'Love, Nell?' he said absently, having skimmed through to the end of the letter. He was sitting, as usual, on the corner of my desk. 'Who's Nell?'

I was admiring my Harecombe Castle Christmas cards, a box of which had at last arrived from the printers in the same post.

'Surely even you remember their names,' I muttered.

The photograph on the front of the card showed the castle silhouetted in black against a splendidly sexy sunset, with lights glowing in every turreted window. I had ordered enough to despatch Christmas greetings to all customers past, present and potential, which took in most of the West Country.

'Ah, she's one of Constance Berisford's bunch,' he exclaimed. 'We've pulled it off. They want to hold the ball here.'

'Well done.' I said, rummaging in the box from the printers. There was also a leaflet to slip inside the card, where appropriate, which gave the amended opening date as mid-April and listed the castle's luxurious facilities. Content if not style surely qualified it for entry in the Booker Prize for Fiction. I surveyed it with authorly pride. 'When?'

'Seventeenth of March,' said Joe.

I put down the leaflet. 'You're joking of course.'

'Nell says here it's the latest they could consider. I tried to put them off until May.' He shot an apprehensive smile towards me. 'She understands our problems but, as she says, they won't need half the castle. Don't look so gob-smacked, babe. The bedrooms don't matter. We can manage as long as we've got the kitchens and the ground floor finished by then. And we will have, won't we?'

'Will we?' I said bleakly. It wasn't the condition of the bedrooms which was worrying me.

'They'll be having a marquee anyway.'

'*Will* be?' I shrieked. 'You mean it's fixed? For the seventeenth of March?'

Joe hung his head. 'I suppose I let them talk me into it. Nell really liked the castle,' he added anxiously. 'They all did. One of them actually came to college here.'

'Oh Joe,' I said despairingly, 'you were supposed to be persuading them, not the other way round.'

'It means money up front,' he said, fixing the soupy brown eyes on me. 'And we'd be filling the place with our future

240

customers all in one night. They're loaded, the Foundation crowd, I've catered for their parties before. They'll have photographers from the local glossy mags — just think of the publicity. We could even invite a few journalists along ourselves if we wanted. Treat it as a gala opening.'

'I've no doubt. But . . .'

Balls, as I remembered Lady Berisford saying, always mean trouble. Suddenly the time for secrets was over. Well, I'd been gearing myself up to this for long enough.

'But what, love?' Joe was saying. 'We can manage, can't we?'

'Maybe you can,' I said. 'But you'll have to manage without me.'

CHAPTER TWENTY-TWO

At that moment, Henry strode in with a clipboard and an air of creative preoccupation, demanding to know where his book of curtain samples had been hidden. He allowed himself to be distracted by the Christmas card lying forgotten on my desk, and squawked with laughter.

'My dears, Manderley to the life,' he exclaimed, and when Joe and I ignored him, went on exasperatedly: 'You know, the last scene in the film. When the house burns down. The castle looks exactly as though it's on fire.'

'What?' I said weakly.

'The film, dimbo, *Rebecca*,' Henry chortled with fresh triumph at this coincidence of names. 'Mind, I can't quite see our Becca as the dead but dangerous *femme fatale*. Maybe — at a pinch — in pearls and twinset in the Joan Fontaine role. But I'm afraid Joe wouldn't do at all for Max de Winter. That needs a strong silent jawline. *A la* Dicky Prescott,' he added with an arch glance in my direction, 'to toss out a name purely at random. And bags I play the mad housekeeper. Oh, pardon me for breathing.' And he hurried out with the curtain samples.

The office was stiflingly quiet after he shut the door.

'I'd forgotten,' said Joe, standing up and folding the letter. 'You always said you had to leave in March. Silly of me really. I'd begun to hope you might reconsider.'

'I would,' I said wretchedly, 'if I could. But on the seventeenth of March, well the eighteenth, for what it's worth . . .'

242

I was discovering how hard it was, after nursing a secret for five long months, to release the damn thing.

'You never talk much about Oliver,' said Joe, gazing at me trustfully as a cocker spaniel. 'To be honest, I'd begun to wonder . . .'

'Oliver has nothing to do with it,' I snapped, but then felt obliged to add: 'Well, maybe he has, but not in the way everyone seems to think.'

'Tell me,' said Joe. 'Maybe I can help.'

Like he helped Cathy Langham?

Joe misunderstood my hesitation. 'How can I twist your arm? Money? A partnership? Would that persuade you?'

I swallowed hard. 'I might be persuadable,' I said. 'But I doubt if the baby is. I'm due to give birth the day after your ball.'

Joe performed the kind of hammy double-take they banned from television sitcoms years ago. Halfway round the desk, arms outstretched to embrace me, he froze in mid-swoop. 'Pregnant?'

'Don't look so dumbstruck,' I said irritably. 'It can happen to anyone. Five months.'

He stared at me, 'Where the hell is it?'

I leaned back in my chair and pushed my stomach upwards. Even so, the bulge wasn't very convincing.

'Well, blow me,' he said. 'Five months?'

I could almost see figures whizzing past his eyes like numbers on a slot machine as he totted back through the calendar.

'Five months and a bit,' I said defiantly. 'A souvenir, you might say, of the Bendy Hall ball. Put it down to Midsummer madness.'

'You didn't – intend to get pregnant, then?'

'Course I bloody didn't.' I realized I was shouting. 'Sorry. Didn't mean to bite your head off. And sorry about the baby too – letting you down like this, I've felt lousy, not telling you.'

No response. The news seemed to have turned him into

243

stone: a pillar of macho incomprehension, no doubt wondering why I hadn't disposed of this little mistake months ago.

'But I want it now,' I declared cupping my hands jealously over the bulge. 'I don't care how irresponsible you tell me I'm being. I'll manage somehow. I want this baby more than anything in the world.'

And then — silly cow — I burst into tears. Not a sprinkling of graceful dew-drops, either, but a fire-hydrant surge of body-shaking, face-purpling sobs, an unstoppable explosion of five months' pent-up emotion. Until that moment, I don't think I'd recognized how fiercely I did want the baby. It had been my problem, not my child. Now I howled luxuriously.

The next minute I was wrapped in a lemon-spiced cloud of cologne and two brawny arms, as Joe knelt beside my chair, hugging me. 'That's terrific, then,' he said, rocking me gently to and fro. 'There, there, sweetheart. Don't cry.'

'I'm really happy — to be pregnant,' I wailed. 'I never knew. But I am.'

'You sound bloody ecstatic,' he murmured. I could feel him laughing. He was rumbling like a house over a tube line. And, after completing the ruin of his starched white shoulder with a few more gills of happiness, I managed a bleary smile myself.

'That's more like it,' he said. 'Pity I've no champagne.'

'Thought you never travelled without it,' I said — and then regretted this cheap snipe (which was only what he'd said to me after turning up that day in Oliver's garden with a bottle) because he stiffened and took his arm away.

'Anyway, I'm not drinking,' I said, blowing my nose.

'You're not, are you? Bloody hell. I should have known there was something up. It — well, I guess it all makes sense now.' Patting my knee, he stood up. 'Better make you a coffee, then.'

'I'll get it.'

'No way,' said Joe. 'Stay where you are. Put your feet up.'

He waved away protests and exited with the kettle. I leaned back in my chair and laughed, dizzy from tears and truth.

Joe, on his return, eyed my belly measuringly again and shook his head before crouching by the skirting board to plug in the kettle. 'And how's Dad feeling about it all?'

That wiped the silly grin from my face. 'Oliver?'

Joe clambered to his feet. 'Jesus, I'm sorry,' he began. 'I just assumed . . . Isn't Oliver . . .'

'Oliver's the father, yes . . .'

And that almost set me off giggling again, it sounded so bizarre. I mean, I hadn't consciously disassociated Oliver from the child. Indeed, when I thought of the baby, I rather imagined Oliver in miniature: a floppy lock of fair hair, a dimpled chin, deep blue eyes. But now, aloud, the juxtaposition of words struck me as comic. Oliver: father. The concepts, familiar enough in themselves, just weren't compatible. Like Winston Churchill and ballet dancer.

'. . . but he doesn't know about the baby,' I explained.

'Doesn't know?' said Joe, pausing with spoon poised over the coffee jar. 'You mean you haven't told him?'

'The child – my getting pregnant – really wasn't his fault,' I said uncomfortably. 'Anyway, Oliver's had enough trauma without my inflicting this on him. By the time he returns from Italy, I'll be long gone from Harecombe.' I raised my chin. 'I don't need his help. I can take care of myself.'

No St Joan ever looked more unflinchingly heroic. Noble little mother faces the world alone. I gazed heavenwards, awaiting the applause.

Joe slammed down the jar sending a spray of coffee grains bouncing across the table. 'Christ! *Women* . . . Have you ever thought about what the child might need?'

I abandoned the martyred droop, sharpish. 'Of course I bloody well have. I think about nothing else. Why am I working here? Don't worry, I can take care of my child.'

'Money.' He spat the word out. 'I'm not talking about money. Don't you think the poor little bugger deserves a father?'

I gasped. 'Are you seriously suggesting I should have

marched Oliver to the altar at the end of a shotgun, just to give my baby a legal entry into the world? Half the kids in Britain these days only have one parent.'

'You needn't tell me,' snarled Joe. 'I'm one of them.'

'That was years ago,' I said impatiently. 'As you once said yourself, there weren't single-parent families when you were born. Just unmarried mothers. Well there's no stigma attached these days to being an unmarried mother, thank God.'

'Unmarried *mother*?' roared Joe, advancing on me like a gorilla whose banana supply is under threat. 'I'm talking about the child.'

'It's my child. It's got nothing to do with you.'

'Too right it hasn't. But don't try telling me this child hasn't got anything to do with Oliver.'

I had never seen him in such a passion.

'Oliver doesn't want me, any more than I want him. I just happened to be passing when he was at a low ebb. And —'

'Want?' he bellowed, so loudly I'd swear the windows rattled. 'It's all want, want want. What about responsibilities?'

That was when I finally lost my temper. 'Responsibility?' I yelled back. 'At least I'm accepting my responsibilities. At least I'm going through with it. Not just dishing out money and thinking I can shelve my responsibilities that way.'

'What?' he roared.

'Well, we know that would be your answer, don't we?'

'Answer to what, for fuck's sake?'

'Come off it,' I snapped. I'd owned up to my guilty secret so it was time he did. 'Let's stop playing games, shall we, Joe? I realized the day of the inquest where the money came from.'

He had planted his mighty fists on the other side of the desk, and was leaning towards me, mouth open, but this halted him in mid-tirade. 'Day of the inquest?' he repeated. 'Are we talking about Cathy Langham now?' He sounded dazed.

'Don't worry. I didn't tell Oliver, and I'm not blaming you for Cathy's death. You couldn't be expected to guess how it would affect her, afterwards.'

Joe eyed me uncertainly, much as, I thought, a charging rhino might eye the foolhardy firer of a tranquilizing dart, and then quietly crumpled into a chair. 'Oh Christ,' he whispered. 'How did we get round to this?'

'I'm sick of lies and secrets. Isn't it time to get everything out into the open?' Actually I was already half-wishing I had left the door on this skeleton shut. 'I'm not criticizing,' I added reluctantly. 'I suppose you did what you could. About the baby . . .'

Joe lifted his head. 'I don't know what you're talking about.'

'Oh, Joe,' I said tiredly.

His gaze didn't waver. 'I had no idea Cathy Langham had even been pregnant, let alone that she'd had an abortion — until Al came out of the inquest and told me. You were with me at the time. Believe me, I only wish I had known before. Maybe if I had . . .'

'Don't lie to me any more, Joe,' I said uncertainly. 'Please.'

'I'm not lying.'

'You paid for the operation. You lent her the money. You told me.'

Joe blinked. 'I lent Cathy three hundred quid . . .' Surely, surely he couldn't have been acting? Stanislavsky himself couldn't teach this masterly transition from bafflement, through suspicion, to certainty. 'She just said she needed it to tide her over. I never thought then — and it's never occurred to me since —'

'But I heard you arguing with Alison, even before the inquest,' I broke in. 'You must have known — Alison too — because you were actually talking about getting rid of it.'

'Getting rid of what?'

'The baby. Or that's what I realized, afterwards.'

'Bollocks,' said Joe.

'But I *heard* you . . .'

'God knows what we were talking about, but I can promise you it wasn't Cathy Langham's child.'

'Alison was telling you to forget it. That no one need ever know.'

He flinched at that — I'd swear I saw him recoil, as though I'd spat at him. But he only said steadily, 'I promise you Al had no more clue that Cathy had been pregnant than I ever did.'

He hauled himself out of his chair and walked across to the kettle. 'You saw what Al was like when she came out of the inquest,' he added over his shoulder as he spooned coffee into the mugs. 'Spitting poison. She never liked Cathy anyway, but hearing that was the final straw. That Cathy could abort Oliver's child, without even telling him she was pregnant . . .'

'*Oliver's* child?' I said faintly.

Joe spun round, a milk bottle in one hand. 'Well, stone me,' he said. 'Even Al never suggested that.'

Joe was outraged. No, it was not his child. He'd told me he and Cathy had had a one night stand, hadn't he? So maybe no contraceptive is a hundred per cent safe and he didn't give a damn if I was walking proof. But that one night had been last autumn and I could bloody well work it out for myself. If the child had been his, Cathy would have wanted money for a Christening robe by June, not an abortion. Well, nearly.

'You came to see her,' I protested. 'To the Gatehouse.'

'For Christ's sake, we've been through all this before. Yes, I came round to see Cathy. Yes, she phoned me. But I'm telling you for the last time, Becca. Our affair, such as it was, began and ended on that one night.'

'So why did she come to you?' I said. 'When she wanted to borrow money?'

'According to Al, she had me down as a starry-eyed sucker who would give her whatever she asked for,' shouted Joe. 'And she was wrong about that. At least, yes, I did lend her money. But I'd no idea what she wanted it for. As a matter of fact, I wouldn't — knowingly — have paid for an abortion. I'm sorry, but that's the way it is. Once a Catholic . . . As Al never lets me forget, I was brainwashed young by the monks.'

I was barely listening. Cathy hadn't aborted her baby because it had the wrong father, I was thinking bemusedly. She'd actually told Oliver the truth. She really had done it for the sake of a job. It seemed I'd finally flung open the closet — and found no skeleton at all.

Joe stomped across and plonked the coffee mugs down on my desk. 'And,' he said truculently, 'I still think you should tell Oliver about this child. God, don't start crying again. Oh Becca . . .'

'I'm not crying,' I said. 'I'm sorry. No, I'm not sorry at all. I'm glad. Glad it wasn't your baby, I mean.'

'I should bloody well think so too,' he muttered, sitting down. 'Look, I didn't mean to shout at you. This whole issue is all, well, a bit of a red rag to a bull.'

I sniffed. 'I don't see why my telling Oliver he's going to be a father should be any concern of yours,' I said, bracing myself for a renewed assault.

But Joe only sighed, leaned across the desk and closed his hands round mine. 'Put it another way,' he said. 'Never mind about Oliver for the moment. Have you thought what you're going to tell the child?'

'Of course I have. When he — it — is of an intelligent age anyway. I shall explain he was conceived in, well, maybe not love, but affection. But that it didn't suit his father and me, at the time actually to marry, live together, whatever. Satisfied?'

'And the birth certificate?' persisted Joe, unruffled. 'What are you going to write in the box where it says father?'

'Oliver Langham, naturally,' I snapped. And then: 'I think . . .'

'My mother put *unknown*,' said Joe. 'I spent half my early life wondering whose name should be in that square. Did I ever tell you I used to dream about him coming to find me?'

'So?'

'Barmy, considering what a young thug I was, the things I used to fantasize about my dad. One week I'd have him as a racing driver, then a footballer, even — don't laugh — an opera

249

singer. Me, who thought Verdi was a make of pasta until I was thirty.' He laughed, but not very convincingly. My hand was crunched tightly between his. 'Anything Italians starred in, you see. Even now, I cringe when I remember Mum's funeral. When Aunty Vi told me this Italian superman had actually been a waiter and now ran a chip shop in Northcliffe-on-Sea . . . She'd always thought I should be told. But she had to wait for Mum to pop her clogs. A chippy-owner in Northcliffe – bloody hell.' He was kneading my fingers. I was beginning to appreciate what a peppercorn feels like in a mill. 'A grown man, and I could have wept buckets. I went to find him, the next day, you know. Not hard to find the only chippy with an Italian name. Tatty bloody joint.'

'Joe, there's no possible comparison. I'll – of course I'll tell my child who his father is. One day. I've kept in touch with Oliver, haven't I?'

'And if, *one day*, that child wants to go and look Oliver up? Like I did? Mind, once I'd seen the chip shop, seen what I supposed was him through the window, I didn't want to go in. Not any more.' Now I could hear his hurt, as well as feel it. He must have realized he was pulverizing my hand, because he released me with a grimaced apology. 'But I'd grown out of my father fantasies by then. When I was a kid, if I'd had even a sniff of my father's whereabouts, I'd have been on my bike and walking into that chippy.'

'I don't have to worry about that yet. The question won't arise for years.'

'And that makes it all right, does it? A strapping eighteen-year-old stranger turning up on Oliver's doorstep calling him Daddy?'

'Christ,' I said. 'I – wouldn't let that happen.'

'Sweetheart, I'm not trying to bully you, but just how do you think you can prevent it? The baby won't be part of you then. It'll have a mind of its own. Wanting to find its father is only natural. You can't pretend Oliver just doesn't exist – or that he doesn't have a stake in the child.'

'It's my baby,' I said fiercely.

'Will the baby see it that way? It's no good telling me my views are out of the ark. All that's been thrown at me before. I've covered this ground a hundred times and I can't change how I feel, which is that a child's better off having two parents at home. I'm even old-fashioned enough to believe in marriage.'

'Well, so do I,' I said sharply. 'In the right circumstances. Who doesn't? Anyway – you're not married.'

That only checked him for a moment. 'Haven't met anyone daft enough to take me on.'

Oh no? And what about Alison Laverick? But all I said was: 'Well, me neither. And it certainly wouldn't be Oliver.'

'I thought Oliver Langham was every woman's dream ticket to the altar.'

'Not mine.'

'Do you mean it, Becca? You're – not just putting on a brave front?'

'Are you kidding? Not even if Oliver were misguided enough to offer to make an honest woman of me.'

'Hell,' said Joe, gaping as though I'd confessed membership of the Flat Earth Society. 'All this time, I've thought you were eating your heart out for him, and –'

'Honesty, Joe, do I strike you as the kind of wimp who sits around pining and knitting bootees? If I'd wanted to be with Oliver, I'd have hopped on the next bloody plane to Italy.'

Joe's face crinkled slowly into the familiar lop-sided grin. 'I bet you would, too. Well, bugger me. This is fantastic, isn't it?'

'It is?' I said. 'I mean, what is?'

'Everything,' he roared. He sprang up and slapped his hand with a bang on the blue letter, lying forgotten on the desk. 'And this business of you quitting in March . . .'

But I didn't want to talk about that. 'You said it was fantastic, Oliver and me?'

'Do you still want to go in the spring?' Joe demanded.

251

I glanced down at my stomach. 'You think I have a choice?'

'Daft ha'p'orth,' he said, undeniably fondly. 'I mean, what are you going to do after the birth?'

'Go to my mother's, although she doesn't know that yet.'

If Joe had behaved with such gentlemanly, unlecherous decorum for the past five months because he believed Oliver and I . . .

'Are you planning to work?' he said exasperatedly. 'Or stay at home to look after baby?'

'Oh, very funny. Sit at home and live on what? I'm not expecting my parents to support me. Of course I've got to work.'

'Then why not stay here in the business with me? Unless —' The sudden droop of his face was clownish. 'I was forgetting. You only took this job as a stop-gap, didn't you? Just to tide you over.'

'No,' I protested. 'I mean, well, maybe, at the start. But it's been brilliant. I really love it. I . . .' I — couldn't continue.

'You do?' said Joe, evidently seeing nothing amiss in my purple face.

'Course,' I gasped.

'Bloody wonderful,' he bellowed. 'That's just what I was thinking. You don't have to leave at all, do you? Welcome, partner . . .'

And he yanked me to my feet, hugging me. I, limp as a dishrag, clung to his beefy shoulder, thinking, God, this truly was a day of confession, a day for acknowledging the devices and desires of our own hearts. As if I hadn't known all along . . .

The door smashed open, and Henry pranced in. He peered over his gold-rimmed half-moons. 'Please don't let me interrupt anything . . .'

'You're not,' I muttered, wishing he was.

'You're not,' said Joe, releasing me unhurriedly. 'Becca and I were discussing plans for the future.' I had enough wit left to glare a warning at him. 'For March,' he went on affably, addressing Henry. 'We've been offered a charity ball. I'm suggesting we take the booking and make it a gala opening for the castle. But the date' — if I could hear the snigger rippling under every word, then so could Henry — 'doesn't quite suit our Becca. A prior commitment. That right, Becca?'

'Shut up,' I hissed.

'A gala opening?' said Henry.

The prospect was intriguing enough to winkle his inquisitive gaze away from me. Most certainly, Henry could promise to have the public rooms ready. While Joe and he argued over marquee sites, I slumped back into my chair and picked up my cold half-mug of coffee.

Dear Oliver, I thought. *Things haven't worked out quite as planned. I mean the job's brill. In running a catering business I may, by chance, have found my vocation in life. About time too. And now I've been offered the post permanently. But along the way — and I promise you sincerely this was not on the original blueprints — I seem to have developed a positively schoolgirl-sized crush on the proprietor* . . .

But that wasn't true. I didn't look at Joe and see stars and hear Mantovani (well, Monteverdi) as the teenaged me had once with Oliver. Nor was there a whiff of the lusciously guilty passion Richard and I had shared. I just — loved Joe. Simple as that. When I'd said I loved the job, I'd damn nearly gone on to say . . .

'Oh, talk to yourself,' snapped Henry. I sat up and tried to locate the brochure he wanted, from the firm which supplied our marquees.

Eventually, he exited with a glance which flickered from Joe to me unnervingly wisely.

'I'd best be off too,' said Joe, and raised his voice. 'Wait for me, Henry. I want a word about the dining room.'

'Must you?' I said, desperately. 'Go, I mean?'

'Late already. Buffet for a hundred and fifty tonight. Two parties tomorrow, and from then on we *really* get busy. Christmas, I ask you — who needs it?'

'I'd like – to talk to you.'

'I've a million things to say to you too, babe,' replied Joe with a warm vehemence which raised goosepimples from my ears to my elbows. 'But think about staying on, won't you?'

I managed a smile. 'Sure. But, I don't know . . .'

I knew what I wanted all right, and it wasn't the kind of partnership he was talking about. I wanted protestations of love, not contractual obligations, shared lives, not profits, the full happily-ever-after works. And I can't pretend this was a dazzling leap of self-discovery. I couldn't remember a time when I didn't want Joe. Simply, with me pregnant, and him showing less ardour than a dead cod, I'd filed away the idea under P for pipe-dreams. I've never wasted time and tears pining for the great unattainables. Even now, as Joe's soppy grin scattered the tidy emotional filing cabinet into fluttering, hopeful chaos, I couldn't ignore the minor inconvenience of being five months pregnant with another man's child.

'Take care of yourself, sweetheart,' said Joe, walking across to the door and blowing a kiss. 'Of both of you, I mean.'

I bounced up from my chair. 'Joe! You won't tell anyone, will you?'

'Mum's the word?'

'Sod off. I'm serious. As long as I can, I want to keep it secret.'

'Oh, I'm great on secrets,' he said, with a curious bitterness. He paused, the door half-open. 'Keep your hair on. I won't tell a soul. Will you?'

I picked up the picture of Harecombe Castle. It did look rather as though it was on fire. Oh, what the hell. 'All right. I'll tell Oliver. I'll – I'll put a letter in his bloody Christmas card.'

Joe's winked. 'Behold,' he said. 'I bring you glad tidings of great joy . . .' and managed to get out of the door just before the crumpled-up card hit him.

CHAPTER TWENTY-THREE

I look back to that December and I see a blur of work. A few things stand out. I remember writing to Oliver. Strangely, it turned out to be the easiest letter I ever wrote to him. I just gave the facts and made clear I didn't expect anything from him. But I got that out of the way early in the month. As for the rest, there wasn't a day Flying Duck didn't have a booking, sometimes several. Joe — at a rare meeting — said he was dreaming of mince pies like giant clams which advanced on him, gnashing their fluted crusts.

I was dreaming of Joe Duff. He would be outside the house, and I would be inside, frenziedly hammering on the window. But he always wandered away, unaware of me. Not hard to interpret this dream. Sleeping and waking, I was screamingly frustrated because I couldn't get Joe to myself.

Admittedly, in real life, he didn't wander off, mysteriously deaf and blind. In fact he was flatteringly tender and solicitous. But snatched telephone calls, or hasty conferences when he dashed up to check progress on the kitchens, were as satisfying to me as a lettuce leaf to a starving man. I devoured them, only to feel hungrier for more.

Even when Joe contrived a night off and roared up to the Stables, there was Henry, who couldn't wait to expand his latest decorative vision. Another working supper. Joe nearly fell asleep at the table and had to be revived with strong coffee just to get himself home.

Poor me. Poor Joe, more to the point. He and his staff

were working flat out, but it was as though they were shovelling money into the castle, which, like a giant furnace, burned it all up, no matter how fast they shovelled. Naturally I told Joe I would come back to work for him after the baby was born — if possible. He thought I was worried about childcare arrangements. Actually I was beginning to doubt if there would be a job to come back to.

I hammered out invoices, prayed they'd be settled quickly and did my best to ginger up the builders. But George — between explaining the latest unforeseen contingencies that were going to cost just a whisker over estimate — was palpably more interested in pantomime plans. *Aladdin*, apparently. I wouldn't have minded quite so much if the panto could at least be expected to be over and done with at Christmas. Nothing so conventional. The Harecombe Village Pantomime — an annual social event of the prestige, locally, of Ascot and Glyndebourne combined — was always staged in February. As yet, George was only auditioning for Abenazer.

My recollection of the plot suggested wicked Uncle Abenazer dodged the work himself and tried to rook his nephew out of a fortune. On that basis, I should have been auditioning to play Aladdin, but I no longer had the figure for tights.

'My my,' said the midwife admiringly, 'we are growing well, aren't we?'

We were. In mid-December we suddenly outgrew even the most forgiving of skirts. It was leggings and ever-baggier woollies. Henry said he hoped some kind soul would buy me a new pullover for Christmas. He was getting bored with that hairy black sack.

'Designer mohair,' I snapped.

'Designed for what? King Kong impersonators?'

However, he poured my orange juice along with his own wine without querying my supposed health kick. His very silence suggested he suspected something. Henry's antennae were super-sensitive: he was a byword for knowing hot gossip a day before it happened. Since he also operated an information dissemination service which left fax in the Stone Age, I was not confirming any suspicions until after Christmas, which was when I had to break the glad tidings to Ma and family. On my last hasty visit home she had observed, complacently, that country air and food must suit me. Ma reads a simple correlation between waist measurement and happiness quotient. Poor innocent. I was not looking forward to Christmas.

A week or so before, an envelope arrived bearing an Italian stamp and Oliver's handwriting. I had to steel myself to tear it open. I need not have worried. It was only a Christmas card which must have crossed in the post with mine. Innocuous seasonal wishes.

Finally, on Christmas Eve, just before leaving for London, I tore down to the village for extra wrapping paper, and missed Joe. There was only a giant teddy bear sitting at my desk, with a red bow and sprig of mistletoe knotted round its huge neck. What's more, Henry had found Joe installing the creature.

'I told dear Joe this was *exactly* what you wanted,' purred Henry. The bear glared balefully at him – and so did I. He beamed. 'Something big and hairy to share your bed, pet.'

'Pregnant?' gasped my mother, on Christmas Eve. *Pregnant?* And – totally unlike Ma – she burst into tears.

'God, I'm sorry,' I said, thrusting a tumbler of sherry into her nerveless hand. 'It was an accident. I –'

'Sorry?' she wailed. 'This is the best Christmas present I've ever had in my life.'

Well, I hadn't expected her to cast me out into the snow, precisely, but nor had I anticipated wild jubilation. Anyone would think she'd never had a grandchild before. About time too, at my age, she declared, waving aside trivialities like the absence of a father. In fact she almost seemed disappointed that I had not intended landing myself in this desirable condition.

'Going it alone is all the rage with women of your generation,' she informed me, worldly wisdom flowing along with the sherry. 'Getting themselves pregnant and then getting on with it. Personally, I've always rather liked men, but' — she glanced through to the sitting room where Dad was snoring contentedly in front of *The Sound of Music* — 'one can see the attractions of dispensing with them. Once they've contributed their mite.'

So, one way and another, it was a jolly Christmas lunch. But after that ... well, it's always the same, isn't it? About Boxing Day teatime the hectic, dyspeptic merry-go-round grinds to a halt. The world has eaten itself into torpor and continues to snooze blearily for weeks. Or so it seemed to frustrated, sober me that year. I watched more films than a Cannes judge, and I had to stick out the whole holiday period *en famille*: not just to complete the visiting rounds (we are a large and gregarious clan), but because Ma was insisting I arrange to return to London to give birth, where she could keep an eye on me and the hospitals were *dependable*. I pointed out Oxford was hardly the Third World in medical provision, but she would brook no arguments. I didn't get my managing disposition from nowhere.

Before I had digested the turkey she was listing likely hospitals. Most of them were, understandably, reluctant to offer guided tours to potential customers at this time of year. God knows what happened to babies inconsiderate enough to wish to be born on December 27. Were they also recommended — as I was in no uncertain terms if I wanted to discuss modern childbirth facilities — to come back after the New Year? Not that there weren't attractions in lingering in a house with central heating, endless steaming bathwater and a mother fussing over my every whim like a broody hen. She would have been happiest to sweep me back into the nest there and then, but I told her I had to get back to work, which was true enough. I did not add I was aching to get back to Joe.

Even so, I stayed longer than I'd planned. It was the bleakest of January evenings when I finally drove round the side of Harecombe Castle again. Too cold to snow properly, but the wind was laced with frozen sleet. I was momentarily cheered to see light spilling into the courtyard and wondered if Henry had returned early. He was spending the New Year with an ancient and beloved aunt in Blackpool (a former *Folies Bergère* dancer, he swore), but no, the light was coming from the theatre and there were strange cars in the courtyard. The amateurs were evidently rehearsing.

The Stables was dark and smelled mustily neglected, with a snowy pile of envelopes behind the front door. I scooped them up and walked in. The fireplace was clogged with powdery embers and the holly over the mantelpiece drooped in post-seasonal depression. Without taking off my coat, I picked up the telephone and dialled Joe's flat. No answer. I knew there were no bookings tonight. I dialled again and let it ring twenty-six times. Bloody hell. Where was he?

I couldn't be bothered to clear out the fire. I would go to bed early and get warm there. I heated myself some soup, and settled down to open the post. Nothing duller than Christmas cards when Christmas is over. Particularly when most of them have clearly been scribbled in guilty haste after receiving yours. I dropped one after another into the bin after a cursory scan. And then found a postcard of the Leaning Tower of Pisa.

Got your card, scrawled Oliver, *but can hardly believe it. Must see you. Can't get away at once, but will come home soon . . .*

I don't think it was worry woke me so much as coffee on top of soup. My bladder was getting tetchier by the day. Besides, if Oliver and I had to meet, then surely, best get it over with quickly. I had fallen asleep assuring myself that natural fathers had no legal rights. That Oliver couldn't muscle in on the act . . . But the next minute, it seemed, I was awake again and a trip to the bathroom was imperative. I got up, shivering, and padded across the landing.

Groping for the light cord, I looked out of the window. The clouds had cleared and the moon was startlingly bright. The cars of the thespians had departed. Only my own little motor glimmered below. This was the view I should have used on the Christmas card, I thought. With frost glinting on every turret and a cold moon scudding across the sky, the castle was fairy-tale pretty.

Then, in the same instant I pulled the cord, I saw a face at one of the windows. One of the Lady Tower windows. Bit higher than me. And I'd have sworn it was staring right back at me. But even as I glimpsed it, I had switched on the bathroom light. All I could see now was my own reflection in the glass. I twitched the cord again, of course, and blinked out into the darkness, but by the time my eyes had readjusted the tower windows were unwinkingly black.

It never occurred to me that I might have seen the shade of Violet Rivenhoe climbing the castle stair as per legend. What did immediately cross my prosaic mind was a police warning about a spate of thefts from buildings under renovation. An entire eighteenth-century staircase had been filched from a nearby mini stately home. I scurried downstairs and dialled Joe again. No answer. I glanced at my watch. Ten past eleven. I slammed down the receiver.

I got as far as pulling on a tracksuit and wellingtons and finding the big torch when my nerve faltered. I wasn't quite such a phlegmatic creature as Henry averred. It was bloody dark out there. He wouldn't go across there at this time of night, alone, if you paid him. But, unlike him, I was not sensitive to *atmospheres*. Burglars on the other hand ... I hesitated, then, feeling horribly self-conscious, I picked up the phone again and dialled – for the first time in my life – 999.

The next morning I walked into my office to find George sitting in front of my desk, ready for our weekly meeting.

This was due to have begun, I blearily realized, a quarter of an hour earlier. George was glowing with punctuality. 'Hard to return to the grindstone after all the festivities and fun, isn't it?'

I growled, and was about to plunge into erudite questions of cornice restoration, when he went on, 'You weren't wandering round the castle last night, were you?'

'Most of the night, as a matter of fact,' I replied tartly. 'Which is why I slept through the alarm. I had the police round.'

It must have been a slack night for the County Constabulary. We had found nothing amiss, but the two officers had searched every last broom cupboard, inspired less by dutiful zeal, if you ask me, than rampant curiosity about what we were doing with the castle.

'Opening in the spring?' enquired one of them with an incredulity I could understand. Personally, I was cheered to see that the stumpy pipes and dead wires in the basement had blossomed in my absence into shiny ranks of cookers and sinks. George had evidently kept his promise to return the lads to work promptly.

When I told him now about the face I had seen at the tower window his own face, momentarily, brightened — suspecting the spectral Lady Violet no doubt — but then settled back into gloom. 'Ah, well, that would be it then,' he pronounced heavily. 'Malcolm isn't best pleased.'

'Why?'

'Follow me,' said George, beckoning with a long-fingered gesture I reckoned he'd been practising for Abenazer. Dumb as any Aladdin I followed him out of the office and to the foot of the spiralling tower stairs. George trotted up. I, more slowly, followed. He paused just below the first half-landing, outside the lowest tower room. 'Behold,' he cried.

Herein lies a magic cave, treasure that your heart will crave . . .
The lines came back to me suddenly. I hoped the Harecombe lot's script was better than the *Aladdin* I'd appeared in years ago.

But George did not open the door to the room. And the half-landing was empty, pale and limpid as quicksand. Propped across it was a dusty, splintering plank. I had tiptoed across this very plank last night with one policemen in front of me, another behind, and only just refrained from whistling an appropriate chorus from *The Pirates of Penzance*.

'So?' I said.

And he pointed downwards. Sure enough, a line of foot-marks was printed across the concrete half-landing so faint I was not surprised we had failed to spot them last night. Now, I wanted to call the boys in blue back. No question, they'd soon concluded I'd been imagining things. By the end of the search I'd begun to agree. But if ever there was concrete proof . . .

George was less elated. 'Malcolm put that skim on yesterday afternoon.'

'Well, it certainly wasn't me,' I said, showing him my size-eight foot. The prints were tiny.

'Nor a copper either,' admitted George. 'And you saw a face in the window?'

'The tall one, next floor. Could it have been one of your lot from the rehearsal? The pass door was open again.'

One policeman had spotted that, adding self-righteously that Mr Duff had been advised to keep the door linking theatre and castle locked. Easier said than done, I'd retorted with a builder doubling as panto villain.

'Far as I know we all left together about a quarter to eleven,' George murmured, studying the floor. 'You know, these footprints don't come back. They only lead one way.'

'There was no one up there,' I said. 'We searched every sodding room.'

George stiffened. He did not care for foul language on the lips of the fair sex. 'Did you look on the roof?'

No, I conceded, we had not actually gone out on to the roof.

'Well then,' said George.

I followed him up the stairs. I'd been out on the roof before. Soon after taking the job, impelled by morbid curiosity, I'd crept up one summer's evening after the builders had gone home.

The staircase curled up beyond the top room to end in a low-jambed doorway. A peeling door was secured with rusty bolts which George yanked back, tutting.

'New push-bar to be fitted here, as per fire regs,' he said. The present door grated open and we stepped into a small well, set into the sloping roof of the tower. There were shallow stairs leading up to the deck of roof-tiles.

Alone, last summer, I had barely stuck my nose above roof-level before, shuddering with vertigo (and a certain disgust at my own ghoulishness), I had retreated, bolting the door behind me. Now I followed George.

The roof sloped gently round from a central, flag-poled pivot. Just like Aladdin's hat. Round the perimeter the battlements, which from ground level looked frail as the points of a tiara, were actually massive and mossy like giant tombstones. An aerial, more symmetrical, Stonehenge, without linking capstones. The gaps between the battlements yawned stomach-lurchingly wide, over a parapet of barely knee height.

Framed in these gaps was a sectioned panorama of the countryside in winter: ploughed fields, the village smoking silently, the river glinting in the distance and an eternity of cold sky. The wind whistled fresh from Siberia. A rook swooped far below croaking loudly, nothing but air in a direct line between me and it. I clutched the iron handrail, a puny lifeline leading, I could only assume – no way was I going to investigate – to the jutting platform of the fire-escape on the back of the tower. I found myself reflecting that in case of fire I might be more inclined to stick around and fry than step between the battlements, over that low stone parapet as required.

And I also found myself thinking of Cathy Langham. Coming up here. Alone. In the dark. Quitting the safety of the handrail . . . Dear Lord. She really must have been brave. Brave or mad.

George, carefree as a sparrow, was wandering round the perimeter of the roof admiring the intricate brick and stone work. 'Beautiful craftsmanship,' he said, stroking one of the carved battlements reverently. He actually had one foot over the parapet, resting – I supposed – on the ledge circling the outside. 'Never see anything like this today. Are you all right?'

'Touch of vertigo,' I said. 'And, to be honest, I find the, um, history of the tower slightly unnerving.'

'You don't think it could have happened again?' said George, positively tripping round the edge, peering between the columns of brick and stone.

'I think we might have noticed something,' I said. 'A blood-ied corpse in the courtyard would be difficult to overlook.'

'Well, there's no sign anyone's been up here,' he conceded, following me down the shallow steps out of the wind, and shutting the door behind us with a safe, satisfying clang. 'So where'd she go?'

'She?'

'Small feet.'

'Maybe she – or a small-footed he – only realized the concrete was tacky when they got halfway across. They came up in the dark, after all.' I hastened down to the landing in question to review the evidence. 'Look,' I said, feeling like the detective in a rep Agatha Christie. 'They started off walking normally – three steps. And then they realized the floor was soft. So – see? – they jumped from here to the stairs. And on the way back down, they just walked across the plank like the rest of us.'

'Fair enough,' said George, nodding thoughtfully. 'But what on earth would anyone want, coming up here in the first place?'

CHAPTER TWENTY-FOUR

'One of the Am. Dram. crowd having a nose round,' declared Joe that evening. 'The locals are dying to see what's going on here. Can you manage this, love, and I'll carry the box?'

I'd been trying to get hold of Joe all day. According to Steve, his assistant chef, he'd gone to London for a party. But at half past seven, to my surprise and satisfaction, he was here on my doorstep with our supper in a box.

'Well maybe,' I conceded, following him into the sitting room. 'The policemen certainly wanted a full guided tour.'

'Oh hell,' said Joe in passing. 'We can't watch the snooker on that. Why don't you get yourself a colour set?'

'This one was here – and it's free,' I retorted, switching the Bakelite tank off and following him into the kitchen. 'Probably a priceless antique. Joe, pay attention. If it was only someone wanting a sneak preview of the hotel, why were they lurking by a window, staring out at the courtyard . . .'

'Ought to be careful with those old valve sets,' observed Joe sagely, 'My mum's went up in a puff of smoke one night.'

'. . . and scaring the wits out of me?'

Joe turned round with a look of surprise. 'You were scared?' He dumped the box to hug me to his chest. Realizing discretion beat the hell out of valour, I batted my lashes and even essayed a little shudder. Plucky Heroine Abandoned in Sinister Castle. Take One. 'Poor old love,' he said. 'I warned you it was lonely out here.' But he soon released me to pick up a

265

bottle and rummage in the drawer for a corkscrew. 'And where was Henry during all the excitement?'

'Blackpool.'

He stopped rummaging. 'Blackpool? I brought food for three. You mean — Henry's still away?'

This time my shiver was entirely uncontrived. 'Until, um, until tomorrow.'

'You're never telling me,' whispered Joe with a wolfish curl to his smile I hadn't seen since that sunny afternoon when, in another life it seemed now, he had strolled into Oliver's garden, 'that we're *alone at last*?' This was drawled, I promise you, with all the sex-dripping innuendo appropriate to this caption on a hundred honeymoon cartoons.

'Looks like it,' I trilled, maidenly shy as any cartoon bride. But maidens aren't six and a half months pregnant.

'About time too,' he murmured. 'Sod the snooker.'

I felt like a child who, accidentally, has lit the blue touch paper on a long-coveted firework, and is now scared stiff because, no question, sooner or later the thing's going to explode.

But we had supper first. Well, Joe did. He had even packed flowers and candles, which he arranged with panache on the rickety table, polishing the chipped glasses and flicking off lights as fast as I switched them on. Had the hi-fi not been on the blink, it would undoutedly have been oozing slinky strings. Instead Joe hummed Puccini's greatest hits as he chopped and sautéed and stirred.

His cooking was masterly as ever, although by then, as I rather meanly observed, anything which wasn't recycled turkey would have tasted ambrosial. But I could only peck through the courses until Joe was moved to ask, over the poached peaches, what was wrong.

'Wrong?' I echoed, like a startled parrot.

'This intruder business has really put the wind up you, hasn't it?' he said, discarding his spoon and stretching his arms wide. 'Come here, sweetheart.'

'I'm fine,' I snapped, attacking a peach. And I jolly well should have been fine. I should have been bouncing on cloud nine. Wasn't this exactly what I'd yearned for, this cosy dinner *à deux* and Joe's eyes glowing brighter than the candles with the unmistakable light of lust?

'I've had a postcard from Oliver,' I said hastily, which was about the last thing on my mind then, but it certainly doused the lusty glow. Joe's arms snapped back to his sides like the jaws of a trap.

'Saying what?'

So I told him. Spinning the story out like Scheherazade.

'Coming home soon?' he repeated, pouring the last of the bottle into his glass. 'That what you want?'

'I suppose so. If I've got to see him, then the sooner the –'

'I didn't mean that,' said Joe. 'I'm asking if you want Oliver back with you.'

'You know I don't.'

'What about the baby?' he persisted. 'What about Oliver? How does he feel?'

A pulse ticked in my throat. 'I've told you, there's absolutely nothing between us.'

'There was once.'

'But there wasn't,' I said impatiently. 'That's the whole point. Oliver was so grief-stricken over Cathy, he didn't know whether he was coming or going. Oh, pack it in, will you?' Joe, predictably, had guffawed like a drain at my all-too-appropriate turn of phrase. 'What I'm saying is he didn't give a fig about me. It was pure chance threw us together – virtually threw us into bed, what's more. And as far as I was concerned it was nothing: a bit of fun, a one-night fling ...' Then I realized what I was saying. Too late.

Joe misread my sudden stricken silence. 'But now there's a baby on the way. Becca, if hearing from Oliver has made a difference to you, just say so. I'll – understand. We'll have a coffee and I'll toddle off home like a good boy. Just like I always do.'

And otherwise? We had reached — as they say — the moment of truth, I was a big girl. I knew what 'otherwise' meant.

Fleetingly, mad as it sounds, I was tempted to cave in and claim Oliver's postcard had changed everything. But the moment of truth is no time to go wading into a whole new mire of lies. I reached across and defiantly relieved Joe of his wine glass. 'I've told you, I don't want Oliver back.'

You hear about people's smiles reaching, or not reaching, their eyes. Joe's grin, I swear, took in his whole sprawling body, ears to toes. I downed the contents of his glass in a single gulp. I don't know what Eve made of the apple, but the thrill to the tastebuds — and the heady shock to the system — of that one mouthful made me wonder, I gasped, whether I wasn't a closet alcoholic.

Joe, rising and kicking back his chair, retorted that if I knew what white Burgundy of this calibre cost, I would bloody well expect to be transported to heaven. Speaking of which . . . how about we go and sit in front of the fire?

'What about the washing up?' I stuttered, which was hardly up to Scheherazadian levels of invention. Besides, she was warding off death. I was only contemplating a fate I'd always found a damn sight more inviting.

'Don't be daft,' said Joe, heading into the kitchen. 'Go and make yourself comfortable.'

I arranged myself in one corner of the small sofa, straight-spined as a Sunday School teacher, and bundled a defensive pile of newspapers on to the seat beside me. But Joe, returning with brandy and a box of lusciously decadent chocolate truffles, made no attempt to join me. Instead, he switched off the standard lamp and stretched across the rug in front of the fire, unfastening a shirt button and yawning.

'Take me,' he whispered. 'I'm all yours.'

Joke. He was already raising himself on an elbow to pick up his brandy. I giggled manically. What the hell was the matter with me anyway? I wanted this man, this lusty grinning animal, more than anything on earth, didn't I? I had tumbled readily enough into much less desirable beds in the past. But that, I was beginning to understand, was the whole point. In the past. In that other life, when I had not been pregnant. Joe and I were not *à deux*. We were two and a half. 'I felt the baby kick this afternoon.' I said.

If this was an attempt to keep Joe at a safe distance by reminding him of my condition, it failed. 'Can I feel?' he said, shuffling across the rug. He positioned his hand over the bulge with the painstaking gentleness of a circus elephant resting a foot on the torso of his lady trainer.

'You might have to wait,' I said lamely. 'Probably won't do it again now.' His hand was noticeably steady. I settled back, willing myself to stop quaking.

'I went up to town for a party yesterday,' he remarked.

'Last night, was it? Steve — said something about a party.'

'At Al's. You remember Alison? Hey — I felt that!'

What he had felt was me twitching at the mention of Alison Laverick.

'She was asking after you,' he said, taking away his hand.

I bounced upright. 'You didn't tell her? About the baby?'

'Do me a favour,' said Joe, and I sank back on to the cushions again. 'Mind,' he added glancing over his shoulder, 'I don't know how long you think you can keep *that* under wraps. Tell her yourself, anyway. She's due for a visit to the parents soon.'

'That's nice,' I hissed. I knew I was behaving illogically, resenting Joe's past lovers even while I was wondering how to fend him off myself.

Joe apparently noticed nothing. 'And she's promised to get across in March, too, for Constance Berisford's bash. Offered to try and place a piece about the castle and our gala opening.'

'Great,' I snarled, and this time he did glance round. 'We — need all the publicity we can get,' I added quickly.

'Too right,' he agreed. 'She came up with another idea, too.

Which I've been meaning to get round to all night . . .' Where-upon he fell silent, staring into the fire. Oh God, he was steeling himself for something. 'With things going the way they are,' he said at length, 'she suggested I could raise a bit more capital by selling my flat.'

Anxiety melted under a deluge of familiar guilt. 'Oh Joe,' I wailed. 'You should have sold the castle when that man of-fered. I advised you wrong —'

'I knew the risks. Contrary to popular opinion. I'm not a complete idiot.'

'But I was only thinking about myself,' I said, determined to make a clean breast of it. 'My own job —'

'We're having a good time, aren't we?'

'Laughing all the way to the bankruptcy court?'

'We'll manage,' said Joe. 'And I daresay Al's right. She usually is. It might help if I sold the flat and — well — moved in.'

'With *her*?' But my consternation was only momentary. Joe couldn't possibly commute from London.

'No, you daft bat,' said Joe, twisting round to face me. 'Here, have a truffle,' Mechanically, I picked one out of the proffered box. 'With you, of course.'

I froze, chocolate halfway to my mouth. 'You mean — come and live with me?' Was *this* it? The long-awaited lunge? This baldly chucked-out proposition?

Joe was grinning. 'Only if you'll have me, babe.'

Never judge a firework by its wrapping. You think you're in for long whispering showers of delight, and a quick sub-nuclear blast knocks you sideways.

I saw Joe's grin wilt. 'It's up to you,' he said. 'Really, I mean, the house is still yours. But there are three bedrooms, or is it four? Mind, if you don't fancy it —'

'Rooms?' I croaked. 'You meant — just — come and live *here*?'

'Only if the flat sells and . . . Becca? What the fuck did you think I meant?'

I gulped. The last time I'd assumed he was after having his shameless way with me, he'd innocently offered me a job. And now? I could feel the blood scalding my cheeks.

'Well bloody hell,' said Joe — and then we both began to laugh. Too loud and long, like children with a joke they don't understand but suspect is smutty.

'Honestly, Becca,' he said eventually, picking up his brandy glass. 'Al used to say I had the sexual finesse of a sledgehammer but, I promise you, even I could do better than *that*. And in your condition, too,' he added self-righteously.

'Actually, Alison once told me,' I said kindly, 'that you were a good lover.'

Joe had taken a sip of brandy, and now broke into a violent spasm of coughing. 'Christ,' he croaked. 'Is that really what women talk about when they're alone?'

'Not in my experience,' I said — with a touch of regret. I was still holding the chocolate truffle. I noticed, without interest, that it was melting. I was remembering what Alison had gone on to say.

'Thank the Lord for that,' Joe muttered.

Joe was a good lover, she had said, *but not husband material.*

He picked up the poker and prodded the red coals. The fire spat and crackled companionably. Shadows flickered across the ceiling and I contemplated my predicament.

'Good?' he enquired *sotto voce*, before dropping the poker back in its bucket. 'Or *very* good?'

I laughed, but felt more inclined to weep. Alison Laverick had defined my dilemma. Joe was not husband material. Six and a half months pregnant, I realized I didn't want just a lover, however good — and I was prepared to believe he was Casanova on wheels — but . . .

'Babe,' said Joe tutting. 'You've got chocolate melting all over your fingers. Don't you want that truffle?' He tried to take it from my limp hand but it collapsed gooily. He sucked the chocolate from his own fingers, then casually licked a remaining blob off the ball of my thumb. My toes curled;

271

reflex response. The surge of lust which rampaged through the rest of me, though, nearly made my hair curl. Shouldn't pregnancy, I thought indignantly, innoculate one against urges like this?

'Tastes better on you,' he murmured, and did not release my hand.

'Joe,' I began.

'Tell me,' he said. 'What's up?'

'Look, don't get me wrong, I really – like you . . .'

'I really like you too, sweetheart.' And with slow tenderness he began kissing my fingers one after another, only pausing between the third and fourth to say it would help if I stopped wriggling.

'Um, Joe . . .'

He relinquished my hand, shoved the newspapers aside, and hoisted himself up to perch on the sofa beside me. It was a tight fit. He wrapped an arm round me. 'Love?'

'It's the baby,' I faltered, which was at least half the truth. 'I can't – not like this.'

'You're shaking like a jelly,' he observed. 'What do you think I'm planning? To pin you down and ravish you?' I managed a wavering laugh. 'Not that I wouldn't like to,' he added. 'Just say the word. But I'm in your hands, sweetheart. You tell me what you want.'

I knew, explicitly, what I didn't want. I didn't want a one-night stand, like Cathy Langham. I didn't even want a long affair, like Alison Laverick. But I didn't want Joe to drink his coffee and go home like a good boy either.

'You see, I'm afraid – of getting hurt,' I whispered, despising every wimpish syllable even as I uttered them. And Joe, silly fool, only protested, raining soft kisses across my forehead, that he would never hurt me. Not physically, I wanted to scream, emotionally. Can't you see my soul's being ripped out, quivering and pathetic like a snail from its shell?

'Relax, little one,' he murmured, nibbling my ear in a most unsettling way. 'We've got all night, haven't we?'

272

And maybe all night was all he wanted. He could jump into my bed now and out again in the morning, casually as cleaning his teeth. Just like I told him I'd done with Oliver. Me and my big mouth. How could I turn round now and announce that the game, for me, had changed? Sorry, ducks, but I'm reverting to the pre-1960s rule book: flings, one-night stands (prim smile) are now offside ... an experienced player, thirty years old and heavily pregnant, announcing she's reapplying for the coy virgins team?

Joe, like a hairy octopus, hugged me closer still.

'So tell me,' he whispered. 'Tell me what you want me to do.'

Marry me. The answer was flashing in my brain like a neon advertising slogan. That was what I really wanted: a husband for me and, yes, a father for my baby ... Bit of a tall order. So I said nothing – but I noticed my mouth was drooping hospitably open of its own accord. As if, while the brain agonized over policy decisions, the body had got bored waiting and was pursuing its own wayward inclinations. I could taste Joe's breath, sweet with brandy and chocolate. I felt my eyes closing and resolutely blinked them open again. 'Joe – I ...'

I heard a car draw up and brake in the courtyard.

'Oh my God,' said Joe, raising his head to listen. 'Not bloody Henry again. Not now.'

'He's ... not due back.'

The engine was idling. The chug-chug of a diesel engine. Unmistakable.

'With a bit of luck,' murmured Joe, stroking a lock of hair off my forehead, 'it's your mysterious intruder returning to haunt the tower. He's welcome to it.'

I shut my eyes. 'I don't think intruders arrive in taxis.'

The car door slammed, but the engine was still ticking over patiently. There was a tap at the front door.

'Don't get up,' said Joe. 'I'll go.'

But I was wriggling free and scrambling, red-faced and ruffled, to my feet.

273

'I think,' I said, 'I'd better go and answer this.'

I lay no claim to telepathic gifts. In six months no one – *no one* – had arrived at the Stables like this: late at night, in a taxi. I walked into the poky, chilly hall, gritted my teeth – and opened the front door.

'Somebody,' said Oliver with the indignation of Baby Bear after encountering Goldilocks, 'is living in my house.'

Somebody else – I had already guessed – would not be sleeping in my bed tonight.

Just me and my teddy bear.

CHAPTER TWENTY-FIVE

Before I could speak, Oliver threw his arms round me. 'God, it's good to see you at last,' he exclaimed, his glasses gouging my forehead as he kissed me. 'I seem to have been travelling for ever. Hey,' he added shyly, dropping his hands to my waist and holding them there, 'you really are pregnant, aren't you?'

Joe's bulky silhouette was blocking the sitting-room doorway. Now he melted silently back into the sitting room.

'You'd − better come inside,' I said to Oliver, squirming free of his embrace.

'What shall I do with my stuff?' he asked. And I registered, dismally, that the taxi driver was piling luggage up behind him.

'Bring it into the hall,' I sighed.

The taxi chugged off with a toot of farewell as I finally shut the front door.

Oliver preceded me into the sitting room, where he found Joe switching on lamps and snuffing candles. 'Oh,' was all Oliver said, but he quivered like a terrier at a rat-hole.

'I was just going,' said Joe, adding softly to me as I walked past him: 'What's a petard?'

'How should I know?'

'I think I've been hoist on one,' he said, swallowing the remainder of his brandy. 'And it's bloody uncomfortable.' He turned to Oliver. 'How long are you back for?'

'For good,' said Oliver, warming his hands over the fire and shivering briskly. 'Who the hell's that guy in my house?'

'A mathematician — Trinity?' I said. 'Didn't Constance tell you?'

He shook his head. 'Have to sort him out in the morning.'

'The morning? Oliver, what are you intending to do to-night?'

'Can't I stay here?'

'Why not go to Constance?' I said wildly.

'For God's sake, I've been travelling since lunchtime.'

'This isn't my place, Oliver,' I said desperately.

'Course it's yours, Becca,' said Joe, and I scowled at him. But he continued imperturbably: 'You can have anyone you like to stay here. For as long as you — or they — like. I'd best get on the road.'

'Should you be driving?' I said, clutching at excuses to keep him here.

'Probably not, so I'll take the back roads and trust in St Christopher. No, love, I must,' he said, pulling on his jacket. 'Don't worry. I can let myself out.'

Which he did. But not before he heard Oliver say, 'Do you want to get married?'

'Of course not,' I snapped. 'Any more than you do.' I heard the front door open, felt the draught round my legs.

'I wouldn't mind,' said Oliver. At least no one could accuse the boy of over-schmaltzing the romance. 'In fact I think we should. For the baby.'

I could have wept. Damn Joe, I was thinking. He's hoist us all on his bloody petard, and now he's shimmering off into the night. I turned and pelted into the hall after him, just in time to see the front door click shut — and nearly went flying over Oliver's luggage.

'Steady now,' said Oliver who had followed me, catching my arm. 'We've got to look after you. I'd better shift this lot. Where's our room?'

'*Our* room?' I shrieked.

Oliver disarmed me by blushing vividly. 'Put me wherever you like,' he stuttered. 'The sofa's fine.'

I made up a bed for him in a spare room. But I told him to leave the bulk of his luggage in the hall. Ready to go tomorrow.

Florence was bloody noisy, said Oliver, when he appeared next morning in the kitchen, yawning. The natives never stopped shouting, the tea was foul, the money came with mind-boggling strings of noughts . . .

Oliver, no question, was one of the school which knows the civilized world ends at Dover. He wasn't remotely aware that what he was saying might be funny. Not that I was in great humour for jokes myself, but I remember thinking – as I cracked an egg into the frying pan – that I wouldn't be surprised if he complained they all bloody well insisted on speaking Italian.

'And,' he went on, pouring himself a cup of tea, 'no one understood a word of my Italian.'

When I asked him how much Italian he actually spoke, he replied indignantly that he'd been familiar with music terms since earliest childhood. I had a vision of Oliver propelling himself round Florence shouting '*Allegro molto*' at bemused taxi drivers. Work was OK, he conceded. He'd completed the research for his paper – well, more or less.

'I can finish it here in Oxford now,' he said, tucking into the fried eggs and toast I put before him like a starving orphan. 'Though God only knows what Constance will say when she finds out.'

'She'll be thrilled to have you home.'

'I doubt it.' Oliver eyed me rather oddly for a moment, before reapplying himself to his plate. 'She fixed the teaching job for me,' he said, between mouthfuls. 'And the digs. She's not going to be pleased.'

Naturally I didn't take this seriously. But when, at my urging, he telephoned her after breakfast, I began to realize he might know his aunt better than I.

I was washing up the breakfast pots but even in the kitchen

277

I could hear Constance's chain-saw of a voice buzzing out of the telephone receiver. Stray words reached me. *Crazy* . . . *Irresponsible* . . . *Oldest friends* . . . *Breach of contract* . . .

'But I hated the place,' Oliver burst out at length. 'You don't realize. I was lonely as hell.'

I'll bet he was too, I thought, touched with a sharp and unexpected compassion: pregnancy makes one blub at the drop of a handkerchief. I never doubted, though, that Constance would be even more sympathetic once the necessary scold had been delivered.

'But it's my house . . .' protested Oliver a little later.

The pitch of her voice upped, and I heard her reminding Oliver it most certainly was not his house. And that she was not in the habit of breaking *her* word. And more at a less audible level. I clattered the pots back into cupboards and waited. Eventually, Oliver put the receiver down.

'Well?' I said, strolling through. 'If you want to load your bags into the car, I'll run you into Oxford.'

Oliver shook his head. 'I can't go to Constance,' he said. 'She washes her hands of me.'

'Rubbish,' I said heartily. 'Not Constance. She adores you.'

Oliver glanced up, looking older and quite uncharacteristically cynical. 'Not after the way I've blotted my copybook.'

'Oliver, this is mad. She may have gone to a lot of trouble to fix you up in Italy but —' He was shaking his head, as though I was talking nonsense. 'Oh Lord, is it my fault?' I demanded. 'Is she cross because you've come here to me?' I began to recount my odd telephone conversation with Constance, how embarassed she had sounded to find me at Harecombe, but Oliver dismissed all this.

'We never mentioned you. She didn't even bother to ask where I was ringing from. She doesn't care where I go, what I do. Anyway,' he added with a flash of petulance, 'why the hell should it be anything to do with you? She thought you were terrific.' He broke off because there was a rattle from the front door.

278

'Thanks, Phil,' I called. 'Oh, do you want a signature?'

Phil, our friendly postman, eyed the cases in the hall with undisguised interest as I scrawled receipt of a parcel for Henry. 'The prodigal's finally showed up, eh?' he enquired affably. Only when I returned to the sitting room did it occur to me the man had sounded as though he'd been expecting Oliver's return.

'Oh, Phil knows everything,' said Oliver, when I mentioned this. 'Cathy swore he was late because he read the mail and spent his round circulating the news. If he knows I'm here, you can bet the world will by tomorrow.'

'But you're not here,' I said stupidly. 'I mean — where are you going now?'

Oliver gazed at me, clear-eyed and earnest as a boy scout taking the oath. 'I've come back to look after you, Becca. And our baby.'

Our baby? Which even now was kicking me furiously. '*My* baby,' I hissed, sinking on to the sofa.

'Why did you write, if you didn't want me to come home? Look, if you don't want to get married —'

'Of course I don't want to get married. The idea's ludicrous. We hardly know one another.'

'Nevertheless, we're responsible for bringing a child into the world. We've got to consider its needs. How are you going to look after it?'

This was a different Oliver from the sad-eyed wretch of six months ago. It was as though he'd grown up, acquired sense and purpose. Grown into fatherhood? My God.

'I can support myself. And my child.'

'Our child,' said Oliver, adding quietly: 'It's not much fun being brought up by nannies. Take it from me.'

'This is completely different,' I retorted. 'Your mother didn't want you.' Oliver flinched. 'I didn't mean that exactly,' I temporized. 'Oh Oliver, you know what I mean ...'

'I'm just grateful you did want this child,' he replied, evenly. 'That you didn't take — the other way out. Like Cathy did.'

He squatted beside the sofa, taking hold of my reluctant hand and forcing me to meet his eyes. 'Becca, when I got your letter it was — well, it was as though everything fell into place, began finally to make some kind of sense. After the whole ghastly tragedy, something good was coming out of it. I mean, I'm absolutely not superstitious, but it seemed almost like Fate. Can you understand that?'

Fate? All armies have God on their side; everyone claims Fate is batting for them. Rot. It wasn't Fate that had made me pregnant, I wanted to tell him, just a dicky mussel and bloody bad luck. But Oliver was so passionately sincere, I couldn't laugh it off. I couldn't even release my hand. I just shook my head. But he went on: 'I lost Cathy, and our child. Now, it's as though I've been given a second chance.'

'No,' I shouted. 'My baby, well, OK, *our* baby, — it's not some kind of substitute for the one you lost. Be reasonable, Oliver. Cathy was your wife. You loved her, you . . . Oh, this is mad.'

'No it's not. I'm not stupid, Becca. I know . . .' He shrugged, looking uncomfortable. 'I know there's no question of love, or anything like that between us. Not yet, anyway. And I swear I won't press you to anything at all. Just let me help you.'

'Oh God.'

'We must talk. Sort out what you want.'

What I wanted, at that moment, was to throttle Joe Duff for landing me in this mess. 'I'm late for work,' I said feebly.

'OK,' said Oliver, releasing my hand and standing up. 'I'll go down to the Gatehouse and see if I can get my bike out of the garage. I can't manage here without it.'

'Manage here? Oliver, I've told you, you can't stay here.'

'Why not? Be reasonable, Becca, it's a spare room isn't it?'

I remembered Joe making almost the same observation last night — but in such different circumstances. I could have wept.

'What will people say?' I protested.

'People? Who the fuck cares what anyone says?'

'Cathy's mother, Oliver, have you thought about her?' I

stuck my stomach out. 'This can't be hidden much longer. And you coming back here . . .'

'Becca, you mustn't get worked up,' he said, with a soothing calm which would have incensed a Madonna. 'I've told you I'll do whatever you want. But, just for the moment, until I've had a chance to sort myself out, *please*. You go into work,' he added kindly, 'and I'll get my stuff out of the hall.'

I walked across the courtyard, wondering how I'd been so easily out-manoeuvred — by *Oliver* of all people. Goliath must have felt like this when the pebble felled him. But I bloody well knew who to blame, and the first thing I did when I got into my office was to ring the architect of this fiasco. No answer from his flat. He was not at Flying Duck either, said Stephen when I rang there.

Now I shut my eyes, imagining the red car wrapped round a tree — or Joe hollow-eyed and wretched, sobering up in a police cell . . .

'He phoned ten minutes ago, actually,' Steve went on cheerily. 'To say he's taking a few days off. Probably still whooping it up in London. You know old Joe . . .'

I couldn't speak. Relief, frustration — fury — were choking me. Steve was saying Joe had asked him to let me know. Thanks, I'd saved him a call.

'My pleasure.' I slammed the phone down.

'Happy New Year,' said Henry, stalking into my office that afternoon and pecking the air beside my cheek. 'Who is he?'

'Ah,' I said. 'You've met Oliver.'

'In a manner of speaking,' said Henry, pulling off his gloves finger by finger and dropping his mac over the back of a chair. 'Ten minutes ago, I emerged from my taxi to find two total strangers in heated discourse on my doorstep. An over-grown schoolboy and a stunted nun.'

'Nun?'

'Something about the eyes,' he said dreamily. 'The peculiarly unfocused light of fanaticism — but a perfectly horrible sludge-coloured coat. She was berating him about a miscarriage of justice, how it was his duty to act —'

'Not Cathy's mother, please,' I said, shutting my eyes. 'Small and mouselike?'

Henry ignored me. 'Believe me, I waited as long as I could. But when the record began repeating itself — stupid police, wilful overlooking of evidence and so forth — I felt obliged to interrupt, and ask if I could possibly enter the house. Perhaps I wasn't at my most tactful. The nun — yes, very mouselike, if one can imagine a mouse in holy orders — exited Courtyard Left. The schoolboy glared at me. "Who the hell are you?" he demanded. Truly — pure Bulldog Drummond. "And what do you want here?" I informed him that, as a matter of fact, I lived here. With Becca Haydock. Guess what he answered? Predictable as a Whitehall Farce . . .'

I sighed. 'He said — he did too?'

Henry smiled dangerously sweetly. 'Tell me it's not true.'

Maybe some things in nature are genuinely incompatible. Among them, as was to become apparent, Oliver and Henry. Everything, it seemed, could be guaranteed to polarize them, from tea and Radio Three in the morning (Henry preferred coffee and television) and onwards through the day. Oil and water. But you can blend the oil and vinegar in your salad dressing with a dash of emulsifying mayonnaise if you wish and, on the same principle, I've always believed anyone can get along with absolutely anyone else — granted a mutual dash of good will, which was lacking here. Henry and Oliver, quite irrationally, had taken against one another on sight. Oh to be able to shake the pair of them together like a vinaigrette.

Oliver's hostility over supper that first evening was blatant — and absurdly misplaced. Only an innocent like Oliver could suspect a Henry of harbouring sexual designs on me. Equally, only a fiend like Henry — understanding perfectly what Oliver suspected — would then go to painstaking lengths to confirm he was right.

'Henry,' I said sternly, trapping him in the kitchen after an interminable hour of Henry *darling*ing me and Oliver grinding his teeth, 'this has got to stop. Oliver's only staying a few days. Be nice to him.'

Henry scowled. 'There's something about that *particular* cast of square-jawed Englishman which is anathema to me. I see, oh, the Marquis of Queensberry crossed with Bertie Wooster. Dim-witted, but stiff with prejudice nevertheless.'

'Rubbish,' I snapped, stacking plates in the cupboard. 'Oliver's sweet-natured, and there have been awful tragedies in his life. Please, Henry. For me.'

'Well . . . I suppose we mustn't upset you. Not in your condition.'

I spun round. 'You *did* know.'

Henry peered quizzically at me over the top of his spectacles. 'The day I arrived I could not but notice the pregnancy manual beside your bed,' he said. '*You and Your Baby* isn't most people's idea of gripping entertainment. Although I have rarely opened a more lurid publication. My dear, the *pictures*. One cannot help feeling the gooseberry bush is a deeply underrated institution.'

'Why didn't you say something?'

Henry raised an eyebrow. 'Apparently, you didn't wish to discuss your, ah, predicament and I, as you know, am the soul of discretion.'

The very innocence with which he said this alerted me. 'Have you told anyone?'

Henry shrugged. 'Does Richard know?'

'Richard?' I shrieked. 'It's not Richard's.'

'Oh dear,' said Henry with a little giggle. 'Silly me.'

I glared at him. 'Who the hell have you been talking to?'

'My darling,' said Henry, 'Blackpool in January is hardly the haunt of the theatrical *beau monde*. No one you know anyway.'

'Give me strength . . .'

'And who,' enquired Henry, 'if not Dicky Prescott, is the lucky father, you naughty girl?'

And so I told him. It was one of the rare occasions I have had the satisfaction of silencing Henry Blayne completely.

The first thing I noticed about Joe's eventual return — apart from the thunder of blood through my pulses and the silly smile pulverizing my cheeks — was the car. No scarlet Batmobile. A little yellow job with even more rust than mine.

He had been away an entire, interminable week — with no word, only a telephoned message to the kitchens — when this foreign vehicle squeaked to a halt beside me in the courtyard, on a bitter breezy morning, and Joe clambered out.

'If I can't sell the flat,' he said, kissing me exactly the way he always used to — as though I were his aunt, 'the least I could do was flog the car. Know what the insurance alone used to cost on that beast?'

'But of course you can sell your flat, if you want,' I said clutching his arm.

How often had I rehearsed this scene — the great reunion — over the past week? But not like this. In my staging, I'd relit the candles, banished Oliver and Henry, crept back on to my sofa and, languorous and rotund as a Rubens courtesan, extended my hand — to tell Joe I was his. Instead, in a bright and breezy courtyard, I was reminding him the Stables was his.

'Don't worry, babe,' said Joe, shaking himself like a wet dog as a particular vicious gust of wind sliced round the castle. My hand, which was still clutching his sleeve, flopped back to my side. 'I'm not going to throw you out.'

'I wasn't thinking of myself,' I protested. 'Joe, where have you been? I've been worried sick.'

Joe glanced round and raised a hand as a plumber and his mate trundled past with a ladder and a shouted greeting. He turned back to me. 'Just thinking.'

'Well, me too. I've been dying to see you again. I behaved like an idiot the night you left.'

Ten minutes of solitary reflection, let alone a wretched

week, had proved how stupid I'd been to dither instead of dally. I'd soon realized I wanted Joe on any terms. Better to love and lose than never . . .

'It was all my fault,' interrupted Joe, before I'd reached even the beginning of this, my big speech. 'I behaved like a bum. I'm sorry, Becca. I'd had a lot to drink. No excuse though. It seemed a bit unfortunate, Oliver turning up when he did . . .'

'Unfortunate?' I wailed. 'It was fucking tragic.'

Joe smiled — but sadly, patting my arm. 'I wasn't best pleased either, at the time. But, look at it this way: if he hadn't arrived . . .' He left the sentence dangling discreetly.

'We'd have ended up in bed,' I declared, back on script now and smiling boldly, ready to be crushed into the octopus embrace.

But Joe hadn't read the stage directions. No lust smouldered in the dark brown eyes now. In fact he looked embarrassed. 'Well, I dare say. So maybe it was for the best, eh?'

The smile was freezing in my face. 'Oliver coming home? Best for who?'

'Is he still here?'

I nodded.

'You were right,' said Joe. 'You've got a baby on the way. I — well, like I say, I'd had a skinful. I got carried away. Becca, I can only say I'm sorry.'

'Sorry?' I echoed numbly. For the first time I realized how cold the morning was. I shivered. 'Sorry for what?'

'You know what I mean, love.'

The smock my mother had insisted on making for me at Christmas was billowing on the wind. Towering over Joe in the middle of the courtyard, I felt like a barrage balloon. And about as desirable.

'I . . . know what you mean,' I said stiffly.

We all know that what seems irresistible viewed through a haze of alcohol and forgiving firelight is a different proposition in the sober morning light. Also, in my case, in a bloody maternity smock. What man in their right mind, I thought, would want me like this? Except, hell, Oliver . . .

'You needed time to think too,' Joe added, locking the car. 'With Oliver coming back. I promise you I've done plenty.'

So had I. More than enough. But Joe was already walking towards the castle. I collected myself enough to trot after him, demanding again to know where he'd been.

He looked at me oddly – apologetically almost. 'Back to square one . . .'

Before he could elucidate, George darted out of the door, and commandeered him to view the kitchens. Ready to cook a banquet for a king, declared George. Wasn't that right, Becca?

I squeezed a wan smile and escaped to my office.

I was cursing myself for so flagrantly laying bare my soul. For scattering my dignity, my self-respect, my principles (such as they were) to the wind. After contorting half a box of paper clips, I concluded I could never face Joe Duff again.

Then he dodged into the office, asking urgently about the time of a lunch booking. I swallowed air like a stranded goldfish and – because I couldn't think what else to do – took out the diary.

And from that moment on we seemed to slip, with terrifying ease, back into the old working relationship. As if nothing had happened.

It was rotten consolation to reflect that nothing – really – had.

CHAPTER TWENTY-SIX

A week later, Flying Duck was finally able to take roost, so to speak, in the castle. However, even if we were now working in the same building, I saw no more of Joe. Or at least, we met often enough, but rarely alone. He moved in a cloud of check-trousered or dicky-bowed acolytes. Moreover I still had Oliver — as well as Henry.

Their frigid politeness to one another was more wearing than pitched battles. Both justified themselves by claiming the other was bad for me.

Oliver said my job was tiring enough for a pregnant woman without Henry's incessant demands. It was true that Henry's creative genie required long and patient nurture. Some artists lock themselves away and suffer in sweated silence. Henry preferred a public arena for his angst. And when he wasn't creating (in every sense of the word), he was only too ready to bitch about Oliver.

'There's something deeply, deeply wrong with that boy,' he declared, cornering me in my office just as I began my lunch.

'Well of course there is,' I retorted. 'You'd be pretty un-happy too if your wife had killed herself.'

'There are murky secrets in his soul. No,' he said, raising an admonitory finger. 'I recognize these things. Unlike you, my little tank, I am finely attuned to the nuances of the human psyche. It's to do with the castle. This is what I sensed from the day I walked in. The mainspring of my design concept.

Buildings can exercise a malign influence all of their own. It was built by one of his ancestors. Oliver Langham,' he concluded dramatically, 'is the latest scion of a Doomed Dynasty.'

Method actors, conscientiously *living* a part to integrate themselves into the personality, I could just about cope with. Method designers, applying the same idea to a building, were another matter.

'Balls,' I snapped. And when Henry tried to pursue the argument, I shut him up by reminding him I was carrying a member of the next generation. Family curses, I said, I could do without.

'Quite,' declared Henry, unabashed. 'Very worrying for you, pet.'

I was worried about Oliver all right — but not as the latest scion of an ill-starred dynasty. He was settling into the Stables far too comfortably. He was anxious to complete his research paper (he claimed) and to this end cycled industriously into Oxford most days. He was also plainly anxious to make himself useful at home. He shopped, cleaned, washed up — and dropped Henry's favourite china cup. But I could only be grateful for his efforts.

When I developed a cold, Henry avoided me like the proverbial plague. Oliver administered honey and lemon, hot-water bottles and sympathy. When I returned from the local hospital brandishing my grainy ultra-sound snapshot of the baby, Henry expressed acid surprise that the sum total of me, Oliver and all this fuss appeared to be only a deformed tadpole. Oliver was as fascinated as I was.

I was at once touched, and appalled. Then, one morning, I rounded the castle to find him at the foot of the tower, staring down at the flagstones with such bleak desolation, I could have wept. He didn't even see me until I touched his arm. Then he spun round, flinching;

'Oh Oliver,' I said. 'You shouldn't have come back here.'

He shrugged. 'You're here,' he said simply. 'I had to. Don't worry, I'm fine. Let's go in. It's bloody cold.'

I found this mute bravery more poignant than the most eloquent outpouring of grief. In fact, Oliver barely mentioned Cathy ever. Inevitably, my proddings that he should find himself somewhere else to live carried less and less conviction. Besides, he assured me he would. Once he'd sorted himself out . . .

I suppose I expected any day he and Constance would make up their silly quarrel and he could go to her. I was tempted to intervene and ring her myself, until I realized this would involve, sooner or later, telling Constance she had an illegitimate great-nephew or -niece on the way. She saw Oliver as her adopted son. Would she be scandalized? Or, worse, would the light of impending grandmotherhood kindle in her eyes, much as it had in my mother's? My nerve failed me — and Oliver stayed.

Besides, I had enough on my hands at the castle, without disentangling Oliver's life for him. More than enough.

'Sod's law,' said my mother philosophically, when I moaned on the telephone that we'd never have the place ready to house a ball.

The basement was bubbling and steaming with activity, the Flying Duck vans were flitting in and out of the courtyard brimming with goodies, but upstairs, correspondingly, progress seemed to lumber to a halt. George and his men, sated with triumph after the rush to finish the kitchens (a mere four months behind schedule) reverted to serious tea consumption only occasionally punctuated by work-breaks. Even so, they managed to mint a fresh daily issue of disaster.

'Soon as the adrenalin stops flowing, things go wrong,' said Ma. 'That's why you're fine being operated on by some red-eyed junior doctor at the end of his forty-eight-hour shift. The guy you avoid is the laid-back geezer who's just had a holiday. It'll come right when the pressure ups again.'

The next day, my beautiful gilt-framed mirror crashed to the floor in the ladies loo. The frame wasn't damaged and we could replace the glass at staggering cost (So what's money? said Joe. A purely imaginary concept for us these days . . .) but Henry blenched like a chameleon dropped in a bath. 'Seven years,' he intoned hollowly. 'Seven years.'

'They smashed a whole box of mirror tiles last Friday,' I said irritably. 'If we add those in we're cursed for the next millennium.'

'A jinx,' pronounced George complacently and went away muttering rhyming couplets.

This *Aladdin*, I observed tartly to Joe, seemed to have been longer in rehearsal that a Bayreuth production of *Götterdämmerung*.

'My God,' said Oliver, when I — unwisely — invited him across one morning to view work in progress. I suppose it takes a certain vision to see through scaffolding and dustsheets to the emerging palace. 'This place used to look quite decent, as I remember it.'

I could hear Henry hissing up in the balcony, like a malevolent barn owl.

'Maybe that boy is responsible for all our problems,' he said dreamily over (my) lunch, a couple of hours later. 'They only started after Oliver arrived, didn't they? He could be the catalyst. A focus for the Forces of Destruction. Innocent in himself but — Going somewhere, angel?'

'I am going to get changed into my one respectable dress,' I snapped. 'Because in half an hour, you may be interested to know, I am going to confront the Forces of Destruction. And, take my word, they've got sod-all to do with Oliver Langham.'

The bank manager had summoned us in to see him at three-fifteen.

'Could be worse,' Joe observed, as we climbed into his car. 'Tea and biscuits. It's when they offer lunch you want to start worrying.'

'Why?'

I was just grateful to secure Joe's company to myself for once — even if only for a car ride to Oxford and back.

'Giving you lunch is like feeding the condemned man a hearty breakfast.'

Joe was right — up to a point. We were not condemned. Or, to put it in the lingo favoured in the plastic-plant world of modern banking, our credit facilities were not being reviewed. Yet. The manager just preferred to meet with his customers, he told us, face-to-face. Impossible, we agreed numbly, to have a meaningful dialogue over the telephone.

In fact, the man was a long-standing customer of Joe's and, in a bank-managerly way, sympathetic. He spent a long time telling us nothing I didn't know. Moreover, he had the kind of voice which makes a speak-your-weight machine sound riveting. We could, he droned, reach a point where we would have to liquidate our assets just to service our debts. And the property market was not as buoyant as one would wish. Bank manager-speak for sinking like a stone. Nothing new here . . .

The only shock came when Joe raised the possibility of selling his flat. This was our hidden ace. I had insisted Joe play it today. The manager, however, did not fall on the proffered injection of capital with the delight I expected. In fact, he delicately advised against selling. I realized, with a jolt, as he drivelled on about the roof over one's head, that this grey-suited automaton was expecting us to go under any day.

Walking back to the carpark, I rattled on feverishly about deadlines and putting a bomb under the the builders. Joe was noticeably quiet. I thought he was upset. When we got into the car, however, he just asked abruptly, 'How's Oliver?' He was twisted round in his seat, to back the car out of the parking space. His arm was resting across my shoulder, but he didn't seem aware of it in the breathless, burning-a-hole-in-the-back-of-my-neck way I was. In fact, he lifted it away, adding: 'I've barely exchanged a word with him since the night he arrived.' He gave an uneasy laugh. 'Maybe he's avoiding me.'

'Oliver should be bloody grateful to you. It's your roof over his head.'

'Don't talk rubbish.'

'I wish he wasn't here,' I said sulkily. 'It's your fault.'

Joe pulled up to pay at the barrier, then turned to look at me. 'Sweetheart, this situation's pretty bloody miserable for me too, you know.'

'It is?'

But Joe was already driving forward again and didn't pursue this enigmatic opening. In fact now he started talking about our finances. I let him weave out of the city, and waited until we were on the road home before asking determinedly, 'Joe, where did you go? After Oliver turned up?'

He didn't answer immediately. Pretended he was concentrating on overtaking a tractor. 'Up North,' he said, as he pulled in again.

'To your family?'

'You could say that.' He shifted back into top gear, and sighed. 'If you really want to know, I went to find my father.'

'You're not serious,' I said, jerking round to stare at him. 'For God's sake, you were the one who persuaded me — *blackmailed* me — into writing to Oliver. By describing a long-lost bastard turning up on his doorstep twenty years hence. And now you tell me . . .'

'I didn't turn up on his doorstep,' said Joe. 'I didn't even intend to go and find him at all, I just drove up North. You know, returning to my roots, like people are supposed to in times of anguish. To think it all through. Bloody true, too. I needed to sort my feelings out.'

'Feelings?' I echoed faintly. It was like reading the letter which informs you that you personally are in line for the one-million-pound jackpot. There must, you think, be a catch somewhere. It took an effort to ask Joe composedly where he'd actually gone.

'Booked into a hotel for a few nights. Fabulous place. No

tea-bags in those rooms,' he said. 'Proper little pots with caddies of leaf, Indian and China. Very classy.'

'Blocked pipes. People'd be bound to empty them down the sink.'

'But the food was crap,' he added with evident satisfaction.

'Joe —'

'Yeah, OK. Well, I hadn't planned to go to Northcliffe, but there I was, not forty miles away and after a couple of days I drove over to the coast.' He paused while he crossed a junction and didn't resume until he had turned into the lane which snaked round the back of the Harecombe Estate. 'The chippy had gone. There's a Chinese there now. So I looked for his name in the phone book. Sure enough, there it was. I found his address — and parked outside, and waited.'

He braked now. We were at the back of the castle grounds, by the Gatehouse. I saw the light in the window and sighed. Constance's mathematician was evidently still ensconced.

Joe snapped open his seat belt and scrambled out of the car. Only to get back in immediately, slamming the door. 'Some fool's left the back gate open again,' he said irritably. 'The lease specifically says this mustn't be used as a public access route. I've told George about it. If they keep leaving it open, next thing you know we'll have half the bloody village using us as a shortcut to the Oxford road.'

'Wait,' I said, as he turned the ignition key again. 'Don't drive in yet. Tell me what happened first . . .'

Joe eyed me speculatively for a moment, then switched off the engine. 'Well,' he said slowly, 'I saw this old guy totter out, and I followed him down to the promenade. I tell you I was beginning to feel like a private eye. But it couldn't have been easier. He goes and sits in one of the shelters for a quiet fag. His sister-in-law won't let him smoke in the house, poor old bugger.'

'So you spoke to him? Did you tell him who you were?'

'I didn't mean to, no.' In the dim, wintry twilight, I saw him grimace. 'I'd got it all worked out, Becca. All I said was I thought he'd once known someone from my home town. Mavis Duff. And he looked at me — and guessed. *Giuseppe*, he said. Can you credit it?'

'Blimey,' I said faintly. 'It's like something out of a film. Was it very upsetting?'

'No,' said Joe. 'That's the whole point. I stared at him, like an idiot — and I didn't feel a blind thing. Of course, he doesn't look like me. Well, he's an old man. Sixty-eight going on a hundred and coughing like a trooper. But I shouldn't think there was much resemblance forty years ago. He tells me' — Joe cleared his throat self-consciously — 'I'm the living spit of his brother.' He twisted round to look at me. 'But he knew about me. That was the real bombshell. He'd always wanted to see me. It was Mum who refused. Once she'd learned he was married already, that was it. Apparently he offered her money but she wouldn't take a penny. And, suddenly, out of the blue — there I was. He . . . Well, if you want the truth, he burst into tears. You said it, babe. Just like the movies.'

I felt weepy myself. I groped for Joe's hand.

'I told him about this place,' he went on. 'He thought it was miraculous, his' — I felt Joe's hand stiffen momentarily — 'his *son* owning a castle. No chance of him ever seeing it, though. The sister-in-law doesn't know how he misspent his youth, and it's too late now. I've sent him one of your Christmas cards so at least he's got a picture. I just hope the poor old sod pegs out before we sell up. If it comes to that.'

'Joe, you're talking about him as though he's a stranger.'

'What else is he?' said Joe. 'Not just a stranger, a foreigner. Forty-odd years in this country and he still talks like he came over on the last . . . Babe? Whatever's the matter?'

'Ignore me,' I sobbed. 'It's being pregnant. Books all warn you. I was bawling at some pictures on the news last night. Puppy — rescued from a pothole.'

'Soft ha'p'orth,' said Joe, unsnapping his seat belt and thrusting his arm round me.

'Why didn't you tell me before?'

'I've not had a chance, have I?' he said unconvincingly. 'And . . . well, all right, to be honest, I thought you'd just say it proved I was wrong.'

'Wrong —' I broke off to sniff loudly. 'Wrong about what?'

'Children and their fathers.' He sighed. 'You said it yourself. If it weren't for my pig-headedness on the subject, Oliver wouldn't be here now.'

He sounded undeniably dejected. As though Oliver's return had been every bit as unwelcome to him as me.

'Even so, I still think you had to tell him. If my mother had only been honest with me . . . Anyway, there I was, first time in forty years, looking at my dad and what did I feel? Sod all. Don't get me wrong,' he added hastily, 'I quite liked the guy. I even forgave him for not being a Formula One driver. I bet he was a bloody good waiter. I took him for a few pints and he was full of tales about his time at the Empire. God, it's another world, the staff they fielded in those days but . . . Oh cheer up, sweetheart.'

He was smiling so soppily — so lovingly.

'I'm fine,' I whispered, settling my head on his shoulder and thinking it would suit me to stay here a bit longer. Like the rest of my life. 'What about you? Are you glad you went?'

'I suppose so. In fact, yes. It made him so happy I almost wished I'd walked into the chip shop years ago. Except the wife was still alive then, so maybe better not. They never had kids of their own,' he added. 'Anyway, there I was. And there he was, crying harder than you, you big softy. The return of the prodigal had nothing on it.'

I could feel the familiar rumble of laughter. 'Oh Joe,' I wailed, casting my arms round his neck. 'I do love you.'

Joe didn't actually recoil, but he didn't speak either. Just went on stroking my shoulder mechanically.

'I'm sorry,' I stammered. 'I didn't mean . . .'

'Of course you didn't,' said Joe, with a heartiness I found acutely painful. 'And you know — well, of course, I'm devoted to you too, sweetheart.'

'You are?'

'Sure, but . . .'

But . . . A long silence.

'There's — the baby,' he said eventually.

The baby. Was that the rub? Joe quite fancied me, but not instant fatherhood?

'I only want what's best for you,' he went on. 'I mean, look at me: the business is going down faster than the bloody *Titanic*. You need someone who can look after you, provide for the baby.'

'I — don't *need* anyone,' I said. Except you, I thought. But not in the way you mean.

'Deserve someone then. Oliver wants to marry you, doesn't he?'

'Not really. It's only the baby.'

Funny, I was thinking. Oliver wants me because of the baby. Whereas Joe . . . Oh, bloody hilarious.

'He'd be a good husband, a good father,' Joe said. 'Dependable. You know, Al always used to cite him as a model husband.'

I vaguely remembered Alison saying something of the sort to me. Oliver was like a swan, she said, mating for life. Faithful. Unlike — Joe? Was that what Joe was hinting?

'I'm not going to marry Oliver,' I said flatly.

Joe turned and stared at me. But, in the gloom, I couldn't read the expression on his face. Nothing so simple and desirable as love. Concern? Not — please, not — pity?

'Well, let's wait until the baby arrives and see how you feel then, eh?'

We drove home in silence.

CHAPTER TWENTY-SEVEN

Next morning I was first down to breakfast as usual and no sooner had I put the kettle on than the phone rang. Sure it was Joe, I pounced on the receiver, avid to apologize for my sulky exit from his car last night.

'Whore,' said a muffled voice.

'What?'

At first, to be honest, I didn't actually catch the word. Only when it was hurled at me again did I realize what was being said. There was an odd, gasping breath, 'You're a — whore. I know your type. Anything in trousers.'

Sheer astonishment held me rigid. I didn't have the wit to move, let alone to speak. Just clutched the receiver, gaping.

'I've seen you — *flaunting* yourself. He doesn't belong to you.' Another noisy breath. 'Get away from Harecombe. And take your — your *bastard* with you.'

That galvanized me. I crashed the handpiece down just as Henry sauntered in, splendid in a scarlet towelling robe. 'Look as though you've been hit over the head, old love,' he observed. 'Any coffee?'

'Henry,' I said dazedly. 'That was a —' I didn't even know what to call it. Poison pen *letters*, but poison phone calls? 'I've just had an anonymous phone call.'

'Was it obscene?' said Henry. 'You might have asked them to hang on until I came down.'

'She called me a whore . . .'

'Oh *she*,' said Henry, losing interest and picking up his news-paper.

'And she said – implied – I'd go for anything in trousers.'

'No,' said Henry. 'Most things, maybe, but –'

'For God's sake, this isn't a joke.' I shoved the telephone away from me, shuddering. Henry folded away the newspaper and walked over to me. 'It's upset you, hasn't it, pet?' he said, putting one arm, weightless as a bird's wing, across my shoulders. 'Come into the kitchen. I'll make a nice cup of coffee and you can tell Uncle Henry all the gory details. I need a bit of excitement.'

I managed a hiccuping laugh, and followed him through.

'Although,' I said after repeating the substance of the call, 'the voice was so muffled you could hardly hear it.'

'Speaking through a tea-towel, I dare say,' said Henry with an air of knowledgeability.

'But – the way she spoke was bizarre. It was, well, so *unconvincing*, as though she could hardly bring herself to say the words. The tone was about as menacing as the Speaking Clock.'

'Ah, well, that's because it was real,' said Henry. 'And proves it was *definitely* not an actor.'

'What?'

'One of the great eternal truths, my love. Real life is twenty times less realistic than The Drama. Haven't you ever got a crossed line on the phone? Sounds so bloody staged and unconvincing I want to interrupt just to tell them how to deliver their lines. Imagine if you'd been playing a threatening phone-caller. You'd have done a cross between Bette Davis and Peter Lorre. Accent?'

'It was so short,' I said, and then: 'Local. Must be. She pronounced it Harkum. Only the locals do that.'

'Well, how interesting,' said Henry. 'So who saw you trolling round Oxford with our butch wonderboy yesterday?'

'Joe?' I said indignantly. 'But he hasn't even got a girl-friend.'

'Oooh, surely someone must be soothing that craggy brow of an evening?'

'Not necessarily,' I snapped. 'And she knew I was pregnant.'

'Well, that hardly narrows the field,' said Henry, eyeing the lump. 'And she didn't name names. Just "he"?'

I nodded.

'A *he* who doesn't belong to you?' His eyes glinted maliciously. 'It couldn't, I suppose, be that word of your condition has reached the Honourable Mrs Richard Prescott . . .?'

'Don't be daft,' I said. 'This woman didn't have an Honourable Haccent.'

'Doesn't Dicky's wife come from this part of the world? Anyone can take off the accent of their home patch.'

'Besides, we — Richard and I — were bloody careful. She never suspected a thing.'

'Goodness me,' said Henry, putting down his cup. 'No — no, honestly, love. I'm sure it wouldn't have gone any further.'

I shut my eyes. 'Just how many people did you tell?'

'What's all this?' said Oliver, who had walked in unnoticed. Henry began, with some relish, to tell him.

'Pamela,' said Oliver disgustedly. 'My God, whatever next? I thought it was too good to be true when she stopped ringing me.'

'Cathy's mother?' I said. 'She's telephoned you? Here?'

'From the day I arrived — well, she turned up on the doorstep then.' I was still gaping. Oliver shrugged impatiently. 'I thought you'd get in a state about it and tell me I shouldn't be staying here. Before now, fortunately, she's put the phone down if anyone else answered — like I do to her.'

'Put the phone down on her?' I squawked. 'On your own mother-in-law?'

'What else am I supposed to do?' said Oliver. 'She just goes round in circles, pestering the police — everyone — to reopen the investigation. Why can't she finally accept that nothing's going to bring Cathy back? Don't look at me like that, Becca.'

'If it was her,' I said, 'then she's found out I'm having a baby.'

'She had to know some time,' said Oliver. 'Anyway, who's to say it's mine?'

'Quite,' said Henry, smiling angelically. 'Shall we spread the word that I'm the father?'

Oliver reddened, opening his mouth to protest.

'Enough,' I said commandingly and stood up, which was getting more difficult by the day.

'My God,' said Henry. 'You look like one of those things arising from the waves.'

'Venus?'

'I was thinking of a hovercraft. You go across,' he said smiling sweetly. 'I'll be sure to take any phone messages.'

'I think Oliver's probably right, though,' I said to Joe later, when he joined me for coffee. I was hoping to be swept into strong comforting arms.

'Pam Metcalfe?' said Joe frowning. 'Why?'

Fat chance. Joe was noticeably careful to keep a full desk-width between us. As though afraid I might assault him.

'Oh, come on. Oliver's back and I'm the size of a house. It's bloody obvious. I wonder if it was her up the tower that night? Maybe she's been watching me all along.'

'No one's been watching you, you daft bat.'

'No? I suppose a ghost made the prints you can still see on the tower landing?'

'That's certainly what I intend to tell the punters,' said Joe. 'I was wondering about the Lady of Shalott. Ghost of.'

'You're a great comfort.'

'Pamela Metcalfe's as frightening as a little rabbit,' said Joe.

'You should have seen my rabbit when she had babies to protect,' I said. 'I've still got a scar on my wrist.'

'Oh for God's sake, Becca.'

300

'I'll tell you what worries me. Suppose she believes I was having an affair with Oliver even before Cathy died. She could easily have convinced herself that's what drove Cathy end it all.'

'Nonsense,' said Joe – but he sounded marginally less sure of himself now.

'I almost wish I could talk to her. Tell her it's not true. The voice *threatened* me, you know . . .'

'Could be any old crank. Someone in the village who's seen Henry and Oliver round the Stables and probably thinks you're running a brothel.'

'Thanks a lot.'

'Look, Becca, there's still an older generation which disapproves of unmarried women having babies, full stop. So why not let well alone?'

'Oliver's convinced –' I began.

'See you later,' said Joe, picking up the tray of cups and departing abruptly.

So much for being enfolded in strong arms.

I can't remember if it was that day or the next Constance Berisford telephoned the castle.

'Becca?' she said, and went on to enquire after my health. That alone should have made me smell a rat. Constance Berisford's style was to plunge into business without pause for breath, let alone social niceties. And Constance, who would not have scrupled to ask the Devil in hell to turn the heating down a notch, took almost five minutes to get round to fixing a date for some of her committee to come and agree final arrangements before the ball. Table plans and so forth, she said airily.

'Of course,' I responded, wondering why this perfectly reasonable request should be tying her in knots of embarrassment. Nevertheless, I was glad she had rung. The time had come, I decided, to open negotiations with Constance over matters far more vital than table plans.

301

But she was already explaining, underlining certain words with careful significance, why Margaret — that is, the former chairman of the ball committee — *insisted* on inspecting the premises herself.

'Dear Margaret can be a little — difficult. She was naturally disappointed that we were unable to secure our usual venue. We've all assured her that Harecombe will be simply wonderful, but . . . Anyway, I can only ask you to do your utmost to accommodate her.'

I assured her we would. Then: 'Constance . . .' I began, but now she was ahead of me in turning the conversation to matters closer to home.

'Oliver's come back to this country,' she said baldly. 'Did you know?'

'Of course I know. Where do you think he's staying?'

There was a pause. 'Good God,' she said flatly. 'Not with you? But, well, you rather implied that your ways had long since parted . . .'

'He turned up on my doorstep at midnight. I could hardly cast him out. And he's still here.'

'Here?' she bawled. 'At the castle?'

'I live in the stable block, didn't you know?'

There was another pause, long enough for me to wonder whether we'd been cut off.

'Stupid of me. I might have guessed Oliver would head for home.' She was talking more to herself than me. 'I had no idea you were actually *living* there,' she added fiercely, as though it were all my fault. 'The boy must be off his head.'

'Well, thanks very much,' I retorted, stung. 'I'm only trying to help.'

'I wash my hands of him,' she said sharply. 'I went to enormous pains to get him to Italy, and now —'

'For pity's sake, Constance,' I said. 'He was miserable abroad, and now he seems to be settling down, working, and —'

'I'm sorry,' she interrupted. 'I'm sure you're acting as you —

well, as you see fit, but — oh Lord, the French are so much more understanding about these things.'

And without another word she rang off.

I gazed bemusedly at the telephone: the French are so much more understanding about what things?

Sex, of course, and everything to do with it.

Constance . . . knows I'm pregnant? I remembered the enquiries into my health. She's heard . . . from one of her tenant farmers? And jumped to entirely correct conclusions as to Oliver's role?

And promptly put the phone down on me.

Maybe Joe was right, I thought sourly. Easy to underestimate how strongly some people still feel about unmarried mothers.

'Poor little bastard,' I murmured to the lump.

'You really must get in touch with her,' I said to Oliver.

It would have been quicker to come shopping on my own but (as Oliver pointed out) I shouldn't be lifting heavy boxes, so he'd climbed into the car with me. A giant supermarket, with a coy Toytown clock tower over the trolley-store, had opened twenty minutes' drive away. Everyone for miles around now shopped here.

'Get in touch with Constance?' said Oliver, following me across the carpark. 'What's the point?'

'The situation's crazy. People — reasonable people in the real world — don't cut off their nearest and dearest for ever.' I yanked a trolley free of its brothers. 'You've got to talk to her.'

'She'll only tell me to go away. From here, I mean. She told me to quit Harecombe for good.'

'Don't you think she might be right?' I said, nipping through the automatic doors. 'Surely, being here for you, well, only keeps the wounds raw?'

'I'm all right,' he said impatiently.

'What about a new job?'

'I've money enough to manage.'

'I'm talking about making a fresh start. A new life.'

'I could ask you the same,' said Oliver. 'Exactly where are you planning to live after the child's born?'

That's when I gave up and applied myself to filling my trolley. The place was swarming. Oliver was willing enough, but lacked the killer instinct required in the shopping jungle. He tended to wander along the aisles like an Elizabethan poet seeking inspiration in the court maze. Eventually, I gave up trying to keep track of him, and worked steadily down my list until I reached the checkout queue. I supposed he would find me.

I stacked my purchases on the conveyor belt in neat classifications. Bottles and solid heavies at the front. Cold stuff together. Soft fruit and veg held back. Glanced round. No sign of Oliver. The till-assistant stretched out one hand, mechanical as a crane, and began to ring through my goods. The previous customer, was still fumbling her receipt into her purse. She had not even begun to pack away her purchases.

I always find myself studying other shoppers' baskets. In combinations of goods, more surely than in combinations of planets, do I recognize kindred spirits. The woman in front was now packing her few goods with leaden slowness into a shabby tartan bag. Margarine, tinned dog food, a single small can of salmon, a packet of custard powder. And I was thinking, in the way one does, God, what a depressing little shop, when she looked up and saw me.

I only recognized her then: the faded hair, the pale, powdery face. Exactly the same moment she recognized me. Pamela Metcalfe.

'You,' she said breathlessly, and clutched her tartan bag to her thin chest, as though to protect herself.

Whore, I thought. Whore. Surely it was the same breathy voice?

'Look, Mrs Metcalfe . . .' I began, and then floundered.

She was staring at me, not at my face but at my belly.

With – I flinched – envy. Searing, miserable envy. Beside me, bags of flour, tins and bottles thundered down the conveyor belt like logs down a river. 'He – hasn't made you get rid of your baby, has he?' she said, and burst into tears.

She was crying on the phone too, I thought. That was why she kept stopping. She couldn't get the words out because she was crying.

'Mrs Metcalfe –'

'He made . . .' In the middle of a packed supermarket, she was standing with tears zigzagging unheeded down her face. 'He made my daughter get rid of hers.'

'What?'

'Didn't you know that? It was all his fault. I should have guessed from the start. He was always going on about his mother and her singing.' She gulped convulsively. 'As if having a baby would have spoiled Cathy's chances. Never heard – such rubbish in my life.'

'It's not true,' I protested. 'Oliver wanted a child. It was Cathy chose to have –'

A cabbage rolled past and thudded into a bottle of fruit juice. Like a bowling alley. What a bloody place for discussing abortions. For reasoning with a woman clearly demented with grief.

'Look, can't we go somewhere else?'

I moved towards her but she shied away, as though I was going to hit her. Besides, paradoxically, we could not have been more alone. Customers were bustling past unseeing; the music trilled on, the assistant tapped her till; and no one was taking a blind bit of notice of us.

'Honestly,' I said. 'You've got it all wrong.'

'Forty-eight pounds, twenty-three pence, please,' chirruped the assistant, and that – ridiculously – made me feel even guiltier. Poor Pam Metcalfe with her piddling three pounds' worth of bits and pieces.

'Wait,' I said to her desperately, handing money to the assistant.

'Hang on,' called Oliver's voice as, apparently unaware of queues, he pushed towards me waving a single packet of biscuits. 'You said we wanted some – Oh God.'

Oh God, I thought too.

Pamela stiffened, and turned to stare at him.

"Scuse me,' said the assistant, cavalierly swinging an arm and sending the remainder of my shopping tumbling and thumping to the well at the end of the counter. She slammed my change on the tiny perspex ledge. 'Next customer, please.'

'I've been telling your *girlfriend*' – Pamela spat the word at Oliver – 'a few home truths. I've got it all worked out now.' Henry was wrong, I thought Real Life was getting too much like The bloody Drama. 'I should've known all along. It was you, wasn't it?'

The timbre of her voice was so peculiar, not a human sound at all.

'It's all right for – *her*. But not my Cathy.'

My rabbit, I thought absurdly. That day I put my arm in the hutch with young. Snowy had actually growled. Just like a dog.

'No wonder you won't talk to me. Too *ashamed*.'

Oh for heaven's sake, Oliver, I thought, talk to her now. Set things straight quickly, you fool. But horror at finding himself embroiled in such a public scene seemed to have robbed him of words – while she looked madder by the minute.

'You were afraid I'd guess, weren't you?'

Suddenly my head was swimming. The overhead lights were beating down like a desert sun. Pamela's tearful face was oozing in and out of focus.

'I know it was you made my Cathy do it. You – *child murderer . . .*'

'No,' whispered Oliver at last, edging back and tripping into a long-nosed woman who squealed and *well, really*ed! away.

The blood was roaring in my head. I couldn't breathe. 'I've got to get some air,' I gasped. 'Oliver, I'm sorry – will you . . .' And I staggered past them and out into the cold clear air.

CHAPTER TWENTY-EIGHT

A couple of breaths and I was fine. I wanted to talk to Mrs Metcalfe. To set her right. But the door I had come out of was an exit only. I had to walk all along the glass front to find the entrance. No sooner had I passed through it than I saw her leaving: scuttling across the carpark and stuffing her tartan bag into the back of the little white car.

Oliver was standing by the checkout like a wax dummy.

Round him, a track-suited couple operating in efficient tandem, loaded shopping into boxes, taking less notice of him than of an inconveniently parked trolley. Would anyone notice if you dropped dead in here? Maybe if the corpse blocked a gangway.

'Get a move on,' I hissed at Oliver and, grimacing apologetically at the young husband, began to clear my own jumble of goods away. 'Did you pay for those?'

Oliver looked down at his hands, and saw the packet of biscuits. I checked the price ticket and fished the exact change out of my purse, impelled less by honesty than by a feeling that, after all this, I could do without Oliver being arrested for shoplifting.

'She thought – she was *accusing* me of making Cathy have an abortion,' said Oliver disbelievingly.

'Yes I know,' I said, smiling through clenched teeth at the efficient young couple and packing my own shopping furiously. 'Bloody ridiculous. We'll talk about it later. In the car. Can you push the trolley?'

'To think *I* wouldn't want Cathy — us — to have children,' he said incredulously, 'just because my mother's career foundered . . . Sorry, where?'

'In the boot, please. Oh, the woman's off her head. I remember Alison Laverick putting it down to the menopause — and God knows,' I said with feeling, 'a change in hormones does funny things to the sanest of us. Don't squash those lettuces. Did you put her straight?' I slammed the boot and walked round the car. Oliver was staring at me across the roof as I unlocked my door. 'Oliver? You did explain to her?'

'I didn't realize what she meant.'

'Bloody hell, Oliver. You must be the only person in the supermarket who didn't.'

'I didn't understand what she was talking about,' he said. 'Until it was too late. Oh Christ, what will she do now?'

I choked back my irritation, telling myself that any man might be struck dumb, confronted with a deranged mother-in-law in a crowded store. 'Don't be silly,' I said, not unkindly. 'What can she do?'

Oliver looked at me for a moment, then shrugged. 'Nothing,' he agreed. 'Sure.'

He didn't sound very sure.

And I remembered my rabbit. However many carrots I slipped into the hutch, she was never the same with me again.

Logic told me Pam Metcalfe was a sad, bewildered victim who couldn't harm a fly. Joe told me the same. Even when I complained the phone was ringing at all hours of day and night and cutting off without a word.

'So let it ring,' he said. That was when I produced the pantomime programme.

George had delivered the programme with profuse apologies for not including a complimentary ticket. But *Aladdin* was booked to capacity. Nevertheless, he added, fixing me with his eye, I was welcome to slip in at the back one night.

Flipping, idly, through the programme, I had deduced the

compiler watched too many films on the telly. The list of credits must have encompassed half the population of Harecombe. There wasn't actually a Grip listed, or a Best Boy, but after the Electricians and Costumiers, we did have a Production Accountant. And Chief Rehearsal Caterer.

Pamela Metcalfe.

'That night after Christmas, when I saw someone in the tower,' I now said to Joe, 'there'd been a rehearsal in the theatre.'

Joe had rolled the programme up into a tube and was holding it like a telescope to his eye, studying his foot. I wished he'd look at me instead.

'If Mrs Metcalfe was at that rehearsal,' I went on, 'she could have slipped through at the end, and climbed the tower.'

Joe rarely came into my office these days. A more fanciful woman might think he was avoiding her.

'She knows her way round the castle,' I persisted. 'She used to be secretary here, when it was a college.'

Why, having secured his company for a few precious minutes, was I blithering on about Pam Metcalfe? But I can't bear loose ends. I'm the kind that feels impelled to pick a scab until it bleeds.

'Look,' said Joe, rolling to his feet and taking his telescope across to the window. 'I accept Mrs Metcalfe might be upset now, what with the baby and that. Perfectly natural. But the phantom foot-printer climbed the tower ages ago. Before Oliver came home, wasn't it? And long before anyone knew you were pregnant. Just tell me, Becca, what would she want up there?'

'She was trying to see into the Stables.'

'What the hell for? There's a most peculiar bird sitting on the clock tower.'

'Because she wanted to know if Oliver was back yet,' I said promptly. 'She knew he was coming home from Italy.'

'Did she now? Maybe it's only a pigeon.'

'Well, what I'm saying is she *could* have known. I've been working it out.'

'Go on. Astound me.'

'Phil Halford, the postman, read the postcard Oliver sent me,' I said triumphantly. 'And then told her.'

Joe spun round, telescope hand flopping to his side. 'Becca? I don't believe I'm hearing this. From you, of all people.'

'Joe,' I said rapidly, 'do you ever feel there's something that hasn't come out yet about Cathy Langham?'

'Oh for God's sake,' he snapped, striding across and tossing the panto programme back on the desk. 'If you ask me, Oliver should take a big box of chocolates round to his poor bloody mother-in-law and have done with this nonsense.'

'No one — listen Joe, I'm talking about you too — *no one* believed Cathy was the type to kill herself, did they? Oliver's forced himself to accept it, but her mother won't. She's obsessed. She —'

'Hogwash,' roared Joe.

'You didn't see Pam in the supermarket. You don't know what you're talking about.'

Joe marched to the door. 'Unlike you, I know exactly what I'm talking about,' he said, and slammed the door behind him.

Always the same, picking scabs. Afterwards you wish you hadn't.

It was a dour drizzly evening when the panto finally opened, but that didn't deter the punters. I emerged from the Stables to see cars circling the courtyard. Some were dropping audience members at the theatre door, others driving under the arch to our newly tarmacked carpark beyond.

I was not going to the pantomime tonight, however. I strode briskly round the side of the Stables and down the back drive, heading for the Gatehouse, with an envelope in my hand. Phil had efficiently delivered the Gatehouse electricity bill to us this morning, presumably because the account was still registered in Oliver's name. I'd volunteered to walk down with it, saying I could do with some fresh air. What I really wanted was a respite from the continuing cold war at home. The lights and bustle faded behind me and I switched on my torch as I entered the wood.

I heard the car before it came over the top of the hill. I was on a steep stretch of the lane, just under the brow. I registered the engine-roar with irritation. Joe was right we really must shut the back gate. Too many people were already using us as a shortcut to the Oxford road. The lane was narrow. I stepped to one side and half turned back towards the castle to watch the car approach, blinking in the headlights.

And suddenly the car swerved sharply. Not away — but towards me. There was a still, almost contemplative instant when I thought quite coherently: This car is going to hit me.

Then I hopped smartly backwards and found myself tripping and tumbling into a ditch. Even as I did, I breathed a whiff of hot engine, the garage-stink of rubber tyres. The car and I had passed within inches of one another. I heard it brake at the next bend, then roar off down the lane.

The baby, I clutched the bulge. There was an indignant kick. And I hadn't fallen heavily, just rolled in the mud. I sat up and prodded myself. One shoe had come off and I had wrenched my big toe. But that was all. The baby kicked again. I wasn't frightened so much as amazed. I couldn't believe what had happened. Not an accident. That bloody car had come straight at me.

I clambered back to the road. As I did so, another car breasted the hill, and I froze. But this one slowed in a civilized fashion and passed me with a companionable wink of its headlights.

As I hobbled up towards the castle, I was rehearsing answers to the inevitable questions. No, I didn't recognize the make of car; no, not even the colour. Pale. But I was almost blinded by the headlights. Number? You must be joking, I was jumping off the road. Smallish vehicle, just the driver. No passenger. No, I didn't see the face. A pale oval. But that face had bloody well seen me. Seen me — and then she swerved towards me. *She* . . .

Oh, I had absolutely no doubt who had been behind that wheel.

I marched straight past the Stables and into the castle, shrieking for Joe. My voice echoed round the hall. I stomped down the corridor, still calling. He appeared at a fast trot up the kitchen stairs. 'Baby?' he roared. 'You're covered in mud.'

'She tried to run me over,' I said. 'Satisfied? I told you it was her. Up the tower. On the bloody telephone . . .'

'Hush, love, hush,' said Joe, putting an arm round me and looking round for somewhere we could sit. We ended up on the bottom step of the hall staircase. 'You're shaking like a leaf.'

'A car drove at me,' I said. 'I had to jump into the ditch.'

'Christ,' exclaimed Joe. 'Didn't I say this would happen? The local yobs have been tearing up and down here all week. Poor old love. Are you hurt?'

'I'm fine. Well, more or less. But this wasn't any local kid. Why didn't they stop? Check that I was OK?'

'Full of booze,' said Joe promptly. 'The Partridge is open all day. You get some bloody lunatics piling in there in their souped-up Escorts.'

'There was only one person in the car.'

'So?'

'Joe,' I said with the patience of one addressing a slow-witted child, 'this car did not accidentally knock me off the road. I turned, the driver saw me in the headlights — she *must* have seen me — and, quite deliberately, swerved towards me. I promise you I am not imagining things. It was Pamela Metcalfe. And, melodramatic as this sounds, she could have killed me. Maybe she wanted to.'

Joe looked embarrassed, as though he didn't know what to say. 'I don't think so, love.'

'What do you mean, you don't *think* so?'

'Well, she's here,' said Joe. 'Pam Metcalfe's in the theatre

313

and she has been for the last half-hour. With Mrs Laverick. Watching *Aladdin*.'

'I don't believe it,' I said uncertainly as I followed Joe up to the lighting box.

'Al dropped them here,' said Joe softly as we slid in at the back. 'She ran them up in her dad's car. Her mum had a ticket for her too, but she couldn't face it. She only got back from the States this afternoon and she'd barely had time to take her coat off. I'm surprised you didn't see her, actually. She said she was going to call and say hello to Oliver.'

'I've an eensy-weensy feeling . . .' carolled a scarlet-lipped, blue-eye-shadowed principal boy with thighs just an eensy-weensy bit too solid for fishnet tights, 'there's someone creeping up behind me. And it's not very nice.'

I knew that feeling. But George — green-faced and talon-clawed as Abenazer — was not driving a car.

'Will you shout if you see anyone, boys and girls?'

The children didn't seem too bothered, but the deferential older generation helped them out. I didn't join in either. I was too busy watching the audience.

Pamela Metcalfe was perfectly visible in the middle of the third row, an empty seat beside her. Mrs Laverick, beyond, elbowed her in the ribs from time to time, encouraging her to join in the hilarity, but her pale face barely cracked into a smile.

'Poor soul,' whispered Joe. 'Al told me it was like persuading a corpse into the car. Apparently, she won't talk, won't go anywhere. Mary Laverick's worried sick about her.'

'Oh hell,' I muttered. 'OK, OK, it wasn't her.' Joe put his arm round me and squeezed my shoulders. 'Not this time anyway,' I added mutinously. 'But someone's ringing the Stables and, you've just admitted it yourself, the woman's behaving oddly, and —'

'Does it matter who was driving?' said Joe. 'You've had a nasty shock. Come on, let's get you home, shall we?'

But 'home', at that moment, promised none of the warmth and comfort usually implied in the term. It meant Oliver and Henry sniping, the telephone ringing — or maybe not if she was in here? Besides, I felt a damn sight happier in here with Joe's arm wrapped securely round me.

'George saw us come in,' I whispered, knowing full well an elephant could come and go unperceived behind the bank of lights in our box. 'If we don't stay to the end, he'll never forgive us.'

So Joe shrugged and settled himself down beside me again.

At first all I could think about was the driver of that car. Not Pamela — so who? All very well for Joe to say it didn't matter. It bloody well mattered to me.

Oh no it didn't . . . Oh yes it did . . .

Old fashioned pantomime is insidiously therapeutic, however.

> When every thought's expressed in verse
> You re-a-lize things could be worse . . .

Gradually, I abandoned speculation in favour of stamping and shouting with the rest. And hissed louder than most on George's entrances.

I was even quite sorry when the cast lined up for the finale chorus, but Joe nudged me in the ribs and suggested we slip out ahead of the rush. My toe was throbbing now, and he gallantly helped me down the stairs into the tiny foyer.

Alison Laverick was standing just inside the door, knotted into the most delectable buttery-yellow trenchcoat. I wondered if I was forgiven for my long-ago tactlessness.

'Back to collect them?' said Joe, cheerily. 'Have you seen Oliver?'

She was staring at me. I guiltily released my arm from Joe's.

'Are you all right?' she said.

Only then did I realize I was still mud-caked from the eyebrows downwards. 'Fell over,' I said.

315

'Knocked over,' said Joe. 'By some maniac down the back lane.'

'Oh,' said Alison. 'Was — was *that* all?'

'All?' protested Joe gallantly.

'Oliver said Becca hadn't returned from posting a letter or something. You might have told me,' she added, glaring at Joe, 'he was at the Stables now. He was worried about Becca — afraid it might be the baby. I didn't realize,' she finished awkwardly, turning to me, 'you were having a baby. Is it public knowledge? Congratulations, anyway.'

I've heard condolences offered more enthusiastically.

Behind the auditorium doors, the applause was finally dying away.

'Stand by,' said Joe. 'Here comes the stampede.'

'I'd better get home,' I said hastily.

I'd had just about enough that night, without encountering Pamela Metcalfe again.

So much for the ripe tranquillity of late pregnancy, as described in the book. But none of my antenatal textbooks bargained for threatening phone calls, or cars driving out of the night, let alone a Henry Blayne running at full creative throttle.

He was always the same before opening nights. And, as far as he was concerned, the Foundation Ball was our opening night. He didn't seem to realize it might well be our closing night too.

'I'm like the best champagne,' he had once confided in me. 'I simply can't give of my best unless the fermentation reaches exploding point.' This meant a little explosion, of one sort or another, daily. I could put up with it — just about — because the results were now beginning to show. The dining rooms might lack curtains still, but they certainly didn't lack style.

'One well-placed light,' Henry had always said, 'is worth a thousand quid's worth of wild silk.'

The hall looked magnificent. Henry's extravagant sweep of

scarlet carpet down the curving stairs suggested triumphal processions with Waltonesque fanfares of trumpets. To me, anyway.

'Murder to keep clean,' said Joe. 'It'll show every crumb. But . . .' He shrugged. 'Maybe that won't be our problem.'

It says everything that we had hired no staff and taken no bookings beyond the ball. We had also — word always gets round — received an offer from a would-be purchaser of the castle. An offer that would leave Joe in debt to the tune of fifty-odd thousand pounds.

'We ought to be inviting a table of estate agents to this ball,' Joe observed. 'Instead of pressmen.'

On March 1, we switched on the newly installed castle floodlighting. Going down in a blaze of glory, Joe called it. More a case of going out with a bang, as it happened. At eleven the next morning, having forgotten to turn the floodlights off, we blew every fuse in the building.

'Christ!' said Henry, rushing into my office with the air of a man driven beyond the endurance of human flesh. 'How am I supposed to work in *this*?'

'I'll make us coffee,' I said placatingly, picking up the kettle.

'Shall I hold a match under it?' retorted Henry. I put the electric kettle down again.

The kitchens, in the basement, were Stygian and empty. The staff had piled out minutes ago with a wedding breakfast for a hundred and twenty. Good job the power hadn't failed an hour earlier. But the gas stoves worked by electric ignition and I couldn't even locate a box of matches. I groped along to a cupboard, found some mugs, and took them across to the Stables praying the electricity hadn't failed there too. God was evidently listening. I boiled a kettle and a pan of water and made a tray of coffees — for all of us, including the team of electricians who had already arrived in answer to Henry's furious summons.

And this is where, as Joe was acidly to observe, the Harecombe Castle Pantomime really started . . .

CHAPTER TWENTY-NINE

'You brought some milk in off the step,' repeated the young constable, looking, quite understandably, out of his depth. 'Here?'

We were sitting in my office.

'Over at the Stables,' I said. 'And there was a hole in one of the bottle-tops.'

'Little beggars, the tits round here.'

'Exactly,' I said. 'So I used the bottle with a hole in the top.'

'All of it?'

'The whole pint,' I said. 'As well as builders and carpet-fitters, we had half the electricity board round this morning.'

I'd carried the tray, steaming in the morning air, across the courtyard and into the castle, screaming that coffee was served for anyone in earshot. Henry was in the hall already. Scowling abstractedly into the gloom, he'd stretched out an arm, grabbed a mug, downed half of it – then screamed.

I didn't drop the tray. Almost, but not quite.

'There's a foreign body in here,' he had said, retching theatrically. 'Grit – God, a mouthful of grit.'

'I found a whole twig in our bottle one morning,' observed the policeman. 'Blooming nuisance.'

I smiled nervously. 'Henry didn't quite see it that way.'

'Someone's trying to poison me,' he had wailed. 'This place is cursed.'

For me, it was like running along a jetty and finding quite

suddenly and unexpectedly it stops. My patience, usually infinite, had come to an end. 'Don't be so fucking stupid,' I shouted.

Henry gaped at me, as one might at a cow which had gnashed its teeth. Then snatched the tray from me. 'No one must drink these,' he said, and I knew I'd blundered. I should have spoken soothingly, offered at once to make him a fresh cup. But I was too cross to care.

'Where are you taking those mugs?' I demanded, panting along the corridor in his wake.

With an imperious swing of the bum, he knocked open the door to the ladies loo, and emptied the mugs dramatically, one after another, into the hand-basin.

Two hours later, as I recounted these events, I could sense the policeman's incredulity. What kind of twerp, he was thinking, would pour away a dozen perfectly good mugs of coffee because he'd found a bit of grit? But he had never encountered a Henry, gearing up for an opening night.

And as the last coffee swirled murkily round the white sink, the lights had flickered back on. I retrieved the tray and empty mugs from Henry. 'I have an in-tray three foot deep in urgent paperwork. I have an appointment at the health centre this afternoon, and in exactly an hour's time, a policeman is coming here to advise me on parking and traffic flow round your bloody marquee for the ball. Nevertheless ... I am going down to the kitchen, to waste another quarter-hour of my precious time making coffee. If you want a cup, I suggest you come and apologize.'

And I slammed the door behind me – or at least I would, if the blasted door hadn't been fitted with one of those vacuum devices which slowed it to a decorous wheeze.

Henry did not apologize. You have to be joking. An hour later, he was cavorting on the sofa back at the Stables, grey-faced and clammy, crippled – he gasped – with food-poisoning.

'Poisoned?' said the policeman faintly.

'He tends to exaggerate,' I said hastily. 'But he really was desperately sick.'

'I guess it would be easy,' said the policeman dubiously. 'Knock a hole in the top of a milk bottle while you're passing the doorstep and drop something in. But it's really not my field.'

'I realize that,' I said. 'I really only mentioned it because, well, there've been one or two other odd happenings here . . .'

'What?' Joe had bellowed when I told him I was going to have an informal chat with the law. 'I don't believe I'm hearing this. Because Henry's thrown a tantrum?'

'It's not that,' I said. 'It's — everything. For God's sake, Joe, there's something funny going on . . .'

'Give me strength,' he sighed, and returned to the figures he was studying. 'Just don't bring me into it. And perhaps,' he added sourly, 'when this pantomime is over, you'll tell how the fuck we're going to pay for the rewiring I've just been told we require. Correction. Must have legally.'

'I had a threatening phone call,' I explained to the policeman. That made him sit up and start scribbling, anyway. I notice he spelled 'whore' wrong. I wondered if that was a sign of poor education or clean living. 'And, since then, someone keeps ringing and putting the phone down. And I was nearly knocked over by a car. Which didn't stop. And — you might remember — there was an intruder in the castle just after Christmas.'

The man eyed me keenly.

'Do you happen to know of anyone,' he said, with evident carefulness, 'who might have a grudge against you?'

Bet your life I did. But Pam Metcalfe had not been driving that car. So I shrugged.

'We've received . . . one or two odd calls ourselves,' he went on, with visible reluctance.

'Oh?' I said eagerly.

'There was a tragedy here at the castle, last year.'

'I know,' I said promptly, waiting for him to mention Pamela. But he didn't. Maybe that would be leading the witness or some such breach of the rule book. I opened my mouth, but couldn't bring myself to name her either. If the police turned up on her doorstep purely on my word, Joe would never forgive me.

His parting shot, earlier on, as I stomped out of the office, had been to tell me I shouldn't get so worked up. Not in my condition. He probably meant it kindly — but that was not how I saw it at the time. 'You think it's my condition that's making me imagine things, don't you?'

'Nothing wrong with that. Perfectly natural.'

'Oh sod off,' I had screamed.

'I love you when you're angry,' he said. 'And when word gets out — as it surely will — that we're in the habit of poisoning people in my establishment, I hope you'll support me in retirement in the manner to which I've become accustomed.'

'I've got to see the policeman about traffic anyway,' I said, and marched out.

And, indeed, the officer and I soon turned — with visible relief on his part — to the positioning of No Parking cones. But, before leaving, he conscientiously offered to have a word with the gentleman who actually drank the coffee.

I escorted him across to the Stables, where Henry, whey-faced and prostrate on the sofa, described his every symptom in Technicolor detail. He did, however, confess his was an exceptionally sensitive digestion. Something I had failed to notice over months of feeding him hearty breakfasts and suppers.

'Pity you rinsed the bottle out,' said the policeman. 'Nothing left for analysis. Anyway, we'll keep an eye on things.' He rose to his feet and shot me a shy, sideways glance. 'Don't mind me asking ...' he said, 'but, those Frosty adverts — aren't you on the telly?'

'Not any longer,' I said. 'I've given up acting now.'

'And not a moment too soon,' hissed Henry, momentarily returning to life.

The policeman grinned. 'Those kids looked a real handful.' He looked down at me. 'And you're having another now?'

Oh shit. I could see the diagnosis of Henry's condition — and of all the other odd little happenings — written all over the police officer's face: theatrical tantrums, hysterical (pregnant) actress . . .

'Thanks for — all your help,' I said.

Henry was noticeably subdued for the next couple of days. Barely spoke to me. Joe robustly insisted it was all a sham. He reminded me of the famous story I'd once recounted to him about Henry and the German Measles. Henry's forehead had been livid with rash one day — I'd seen it myself, fearful scarlet — but he'd been fit as a flea the next. Once he'd won the argument with the director.

But I was unnerved by Henry's uncharacteristic silence. It was a relief when he bounded into my office after a trip to the village, looking quite his old self. In fact he was radiating malicious glee. 'Guess what I overheard in the post office?'

I smiled. 'Amaze me.'

'They'd heard all about our poisoned milk and my brush with death. And the chief suspect?'

My smile froze. 'Oh God Henry. What are people saying?'

'Oliver.'

'Oliver?'

'Well,' said Henry, shedding his mackintosh and settling comfortably into the chair opposite me, 'you know his erstwhile mother-in-law has been telling everyone who'll listen that he murdered Cathy?'

'You are joking, aren't you?'

'Phoning the police station daily, according to my source. And when the police eventually told her, in the kindest possible way, to get lost, she went public. Denouncing him to the world.'

'Jesus,' I breathed. No wonder my policeman had asked, so carefully, if there was anyone with a grudge against me. 'The woman really is unhinged.'

'That's just what everybody else was saying — until you brought the police in.'

'Henry, you told me you'd been poisoned.'

'In your stead, evidently,' he said. 'And precious little thanks I've received so far, if I may —'

'What do you mean, in my stead?'

'Well, darling, because the village *tricoteuses* are wondering if Oliver isn't perhaps a serial wife-killer. With both of you expecting, too. After all, some men — observed a hag in the most vile puce anorak — some men can get very funny, *you know*, about pregnancy, and —'

'For God's sake, Henry, this isn't a joke. It's Oliver they're talking about.' Then I shut my eyes. 'Oh Lord — do you think Oliver's heard the gossip? He's been very odd recently, have you noticed? Withdrawn . . .'

'So what's new? I've always found the little papa-to-be strangely sinister,' responded Henry with relish. 'I caught him yesterday staring out of the window at the courtyard. As though X marked the spot. Creepy,' He gave a theatrical shudder.

'He loved Cathy so much. Can't you see that? He's still absolutely devastated by her death.'

'Moment of madness. A *crime passionel* as the French would would say, and let him off with six months and a warning.'

'Don't talk rubbish, Oliver wasn't even here when she jumped. He was miles away in Oxford.'

'Shame,' said Henry shamelessly, and added: 'Not that I see the boy as the murdering type, I admit. Dear Joe, now, I could imagine casting a lifeless body over the parapet in a fit of dark Italian passion. Hardly Oliver. Anglo-Saxon to the core and explosive as cold rice pudding. But hidden some-where there may be a deep vein of chilly insanity. Dear me, I hope not of the *hereditary* variety . . .'

323

'Shut up,' I hissed. 'Oliver loved his wife.'

'Well ninety-nine per cent of all murders take place between —'

'Shut up,' I screamed.

'Pregnancy has done terrible things to your sense of humour, pet,' said Henry, flouncing out.

Just tell me what there was to laugh at in those last days.

Joe clearly thought I was half way round the twist; the castle was as ready to house a ball as to sail the Atlantic; and there was Oliver. He knew what Pam was saying. He must have done.

The silent phone calls were fewer now, but he was there, virtually sitting next to the instrument, when it rang late one night, and he conspicuously waited for me to pick it up. I was beginning to think I could actually recognize the breathy quality of the silence.

'Mrs Metcalfe?' I said sharply. 'Pam, look, this has got to stop . . .'

She — whoever — put the phone down. I caught sight of Oliver. He was wild-eyed as a cornered hare.

No wonder he fled to his library in Oxford at every opportunity. Who could blame him? I just wished I could stop him pressing me, when he was home, to think about the future, our child's future.

'We could go away from here,' he said. 'London — anywhere you like.'

'My job's here,' I protested.

'What job?' Oliver said scornfully. 'The business is on the skids, isn't it?'

'Please,' I said. 'Not now.'

My last days at Harecombe galloped past as I tried to get everything in order. My last nights, on the other hand, dragged long and cold and miserable. The baby had settled on a nerve in my spine. It wasn't that which kept me awake, however, so much as aching longing for Joe. He — and I was not imagining this either — frankly avoided me.

The day before my mother was due to drive up from London and take me home, I staggered down to breakfast with a heavy heart, black-ringed eyes, raging backache and a sheaf of lists. It was Monday morning, with the ball only five days off.

Between mouthfuls of tea, I ticked item after item on lists, trying to block out the cheery babble of Breakfast Television. I've always found television in the morning as degenerate as cocktails with the cornflakes, but Henry would insist.

'Tables: arrival of,' I muttered, ticking furiously, 'Cloths . . .'

'"Even if the whole world seems to be collapsing round you today, keep smiling . . ."'

Not only did Henry insist on having the television switched on, he then ignored it every morning to read his grubby tabloid newspaper.

'Why aren't you in your bath?' I enquired.

'The little papa got in there first,' said Henry, putting aside the paper briefly to glare at me. 'I am forced to postpone my ablutions until the prehistoric plumbing in this place can reheat its customary two cupfuls.' He raised the paper again. 'Pay attention, pet, this is yours I'm reading. Got that bit about the world collapsing? "You must be ready to take the rough with the smooth" — promises, promises, give me a bit of rough any day . . .'

Table plan: were they doing that, or were we? Any minute now I was going to scream . . .

'"Chin up. A surprise development on the romantic front may sweep you off your feet."' Henry looked at me and snorted with laughter. 'An amorously inclined bulldozer, presumably.'

I scowled back and he shrugged and disappeared behind his paper.

I didn't want any bloody surprise developments. I wanted Joe Duff. Just as he was. But within twenty-four hours I was leaving for London. I hadn't even packed. A row of baby clothes was airing in the sitting room. Little stretchy towelling things like skins waiting to be stepped into. Impossible to imagine a small body kicking inside there. Impossible to imagine any kind of future at all beyond this weekend, when the ball was certainly going to arrive – and the baby was supposed to.

I clambered to my feet, announced that Henry could wash up the breakfast pots, and lumbered out of the house. Ironically, given the bleakness of my mood, it was a deliciously mild spring day. Feathery clouds scudded across a pale blue sky. A flag rippled gaily from the top of the tower. On an impulse, I walked past the tower door, and round to the front of the castle. My cloud of daffodils danced and nodded in the moat. They'd be finished by the time I got back – whenever that was going to be. And next year, we might not be here to see them flower again. Oliver was right about that. And where then? I was wallowing in melancholic contemplation of my uncertain future when, out of the corner of my eye, I saw Pamela Metcalfe.

She was a long way off, only just entering the main gates, but I knew exactly and instantly whose that slight figure was, marching towards me, purposefully.

No waiting to see the whites of her eyes. I ran – stupid in my condition – but I ran round the castle, slammed the tower door behind me, and panted into my office.

Joe, to my surprise, was in there already, perched on my desk, studying a letter.

'Pam,' I panted. 'Out there, in the grounds.'

'Yes?' said Joe.

'She's walking up to the castle.'

'Where else would she walk her dog?'

'She didn't have a dog with her,' I said. 'She . . .'

She was what? Looking purposeful? What could she do to me, anyway? Besides, the last thing I wanted now – with only twenty-four hours before I left – was to be side-tracked into further bickering over Pam Metcalfe.

'Sorry. Silly,' I whispered. I was still breathless from my canter round the building.

326

'That's my beautiful girl,' said Joe absently, returning to the study of his letter.

Beautiful? I was beautiful as a beached walrus. I flopped into my chair which exhaled air from its pneumatic tube in a prolonged, protesting fart.

Joe, on the other hand, was almost unrecognizably smart: shaved, after-shaved, dark-suited, crisp-shirted and sober-tied. Looking, I thought vaguely, like a Mafia hood about to attend a Family funeral. Looking, I thought with more certainty, positively edible. Sweep me off my feet, I thought, remembering my horoscope. Feel free.

'What's with the suit?' was what I actually said.

'Constance Berisford and her cronies on the ball committee arrive at ten,' said Joe. 'You told me to dress up and be on my best behaviour.'

'Shit,' I said, and he glanced at me in surprise. 'I'd forgotten they were coming this morning.' I shut my eyes in anguish. 'What else have I forgotten?'

'Nothing,' said Joe, soothingly. 'You'll be back before I'm through Volume One of your collected lists.'

He stood up, and after a moment's hesitation began to tuck the letter away in his inside pocket. I could tell at once, by the shifty way he folded it, there was something wrong.

'What's that?' I demanded.

'Nothing. Letter from the bank.'

'Saying what?'

'Don't let's worry about it now, eh? Talk about it when you get back.'

'Joe, if it's bad news I want to know now.'

With an air of reluctance, he lowered himself on to the desk again. 'Look, sweetheart. Even if we have to sell this place and, OK, I admit, it looks like the writing's on the wall . . .'

'Oh my God,' I whispered.

'It's not the end of the world.'

'You know how much the last offer was. You're going to finish in debt to your eyeballs if we have to sell now.'

'That offer was just a try-on. Even the bank manager called it derisory. Harecombe's worth a whole lot more.'

'If there happens to be an eccentric millionaire itching to waste his cash on a half-converted folly with dicky wiring.'

'Bound to be.' He grinned. 'The world's full of nutters. Let's pray a rich one comes our way.'

'Joe, you're talking as though you want to sell the castle.'

He shrugged and studied the toe of his shoe. 'Well yeah, I guess, in the end, I won't be sorry to see the back of this place. Will you?'

I gulped. I couldn't speak.

Joe saw and pulled a wry face. 'Don't look so stricken, babe. We've always got the catering. We can take our time looking for somewhere else. A bit less ambitious next time. What about a nice little transport caff?' I tried to smile and failed. He took my hand. 'That's if you want to stay in business with an incompetent bugger like me.'

I clutched his hand tightly. 'You know I do.'

'Well then. What's money? Oh come on, love. You look wetter than a month of Sundays.'

He slipped off the desk and crouched beside me, thrusting his arm round me — well, as far round me as an arm would go by then — and began mumbling a soothing mixture of nonsense and kisses into my hair. Naturally I turned my face up to kiss him back. Didn't think twice. As far as I was concerned, kissing Joe Duff was the most obvious and desirable activity imaginable.

So there I am head on his shoulder, face lifted to his, eyes blissfully shut, lips puckered — and nothing happens.

After a while, I felt obliged to open my eyes. Joe's face was only inches from my own — well I'd known that. I'd been sharing his every breath. He was staring down at me rather as — I could only imagine — someone might stare down at a beloved corpse, recently deceased. His face was soft with the kind of tragic fondness you feel for someone who's left for a different and unreachable world. I blinked a couple of times.

The curious expression vanished. And, with gentle care, he began unpeeling me from his shoulder and detaching his arm from my waist. 'Sorry, love.'

'Sorry?' I squawked dizzily. 'Joe, just what are you apologizing for? I thought you were going to kiss me.'

At that moment footsteps clattered past and George began whistling 'Delilah' outside the door. Joe chuckled, but I was in no mood to be amused.

'And what's more,' I added, 'I bloody well wanted you to.'

'Hell, Becca, do you think I didn't?'

'How should I know?'

'Look, babe . . .' Joe sighed and clambered to his feet. 'This is hardly the time or place, is it?'

Nine-thirty on a busy Monday morning with a builder whistling outside the office door. No it wasn't. But I felt like – in fact, given my size, only too like – a great ship, inadvertently launched down the runway. Once she begins to move, there's no turning back. Only a slow, inevitable gathering of momentum.

'Just when is the right time, Joe? I'm sorry, but I've got to know where I stand with you.'

He shrugged. 'Becca, you know how I feel.'

'No I don't. That's the whole point. I don't know at all.'

'We've – well, we've taken it for granted, haven't we?'

'Speak for yourself. What am I supposed to take for granted? You've never said a dicky bird.'

Joe gazed at the ceiling. 'OK,' he conceded, with the air of a man well and truly cornered. 'I'm saying it now. I love you.'

An orchestra should have begun to whisper a weepy piano concerto. Instead, outside, George broke off to shout for an electrician.

'You do?'

'Don't be daft, you know I do. But . . .'

There always had to be a but, didn't there?

'Look, love,' Joe began – and then stopped again.

I was once in the prompt corner for a show starring a

329

distinguished but elderly actor who dithered agonizingly over every line. I used to believe only my concentrated beam of willpower got him through the performance. I was gazing at Joe with the same intensity now.

'If it's possible,' he burst out. 'I mean, if it's what you still want, once you've had your baby . . .'

He walked over to the window. Old Robert always used to rearrange the pots on the mantelpiece when he was stuck for words. But now I didn't have the script in front of me. I could only wait and pray.

'Then of course,' he went on, 'there's nothing I want more than . . .'

To spend the rest of his life with me?

'To – share the rest of my life with you.'

Dear Lord. Almost word perfect.

But I sank numbly back into my chair, wondering why, if this was the happiest moment in a girl's life, I didn't feel happier. Probably because Joe sounded miserable as sin.

'We seem to have got everything back to front, don't we?' he said, glancing uneasily at me over his shoulder. 'Instead of tumbling into bed, we jumped straight into the comfortablest of middle-aged partnerships; no rows, plenty of laughs, great working relationship – no sex. Mind, I hope we don't end up like that. I fancy a debauched dotage. I was thinking we'd potter our way backwards through the child-rearing years. In the end we might even get round to a honeymoon.'

Honeymoon?

Richard had always complained of my need to have everything cut and dried. Black and white. Not a shred, he said, of poetic ambiguity in me.

'Joe.' I began doggedly. 'You – say you love me . . .'

'Course I do.'

'But, well, it's not just me, is it? There's the baby. What I mean to say is . . .' Here we go. Now or never. 'Joe, was that a proposal of marriage?

'Well . . .'

330

Oh Joe, I was thinking, just say yes. Please. No more buts. We've gone — Christ, I've *pushed* you — too far to turn back now. Say no now and I swear it'll be me climbing the Lady Tower next . . .

'Oh Becca,' he groaned, turning to look at me.

I recognized the voice and face of a man driven beyond endurance.

In the blackest flood of despair I'd ever known, I couldn't even cry: In fact I clenched my mouth into a wan smile. For once, just this once, my mother would have been proud of me.

'Don't worry . . .' Whose was this quavering soprano voice? It sounded nothing like mine. 'I shouldn't have — cornered you like this. It's all right.'

'All right?' shouted Joe. 'Of course it's not all right. Oh Becca — love — what the fuck are we going to do about Oliver?'

CHAPTER THIRTY

I was so geared up for heroic martyrdom, it took a few moments for his words to penetrate.

'Oliver?' I echoed dumbly. 'What's Oliver got to do with it — with you?'

The desk lamp flickered off and then on again, and George shouted something inaudible to one of his cohorts.

'For Christ's sake, everything,' said Joe. 'Face facts, sweetheart.'

'Joe, I've done what you wanted, Oliver knows about the baby. The baby — will know him. But you said yourself: children don't automatically feel anything for their natural father. It's not genetically imprinted like blue eyes. I don't see —'

'This is nothing to do with the baby,' interrupted Joe passionately. 'I'm talking about Oliver himself. What can we do?'

I sank back into my chair, staring at him. 'Why should we have to do anything? I've been feeding him, you've been housing him, but he's a grown man, Joe. The day's got to come when he sorts himself out.'

'Have you seen the way he looks at you?' The classic question of a jealous lover. But Joe didn't sound in the least jealous. He sounded desperate. Strangely, the effect of this on me was calming.

'Oliver isn't in love with me, if that's what you mean.'

'No?'

'I'm his friend. He's deeply unhappy. His wife's dead — and

so is her child, the child he really wanted. Even his aunt's given him the boot. Where else can he turn? Oliver needs someone — anyone. He doesn't love me in the least.'

'He wants to marry you, doesn't he?'

'You can't get married on friendship.'

'You can't,' responded Joe bitterly, 'get pregnant on it either.'

'Oh for God's sake, there was no love then — on either side. I've told you all this. He was half-dead with grief over Cathy, like a man drowning. I just happened to be a passing lifebelt.'

'If you say so,' said Joe. 'And am I going to be the bastard who whips the lifebelt away from him?'

A silence, punctuated by a quiet tapping on the wall.

'I am not, actually,' I said, 'an inanimate object to be given, or taken. I have a choice in the matter. And I choose you.'

'Do you think that makes it any easier for me?' demanded Joe.

'Why should it be so difficult?'

There was a quiet buzz of chatter outside the door now, too quiet to catch the words.

'I just feel,' said Joe slowly, 'that I've inflicted enough misery already on Oliver Langham.'

'I suppose you're talking about Cathy.'

No answer.

'Just because you had a fling with her, and Oliver was upset?'

Joe was staring out of the window pretending to be deaf.

'Is one — fuck so very important?' I demanded, forgetting to maintain the tone of calm reason.

The buzz of chatter outside broke off abruptly, then resumed with the volume ostentatiously upped. I bit my lip.

'No,' said Joe tiredly. 'One fuck isn't. At least, I never used to think so. Probably my big mistake. I've learned that lesson the hard way. Marry me, babe, and you're getting a reformed character.'

'I don't know what you're talking about.'

'Nothing,' said Joe, 'Forget it.' He glanced out of the window again. 'There are two cars pulling up out there. I must go.'

'How can I forget it?' I shouted, in a wild rush of panic that he might walk out now, with everything unresolved. 'That woman bloody haunts us, Christ, there are times when I wish I'd never come to this place . . .'

I didn't mean it. Angry panic talking. If I'd never come to Harecombe, I would never have met Joe again, and that made everything worth it. A hundred times over.

'Yeah,' said Joe. 'Why do you think I want to sell? Every night I go to bed wishing I'd never set eyes on Harecombe Castle, but what's the use?' Unlike me, he wasn't angry. He spoke with melancholy seriousness.

There was a tap at the door. 'Sorry to interrupt, guv,' called George. 'But there's a party of women knocking at your door.'

'OK, OK,' shouted Joe, and turned back to smile at me. 'I'll go throw myself to the lionesses.'

'Do you often wish,' I said tightly, 'that you'd never set eyes on me either?'

'Oh, for heaven's sake,' said Joe, and hurried out, leaving a wake of expensive cologne and a burning sense of shame in me.

I don't like rows. At least, I don't mind a few lustily hurled insults in a squall that blows itself out in seconds. But this had been cold and sour – and unresolved.

How could I float off into the sunset, wall-to-wall Mozart and serene pain-free childbirth if I was at odds with Joe? But the ladies of the ball committee seemed to have established themselves in the hall for the day. I kept tiptoeing to the end of the corridor. The chatter – questions, arguments – wound on endlessly.

'Please,' I hissed under my breath, 'shut up, all of you . . .'

By the third visit, I'd established it wasn't the whole committee pitching in. There were four women present, and the only one causing trouble was an old battleaxe in a fur coat, so mangy and motheaten you couldn't imagine what poor animal it had ever belonged to. A starving rat possibly. The current wearer had a prominent nose, deep-bagged eyes and a crimson velvet toque. She reminded me of Henry's late and unlamented parrot, and not only to look at. She was every bit as raucous, deaf to blandishments, and ill-tempered as Percy at his worst. Even Constance Berisford seated beside her on the sofa was cowed into silence.

'He who pays the piper,' the parrot crowed more than once in my hearing, 'is entitled to call the tune.'

Henry's bird used to croak 'fuck off' with more charm and less regularity. I could understand why Joe was murmuring diplomatic nothings — to little effect, mind you. She, as she reminded us, was the paying customer. What I couldn't understand was why her fellow committee members didn't throttle her.

Eavesdropping, I'd gathered the tombola could not be relegated to the smaller dining room, and that the shape of table we'd ordered for the marquee would not have been her choice. She had got on to music when incautiously I stuck my head too far round the corner.

'Becca,' shouted Joe, sighting me. 'You booked the band. Can you tell Lady Bracknell —'

'Brickhill,' she snapped. I glanced at Joe, but he hadn't intended to be funny. Lady Bracknell sounded right. Played with a gusto which would make Edith Evans look milky.

'How can I help?' I said, walking down the hall towards them.

The beak pointed in my direction. 'I've never heard of this ensemble.'

'Becca!' exclaimed Constance Berisford, springing to her feet with an abruptness which startled even the parrot into temporary silence. 'Child, are you *pregnant*?'

This at least made Joe smile. 'No, no,' he murmured, 'she just has a healthy appetite.'

There was a flutter of sycophantic laughter from the two other women.

'Surely,' I stammered, 'you knew I was having a baby. Didn't you?'

'Tell me about Mr Ted Vernon,' commanded Lady Brickhill. 'And his *Sound* . . .' She had a spot of rouge on each withered cheek like Mr Punch. I imagined she could have put a big stick to good use. 'Do sit down, Constance,' she added irritably.

'Good God. Is — is this why Oliver came home?' demanded Constance, ignoring her.

The other two ladies of the committee, one a stout matron of Constance's age, the other a fair-haired lump of indeterminate years in a staggeringly ugly yellow coat, were coughing and fiddling with their handbags. But they were hanging on every word. I wasn't surprised. This must be vastly more interesting than table plans.

'Well, in a way,' I said uncomfortably, looking at Joe who pretended to be studying his notes. The pig. 'I didn't ask Oliver to return, I assure you. He didn't much like Italy anyway. I . . .' I was floundering.

'I think,' said Constance austerely, 'we had better have a chat, Becca.'

Come to my study at noon, said the headmistress.

'But not now,' snapped Lady Brickhill. 'This is a band and not a dis-co-theque, I trust?'

I made appropriately reassuring noises, but I was covertly studying first Joe, then Constance Berisford. Joe was pretending to pay attention, but his thoughts were miles away. As for Constance: she wasn't even pretending to listen. She was twiddling her rings, steeling occasional, uneasy glances in my direction. When the battleaxe finally let me off the hook, I mumbled excuses and fled. Before I'd reached the door, Lady Brickhill was saying loudly that she hoped some decent lighting would be installed in this gloomy barn. I thanked God Henry wasn't within earshot.

I needed to escape for more than one reason. By now I was tripping to the lavatory every ten minutes. Henry had said recently he would never have queried the tacky opulence of the ladies had he realized I was intending to take up residence in there. My operatic mirror was restored, a chaise longue was upholstered in velvet the silky green of a mallard's neck, and there was even a line of scent bottles asking to be sprayed. I took a squirt of Dior, after rinsing my hands, and opened the door back into the corridor.

The voice wafted inexorably up from the direction of my office. 'Becca? Excuse me, young man, is Miss Haydock in that office?'

Constance was looking for me. I shut the door again and collapsed, panting like a trapped animal, on the chaise longue. Not now, I was thinking. Not today. But the door opened and I braced myself for Constance to goose-step in. In fact, what appeared was the mousy lump in the yellow coat. She began walking through to the lavatories, then stopped, evidently having seen the stricken look in my face. 'Are you all right?' she said.

'Fine,' I replied breathlessly.

To my surprise, she sidled across and sat beside me on the chaise longue. Her ankles were even puffier than mine. I found this comforting.

'I say . . . I'm sorry about my mother,' she said, and for a dazed moment I thought she was talking about Constance, until I remembered Constance was childless. 'She's missed nearly all the meetings and she does, well, rather feel the need to put her stamp on proceedings.'

This was an unglamorous Gwendoline to the parrot's Lady Bracknell?

'Her illness makes her tetchy,' she said anxiously. 'But her bark's much worse than her bite. Well . . .' she gave a nervous laugh, 'her bite's pretty fearsome too, but honestly the rest of

337

us all think this place is marvellous. As soon as I saw what you were doing here, I couldn't resist. I'm afraid I rather twisted Joe's arm to let us come, and now Mother . . .'

Honestly, I began feebly, it wasn't her mother . . .

'I ought to bring her in here,' she swept on, waving an admiring hand round my pet domain. 'Out of this world. I'm so envious. I much prefer,' she added with an endearingly guilt-stricken glance down at the ghastly yellow coat, 'dressing houses to — bodies. So much more manageable. Don't you find?'

I looked down at my own faithful black sweater, à la King Kong, and said ruefully that at the moment I didn't have a lot of choice as far as bodies were concerned.

She giggled like a little girl. 'When's baby due?'

I told her. A great breacher of social barriers, obstetrics. Total strangers swap intimate anatomical details with unblinking enthusiasm. Time passed, Constance did not appear, and I breathed more normally, soothed by the womanly chat. She'd much preferred her second labour, she told me — as we continued our discussion in raised voices over the oak door — and, golly, were these tiles Italian marble? Fabulous. She'd never been able to afford the real thing.

Second time round, she'd let them inject her (she loved the brass bolts too) with pethidine. Heaven on wheels, she assured me, emerging with a shy smile and walking across to the hand-basins. She'd only wished they'd given Richard a shot because, no question, her husband had been in a worse state than her.

'A sensitive plant, my beloved,' she went on, sniffing the soap with appreciation.

And all at once — about to say merrily that at least I wouldn't have a husband to worry about — I stopped because I had a terrible, if quite irrational, premonition of what was coming next.

'He's an actor,' she added. 'I think all actors are a bundle of nerves. They can't help it, you know, poor darlings.'

What do you do? Of course there are a hundred — probably even a thousand — actors called Richard. They're probably all a bundle of nerves according to their wives. But, leaving no space for hopeful ambiguity, she said: 'I'm Nell Prescott, by the way.' She held out her newly washed hand for me to shake.

The Honourable Helena, I thought. Cancer Foundation Lunch second Thursday of every month. Staying with Mama. Why be surprised they shared charitable interests?

'I don't know if you'll still be around by Saturday night,' she said, shaking my hand. 'So I'd better wish you good luck now, ah . . .?' She smiled enquiringly.

Wild ideas of giving false names galloped through my thoughts — only to be rejected. Too bloody silly. She'd find out soon enough.

'Becca,' I croaked. 'Becca Haydock.'

And, right on cue, the smile vanished.

'Haydock?' she began. Her face twisted as though she was in pain, but I realized she was not looking at me. Her head had turned towards the door. 'Oh Lord, is that Mother?'

I'd never imagined I would be grateful to the noisy old parrot, but I was then. 'I think she's calling you,' I said helpfully, opening the door.

The squawked 'Helena! Helena!' was unmistakable now. The Hon. Hel. squared her shoulders and, with some inaudibly mumbled farewell, hurried past me.

I resisted an impulse to collapse on to the sofa again. There was, I told myself, no reason she should connect me with her husband. No reason at all. Unless Henry's gossiping tongue . . .

In another mood, on another day, I could even have found the situation funny. Surely it was comic: wife and ex-mistress unknowingly swapping confidences. But, for pity's sake, I liked the woman. This shy creature, giggling about her awful coat — this wasn't the Hon. Hel. Not as I knew her — or rather, had never known her. I felt sick with guilt, and found myself praying my name meant nothing to her. That it was just her mother's summons which had blighted her sunny smile.

I practised deep breathing until I thought I could emerge without encountering either her or Constance. The corridor was quiet. I walked into the hall. Deserted. Only a tray of empty coffee cups and a pile of programmes on the table.

'Joe?' I shouted, and walked back into the main corridor, still calling him. The *Marie* bloody *Celeste*. Even George had vanished. 'Joe?' I bellowed at the top of my voice.

Oh God, I thought, don't say he's gone out somewhere. I hurried past my office and out of the tower door. His car was still in the courtyard. I felt dizzy with relief. I leaned on the bonnet for a minute, panting. I was just about to return indoors and resume my search, when a flicker of light from the Stables caught my eye. From the sitting-room window. I squinted – and at that moment, the whole window seemed to blaze orange.

'It's on fire,' I breathed disbelievingly. And then began screaming: 'Fire! Fire!'

Joe rounded the side of the castle at a fast trot. 'You're joking,' he said, jerking his head round, staring up at the tower. 'Where?'

'Not here, the Stables,' I shrieked.

We both ran across the courtyard. Or rather Joe ran, and I bounced and puffed in his wake. *Manderley*, I was thinking in wild panic. Henry laughing about Manderley. The house – set on fire by a jealous old woman, wasn't it? Jesus, *Jane Eyre*: Mr Rochester's house set alight by the mad wife – with Mr Rochester in there . . .

'Oliver!' I screamed, as I caught up with Joe outside the front door. 'Oliver – is he in there?'

A spectral figure streaked past the landing window, then a face appeared in my bedroom, to be replaced by a fist hammering against the window-frame, which eventually swung open.

'My God,' squealed Henry, leaning out, 'I'm in the bath. What's happening?'

'Oliver?' I yelled, 'Where's Oliver?'

But Henry had disappeared again.

'Oh Christ,' breathed Joe opening the front door and meeting a wall of oily black smoke. Even as he did so, Henry stumbled down the stairs, coughing, and staggered out into the courtyard. He was clad only in a bath towel with, incongruously, his feet stuck into wellington boots.

'Where's Oliver?' I wailed.

'Out,' croaked Henry.

'Are you sure?'

'Becca, I have escaped immolation by seconds, and all . . .' He broke off to cough. 'All you can do is interrogate me. He bolted into town.' Henry wrapped the towel round himself more tightly. 'When Mama-in-law called.'

'Pam,' I gasped, turning to Joe. 'It's her. I told you she was coming up here, and now she's done this.'

'Don't talk daft.' Joe was peering through the window. 'No flames now. Must have been the curtains went up like that. Shall we call the fire brigade or –' he grinned – 'think of the insurance and have a cup of tea first?'

'All my stuff, all the baby's things are in there,' I shrieked. 'We can't just watch the place burn down.'

'Joke,' said Joe. 'I'll have the firemen here in no time.'

'They'll be too late. Everything I got for the baby, it'll all be destroyed . . .'

'Don't look at me,' said Henry, coughing.

Joe was already heading back to the castle but now he paused, and returned to take another look through the sitting-room window. 'Oh well, if I must,' he said. And with a great air of reluctance, he stripped off his jacket.

'What are you doing?' I squeaked.

'My hero,' murmured Henry admiringly.

'I'm no bloody hero,' retorted Joe. 'Far as I can tell, there's nothing much alight. I'll see what I can do. But I'm not wrecking a good suit.' He tied a handkerchief over his mouth.

'Hi-ho Silver!' carolled Henry.

341

'Be careful,' I said, catching hold of Joe's arm.

'You're talking to a devout coward, sweetheart,' he said opening the front door. 'One flicker and you won't see me for dust.'

Henry and I shuffled along to squint through the smoky glass of the window. Joe hurried to the cupboard where the fuse box was housed. The corner lamp went out. Then he vanished into the kitchen for what seemed like an eternity.

I was beginning to panic when he re-emerged into the sitting room carrying a bucket of water and, as far as I could make out, the kitchen curtains over his arm, sodden. He draped them over the television set, then emptied the bucket over them and began stamping purposefully on the surrounding carpet.

'Dear me,' said Henry thoughtfully. 'I did notice the television was smelling a little strong.' He shivered and walked back to the front door. 'Safe to enter?' he called. 'Or shall I resign myself to triple pneumonia?'

I pushed past him into the sitting room.

'Help yourself,' said Joe, and Henry clumped off up the stairs. 'Panic over. All out now.' Sooty-faced, Joe was staring down at the television which was smoking poisonously. 'That was your fire. Bloody death traps these old valve sets.' The room stank. A blackened tatter of fabric was all that now dangled from the curtain pole. 'Don't say I didn't warn you,' he went on. 'My mother's went up just the same.'

I ignored him. The little white towelling jumpsuits had been airing nearby. I picked one off the back of a chair. Both tiny legs had been burnt away to pathetic scorched sockets. It was enough to make any woman hysterical.

'She wanted to hurt my baby. She could have killed both of us.'

'No one tried to kill anyone,' said Joe impatiently, stripping off his shirt and tutting at the soot. 'Except me, letting you keep this old telly. Never get this shirt clean again.'

'Pam Metcalfe was here.' My voice was rising. 'I told you

342

she was coming up here to – to do *something*. And Henry said she –'

'Calm down, love,' said Joe, walking over to me. I was frightened, momentarily, that he might slap my face in the approved manner for dealing with hysterics, but he clamped an arm round me and pushed me into the kitchen, away from the stench of smoke.

'I'm going,' I declared. 'Now. I'm not waiting around here for her to try again. I'm driving myself to London this minute and –'

'You're driving yourself nowhere,' said Joe. 'Henry? For Christ's sake, where's he vanished to?'

Henry appeared in the kitchen doorway, clad in a dressing gown and slippers now, a white handkerchief pressed over his nostrils, announcing that the damage to his lungs might prove fatal.

'It wasn't even you she was trying to kill,' I wailed.

'Give me strength,' muttered Joe. 'Henry, what's all this nonsense about Pam Metcalfe coming here?'

Henry emerged from the handkerchief. 'She didn't come in,' he said, with a distinct twinge of regret. 'Oliver saw her across the courtyard and was off down the back lane on his bike at Tour de France speed. Hardly the way to behave to one's mother-in-law, but perhaps under the circumstances . . .' He smiled thinly. 'My natural courtesy impelled me to invite her in for a cosy chat, but to no avail.'

'When?' I shrieked.

'Hours ago,' said Henry impatiently. 'I've done half a day's work since then, and *finally* found time for my bath. I'd just switched the lunchtime news on, toddled upstairs and –'

'There we are then,' said Joe. 'Something blew inside the set and set light to the curtains.'

I looked through to the sitting room. What did I expect to see? A black ball, labelled 'BOMB', with fuse still smoking? A petrol can? The charring was – indisputably – confined to a small circle round the television. I gulped. 'Sorry,' I muttered. 'You must think I'm going crazy.'

343

'Come here, you nutter,' Joe said, hugging me close to his hairy chest.

'All this excitement,' said Henry, 'and naked flesh too. I think I may faint.'

'Oh shut up,' I said into Joe's shoulder.

And, just as I began to give great heaving sobs of relief, my waters broke.

Henry, when he realized what was happening, burst into tears. Joe started laughing. Told me it would have been more useful if I could have managed it five minutes earlier when he was extinguishing the flames. Then, after ringing the local hospital, he bundled me into his car.

God knows what they thought of the pair of us. Joe looking like a coal miner. Me tear-streaked, breathless already with contractions which seemed to be galloping even during the short car journey. And I was indignant — that's what I chiefly remember. This was not how it was supposed to happen according to my textbooks. I had not taken the soothing bath. Not packed the poetry books. Not psyched myself into the correct condition. I was a filthy, shivering wreck.

'I don't want medication,' I announced before giving my name. 'Or unnecessary surgical intervention.'

'She may not, I may need both,' Joe said.

The sister on admissions smiled with the world-weariness of one who has heard all the jokes before.

'Is the father staying with you for the birth?' she asked.

'He's not the father.'

'Step-father,' said Joe promptly.

'What?'

'Well, that's what I am, aren't I?'

'You're Mr Haydock?' said the nurse.

'If that's what she wants,' said Joe large-mindedly. 'Or she can be Mrs Duff. Up to her.'

'You're her husband is what I meant,' said the nurse.

'Not yet,' said Joe, smiling soppily at me. 'But I'll have to marry her now, won't I?'

'Will you?' I said.

'And will you be staying for the birth, Mr Duff?' asked the nurse at the same time.

'Course I will, you daft bat,' said Joe.

It was not clear which of us he was answering. The nurse ticked her form and I was in no condition to argue.

ENTR'ACTE

The problem with consuming a feast in the main interval is that the audience thereafter falls into a dyspeptic torpor. I feel sorry for the poor buggers up there, acting their little hearts out; but if Irving and Bernhardt had been giving a double act, it would still have been a struggle to stay awake for the last forty minutes. My thigh must be blue I've been pinching it so hard. Finally, in a brief hiccup between the closing scenes, I murmur something fatuous about Linda possibly getting nervous on her own in the Stables, and slip out of my seat. Joe doesn't even protest. I've always understood horses can sleep with their eyes open. I suspect he may have mastered the same trick.

The cool evening air is delicious, the courtyard dark and silent except for the musical tinkling of the fountain. I'm tempted to linger here, but feel obliged to look in at the Stables. Linda, unsurprisingly, is neither nervous nor alone. She has been joined by two pyjama-clad boys. They are devouring potato crips and a horror movie on video.

'Get a load of this bit,' chortles one of her young friends, expertly whizzing the film backwards. The picture steadies on a smiling mother. She has wandered away from a pram to play ball with an older child. The camera slowly pans left. A spider, the size of a cow, is plodding grimly towards the pram.

'Brill,' whoops Linda. I sometimes wonder if childcare is the right career choice for her. The spider's hairy and monstrously magnified jaws scissor wide over the frilled pram canopy. I just manage to get out of the room in time. Sweat is breaking out on my forehead, although I know I'm being silly. Even as I shut the door a shift in the soundtrack music suggests rescue has arrived in the nick of time. It generally does in films.

Because the hall is dark I can't see the changes, the new carpets, the different furniture. It has become once again the hall I remember — and dream about. I dream about this house often. Queasily, I feel I've tumbled into one of my own nightmares. I don't know what impels me to creep up the stairs. The need to lay ghosts? Anxiety? Or common old curiosity to nose round a house while the owners are out? Whatever, I ignore the room I've been lent for the night. The room that was Oliver's once — is still Oliver's in my dreams. Instead, I push open the door to what used to be my room. Mine and — so very briefly — Henrietta's.

My daughter Henrietta was a lusty nine pounds five ounces of purple-faced perfection when she finally squeezed into the world. When the midwife cried that it was a little girl, I could see Joe's mouth opening and closing silently and I thought for a second, my God, something terrible has happened.

It hadn't, of course. Joe was dumb with tears.

'Looks just like her dad,' said the midwife, who had visibly taken a shine to Joe during the last six hours.

Face crumpled like a prize-fighter's, fists clenched, with a dark wet mat of hair: I could see what she meant.

'Josephine,' I croaked besottedly.

'Olivia?' whispered Joe, eyes streaming as a small fist locked round his finger.

And that was how I came up with Henrietta. A murmured joke which stuck. Henrietta, Giuseppa . . . Olivia. Joe insisted. And within an hour of the birth she was visibly Oliver's child. The mat of hair dried to a blondish mop. Her eyes proved to be exactly his shade of deep, slately blue and most unmistakable of all was the dimple in her chin. At least it proves wrong those cynics who claim family resemblances, in babies, are mere fond imaginings. Believe me, the very last person to whom I wanted to trace any likeness in my daughter was her father.

Oliver came only once to the maternity ward to view – *his* daughter. There. I can say it now. His daughter. At the time, the words would have stuck in my throat. It would have been even worse if he had made any attempt to lay claim to Henrietta. To my passionate, possessive relief, he did not. The first time he actually saw her, he reminded me of a little boy viewing someone else's pet hamster, which he fears may bite. Poking a timid finger towards her. Nervously exhilarated when her eyes blinked open.

'She's exquisite isn't she?' he had whispered. 'I can hardly believe something so beautiful – so perfect – has come out of it all . . .'

I had no doubt what he meant by 'it all', but I pretended not to hear. I steadfastly refused to connect my daughter with his tragedies. So, maybe if it wasn't for Cathy's death, I wouldn't have been cuddling Henrietta then. But once you allow yourself to be seduced into the 'what if . . .' maze, you can wander for miserable eternities. Queening it on a mountain of snowy hospital pillows, surrounded by flowers and cards, I was totally happy with present realities. Happy, innocent and heedless as the mother in the spider video.

It's a warm night now but I'm shivering. However fervently I might have begged Henry to forget the past I find I'm thinking about nothing else. I'm glad this room has changed. I don't think I could have borne to come in here otherwise. The old murky beige walls are now Wedgwood blue. Blowsy peonies droop over curtains and bedhangings. Very tasteful. Very pretty in fact. And quite unrecognizable.

Only the view from the window is unchanged as I gaze out. The tower is exactly as I see it in my dreams and I jump because something is moving in the courtyard below. A – peacock? Good Lord, it is too. A peacock is strutting across the empty tarmac. Henry, I think. That bird is undoubtedly

Henry's doing. But at least, this time, Henry has managed to banish cars from the courtyard.

'Enough, darling girl,' Henry had hissed, the umpteenth time I'd rung him from the pay-phone in the maternity ward. Well I had to keep phoning, didn't I? They were all too busy to come and visit me. 'The sun will not fall out of the sky just because you're not here to remind it to shine.'

Maybe, but my shiny no-parking cones would have been arranged round the courtyard, as recommended by my friendly policeman in time for the Foundation ball — exactly as they have been tonight.

They were forgotten fifteen months ago. And as a result, on that dark and blustery March night there were cars everywhere. The weather was evidently too wet and too cold for the patrons of the ball to risk venturing round to the carpark — so they squeezed their vehicles into every available corner from the main gates upwards.

The congestion meant that, in the end, the ambulances had to drive over the grass. One nearly sank in the mud, and it seemed the stretcher had to be carted for jolting, agonizing miles. I wasn't even trying to watch what was going on — I was too distraught — but I couldn't help seeing, when they'd eventually got the stretcher inside the back of the van, that the ambulancemen pulled the blanket up over the face.

Such a clichéd way of signalling death. Decent telly directors these days will do anything to avoid it. I suppose real death is never clichéd. I'd never seen anyone die before.

I feel sick at the memory. But how can I help thinking about it? Sometimes it seems to me that everything — *everything* — has happened in one, unbearably long night of feasting and revelry. Joe and Cathy got together for their ill-fated fling after a banquet; I met Joe and Oliver on the night of one ball; then all of us were gathered here nine months later for another. And now tonight? The glitzy frocks and bow ties are out, the champagne frothing again. I glance guiltily at my watch. Nearly ten o'clock. Must get back to the theatre before the end or Henry will kill me.

349

Henry was summoning me across to the castle that night as well. The night of the Foundation ball. It was a bit earlier, I think, as I stood by this very window with the curtains open just as they are now, nursing his little goddaughter-to-be and watching the comings and goings.

During my absence, the castle had sprouted a cherry-striped marquee out to one side. The effect was curiously indecorous, like an old lady blowing a whopping balloon of bubble gum. All afternoon, people had been scurrying round, shouting, carrying, cursing: clowns round the big top, with Henry the strutting ring-master. He was doing my job. Henry had in fact observed smugly to me that it was always hell to watch your understudy go on. If the understudy was bad, he said, you suffered for the play. If, on the other hand, the understudy was *wonderful* (naturally thinking of himself in this context), then you suffered a thousand times more . . .

But he was wrong that night. I was quite happy to let him get on with it. For about the first time in my hyper-dutiful life, I didn't give a stuff. I had Henrietta — and I had Joe. Not that Joe and I had made any public pronouncements. But my mother, telephoned from the maternity hospital by a tearful stranger with the news she was a grandmother, had drawn her own conclusions.

That Henry, too, had his suspicions was only too clear from his phone call that night, when he was so insistent I hurry across to the castle. Which is exactly what I do now, shaking off lingering ghosts as I run down the stairs. Last year, I was less willing to jump at Henry's bidding.

'It had a dying fall . . .'

or

TWELFTH NIGHT WITHOUT END

CHAPTER THIRTY-ONE

'Tell him I can't,' I called distractedly to my mother, who had answered the phone and bellowed Henry's imperious summons up the stairs. 'She wants feeding.'

There was a pause, then Ma appeared in the doorway to say Henry insisted on talking to me. So, reluctantly, I handed Henrietta, mouth opening and closing like an expectant goldfish, into her grandmother's doting arms and went downstairs to the telephone.

'I've got a surprise for you, pet,' Henry said. 'You must come at once.' He giggled. 'Like the famous telegram: *All is discovered. Flee at once . . .*'

'My baby's starving.'

'Well, feed her first if you must. Then come.'

Behind his voice I could hear the band playing. 'Are you kidding? With that mob? I'm in my tattiest old track suit. And it's no good telling me to change because nothing fits and —'

'Just come to the Tower Bar,' he said impatiently. 'They'll all be in the tent, whooping it up to the Ted Vernon Sound — and by the way, darling, where *did* you unearth *them*? I'd always understood the orchestra went down with the *Titanic*, and yet we appear to be employing the survivors.'

'No, Henry.'

The cunning crept into his voice like mist curling across a landscape. 'Dinner's finished. Joe has emerged from the steaming underworld and is circulating among his guests looking perfectly *gorgeous* in his tuxedo. I've been talking to a charming lady journalist, called, now, what was it?'

'Alison Laverick?' I suggested. I knew she was here. I'd got back from the hospital to find – surprisingly – a handsome basket of flowers she'd brought round this morning.

'That's the one. Divine little black velvet number. Joe was admiring it too. He did say, as a matter of fact, that he hoped you might sneak across for a drink, but I daresay he's so busy practising, ah, public relations with the press corps that he wouldn't really notice . . .'

I hesitated an instant too long.

'Ten o'clock,' he said promptly.

'It's quarter to ten now, for Pete's sake.'

'Ten-thirty then. Got that? Ten-thirty sharp in the bar. Toodle-pip.' The phone went dead.

Oliver, who was reading by the fire, glanced up. 'You're not going out, are you? There's – something I want to talk to you about.'

I took a deep breath. Turned to face him. 'There's something I want to tell you, too.'

'Oh?' said Oliver innocently. 'What?'

I'm marrying Joe Duff. The words were there, the bullet loaded, but I couldn't pull the trigger.

'Another time,' I said cravenly, backing out of the room. 'Henry insists I go over for a drink and I must get the baby fed.'

Ma was clucking fondly over the cot. 'See if you can persuade Oliver to come with you,' she suggested, handing Henrietta to me. Ma of course had lost no time in adopting Oliver. Wendy to the world's lost boys, my mother. 'The poor lamb needs cheering up.'

'The poor lamb,' I muttered, already repenting my cowardice, 'needs to bloody well pull himself together.'

And while Ma went down to lavish further tea and solicitude on her new protégé, I applied myself to the serious business of feeding his daughter.

*

It's a commonplace to say you're transformed by the birth of a baby. Course you are. And of course I was. Add to the revelations of motherhood the delicious prospect of a future with Joe and I was flying high on post-natal exaltation.

I looked back on my pre-birth self with incredulity — and shame. My behaviour had been *paranoiac*. A burned-out telly, a carelessly driven car, a bit of grit in a milk bottle ... I cringed. Not just at the memory, but also at the realization that Henry would dine out on the stories for years.

Worse: I'd blamed it all on poor Pam Metcalfe. Perhaps it was inevitable that, with a daughter of my own, I now discovered in myself an almost painful compassion for the woman.

I sat on the bed that night, Henrietta at my breast, watching her eyes crumple as she sucked. If anything happened to my child, well, murder would be the least I was capable of. All Pamela had done was mutter a few pathetic threats down the telephone, maybe wandered round the castle a bit. Who could say? Who cared? The Change does funny things to a lot of us, and the past nine months had taught me sympathy for anyone at the mercy of their hormones.

I even understood the ludicrous accusations she had flung at Oliver. Grieving people need a scapegoat. If she'd convinced herself Oliver was behind the abortion, then it was obvious she'd move on to blame him for not foreseeing the tragedy which followed. To blame him, in other words, for Cathy's death.

Poor Pam. Oliver, inevitably, was the villain of the piece for her. But if only in his own grief, he'd made some attempt to understand hers, she would never have worked herself up to such a crazy pitch. Instead, he'd given her cause a-plenty for her paranoia. Unlike me, she'd had every justification for her crazy ideas.

And, as I had told Oliver when he came to see me in the maternity ward, only he could unravel the tangle now. Eagerness to make amends for my own barmy behaviour made me all the more vehement. There must be no more putting telephones down on his mother-in-law, I told him, no more running away: he must . . .

Well, I didn't quite say *do the decent thing*, but that was the general thrust. Oliver hadn't argued, but he hadn't visited me in hospital again.

I lifted a sated Henrietta to my shoulder and walked over to the window, rubbing her back gently.

'Maybe Mummy could have been more tactful,' I whispered in the daft way one does talk to babies. And went on to ponder silently, for the umpteenth time, the most tactful way of breaking the news to him about Joe.

I did actually notice a slim female figure, raincoat over her head, emerging from the doorway at the foot of the tower. I assumed it was someone going out to one of the cars, and hoped they got soaked. Serve 'em right for parking in my courtyard.

Henrietta emitted a loud burp and I returned to admiring her drowsy face before, eventually, laying her in her cot. When the door opened behind me, I thought it was Ma and didn't even look round until a tentative voice said, 'Hello?'

Alison Laverick was standing in the doorway, mac over her arm now. Henry was right. The black number was so slinky I rather sourly doubted whether it would have closed round one of my thighs.

'The front door was open,' she whispered. 'So I – I just came up the stairs. Sorry, did I startle you?'

I began thanking her for the flowers but she cut me off, murmuring, curiously I thought, that it was the least she could do.

'Come and see the baby,' I said, and she dropped the mac over a chair and teetered across to the cot on lethally high heels, making the kind of cooing noises people do make over infants, while scarcely bothering to look at my little treasure.

'Oliver told me how beautiful she was,' she said, 'when I called this morning.'

I tried not to grind my teeth as I tucked the guilt tenderly round *my* daughter and asked how the ball was progressing.

'Ghastly. The press table's full of old hacks getting pissed out of their heads on free booze. But I ended up sitting next to your friend, Henry.'

She announced this as though it was terrifically important and I glanced round. 'Henry?'

'We talked about — a lot of things. And he told me now frightened you'd been. Because you thought Pam Metcalfe —'

'No,' I wailed, straightening. 'Spare me. I may have acted like a prize idiot but it's Henry's fault as much as mine, and if I hear him telling the poisoned milk saga just one more time . . .'

'God, I don't blame you,' Alison said with a flickering smile. 'I'd be rattled if I thought Pam had it in for me. She's off her fucking trolley. That's why I thought I'd better come and set your mind at rest.' She heaved a great sigh. 'It was me yer honour. Me what done it.'

I had returned to gazing at Henrietta's crumpled rosebud face. Now I looked up in complete bewilderment. 'Done *what*?'

'Tried to kill you, of course. Supposedly.'

And she began to laugh.

'Tricky for you,' she gasped. 'What do you say to your supposed assassin? Off the social map, eh?' She was laughing so heartily she capsized on to the bed. So, less precipitately, did I. Alison leaned towards me and I caught a faint whiff of whisky. 'Girl talk,' she whispered. 'Heart-to-heart about boy-trouble on the old candlewick bedspread. All we need is bobbysox and curlers.'

'Al, is this all some sort of a joke? Surely, the milk business was nothing but —'

'Who's talking about bloody milk? I'm talking about the night of the panto. It was me.'

I was glad I was sitting down.

'Driving the car? *You*? I don't believe it.'

She gave a take-it-or-leave-it kind of shrug.

357

'What were you doing down the back lane anyway?'

'Going to see Oliver,' she said with alarming promptness. 'I assumed, when they said he'd come home, he'd be back at the Gatehouse. So I was driving down there, and I saw you.'

'You *did* see me,' I exclaimed. 'I said all along the driver had seen . . . Bloody hell, Alison, you drove straight at me.'

'Rubbish,' she said, but she sounded less insouciant. 'Pure accident. Dad's car. I'm not used to automatics. I slammed both feet down at once and the bloody thing jumped forward.' She grinned. 'Shit, Becca, I was so relieved when you walked out of the theatre later on, unscathed. Oliver had been working himself up into a real lather of panic and —'

'So why didn't you tell me it was you? For Christ's sake, why didn't you stop at the time? To see if I was all right?'

She eyed me for a minute, then flopped sideways and began yanking threads out of the bedspread. 'I knew I hadn't touched you. A bit of mud never hurt anyone. I thought . . .' She sighed. 'Oh well, OK, it was accidental the way the car jumped forward, but just at that moment I thought a tumble in the mud served you right. I've a terrible temper.'

'Served me right for what? What had I done wrong?'

'Nothing,' muttered Alison, demolishing the bedspread faster. 'Oh, you know what I mean, Becca. Look, I've said I'm sorry.'

'I bloody don't know.'

'But I told you. Last summer. When I came round to Oliver's.'

I heard the band strike up a new number across in the marquee, a rhythmic hiss, faint as the spill from headphones. 'Oh,' I said.

Henrietta stirred, and I sprang up and went to the cot. An excuse. Thinking time. I fiddled with the quilt before saying, 'You told me about Joe and you. How he . . .' Wasn't the marrying kind? But he was marrying me all right. 'How, um, you'd wanted to get married and —'

'Bullshit.'

I wheeled round.

Alison looked as though she couldn't believe my obtuseness. 'Becca, I told you I wanted a child.'

'You — what?'

'I want a baby,' she snapped, sitting up. 'Why do you think I can hardly bear to look at yours? I want one so badly it's like a physical ache.'

I gaped at her. 'Well — why not have one?'

She began to laugh again, but there was a jagged edge to the mirth now. 'Ever thought about the logistics of getting yourself pregnant? Without a regular partner? In these AIDS-conscious days?'

'I did it accidentally . . .' I began, then saw her face and shut up. Like talking about your new diet-plan to a starving peasant.

'I planned it so brilliantly,' she said. 'The holiday in Spain. I invited Joe and he said sure. But, once we got there, and he was lying on the hotel bed like the over-sexed hunk of machismo he is . . .'

I gulped.

'. . . I was dumb enough — Christ, how could I have been so dumb? — to tell him what I wanted. Which was, in that fortnight, to get myself pregnant.' She glanced up. 'That sound unreasonable to you, Becca? I wasn't after marriage, didn't want a penny, didn't even want his name on the birth certificate. All I wanted was a few lousy sperm.' A fat tear squeezed out and trickled down the side of her nose. 'Know what he said?'

'I can guess,' I said wonderingly. 'A child deserves two parents? Or at least to know their father?'

'Pompous bastard,' she interrupted, rubbing the tear away furiously. 'Whisky. Always makes me maudlin. What a holiday. Joe wouldn't fuck without contraception, I wouldn't fuck with it. Comic, isn't it?'

'Sounds like a nightmare.'

'You don't know the half of it. I tried getting him drunk to have my wicked way. What a farce. And — God, I'd forgotten this bit – he actually started smoking. Filthy cigars because I couldn't stand the smell. We fought and fought until we stopped speaking altogether. A syringe in a clinic's got to be easier, hasn't it?'

She blinked away more tears. 'I'm thirty-seven now. I've made my mind up. I'd have sooner, well, known the father. But too bad. It's got out of hand. I mean, I can't go knocking people off the road, can I?' She gave a brittle laugh. 'Just because, when they turn round in the headlights, I see a great lump of baby.'

'That was all it was?' I said, amazed. 'Seeing I was pregnant?'

She jumped to her feet, and strode over to pick up her mac. 'You seemed to have got *everything* I wanted,' she said. 'But that was hardly your fault.'

Everything? She must mean Joe, she must have guessed, and yet . . .

'Jealousy's cheap,' she said. 'I'm ashamed of myself. Oliver told me the baby has, well, not exactly made up for everything, but, oh, you know . . .' She bared her teeth in a painful attempt at a smile. 'How wonderful. I'm very happy for you. Truly.'

'You'll – have your own babies,' I said helplessly.

'Bet your life.' She pulled on her mac. 'But I'm going to have a drink first. A large one. Want a drink with your nearly-killer?'

'Hell,' I said abruptly. 'What time is it? I promised Henry I'd meet him in the bar at ten-thirty.'

'See you in a minute, then,' she said and, blowing a kiss in the direction of the cot, vanished.

I looked at a wardrobe full of pre-pregnancy clothes, then at my waist, and pulled out instead my prettiest smock. Well, I'd thought the flowered pattern was pretty. Henry had said I looked like a sofa – but a very *expensive* sofa, he added kindly. Now I looked like a junkshop couch with half the stuffing knocked out of it. Ah me. There was barely time for a smudge of eye-liner and a comb through the hair — and that was a wasted effort because there was a drenching hurricane blowing across the courtyard. I staggered through the doorway at the foot of the Lady Tower like an Antarctic explorer reaching base camp, and slammed the door behind me.

Once inside, I was enveloped in the perfumed, cotton-wool warmth of an upmarket department store. Extraordinary the difference people make to a building. The castle smelled quite wrong now. When I'd first walked through this door the place had stunk of dust and damp, with overtones of disinfectant. Then of plaster and paint. Latterly — delightfully — of wax polish and new carpet. Now, the air tasted of brandy, cigars and face-powder. Cloying.

I hurried past the entrance of the bar to glance into the hall: empty, but with the thrilling emptiness of a theatre foyer when the play's in progress. I heard voices approaching from the small dining room, whose French windows gave into the marquee, and dodged back into the passageway.

In the Tower Bar, after all my frantic haste, no bloody Henry. But at least the room wasn't crammed with glamorously clad ball-goers, which was what I'd feared. I was grateful to find only one man there buying drinks. He glanced at his watch and I suppose I registered the familiarity of the set of the shoulders — slightly over-square. Recognized the lustrous hair which was a millimetre too long at the collar: the unmistakable cut of one who was young in the sixties. But, as I walked down the couple of steps and across to the bar, nodding at Tom, the barman, I assumed only that his customer was someone I knew locally. My mouth was open, polite greeting at the ready, when the man glanced round and saw me. My greeting withered to nothing — but if I was mildly taken aback, he looked utterly horrified.

'Rebecca!' he croaked.

Of course. I should have guessed. Henry's little surprise.

'Hello, Richard,' I said.

361

CHAPTER THIRTY-TWO

There was a scuffle of feet in the doorway and Henry sprang into the bar like the Demon King.

'Say *money*, my darlings!' he cried. We both gaped and there was a flash from a diminutive, leather-jacketed photographer crouched beside him.

'Caption: "Touching Reunion",' Henry dictated to the photographer with malicious relish. '"Boyishly handsome thespian Richard Prescott shares a joke" – it's always sharing a joke, isn't it? – "with his erstwhile close companion, Queen of the Pitza-Bitza . . ."'

'Well done, Henry,' I interrupted. 'Very funny.'

Richard was looking even less amused.

'Buy me a drink, Dicky,' said Henry coyly, 'and we won't print.'

'Piss off,' I said. 'I could have told you Richard might be here. I met his wife the day I went into hospital.'

'You *what*?' gasped Richard.

'Spoilsport,' retorted Henry. 'I could have been the first known mortal to extract a drink from Richard Prescott.'

'Go torment some other poor bugger,' I said.

'Come, Trevor,' said Henry to the photographer who had paused, pencil hovering over his notebook. 'We will go in search of more grateful subject matter. Richard: that maroon bow tie you have round your neck.'

'Yes?'

'It's a mistake.'

'My God,' breathed Richard when Henry had shepherded the photographer out. 'The bastard lured me in here, you know, with some fatuous tale of a lost gem of a theatre.'

'Oh, that's true enough.'

'And all along he was plotting . . .'

'No wonder he sounded gleeful on the telephone,' I said. 'I should have guessed.'

'How do we get hold of that picture?'

'Don't be draft. What d'you think he's going to do?'

A posse of dinner jackets milled through the doorway, guffawing and groping for wallets as they reached the bar.

'This place,' whispered Richard darkly, 'is crawling with journalists.'

'You have to be famous to interest the press.' Then I saw Richard's expression. 'Which I'm certainly not. I've never even rated a mention in a gossip column,' I added with a tinge of wistfulness. 'Let alone a tabloid full frontal exposé.'

'Let's keep it that way,' said Richard snottily. 'Now, if you'll excuse me I must rejoin my party.'

'Oh come on. You might at least ask how I am.'

Richard eyed me as a Tsar might an importunate serf. 'You're hardly dressed for the occasion.'

'I'm not attending,' I said. 'I work here. Where's Nell?'

'What?'

'I told you. We met at a committee meeting.' Then I added, with a twinge of anxiety, 'She didn't mention it?'

'Of course not.'

'I met your Ma-in-law, too,' I continued, relaxing again. 'Honestly, Richard, I used to think you were exaggerating about how awful the old cow was, but I realize now —'

'For Christ's sake,' said Richard. 'She's here.'

I glanced round, but there were only the dinner jackets and Tom the barman, busily filling glasses and pretending he was deaf to our conversation. He was a poor actor.

'At our table,' Richard muttered.

'A family party? How delightful.'

Richard seemed to see me for the first time. 'You've put weight on,' he said, with the self-righteousness of one who never eats protein and carbohydrate at the same meal.

'I've just had a baby. What do you expect?'

He started so violently he spilled some of the gin and tonic he was picking up. 'Keep your voice down, will you?'

'Richard? What's up with you?'

'Someone might see us.'

'So? We're only talking.'

But he picked up his drinks and made for the door. His escape route was blocked, however, first by more thirsty revellers and, behind them, Constance Berisford, flanked by Henry. Constance paused on the threshold and peered from side to side like an inquisitive budgerigar on its perch.

'Ah! The very person I wanted.'

I won't say I cowered, but my pleasure in the evening was dwindling fast. Lady Berisford, however, advanced not on me, but on Richard.

'I thought he'd still be here,' said Henry smirking. 'There's so much to catch up on when one is talking to a *very* old friend.'

'Shut up, Henry,' I breathed.

'Becca. Good. I wanted to see you too,' Constance called. But, to my relief and surprise, she turned and plucked Richard by the sleeve. With visible reluctance Richard followed her as she elbowed an imperious passage between the bodies crowding the bar, and he was forced to put down his glasses once again, a few feet along from me.

'How are you, Lady Berisford?' I heard him say. He was smiling glassily. 'And Sir Michael?'

I gaped. But if his wife knew Constance, then why shouldn't Richard? It's disconcerting, nevertheless, to discover that two people from entirely separate compartments of one's own life, from different worlds even, are not merely acquainted, but — to judge by the exchange of polite enquiries — old friends.

'But what I wanted to talk about,' Constance announced,

characteristically cutting the niceties short, 'was your mother-in-law. One hesitates to ask outright — naturally one is delighted to see Margaret up and about again — but . . .' She did not sound delighted. She drummed her fingers on the bar. 'The thing is, Richard, when Margaret was on, as it were, her deathbed, she talked about giving us, that is the Foundation, some money.'

I missed Richard's response, but he'd set his jaw in the way he always did when displeased.

It was like being at the hairdressers. I could keep them under observation in the mirror at the back of the bar. I leaned forward on the pretext of ordering a drink. After nine months on the wagon, and confronted with this cornucopia of bottles, I was dazzled, like a child let loose in a sweetshop.

'In fact, a staggering amount of money. Well,' Constance said frankly, 'it staggered me.'

I stopped pondering the galaxy of bottles to listen more closely, wishing I could hush the chatter behind me.

'For twenty years I've been running that woman to and from committee meetings because I thought she couldn't afford a taxi.' Constance's voice sliced effortlessly through the buzz of conversation. 'You can imagine how I felt when it emerged she could charter Concorde and tell 'em to keep the change. This was when she summoned our treasurer and me to the house,' she added, taking a cigar from her evening bag. Richard, gallant as ever, seized her lighter and ignited it. 'It was after the bad attack last June,' Constance resumed, puffing furiously. 'When she really thought her number was up. Understandably, she wanted to avoid paying the iniquitous sums the Chancellor would be demanding. In the event of . . .' Unusually for Constance, she left the obvious unsaid, and tapped a silver fragment of ash from her cigar. 'I'll be honest with you, Richard.' Her eyes opened wide — but not nearly as wide as mine. 'When we heard the amounts involved we were dumbfounded.'

There was a sudden lull in the noise as one party gathered up their glasses and departed.

'Yes,' said Richard grittily. 'I think we were all – a little taken aback. When the facts emerged.'

Henry was at the other end of the bar. I'd thought he was talking to the woman beside him, but now I caught sight of his face, reflected between two whisky bottles. His eyebrows were lost in his hairline. With an air of nonchalance, he picked up his glass and drifted to my side.

'My dear boy,' continued Constance, blithely disregarding possible eavesdroppers, 'I should imagine it hit you two as an absolute bombshell. When I think how Nell has had to scrape and save to bring up those boys with never a penny from her mother. It's positively scandalous.'

'And *truly* shall the darkness be made light,' murmured Henry in my ear. 'The legal wife is discovered to be a mighty heiress one day. Out goes the mistress the next. That's my boy. That's the Dicky we all know and love. Oh poetry. Oh rapture. Oh my, oh my . . .'

Richard, puce-faced, mumbled something inaudible, but Constance continued to address him with her customary public meeting clarity. 'I mention it now only because, if Margaret still wants to rescue something from the taxman, you might alert her to get a move on. I must say, we've worked our socks off to accommodate her in the matter of this ball. Becca over there will back me up on this.'

I jumped like a rabbit, and ordered a vodka and tonic. I don't even like vodka. It just happened to be the bottle next to Richard's outraged face.

'Do you two know each other, by the way?' bellowed Constance. 'Same line of business aren't you? Becca Haydock, Richard Prescott, but . . .' she went on, turning back to Richard and matters in hand, 'although there was talk last year of Margaret underwriting the cost of this jamboree, we haven't heard a word since. What? Forgive me, Richard, shockingly deaf these days.'

Barely more distinctly, Richard said something about his mother-in-law now regretting the disclosure of her financial position.

'I dare say she is,' agreed Constance heartily. 'But has it shamed her into making anything over to you two yet?'

From Richard's face in the mirror we gathered it had not. He added, more loudly, that he must rejoin her and Helena.

'A leopard doesn't change its spots, I suppose, on account of the odd intimation of mortality,' sighed Constance. 'How's her health?'

'A medical miracle, according to the doctors,' responded Richard, with perfectly audible bitterness.

'My poor boy,' said Constance. 'A large malt, barman. Richard?'

'I really must return to my table but an Armagnac if you insist,' said Richard without drawing breath.

'That's our Dicky,' whispered Henry, with the face of a python who has swallowed a particularly satisfying meal. 'That man would take a drink from Lucrezia Borgia as long as she was paying. And now for a flutter in the dovecot.' He raised his voice. 'Richard, dear boy, you must let me help you carry those glasses. I simply cannot wait to meet the heiress. And her charming mama.'

Richard snapped that he could manage, clattering his glasses jealously on to a tray which Tom, a perfect barman, had supplied on cue. Shouldering past Henry, Richard then collided with Alison in the doorway before making his escape.

Al paused on the step for a moment, scanning the crowd, swaying slightly, like a thin black blade of grass. 'There you are,' she said, joining me at the bar. 'Drink? Another large whisky for me, please. Same for you, Becca? Or' — her face twisted into a bitter little smile — 'would that spike the baby's milk?'

The interchange caught Constance Berisford's attention, which she fixed once again on me, and strode across. 'Becca. You've had the baby.'

'Well, you might be forgiven for thinking otherwise,' said Henry, eyeing the billows of the smock. 'But, take it from me, she was the size of a —'

'Shut up,' I said and listed name, weight and date of birth.

'And Oliver?' said Constance stiffly. It was as though she could barely bring herself to name her nephew. 'How does he feel about it?'

'Over the moon,' said Alison, sounding as though she might weep. She took her whisky from Tom and gulped half of it.

'Oh hardly,' said Henry. 'Oliver looking at the brat reminds me of a neurotic monk — a Jesuit, I daresay — staring at a statue of the Virgin Mary. With a kind of holy despair.'

'Where is he?' demanded Constance.

'Sitting by the fire,' I said, 'with my mother.'

'Christ, that's awful,' declared Al. 'He should be here with us, celebrating.'

'Quite right,' said Henry, surprisingly. 'Why don't you go and fetch him, love?'

Al glanced at him uncertainly and stirred her ice cubes with one long finger. 'I might — just do that.'

'You can try,' I said, 'but I doubt if he'll come.'

Constance drained her glass purposefully. 'I shall go and talk to him myself.'

I glanced at Henry, who raised his eyes heavenwards, then put his arms round the shoulders of both Constance and Alison. 'I've got a better idea, old loves,' he said. 'I'll go and fetch the little papa myself.'

'Bring him to me,' said Constance. 'Tell him I want to talk to him. *Must* talk to him. And I think you should be with us, Becca,' she added magisterially.

I swallowed the rest of the vodka in one panicked gulp. 'I'll just — um — find Joe first.'

'In the tent,' said Alison. 'Probably draped round some tart with big tits if he's on his usual form. I think I'll have another of those, please . . .'

*

Dressed as I was, I didn't want to venture beyond the french windows leading into the marquee. But there were two convector heaters in the connecting tunnel, blasting hot air like giant hair-driers. It might have suited the gaggle of bare-shouldered women drifting past, but I could feel my cheeks cooking to crimson. So I crept after them into the crowded ballroom, sidled round the silk-ruched walls and dived for cover beside the bandstand, which was flanked by a flower display the size of a Mini car. I peered out through the foliage.

Joe was at the other side of the marquee. White-jacketed, with navy shirt and red carnation, he was padding from one table to the next like the proprietor of a casino. I willed him to look in my direction, but he was too busy shaking hands with the men, kissing the women. Smooth bloody operator.

Even a waiter, darting to and fro in his tail-coat like a swallow, failed to see. Only the pianist noticed my frantic gesturing behind the massed begonias and raised a hand in friendly salute — without missing a beat.

He'd pounded through another dance and a half by the time Joe drifted close enough for me to call him. At least then he hurried across to my shady corner, arms outstretched, nearly tripping over a speaker wire in his haste. 'How's my baby?' he said, kissing me.

'We're both fine,' I said, kissing him back with fervour. 'Oh Joe, Alison came to see me, and —'

But immediately Henry loomed up behind with an arch smile. 'Kissing behind the bandstand? Really, children.'

'You're haunting me, Henry,' I said grimly.

'Henry's been fantastic,' said Joe. 'I don't know how we'd have managed if it wasn't for him.'

Henry nodded. 'Honesty compels me to agree. And for my final *coup de théâtre* . . .' He gestured towards the marquee entrance. To my surprise I saw Alison shepherding Oliver to a table.

'How did you swing that?'

'I told Oliver his aunt was on her way over and handed

369

him a jacket and tie. By the by, your mother says Henrietta's asleep and you can enjoy yourself. You see,' he added with a soulful glance towards Oliver and Alison, 'I scatter goodwill and contentment everywhere.'

Alison was pouring a glass of wine for Oliver with notable, if noticeably unsteady, goodwill. Oliver looked content as a heretic at the Grand Inquisitor's tea party.

'Not the boy,' said Henry, when I pointed this out. 'My dinner companion. The love-lorn lady journalist.'

'Love-lorn?' I demanded, clutching Joe's hand.

'Oh, the bitter-sweetness of love unspoken and unrequited,' sighed Henry. 'She and I wept together, metaphorically, into our crèmes brûlées. My heart was wrung, even while I deplored her taste.'

Joe was quicker on the uptake than me. 'Are you talking about Oliver? Al and Oliver?'

Henry raised his eyebrows expressively.

'Alison?' I shrieked, so shrilly a passing dancer glanced round at us. What was it Al said? That I had . . . *everything* she'd wanted. 'Al confided *this*? In . . . *you*?'

Henry glared at me. 'Alison confided the barest threads, but enough for a sensitive soul to perceive the hidden tapestry of, ah, human tragedy beneath those few words.'

'Or embroider it yourself,' I retorted.

Henry smirked. 'So clever in some ways, dear heart, and so obtuse in others. Believe me: Alison has yearned for the boy ever since his wife was alive. And no sooner did Cathy conveniently quit the mortal coil, than you appeared and filched the unlikely object of desire. One could hardly blame Alison if she actually had tried to murder you. Don't gape so, child. It triples your chin.'

'I – I can't believe it.'

Joe gave an oddly bitter laugh. 'Hell, I can. Al's moved heaven and earth to protect him. I should have twigged right from the start.'

'Such a charming girl,' sighed Henry. 'Wasted on an Oliver.'

'But this is good news,' I said. 'Isn't it? For us?'

Joe shrugged. 'Not unless Oliver happened to feel the same.'

Henry waved this caveat aside. 'A Mozartian finale to the evening.'

Since Ted Vernon and his Sound were belting out '*My Way*' at the time, I didn't follow and said so.

'All the protaganists are gathered for the closing sextet,' declared Henry. 'Richard, like the Count in *Figaro*, is faithfully returned to his wife. Bonded, one feels sure, for eternity — knowing Dicky — by the prospect of money. I, ah, the high priest Sarastro, have cast together the poetically tragic Tamino and Pamina in the persons of Alison and Oliver. *Magic Flute*,' he added kindly. 'There remain only our heroine and hero. Now, in which opera do I cast you two?'

'Spare me,' I muttered.

'This is a night of happy consummations,' he said, gesturing imperiously at the band leader. 'So shall we announce, at last, the long-overdue event which will legitimize my poor god-daughter?'

I began to protest, only because I wasn't having my engagement announced while lurking behind a pot of begonias in a maternity smock, but Joe positively leaped forward and grabbed Henry's arm. 'For Christ's sake pack it in,' he snapped, so forcefully the drummer craned round to see what was going on and I felt a sudden inclination to burst into tears.

'Dear me,' murmured Henry with a twinkle of malice. 'Do you know, I never thought of *Don Giovanni* . . .'

'For the last time, Henry,' I snarled. 'Shut up.'

'Only trying to help,' said Henry, and departed across the dance floor in the direction of Alison and Oliver, bowing to the dancing couples with truly eighteenth-century grandeur. 'My Way' finished to a scattering of applause and the band plunged straight into another number. Evidently a popular choice. Two couples from the table nearest were stubbing out cigarettes, shedding shawls and heading for the floor.

'Joe?' I whispered. 'You do want to marry me?'

'You know I bloody do,' said Joe, but his gaze abruptly swivelled past me. 'Do we want to talk to Constance Berisford?'

'No – why?'

'She's bearing down on your left now, looking like a thundercloud. Nothing for it. We'll have to dance.'

'Are you kidding? Dressed like this?'

'I'll pretend you're not with me,' he said, wrapping an arm round my waist and firmly propelling me past the herbaceous border and on to the dance floor. 'That's done it. She's headed off for another table. And ah two, three, four . . .'

I blinked in the spotlights and had to conquer an impulse to cut and run. But, as I reminded myself, anyone who has queued regularly in a BBC canteen dressed as a green furry kangaroo should not be fazed by a trot round a dance floor in a billowing sofa-cover. With a partner several inches shorter than herself.

I straightened my back, sloped my shoulders, tilted my head back, pinned my mouth into the glossy beam favoured by the ladies on *Come Dancing* and melted into Joe's arms. Anyone watching me, I thought fondly, must inevitably imagine the eighty-eight yards of tulle and the galaxies of hand-stitched sequins. It's simply a question of acting the part with conviction.

'Becca,' said Joe after two or three minutes of this. 'Pardon me for asking but – *can* you dance?'

'Only the waltz,' I hissed through the smile.

'This is in four time.'

'I know *that*.'

'Could've fooled me.'

I continued to smile graciously round the floor. Saw Constance staring at me and pretended I had not. Saw Richard, who pretended not to see me. Alongside him, his mother-in-law, hideous in mould-green, was lecturing Nell, who also caught sight of me and looked surprised. I lifted my hand from Joe's shoulder but her attention had been reclaimed by Mama.

'Sweetheart,' whispered Joe into my ear. 'I'm the one who's supposed to go forward.'

'At my height you only ever get to learn the man's steps.'

'Then a little double-chassé here, I think,' said Joe, suddenly releasing me and tripping alongside with footwork so fancy I was shocked into immobility.

'Where'd you learn all this?' I said, when Joe whirled me back into his arms with the confidence of a practised gigolo.

'Just one of my hidden talents. There's so much you don't know about me.'

That, at least, turned out to be true.

I felt him stiffen, and looked over my shoulder. Alison was stalking across the floor, with reckless disregard for chasséing couples. 'Is this true?' she demanded loudly in my ear. 'What Henry's just told me?'

It was Joe's turn to adopt a glassy grin now, which he shone round passing dancers while seizing Alison's elbow.

'Take your filthy hands off me,' she snapped, squirming free and losing a high-heeled shoe in the process. 'Is it true?' she repeated, swaying wildly as she tried to thread her foot back into the shoe. 'Henry says that you're dumping Oliver for — for *this*?'

The dance finished with a prolonged, twirling cadence.

'I think we've provided enough entertainment for one evening,' murmured Joe, through teeth still clenched in a smile, as he shepherded Alison inexorably off the dance floor.

I followed, with Alison twisting round to whisper furiously, 'You're as bad as Cathy. Worse — you've actually got Oliver's child.'

I tripped into a chair and had to stop and apologize to the occupant before I caught up with Joe and Al in the marquee entrance. 'What's this got to do with Cathy?' I demanded breathlessly.

'It's only exactly what she did,' snarled Alison, turning to face me. 'Dumped Oliver and ran off to this bastard.'

373

'Please, Al,' breathed Joe.

'Cathy never left Oliver,' I said, looking from her to Joe. 'I mean I know she and Joe —'

'Oh yes she bloody well did,' snapped Alison. 'Or she tried to. The night she killed herself.'

'Al, if you want to make a scene,' said Joe quietly, 'I can't stop you, but not here in a public passageway, *please*. Come through into the . . . Amanda, hello, love, how are you? I'll — I'll be over for a word soon.'

The woman smiled and nodded and, glancing curiously at Alison and me, passed on into the marquee.

'I don't believe any of this,' I declared to Alison. 'You've had a lot to drink.'

'Well, Joe?' she demanded. 'Am I right?'

'For Christ's sake, Al,' whispered Joe urgently. 'Oliver —'

'Don't give me that,' she screamed. 'No one gives a fuck about poor bloody Oliver except me. As for Cathy . . .' She grabbed my arm — whether to secure my attention or steady herself wasn't clear. Her fingers dug painfully into my flesh. 'As soon as the little cow heard Joe'd got this place, know what she did? Packed her bags, ran Oliver into town and turned up on lover-boy here's doorstep, and —'

Suddenly she released my arm. Her face melted from fury into ashy consternation. She was looking past me as though seeing a ghost. 'Oh God . . .' she whispered.

'Packed her bags?' Oliver's soft voice said incredulously, even before I spun round to find him standing behind me. 'Cathy — was leaving me? That night?'

Only Joe had seen Oliver's approach. Now he shut his eyes in despair.

'Well done, Al,' he said quietly. 'Finished now? Or is there an encore?'

CHAPTER THIRTY-THREE

'That bloody letter,' Oliver said dazedly. 'I'd never understood why Cathy wrote me that letter. It was in her pocket. Saying she was sorry and . . .' He stared at Joe, his voice rising. 'She wasn't talking about killing herself at all, was she? Well, Christ, I always knew she wasn't. She was sorry – for *leaving* me? For coming to you?'

Alison burst into tears.

'For God's sake,' said Joe. '*Please* can we get out of here?'

He strode ahead, with Oliver following. 'Her mother – from the start – kept harping on about a suitcase, clothes . . .' Oliver was saying.

Alison stumbled past me, grabbed Oliver's arm. 'Don't,' she whispered. 'Don't torment yourself.'

Oliver shook her off and followed Joe into the hall. It was empty and echoing, a log fire slumbering in the fireplace. Only a waitress lurked behind the staircase, enjoying a quiet cigarette, which she stubbed out as soon as she saw Joe. She needn't have bothered. Joe marched straight through to the bar which, thank God, was temporarily emptied. Even Tom had quit his post.

'Cathy's suitcase,' insisted Oliver. 'Alison said Cathy packed her bags . . .'

I had once seen a woman emerge from a mangled car after a road accident. Her husband was still inside, but she asked obsessively about her shopping in the boot. Whether the bag had spilled. Whether the frozen goods were melting. It was as though she could not face more terrible truths. I thought Oliver was behaving in the same way.

'Tell me,' he persisted. 'I want to know.'

Joe slumped against the bar, head in his hands, but he was *nodding*.

'Joe,' I waited. 'What is all this?'

I felt dizzy. I wanted to wind the whole evening back to the beginning and play the scene again. None of this could be right.

'Cathy – left her things with you? What the hell for? Why didn't you say?' Oliver grabbed Joe by the shoulder, forcing him to turn and look at him. 'Did you get rid of them, for God's sake?'

'It was me told Joe he must get rid of the suitcase,' said Alison. 'I thought it was for the best. I'm so sorry, Oliver. You were never supposed to find out.'

'But I was desperate to know where Cathy went that night. After she dropped me. And why she'd suddenly insisted on running me into Oxford,' said Oliver. Only then did any sign of pain confort his face. 'She was coming to – you, you *bastard* . . .'

Joe flinched. 'I wish I could say no.'

So did I wish he could say no. I'd believed Joe. I'd believed the story of a drunken one-night fling. But Cathy Langham had gone to Joe the night she died . . . *The night she died?*

'Becca? Will you come home?' I realised Oliver was talking to me.

'I'll come,' said Alison. 'I've got to explain to you, Oliver. You must've thought I was mad, talking all that rubbish at the inquest. But I was only protecting you. Believe me, I –'

Oliver shuddered away from her and she crumpled on to a bar-stool like a puppet whose strings have been cut. 'Becca?' he said.

'Soon,' I said. 'I'll follow you in a minute.'

Oliver turned and walked swiftly out, barely checking as he collided in the doorway with the returning bartender. Tom, his fists bristling with small bottles, took one look at us, pulled an expressive face and vanished again. I heard the crash of the tower door behind Oliver. Then I turned to Joe.

'You lied to me.'

I wanted him to shout back. To roar denials.

'You told me – all you told me was that Cathy telephoned you. That evening.'

Joe shrugged. 'She did.'

'And you invited her round?'

'You may well ask,' muttered Alison.

'Shit, no,' said Joe. 'We hardly spoke, she rang off in such a hurry. I'd no idea. An hour later, I opened my front door and there she was. With a bag in her hand. Saying she was leaving Oliver.'

'Sure of a warm welcome from lover boy here,' snapped Alison.

'What was I supposed to do?' said Joe. 'I asked her in. Offered her a drink. I couldn't take it seriously. I thought she'd just had a row with Oliver, I tried to tell her she'd be mad to leave her husband, like this – for me. I mean, we hardly knew one another.'

'Well enough to fuck.'

'Al, *please*. It was excruciating. The girl was in my house, virtually *offering* herself to me.'

Offering herself to him, I thought. Like I had.

'She wouldn't listen to reason. In the end, I found myself telling her I was going on holiday next morning. It was the kindest way I could think of saying no.'

Alison tittered sourly. 'You'd have done better to stay at home with her, wouldn't you?'

Joe turned on her furiously. 'Do you think I haven't thought that a hundred times? Oh Lord, Becca, I don't mean –' He broke off and I glanced round. An elderly woman, trailing magenta chiffon, had appeared in the doorway. 'The girl stormed out,' Joe went on in a whisper. 'Hysterical. Swearing she'd make me sorry one day.' Then he looked beyond me, face pinned into a smile. 'Tombola? Yes, sure. Across the hall, door on your left.' The magenta chiffon wafted out again. 'I'd no idea what Cathy intended. Well, of course I hadn't. But, honestly, I never suspected — never dreamed in a million years — Cathy felt so much for me.'

'Sentimental claptrap,' snapped Alison, clambering to her feet. 'Cathy Langham never loved anyone except herself. She didn't give a fuck about Joe. It was this place she wanted, wasn't it, Joe?'

He shrugged and Alison smiled grimly, turning back to me. 'If you ask me, the moment I told her Joe had bought the castle, she started thinking. It was that afternoon, when I found her up the tower. One minute she was threatening to jump, the next she was bright as a daisy, tripping home to the Gatehouse. Well, she'd had a brilliant idea, hadn't she? Solve everything. An opera festival no less, in the theatre here. Rescue the company from bankruptcy by giving them a home at Harecombe. Joe Duff, well known opera-lover, well known every kind of bloody lover, was going to bankroll her operatic career, just like old Rivenhoe indulged his actress wife. It's true, isn't it, Joe? Isn't that what she suggested when she turned up at the flat?'

'Pipe-dreams,' said Joe. 'Mickey Rooney stuff: let's put the show on right here ... Besides, everyone gets grand ideas about that theatre. Becca did, didn't you? And look at Henry. He —'

'But that's what Cathy wanted,' interrupted Alison. 'Wasn't it? And she had you down as the kind of sucker she could twist round her little finger.'

'We've been over this time and again, Al. And you're wrong. Would she have killed herself in that horrible way — a girl like Cathy — just because I laughed at a crackpot idea?'

No, I thought. The Cathy Langhams of this world don't kill themselves for a thwarted idea. And what had made me, even fleetingly, think of climbing the Lady Tower? The fear that Joe, on the point of proposing marriage, would back down.

'She didn't mean to kill herself,' snorted Alison. 'She just wanted to scare the shit out of you.'

'I don't believe it,' said Joe.

Neither did I. It seemed my destiny was for ever yoked in parallel to Cathy Langham's.

'Cathy was in love with you,' I said flatly. 'You turned her down. She came back here and killed herself.'

'Crap,' said Alison, and she burst into drunken tears again and ran out of the bar.

And then there were two.

I felt unnaturally calm. Good in a crisis, that's me. At least now I knew the worst. Somehow – *somehow* – we were going to clear up this sordid mess of lies and half-truths.

'Her things,' I said. 'Pamela was right all along. Cathy really had packed her case. What happened? Did she forget it?'

'Christ, Becca, she pelted out like a madwoman. I downed half a bottle of Scotch. The case was in the hall. I didn't even find it until the next morning.'

A bald head appeared. Asked if anyone was serving.

'Course,' said Joe, hopping round to the other side of the bar and seizing a handful of glasses. The man began to order drinks for half the marquee. I could have screamed. Eventually he staggered off with his loaded tray.

Joe plonked down two more glasses, poured whisky into them and handed me one. 'What could I do?' he said. 'You tell me. Take her stuff round on my way to the airport at crack of dawn next morning? Knock on Oliver's door? Sorry mate, your wife left this in my flat last night?'

'And when you did eventually come out to the Gatehouse, you found me instead,' I said. 'I even remember the boot of your car was open. Were you bringing the case back then?'

'Course. With a bottle of bubbly to make amends. I mean, soon as I got back from Spain, I rang the girl, but the answering machine was on nonstop. I couldn't risk turning up and finding Oliver at home. So I waited until I was pretty sure he'd be in school.'

'And sneaked round, looking through the hedge. I thought you were acting shiftily, even at the time. And — eventually — I told you Cathy was dead.'

Joe downed half his whisky in one gulp. 'I couldn't believe it. I drove like a maniac to Heathrow and told Al the lot. I didn't know what the fuck to do. She was the one who said, if the police didn't actually come to me, I should just get rid of the bag and keep my mouth shut. I mean, I could see she was right. How would it help Oliver — anyone — to know Cathy had been leaving him the night she killed herself? It could only make things a hundred times worse. So we shut up and . . . Oh Tom, hi. I've — been holding the fort. Got some tonics, have you? We're nearly out.'

Tom looked from Joe to me warily, and returned to his station behind the bar. Joe refilled his glass and walked round to join me.

'But why didn't you tell *me*,' I whispered.

'Think I didn't want to? I couldn't. Not without Al agreeing.'

It was as though Tom's return was the signal for the room to fill up again. We edged down the bar away from the crowd.

'She'd made out at the inquest Cathy had been set on suicide all along,' said Joe. 'I'd got rid of evidence. We were bloody conspirators.'

I noticed that his carnation had fallen to the floor. It was bleeding red petals. I knew how it felt.

'Well, at least now,' I said slowly, 'I understand why you were so concerned about Oliver. You felt guilty.'

'Guilty? Becca, since he came back, the guilt's been *unbearable*. Whatever Al says, Cathy walked out of my house swearing she'd make me sorry. And I just let her go. She drove back here and fucking killed herself. Oliver's wife. I've wanted to throw myself at his feet, beg him to forgive me.' He smiled bitterly. 'I remember you once said he should be grateful to me for giving him lodging here. Christ Almighty. I'd give him the whole castle if I thought it would make amends.'

'And instead, you had me. Flinging myself at you. Just like Cathy did. Must have felt like history repeating itself.'

'I never think of you in the same — *world* as Cathy Langham.'

'No? Except that we both, in your book, belonged to Oliver.'

'How could I cheerfully talk about marrying you when I've already wrecked the man's life so completely?'

'Oliver doesn't love me.'

'I wish I could be so sure of that.'

A thread of music wafted in through the open door. I recognized the tune. 'After the Ball is Over' . . .

The ball was over as far as I was concerned.

'I think I should go and talk to Oliver.'

'Not just yet,' said Joe. 'Or — look, I'll come with you . . .'

'Better not.'

'I love you,' said Joe, and a fat man broke off from his conversation at the bar and looked round, blinking.

'I know,' I whispered.

I could taste tears salting the back of my throat, but I swallowed grimly. I was not going to contribute any more histrionics to this spectacle. I walked to the door. Joe followed, but his arm was grabbed by the fat man who demanded to know when the restaurant was opening. I walked out alone.

Ted Vernon was crooning into his microphone now: '"Many a heart is aching, If you could read them all; Many the hopes that have vanished . . ."'

. . . After the ball. There was already, I reflected, a scrapheap of aching hearts and abandoned hopes — with another two hours before the ball was actually over. I was hissing the song between clenched teeth as I opened the tower door into the courtyard. The icy blast silenced me. The wind was so cold it seemed to have frozen the rain out of the sky. There was a moon visible now, with clouds whisking across at a fierce gallop. I lowered my head against the tempest and began to thread a path in and out of the vehicles packing the courtyard, smug as stag beetles with their phone antennae poking up.

I did actually notice the car pulled up on the grass. Only because its sidelights had been left on. Anyone who parked on my lawn deserved a flat battery, I thought viciously . . . *after the ball.*

It's hard to remember the order of things then. People recounting catastrophes always claim everything happened at once. Well it did. But also in a kind of slow motion. I glanced up at my window — Henrietta's window — and saw the overhead light switch on.

Oliver, I thought with angry certainty. The silly clot will wake her up, and I've got to talk to him, not tend to a grizzling baby. And indeed, at that moment Oliver appeared at the window. He seemed to be fumbling with the clasp. What the hell was he opening the window for on a night like this? And then I knew something was wrong. I've never felt a surge of adrenalin like it. Something was wrong with my baby. He was shouting. I could see that, but couldn't hear anything until he managed to bash the window open.

'She's gone,' he was bellowing. 'Where's she gone?'

My mother was framed in a halo of light at the front door almost in the same split second. She was pointing. 'Over there!'

Even as Oliver roared 'Hey, you!' I saw the woman. She'd been crouched behind one of the big Volvos. Now she darted out. And she was carrying a cot. Henrietta's cot. She was making for the car on the grass. A white car, I saw belatedly. With stripes down the side . . .

I ran like fury across the courtyard, shinning my legs on bumpers, crashing into wing mirrors, shrieking, desperate to get to the little car first. Burdened with the cot, she had no chance of racing me. She jerked to a halt, swung the cot round and headed instead for the castle. Oliver pelted out of the Stables and joined the chase. She got to the castle first. The tower door was open. She slammed it behind her, but not before I'd seen her face clearly in the light. Not tearful now. Not frightened. Just grimly purposeful.

382

Pamela Metcalfe.

Oliver reached the door before me.

'No,' I was screaming. 'Don't chase her! Don't frighten her — she can't get away . . .' But my voice was whisked away on the wind and Oliver vanished into the castle. By the time I arrived, sobbing and panting, there was no one in the lobby. I dodged into the Tower Bar. Empty. Across to the hall. Two elderly men warming their bottoms in front of the fire, brandy glasses in hand.

'Has a woman come through?' I shrieked. 'Carrying a baby?'

They stared at me as though I was demented. And then Nell — Helena Prescott of all people — hurried towards me, hands outstretched.

'I *knew* I recognized the name,' she was saying, smiling warmly. 'I remembered the minute I saw you on the dance floor. You were once in a play with Richard, weren't you?'

'Joe!' I wailed, ignoring her. 'Where's Joe?' And at that moment, thank God, he emerged from the corridor. 'She's got Henrietta,' I babbled. 'You thought I was mad. But now she's done it. She's got Henrietta.'

I expected Joe to argue, to tell me not to be foolish, and I knew I would scream. But he didn't. 'Where?' he said.

'They've — not come through here,' I panted. 'She must have gone . . .' I moaned. Of course I knew where she'd gone. Joe followed me as I pelted back to the foot of the tower staircase. 'Oliver was chasing her. Stupid bloody fool. He should have known — guessed . . .'

'Hush,' said Joe, taking the spiral steps two at a time ahead of me. 'Are you sure they're up here?'

I heard a tiny cry coming echoing down. 'That's her,' I sobbed and overtook Joe, racing up the stairs. Behind me, he was pausing, checking the doors on each landing. But the rooms were empty. Of course they were. Only builders' tools and paint pots. I knew she wasn't there. I didn't stop. I knew where Pamela was going. By the time I reached the top landing, I could hardly breathe. The door was swinging open, with a frozen wind slicing down.

'No, God,' I prayed. 'No, God, please. Not my daughter. She couldn't . . .' When I heard another wavering cry I could have fainted with relief. I felt drunk, light-headed. I'd been sure the madwoman was going to throw her over. Just as her daughter threw herself over. I ducked under the arch and walked unsteadily up the shallow flight of steps on to the roof.

At first, I could see nothing. Only the great carved battlements silhouetted against the orange glow of floodlights. Then I saw Oliver, leaning against one of them. Frail, white and still as a corpse. And on the other side of the roof, Pamela. She was crouched by a battlement, on either side of which yawned infinite space. The carrycot was resting on the tiny, knee-high parapet between two battlements, black against the floodlights. Rocking gently. Balanced, it seemed, although she was clutching the handles.

'Don't come near,' she hissed.

Behind me, I heard Joe pant up the steps. She looked over my shoulder, and her face contorted.

'Send him away,' she ordered shrilly. 'Get him to go — and shut the door.'

'My baby,' I croaked.

'Tell him to go away,' she shrieked. She was so close. If I threw myself full length I could touch the cot. But I couldn't move. I couldn't even breathe. Couldn't Joe spring? Overpower her?

But behind me I heard Joe retreat, and the door clank shut. My hero. My bloody hero. It was his fault we were here now. I'll never forgive him, I swore, never . . .

And then stifled the thought. As if it mattered now. Nothing mattered except Henrietta. I could taste blood. I'd bitten my lip. I was alone, with Oliver — and a madwoman holding my child.

'Please,' I whispered, as levelly as I could. 'Please — my baby.'

'She'll be all right,' said the woman, 'if you do what — what I say.' To my horror I saw the black outline of the cot shift, but it was towards her, not over the edge. She threaded an arm through the cot handles to free her hands, and began groping in her handbag, glancing up after a minute to hiss, 'Don't move. Either of you.'

I glanced at Oliver. He was frozen still.

'We won't,' I said, and tried to sound as reassuring as I could. 'We won't do anything you don't want.'

Awkwardly, clinging to the hand rail, I sat down on the wet, sloping, tiled roof. I was barely ten feet from Henrietta's cot. She was within millimetres of death. 'We won't do anything,' I repeated.

Pamela Metcalfe ignored me, fumbling in her handbag. The cot shifted again, and my heart stopped beating, but the handles were still looped over her arm. She produced what looked like a small box. I heard the click of an electric switch, and she sent the thing scudding across the wet tiles towards Oliver.

'Don't touch it,' she snapped. It was a cassette tape-recorder. A dictating machine. An office toy. 'Just talk close to it,' she said to Oliver. 'Loudly. Or . . .'

The silence was more appalling than a threat.

'What do you want me to say?' whispered Oliver. He, too, was staring fixedly at the cot.

'I want you to describe exactly how you killed my daughter,' said Pamela Metcalfe.

I nearly cried aloud. If it was me, I'd confess to anything — anything — to get my baby back from the brink. Oliver wouldn't have the wit. 'Please, Mrs Metcalfe,' I began gently. 'He didn't kill —'

The woman jerked round to glare at me, yanking the cot with her, and I shut up. I even stopped breathing.

'For Christ's sake,' shouted Oliver. 'Stop it, Pam. Whatever you say. It — it was all my fault.'

'You killed my daughter. Say it.'

I could hear Oliver's breath. A long shuddering sigh. He glanced across at me, and then away, up at the moon.

'Yes,' he said. 'I – killed Cathy.'

CHAPTER THIRTY-FOUR

I didn't believe him, of course. It was a charade. A preposterous piece of theatre. The roof was even raked like a stage. She and Oliver were the players. Henrietta — oh God — the merest prop. And I was the audience.

A helpless, terrified audience with no confidence in Oliver's ability to sustain his part. Already, he seemed to have run out of invention. He was leaning against the battlement, staring across at the cot which creaked with every buffet of wind.

A stage, floodlit in orange from below, the backcloth an ink-black sky. The moon rolled out from a scudding cluster of clouds. Big and round and creamy. People go mad at the full moon, I thought. Below us, I could see a glowing, cherry-striped corner of the marquee, could hear the headless buzz of people, the chugging beat of the band.

The woman suddenly turned on me. 'Are you pretending you didn't know?'

I looked from her to Oliver and back. I would have answered anything to please her. But her face was dark. I didn't know what she wanted me to say, So I opted, despairingly, for the truth. 'No,' I whispered. 'I mean — no, I didn't know.'

'Liar,' she spat.

Oh God. Wrong answer. A blast of wind made the cot rock and me catch my breath. Keep tight hold of that cot, I wanted to shriek. Just hold on to my baby.

'They wouldn't believe me,' she said bitterly, staring down at the cot. 'No one. It was crazy. As if a mother doesn't know

387

her own child, I knew Cathy would never — *never* — do anything like that. But the police only told me to go away. They thought I was mad.'

I'd once played stewardess in a video aimed — if you can believe this — at teaching businessmen to cope if their plane was hijacked. Try to establish a rapport with the terrorists, was one suggestion. God Almighty: could Pamela Metcalfe have anything in common with an international terrorist? 'The police thought I was — a bit mad too . . .' I croaked. Only that she was holding a life in the balance. 'When I told them someone had been up this tower,' I continued desperately. 'Watching me.'

The woman looked up. 'Watching *you*? Don't be stupid. It was him, I wanted to see if he was back yet. Phil told me about the postcard.'

The marquee cracked and boomed in the wind like the sail of a ship. I realized, detachedly, that my fingers clenched round the icy metal rail of the fire-escape were already sense-less with cold. I told myself Henrietta was well wrapped-up. And that babies were famously robust in low temperatures. Abandoned infants survive hours, dumped on doorsteps, even in rags — don't they?

'You — frightened me,' I said breathlessly.

Just keep her talking, I thought. The longer you keep them talking, the less likely they are to do something unexpected. 'And you phoned me, didn't you? But everyone thought I was imagining things. I suppose they said you were imagining things too?'

'*They* . . .' She made a noise of contempt. 'When I found the case gone, and her pink dress, well, I knew then. I told the police. Cathy wasn't after killing herself that night, I said. She was leaving him, that's what she was doing. And I knew *someone* had got rid of her things. Whatever *they* said. And it was him,' she declared. 'No wonder he wouldn't ever talk to me. All the time he was playing the innocent, he knew exactly what'd happened to her crocodile case.'

'But I didn't,' said Oliver, suddenly coming back to life. 'Becca, you know I didn't, Joe said —'

'Maybe you've forgotten,' I broke in, willing the stupid bastard to understand that he must play along with the woman, whatever crazy things she accused him of. 'Maybe —'

Oliver looked at me as though *I* were the madwoman. 'What does the suitcase matter now?' he said. 'She knows. For Christ's sake, I'm admitting it, aren't I?'

Below us, I heard a rumble of applause and shouting in the marquee. Someone had drawn a raffle.

'Oliver?' I whispered. 'You can't be saying ... not really ...'

'Can we stop this fucking charade now, Pam, please?' said Oliver. 'Go down. Get the police. Whatever you want.'

The woman snorted. 'So your aunt can sort it all out for you again? Pretend it's me that's —'

'Constance?' I gasped. '*Constance* knows that — that you ...' But it was impossible. I was physically incapable of saying the words. The whole idea was too fantastic. Too absurd.

And then, suddenly, the lights went out.

'What's going on?' demanded the woman. At first I couldn't see anything but I could hear the cot scraping on the stone and my heart was thumping in my throat.

'Time switch,' I lied wildly. 'The floodlights automatically go off — at something to midnight.' I'd no clue what time it was now. And even as I spoke, I cursed my stupid tongue. Living in the village, Pamela must know that the floodlights went on and off randomly, whenever someone happened to pass the switch. But she seemed to accept this, because she was turning to me, saying angrily: 'Don't try telling me you weren't part of it too.'

My eyes were adjusting to the dark. Strangely, I could see her face more clearly now, because there was no floodlight behind her. And all I could think was: Is Oliver saying he really did it? He's not acting? He — *Oliver* — really killed his wife?

389

'Becca doesn't know anything,' he said tiredly. 'I promise.'

A crime of passion. A *crime passionel* . . .

'More lies,' she spat,

The French are so much more understanding about these things . . .

'She was there,' said Pamela flatly.

'No,' I wailed in panic. 'No . . .'

'In Tesco's. You were there,' Pam had twisted round to me again. 'When he finally admitted it. You'd been standing there at the checkout, woman.'

'What?' I said dazedly. But I could remember the scene clearly enough. Me, hugely pregnant; Pamela, in tears, screaming at Oliver that he'd made Cathy get rid of *her* baby, that he was a child-murderer . . .

'You ran out,' said Oliver flatly. 'And I didn't realize it was the abortion she was going on about. I lost my head. I just assumed she knew everything. Knew that —'

'You murdered my daughter,' Pamela shrieked, and even above the wind, even above the inane buzzing of the microphones, I heard Henrietta whimper a protest at this banshee wail. I couldn't contain myself, I started towards the cot.

'Sit down,' Pamela gasped, scrambling to her feet, lifting the cot aloft. 'He admitted it to me then. In the store. He said — can you believe this? — he said he was sorry. Now he's going to tell everyone. Or he really will be sorry.'

I crouched back on the tiles, clutching the rail again. It was so cold it burned my hand. 'Whatever you say.'

'The police — no one — believed me.' She was swaying to and fro, the cot banging against her side in the wind. 'In the end I came up to find him, to *beg* him, one last chance, just to tell me. What happened to my daughter . . .'

The day of the fire, I thought. The day I went into labour. The day I saw her, marching up the drive, full of purpose.

'But he ran off on his cycle. And that's when I made my mind up I was going to make him talk. Now I've got *his* daughter, he's got to.'

Mine, I wanted to bawl. Not his daughter, *mine*.

'Please,' I whispered. 'Don't hurt Henrietta. I promise, I didn't know anything.'

Pamela looked at me. She didn't say anything but she crouched down again, leaning against the battlement. The cot tilted further towards her. Away from the edge. A foot from death maybe, rather than an inch.

'It's all *his* fault,' she muttered. 'All this.' And only then did I realize the woman was actually terrified — as terrified as I was. 'I was taking the baby home,' she said. 'It's him made me come up here. So — so he'll just have to do it here. When it's all on the tape, you can have the child.'

They were very clear about it in the video. The most dangerous terrorist is a frightened terrorist. Fear makes people irrational, unpredictable, crazy. 'For God's sake, Oliver,' I said. 'Tell her whatever she wants to know. Quickly.'

'And when it's on a tape,' she said. 'Even his aunty won't be able to do anything. Not this time.'

'Constance — really knew?' I said faintly.

Oliver's hair was streaming silver in the wind. 'She guessed. At the inquest.'

'And there she was afterwards, chatting with the judge, friendly as you please. And the way she looked at me . . . I knew it was all wrong.'

'I went to find Constance straight away,' said Oliver desperately. 'When — when I realized Cathy was dead . . .'

There was a low, shuddering cry. For an instant I thought it was Henrietta, but the sound came from Pamela. There were tears glimmering on her face. Oliver glanced towards her. 'Afterwards,' he whispered, 'I ran down to the Gatehouse, got on the bike and rode like crazy into Oxford. I knew Constance'd sort everything out. Get the police, I mean. That's what I intended.' His voice rose. 'But she wasn't bloody there. There was no one in the Lodgings. And I remembered they'd gone to some dinner in London. So I went up to bed. And took sleeping pills. I told you, Becca. A whole bottle. Cathy'd said they were sleeping pills anyway.'

'Cathy never touched sleeping pills,' declared the woman.

'She'd been given them at the abortion clinic,' said Oliver. 'Not very many. And they can't have been much good, can they? I didn't die. I wanted to die. But the next thing I knew, Constance was shaking me. Morning. I — Christ, I felt as though my brain had been shredded. At first I couldn't even remember what had happened. I really thought it was some kind of nightmare.'

He shook his head dazedly.

'And, you see, the police seemed to think they knew everything. Took it all for granted. They hardly asked me anything. Just kept saying how sorry they were. I — honestly, I almost wondered if they were right — and I was going mad. And Constance looked after me. Stopped them bothering me too much. I just let it happen. I didn't care. Soon as I could, I came straight back here. Constance couldn't stop me, I — I was going to kill myself.'

'But you didn't, did you?' hissed Pamela,

The wind direction shifted abruptly. The sound of the band dimmed and I could hear quite distinctly the faint whirr of the tape-recorder lying on the tiles.

'Didn't have the nerve.' His voice was bitter with self-loathing. 'Cathy was right about that. I kept thinking — how to do it. And every day, every minute, I expected the police to knock on the door. Arrest me. But they never did. And then there was the message on the machine about the ball, the madrigal group. I thought . . .' He gave a wretched whisper of laughter. 'I thought Constance would never forgive me if I let Uncle Michael's college down. And you see, I'd made my mind up — I was going to tell her the whole story. That night. Really I was. But I met you, Becca. You never gave me a chance to see her. And later,' he said, almost pleading with me, 'you remember, you said however Cathy had died, it didn't matter. Nothing could bring her back. And I began to think . . .'

I could sense Pamela stiffening. 'I know, I know. So you never actually told Constance.'

'But at the inquest — stupid really — listening to the evidence, she heard me say Cathy had driven me into Oxford that night for the bloody choir practice. And, God alone knows why, she remembered finding my bike chained at the bottom of the stairs in the morning. The morning after. And realized it shouldn't have been there — not if Cathy had given me a lift in the car. And she just looked at me . . .'

He shuddered.

'She knew. Constance could always tell when I was lying. When the inquest was over, in the courtroom, she said — she just said she didn't want to know. Wouldn't let me tell her — explain anything. Said if she didn't actually know anything, she wasn't breaking the law. She told me I had to go away.'

'Not breaking the law?' cried Pamela Metcalfe. 'She knew he was a murderer and all she did was send him off abroad?'

At first I didn't hear a sound. I just felt a tremor in the metal railing I was clutching, and jumped. Then another. Someone was climbing up the fire-escape.

'And what happened?' I demanded noisily. 'Tell her, Oliver, about the day Cathy died. Please.' Anything to drown the faint metallic thuds I could hear now, as well as feel. 'Speak up,' I added wildly. 'So it goes on the tape.'

But he didn't speak up. He didn't speak at all. He leaned against the battlement, gazing up at the moon like a fucking statue.

'That afternoon: you'd cycled home from school specially, hadn't you? To see her.' I was babbling, but at the top of my voice, bellowing every word, terrified of silence. 'Cathy — Cathy was upset about the opera company, wasn't she? And she'd climbed up here, up the tower, but you — you and Alison — persuaded her down. And then she drove you into Oxford. For Christ's sake, Oliver, did you actually go to the choir rehearsal? Or was that all a lie too?'

'No,' he protested, stung at last into speech. 'Of course I went to the practice. It was when I came out — Cathy was parked across the road. Waiting for me. God, I was relieved. I'd been so worried about her.'

Pamela snorted. And at that moment, out of the corner of my eye, I saw Joe appear at the top of the fire-escape and dodge behind one of the battlements. Joe, barely visible in his dark blue shirt. Joe? What the hell was he trying to do? He was miles from Pamela. Miles from Henrietta . . .

'Cathy said she'd had a marvellous idea. A surprise. I'd got to come home with her. But when we got back to the Gate-house, she wouldn't let me out of the car. She darted in – said there was something she had to collect. Something in the house I mustn't see now. She – she was laughing . . .'

For a moment I thought it was a shadow passing between two of the battlements. Only when it vanished behind the second, noiselessly, did I realize the shadow was Joe. Dear God – he was walking round the tower. Round the outside. Along that tiny ledge in the howling black night. I nearly groaned aloud. Oh my poor bloody would-be hero . . .

'It was the letter, wasn't it?' Oliver was saying wonder-ingly.

I willed myself not to look beyond Pamela. Not to look in Joe's direction. Willed my face into blankness.

'I never realized that before tonight. She'd written the bloody letter, left it there for me, because – she was leaving me. She must have gone in to find it. Christ, I can see her now, coming out of our front door, stuffing something into her pocket . . .'

'Speak up,' I hissed, 'Oliver, *please* . . .'

Joe passed silently across the next gap. For an instant, incongruously, I remembered that sunny afternoon in Oliver's garden. Joe dodging between the gaps in the hedge, grinning. There wasn't an eighty-foot drop behind him then.

'She got back into the car. Drove up here to the castle like a mad thing and insisted we went into the theatre. I didn't know what the hell she was playing at.'

The moon came out again and suddenly I glimpsed Joe's thick fingers pressed round the corner of a battlement. As though he were hanging on with his fingernails.

'She marched up on to the stage and told me I was looking at her wonderful idea. We were going — this is what she said — we were going to buy the castle. I knew then she'd run mad. Mad or drunk. We were going to buy the castle, she declared. I could turn it into a school, if I wanted. Run it myself. That was better than working for cranky old nuns, wasn't it? And the theatre was going to be an opera house. Like — oh God — like Glyndebourne, she said.'

I heard a stone rattle from Joe's direction and said loudly, 'But the castle was sold already. Joe had bought it.'

'Oh she told me that. But there was some fuss about the lane, access — I can't remember. Anyway, she said Constance could stymie b-bloody Joe Duff's plans because of it. And when I asked where we could possibly get the kind of money this place would cost she said Constance again. That Constance would give me anything I wanted, if only I asked. I mean, she was talking wildly. I tried to reason with her, but she wouldn't listen.'

Out of the corner of my eye, I saw Joe's head appear, then duck back again. He was behind Oliver now. If he moved, Pamela would see him. She'd have to see him. I was in agony. That he would fall. That Pamela would look beyond Oliver.

'In the end, I just had to say no. Christ, I should have agreed. Agreed to anything. Just to stop her. But I didn't. And that's when she said she would leave me. That — she wanted to anyway.'

'She should have left you,' muttered Pamela uncertainly. 'You were too old for her.'

'I said . . .' he began, then took a shuddering breath. 'I said if she left me, I'd kill myself. And she said, right, do it. And got the pills out of her handbag. Here, she said. Swallow them. Do it now.'

There was still no movement behind him. Joe had fallen, I thought. But we'd have heard. Oh God.

'She told me I was useless. Useless husband, useless — lover. And she ran off the stage, out of the theatre. I chased after her.' Oliver was talking faster, gabbling. I wondered if he knew Joe was inches away from him. 'She came up here. To the top of the tower. I was scared out of my wits. I thought she was threatening to jump again, like she had in the afternoon. But no. She said, if I couldn't face pills, then why didn't *I* jump. Didn't I have the guts? She did — she said. She could have done it this afternoon. I told her — please — not to be so stupid. To come down . . .'

Henrietta murmured. Pam glanced down, and in that instant I saw Joe slip across the gap beside Oliver. Only three more battlements before he was within touching distance of the cot, but Pamela's head was up again.

'I was crying,' said Oliver. He was crying now. 'She kept saying unless I asked Constance to give me the money, then she would leave me. I said it was impossible. I'd give her everything I'd got but this was crazy. And she said, right, she bloody well was leaving me, so I might as well jump. If I loved her, if I meant it when I said I couldn't live without her, then . . .'

The bitch, I thought. The heartless self-obsessed bitch.

'I told her again and again not to be so ridiculous. And she said when I knew what she'd done yesterday I'd change — my tune. And —' His voice was cracking up with sobs. 'That's when she told me — about the abortion.'

Pamela groaned, so loudly I nearly jumped to my feet, convinced she'd seen Joe. But she was staring down at the cot, rocking it to and fro on the low parapet.

'I said, why? And she told me she wasn't going to be like my mother. Ruining her career for a child. If my mother could have in those days, she said, she'd have aborted me, wouldn't she? And that would have been a . . .' Tears were choking his words. 'A good thing for everyone.'

Pamela's head jerked up. I saw her thin face was shiny with tears too. 'And so you pushed her.'

And she deserved it, I thought.

'No,' shouted Oliver. 'No. Of course I didn't. I — I knew

she couldn't mean it. I wanted to hold her. To tell her not to be so bloody stupid. And I – I don't know what happened. The roof – look – it's slippery as hell. She just seemed to lose her footing all of a sudden and . . .'

'It's a lie,' breathed Pamela uncertainly.

Joe appeared behind her.

'I knew no one would believe me,' Oliver was shouting. 'But I hardly touched her. I was trying to grab her, but she twisted away screaming and –' Oliver broke off open-mouthed.

Knocking Pamela flat in a flying rugby tackle, Joe landed face down on the roof with a terrifying thud, one heavy arm pinioned across the cot and Henrietta, who wailed loudly.

But I was shrieking even louder, bellowing my head off, from terror, relief, sheer exploding hysteria.

'What did you do that for?' Pamela was screaming. 'I wouldn't have hurt the baby, I –' Then she saw Oliver.

I'd swear he was only hurrying over to the cot, to Henrietta, but he kicked the tape-recorder and it went skidding down to the edge of the roof.

'No,' Pamela bawled, shoving Joe's arm aside and scrambling to her feet. 'No . . .' And she grabbed Oliver's sleeve. I'm not quite sure how it happened but it seemed Oliver for a long time was swaying, gentle and slow as a tethered balloon, with the shallow stone parapet behind his knees. He spread his arms, tried to grasp the battlements on either side. I saw his fingers curl into claws and scrape painfully across the stone. Hanging on for seconds – an eternity it felt like – but less time than it took me to charge across to him.

'No . . .' screamed Pamela Metcalfe again.

But with a faint, despairing cry, Oliver fell into the night.

CURTAIN CALLS

A great while ago the world began . . .

Only the clown remains on stage.

With hey-ho, the wind and the rain . . .

He sings with the harsh, reedy wobble of an actor who knows he's not really a singer but is doing his damnedest to kid you otherwise.

But that's all one, our play is done . . .

Maybe, but you can bet your life the evening's entertainment is not. That's always the catch with these gala nights. Everyone from the tea-boy upwards is going to be presented with fieldfuls of flowers (protesting that they don't deserve them), and then there are the inevitable speeches . . .

And we'll strive to please you every day.

Every day for the next three weeks, that is. At seven-thirty nightly, five p.m. on Fridays and Saturdays with dinner interval, no matinées. There were endless arguments about this opening production. My bright initial notion was doing the *Dream* out in the grounds, but I do accept that was dotty. You don't raise millions of pounds to restore a theatre in order to perform in the garden. Henry favoured *Love's Labour's Lost*. Richard (inevitably) wanted one of the tragedies. The Trust Committee were pushing for *Comedy of Errors*. Which, said Henry sourly, had a certain poetic appositeness for a committee choice.

Joe, beside me, has been comfortably asleep for twenty minutes at least. He's missed all the joyful reunions of couples, but the salvo of applause when the clown finally minces off the stage, mock-curtsying, disturbs his slumber. His eyes blink open to see me glaring at him.

'Love you,' he murmurs.

The curtains shimmy together.

And I love him. God, how much I love him. I did anyway, even without his absurd, breathtaking heroics up on the tower that night.

'Is it over at last?' he says.

'Over at last,' I reply, heartfelt.

Tabs shoot upwards now to reveal the whole company. Clasped hands, tearful faces, rapturous applause.

I'd still have loved him even if he'd murdered Cathy Langham personally. She deserved it, if you ask me. In retrospect, it amazes me only that no one actually did. Joe isn't as bloody-minded as me. It was Joe who insisted we subscribe for the seat in her memory. He was just so pathetically grateful to discover he had not been the cause of her death.

Another bow. In unison. Admirably democratic this company. There may be a couple of famousish names standing up there in the line but they are not going to take individual calls. The Drama is not like opera. Instead all the actors now loose hands and begin applauding too. For who is walking on — or rather sidling on, for all the world as though he were being shoved, reluctantly, into the limelight — but our director? Echoing cries of *'bravo, bravissimo.'*

Oh brave Richard. Splendid in your blue velvet coat. But, although I am applauding as loud as anyone, I fear Henry was right. You do match the curtains almost uncannily. However, the rest of the audience obviously think the jacket is jolly fine, and cheer even louder.

The volume is fuelled by relief, if you ask me. The

deliciously shared recognition that we're on the home straight, heading for the loos and the booze we know is waiting for us in the hall of the castle. The Gala Reception, my dears. Which equals middling white wine and a scattering (as if we hadn't eaten enough already) of tasteful canapés. Courtesy, you may be sure, of Flying Duck Ltd. Proprietors, Mr and Mrs J. Duff.

Today's staff in the castle kitchens aren't quite up to this sort of catering. More geared to Ye Olde Roast Beef of England for wealthy — *very* wealthy — tourists following the stately home B. & B. trail. It isn't even called a hotel. Just Harecombe Castle. An English gentleman's residence which happens to have ten letting bedrooms and a nice line in silver-salvered bacon and eggs. And, as Joe says, who are we to knock it? This kind of set-up is a lot less work and a bloody sight more profitable than running a decent restaurant. And what's money anyway? Oh, roll on the canapés.

Not yet.

'Speech . . .' the audience are roaring, and Richard is glancing round with prettily timed uncertainty.

'I — I am so very happy to welcome you all here,' he begins very softly, which ensures the restless buzz of chatter is silenced pronto. The mellifluous timbre of Richard's voice trembles with emotion. 'On this special, this *magical* night. The consummation of so many dreams, so much hard work, such generosity . . .'

He is not ad-libbing. And no, this is not cynicism on my part. As Linda, my help, tucked Henrietta into her borrowed cot in the Stables and I powdered my nose, we clearly overheard him rehearsing in the bedroom next door. Every faltering syllable, every pretty hesitation. The emotional crack in the voice always was one of his best tricks. 'For an actor, there is nothing like playing to a house full of — *friends* . . .'

Nothing worse, if you ask me. But Richard is using the word 'friends' entirely euphemistically. He means sponsors, which is not the same thing at all. You have to admire Nell's skill. Years of serving on charitable committees have turned her into an ace fund-raiser. The way she's persuaded local grandees to part with their lolly, this theatre may even turn in a profit if they're not careful.

'And I'm sure,' Richard is continuing, with a glassy smile, 'first of all, we would all like to pay tribute to the mastermind behind the restoration of this Victorian gem.'

Henry, in his immaculately cut cream dinner jacket is tall, distinguished and magnificent. His slow bow is a three-second essay in the art of performance, encompassing dignity, humility and grandeur all in one stately sweep. An education for any aspiring actor.

On second thoughts, with Henry as resident designer they should be in no danger of serious profit. He accepts his bouquet as graciously as the applause, although I, for one, can tell from his smile that he thinks pink carnations frothing with gypsophila are the height − or depth − of plebeian taste.

He steps forward, effortlessly upstaging Richard, whose smile becomes noticeably glassier. Henry − unscheduled, but I have no doubt equally well-rehearsed − is indeed seizing his opportunity to say a few words. Oh hell.

'I told them to put the choux balls in at ten-fifteen,' whispers Joe. 'Any more of this lark and they'll be cremated.'

'Shall we start hissing?' I suggest.

'Friends . . .' begins Henry.

Romans, countrymen, I think, sinking lower in my seat.

'First of all, I feel I must take this opportunity to extend my personal and heartfelt thanks to a man very dear to all of us . . .'

I glance uneasily at Joe. He shrugs.

'Our noble Master Craftsman, whose hard work and dedication to The Theatre . . .'

Et cetera, et cetera. I breathe again, and even smile and begin clapping. Because this is surely George's ultimate moment of glory. He strides out stiffly to take his bow in front of this glittering house in tails and tears.

Well done, Henry, I think, as he goes on to list other

worthies among the workmen. Henry has every reason to be grateful to George. Somehow, along with the mammoth task here, not to mention the transformation of the Stables, George has found time to superintend the civilizing of the Gatehouse in accordance with Henry's requirements. The result is a charming study in rustic simplicity. You'd swear the rose had been rambling over the door for centuries. Henry calls it his Petit Trianon. He, Miranda the dog, and two Siamese cats are idyllically happy as Constance's new tenants.

'Naturally,' Henry continues smoothly, 'it is impossible — and I'm sure Richard would not expect it of me — to list all the many, many people who have contributed to the success of this enterprise . . .'

Richard certainly would not. He has them all listed in his own, so carefully prepared, speech and I could swear he is grinding his teeth up there but, short of thrusting Henry aside, he can do nothing other than wave a graceful assent. He need not have bothered. Henry is already away again and — damn him — looking in our direction. He is deliberately tormenting me.

'Contributions made,' coos Henry, 'in so many *different* ways . . .'

'Like by dropping dead?' mutters Joe.

'Some contributions beyond estimation . . .'

'Oh I dunno. I'd estimate about half a million quid,' adds Joe in a grim undertone. Thinking, no doubt, that this is what we were eventually paid for Harecombe. Enough to settle our debts and us in a little bistro outside Bath. A small legacy from Joe's dad helped too. The Wild Duck, if you're passing.

'Theatres are, of course,' says Henry, switching tack with alarming abruptness, 'notoriously haunted places. So too, are castles. Surely, therefore, Harecombe Castle Theatre should be able to claim at least one ghost within these ancient walls. In fact, tonight, it pleases me, as I'm sure it will you, to imagine a whole cluster of benevolent spirits, the dear departed, watching over our enterprise . . .'

'Oh my God,' I hiss. 'Can't someone shut him up?'

'. . . and I'm sure Richard will forgive me, if I pre-empt him in expressing my own personal tribute to one man more closely associated with Harecombe Castle than any of us.'

I catch my breath and Joe rolls his eyes comically in my direction.

'It was, after all,' says Henry with a glittering smile, 'his ancestor who was responsible for building both castle and this exquisite theatre in the first place.'

He certainly has his audience riveted in a way any of the actors might envy.

'Montague Rivenhoe, if his shade haunts us still, will, I believe, have been proud tonight of his descendant; his great-great-grandson, whose settings of the Bard's songs have added so immeasurably to our pleasure. Ladies and gentlemen, the Musical Director of the production, Oliver Langham.'

Joe gives a sardonic crack of laughter, and I'm furiously hissing, 'Bastard! bastard!' at Henry, even as I applaud Oliver.

Oliver looks as though he had stepped straight out of a Renaissance canvas. Clad in velvet tunic and tights, a feathered cap bobbing over one eye, he looks like a court musician painted by, say, Raphael. The Roman nose helps. And I'm not surprised the middle-aged matrons around me are clapping so vigorously: all that cycling has given him a great pair of legs for tights. Naturally, he doesn't see himself in that light. He was grotesquely embarrassed by Henry's insistence that he must dress up to conduct his Renaissance Consort. Which was why, despite everyone's entreaties, he stubbornly refused to venture into the public gaze and join us for the dinner interval. Alison sneaked a sandwich backstage for him.

His bow is clumsy and fast. In fact, to look at him edging backwards, you might think he was limping, but it's only self-consciousness. His injuries from his fall were minimal. Grazed hands and a sprained ankle. The ambulancemen wouldn't even admit him into the first ambulance, to Alison's vituperatively expressed fury. But he was, they told her, barely bruised.

The same could not be said of the marquee. In cushioning his fall like a giant safety net, the roof ripped across and several thousand pounds' worth of damage was sustained.

Oliver has melted back into the line-up of actors, but Alison and Constance, side by side in the row in front, are continuing to applaud with the shameless noisiness of doting aunt and six-month-wedded wife.

It must be love, Joe observed in awe, if it got Al off the vegetarian kick. In fact, from the moment Oliver fell off the tower, she's hardly left his side. It was inevitable he would succumb, although, according to Alison, she was the one who had to pop the question. But his happiness now — he's peering shortsightedly from the stage, trying to see his wife — is touchingly transparent.

Even poor Pamela Metcalfe is applauding. She is sitting — where else? — in the Cathy Langham Memorial Seat. They let her off lightly: probation, treatment for depression. God knows, it was my child and I didn't want her hounded. Pam had suffered enough. What's more, she's working here at the castle once more. Secretary to hotel and theatre and, according to Nell, a treasure beyond compare. She only stops clapping when Henry opens his mouth again.

Oh Henry, I think. Please shut up. Richard is stepping forward with the same idea — but to no avail.

'All of us in this theatre tonight,' pronounces Henry with magnificent aplomb, 'owe a very great deal to Oliver. See — he blushes with typical modesty. But without Oliver, I believe I can safely claim, we could not *possibly* have enjoyed this evening's entertainment . . .'

There is a ripple of embarrassed laughter from those in the know, which appears to include most of the audience. Joe shamelessly joins in.

'For Christ's sake,' I whisper, but already Henry has passed seamlessly on — to Richard's silent fury — with his remaining credits. All blessedly innocuous.

Henry is right of course. We wouldn't be here at all, were

it not for Oliver. When Oliver thudded on to the roof of the marquee it was — Henry told me later — like the end of the world. The lights went out. Ruched silken canopies collapsed smotheringly over the dance floor. Everyone was screaming their heads off in the pitch black. In that instant, declared Henry, he became a Catholic.

In that instant, or perhaps the ensuing mêlée, Lady Brickhill — frail, foul-tempered, fabulously *rich* Lady Brickhill — suffered her final, and fatal, heart attack.

The ambulancemen did their best, but by the time they reached her she was beyond resuscitation. They tactfully didn't tell the shocked Nell. They waited until they were in the van before covering the face.

And Henry had the decency to wait until after the funeral — oh, until at least the morning after — before advising Nell on her next move. With that massive, monstrous inheritance. Left — entirely — to herself. Not a penny had been willed to Constance's charity; not a sou, in fact, to anyone else in the world. Nell Prescott unexpectedly and, bless her, *unwillingly* found herself in command of a fortune. She was too dazed even to think about it. Until Henry turned up on her doorstep, suggesting the perfect, nay heaven-sent, investment opportunity . . .

'And finally,' says Henry, checking Richard with one up-raised hand, 'I think we must now welcome the Chairperson of our Theatre Preservation Trust, the beautiful chatelaine of Harecombe Castle, Richard's wife and our very dear friend . . .'

Nell is actually in the audience, and protests hotly as she is dragged to the stage. Poor woman. No acting here. She really doesn't care for the limelight. But she looks wonderfully pretty in royal blue taffeta. Henry has also taken over supervision of her wardrobe. She's been delighted to let him. She and Henry are the very dearest of friends.

'So kind . . .' she murmurs.

Having bought the castle from us, she simply adores running her stately bed and breakfast joint. It's such *fun*. She

405

revelled in transforming the Stables into a deliciously cosy nest for her sons and husband: she always did prefer dolling up buildings to bodies. And, most of all, she has been utterly delighted to enable Henry and Richard to restore their theatre. A toy, as old Sir Monty Rivenhoe himself intended it, to keep a spouse happy and at home. She accepts, blushing, her own huge bouquet of flowers, a loving kiss from Henry − a loving kiss from Richard.

Henry bows gracefully and, thank God, steps back at last. Richard can hardly believe his good fortune. He is clearly about to resume where he left off, but − amazingly − Nell interrupts.

'I think,' declares the owner of Harecombe Castle − the Chairperson of the Theatre Preservation Trust, our hostess − taking her husband's hand, 'that we must hurry through to the hall, where our supper is waiting.'

A muffled cheer from the audience means Richard is unable to argue. Nell and Richard, hand in hand, process off the stage and up the centre aisle, with the actors pairing off behind them. Henry pauses by our seats. 'Such a credit to me,' he murmurs. 'And, do you know? I believe she was right in the end about the play.'

It was Nell who wanted *Twelfth Night* for the opening production. And carried her point in the face of the massed opposition of Richard, Henry, the committee . . .

'She who pays the piper,' sighs Henry, helping me to my feet, 'is learning wonderfully fast.'

ROSE TREMAIN
SACRED COUNTRY

Winner of the James Tait Black Memorial Prize

At the age of six, in 1952, Mary Ward, the child of a poor
farming family in Suffolk, has a revelation. She isn't Mary.
She's a boy. An inexplicable mistake has been made and,
somehow, it will have to rectified . . . So begins Mary's heroic
struggle to change gender, while all around her others too fight
to discover a place of meaning in a savage and confusing world.

'Brilliant . . . a strong, complex, unsentimental novel, luscious in
some passages, wonderfully restrained in others'
Times Literary Supplement

'Rose Tremain writes comedy that can break your heart . . . Her
book is one to admire and enjoy. It is funny, absorbing and
quite original. I've read nothing to touch it this year'
Literary Review

'Hypnotic . . . curiously beautiful and strikingly original'
The Spectator

'A remarkable novel . . . The product of a truly original mind,
whose inventions are magically unforeseeable'
The Times

'A strange and magical book . . . wholly capitivating'
The Daily Mail

'Meticulous storytelling, period re-creation utterly convincing.
A considerable work'
Melvyn Bragg in The Sunday Times Books of the Year

MELVYN BRAGG
AUTUMN MANOEUVRES

Jimmie Johnston first became a Labour MP in Cumbria when there was a brave new post-war world to build. Now, in the late '70s, another General Election looms but he is no longer so optimistic. And as he fights to keep his seat, his family begins to fracture around him and scandal threatens. In this absorbing and fast-paced novel, Melvyn Bragg's portrait of the mood and politics of the era remains as pertinent today as on its original publication.

'Melvyn Bragg is quite simply one of the best writers we have . . . He has a rare steadiness of vision, a listening attentiveness to the predicament of the individual, and a sense of time, place and history'
The Sunday Telegraph

'Very good, very pleasurable and very authentic . . . an extremely well-timed book'
Anthony Howard

'A gripping novel . . . There is a demonic streak in Bragg's imagination, something excitingly macabre'
The Listener

'There are certain writers – Lawrence, Hardy, Bennett – whose novels seem to grow from the very soil that nurtured them. Melvyn Bragg is one of them: his characters' roots are firmly in Cumbria . . . The writing and characterisation are powerful'
The Daily Telegraph

'Melvyn Bragg is an experienced and skilled professional writer, who knows exactly what he is doing . . . a highly competent piece of storytelling which holds the attention to the end'
Times Literary Supplement

JANICE ELLIOTT
CITY OF GATES

No one in Jerusalem can remember a time when Eugenia Muna's guest house did not exist. And though the city is threatened anew by enemies within and without, Madame Muna has seen it all before, from the Crucifixion to Saddam's missiles. In this intricately wrought n0vel time past, present and to come, the miraculous and the everyday, humour and tragedy are contained in a story which affirms the power of love, both sacred and profane.

'A literary entertainment of the highest calibre, the kind of novel which demands to be re-read so that a few more pieces of the glittering puzzle can be put in place'
The Scotsman

'A most unusual and deeply-felt novel'
Financial Times

'An accomplished and ambitious work with an admirably succinct and fast-moving narrative pace'
Times Literary Supplement

'She manages to convey the political, historical and spiritual complexity of the place without losing touch with a strong set of characters . . . How many more novels does Elliott have to write before she achieves the wide popular recognition she deserves?'
The Spectator

'A gem of a novel'
Today

'Janice Elliott is one of the most accomplished literary stylists at work in this country . . . She writes like an angel'
The Times

sceptre